MW01012089

GRACE OF THE EMPIRE STATE

GRACE OF

THE EMPIRE

STATE

A NOVEL

GEMMA TIZZARD

G

Gallery Books

New York   Amsterdam/Antwerp   London   Toronto   Sydney   New Delhi

G

Gallery Books
An Imprint of Simon & Schuster, LLC
1230 Avenue of the Americas
New York, NY 10020

First Gallery Books hardcover edition January 2025

GALLERY BOOKS and colophon are registered trademarks of Simon & Schuster, LLC

For information about special discounts for bulk purchases, please contact Simon & Schuster Special Sales at 1-866-506-1949 or business@simonandschuster.com.

The Simon & Schuster Speakers Bureau can bring authors to your live event. For more information or to book an event, contact the Simon & Schuster Speakers Bureau at 1-866-248-3049 or visit our website at www.simonspeakers.com.

Interior design by Hope Herr-Cardillo

Manufactured in the United States of America

10 9 8 7 6 5 4 3 2 1

Library of Congress Cataloging-in-Publication Data is available.

ISBN 978-1-6680-5694-3
ISBN 978-1-6680-5696-7 (ebook)

For my parents

PROLOGUE

The crane derricks had all stopped moving, which was more discon-
certing than anything else, as she stood poised, higher than she or
almost anyone else had ever been before, her toes pointed, ready to take
her first step. She breathed out through her mouth, clearing her mind,
blocking out the hum of noise behind her, below her, where men's voices
scrambled over one another to be heard. They couldn't help her now.

The wind whipped around her face, stealing her exhaled breath and
ruffling her hair, chilling the back of her exposed neck. She flicked her eyes
down. So far down. The street was hundreds of feet below her, a dizzying
distance that made her stomach lurch and swoop, and the moment she
stepped out along the crane arm, there would be nothing at all between
her and it if she fell. The cars looked like tiny toys, the people no more
than moving specks. The buildings around them, set out in their neat grids,
resembled a toy village, something a rich child might receive for Christmas, wrapped in a red velvet bow. But it was real. All of this was too real.

"Okay," she whispered to herself. "This is it."

She placed a hand over her heart, feeling the rhythm of its beat, and
breathed deeply until she felt it slow. She nodded once to herself, then
stepped out along a metal beam no wider than her foot. With her arms
out at her sides for balance, she tensed the muscles in her core to keep her
movements tight and compact, concentrating deeply on her connection
to the beam and grounding her foot to it.

"Wider than a tightrope," she murmured to herself as she stepped again. She could do this. She had walked wires, and it was the same skill, no matter the height. Another step. She really was out on her own now, the safety of the half-finished building disappearing behind her.

"Just another dance," she whispered, as she took another deep breath and lowered her shoulders from up around her ears, relaxing into her body the way she would before dancing. It worked; the next step was lighter, surer. "Nearly there," she coached herself, as her eyes flicked up from the beam and out toward the horizon, New York City sprawling around her. "Some view," she breathed.

She took another step, the wind whistling around her, and the crane arm creaked. Her breath caught in her chest and she froze, suddenly terrified, as her brain finally realized what her body was doing. She fought for balance. Paralyzed with terror, three hundred feet above the city, she cleared her mind once more, forcing out all doubt. She couldn't turn back now if she wanted to. There was only one way to go, and she had a job to do.

She stepped forward.

TUESDAY, JUNE 10, 1930

Grace O'Connell flew into the dressing room, pulling her dress off over her head.

"We keeping you from something?" A moon-faced girl down the bench leaned back to catch Grace's eye, smile on her face, lipstick tube in hand.

"I'm not late," Grace called back, stripping down to her underwear and hanging up her dress. Hopping as she pulled on her shoes, she cleared a space in the clutter of hats, props, and makeup lying on the wooden bench running the length of the room and lifted her leg to stretch. Reaching for her toes inside the newly shined black shoes, she felt the familiar pull in her back and neck. She held it for a moment before straightening back up in one slow, fluid movement.

"Dancers! Five minutes!"

All hell broke loose among the fifteen women in the room as they rushed to get ready. Half-dressed girls snatched their costumes from their markers, elbows flying as they tripped over each other with good-natured screeching and laughter. Material flew in a tornado of color as outfits and hats were yanked from rails to the bench and back again in a tumble of limbs. Dancers scrambled toward the mirrors, powdering cheeks and rouging lips, fastening shoes and warming their bodies.

"Hey, Gracie!" A woman slid into place next to Grace at the dressing table bench, knocking her and making her hop again. The naked bulb above them lit the new arrival's meticulously painted features, the air immediately filling with the floral scent of her perfume. Leaning close to the mirror they shared, she added a beauty spot to her cheek.

"Ready for another night of high jinks and high kicks?" Her grin in Grace's direction was pure mischief.

"Of course." Grace swapped legs to complete her stretching.

Lillibet Lawrence was the self-proclaimed star of the show. The only one among them to give herself a stage name, she was Lily Lawrence to her audience and Betty to her friends. Even though she wore the same outfits and did the same routines as the rest of them, in her mind, at least, she was the draw.

"I have a new fur for you, courtesy of John," she said, expertly lining her lips even as she talked.

"Thanks, Betty, but you really don't need to give me your things."

Betty waved her away. "You're doing me a favor. It's not my color."

She pouted her full lips and wrinkled her small nose as she examined her handiwork in the mirror, turning her head one way and then the other. Pretty enough, she knew how to make the absolute best of her features. With a body shaped like a violin, she was used to attracting attention, and always wore a higher heel than the others to make herself taller.

"I hate this hair," she complained, frowning. She jammed down her blue cap to cover as much of it as possible. The dancers at Dominic's all had brown hair. For reasons best known to himself, Billy "Texas" Laredo, the club owner, not only preferred it, but insisted on it. In the eight months she'd been on staff, Grace had seen girls use everything from henna to boot polish to get around the rule. Betty was one of the few girls who, thanks to many male admirers, could afford a wig. She tugged it resentfully, making sure every wisp of her blond hair was covered. The rule made her furious; she had almost come to blows with Texas over it more than once.

"It's our thing, makes us stand out," he'd said once, cigar clamped in his jaws, smoke forming a wreath around his head.

"Nobody ever stood out by looking all the same," Betty had fumed.

Grace never had to worry about the rule. Her hair was the color of polished walnut and had a natural shine. As she pulled her own cap on, her curls crackled in protest, a consequence of the liberally sprayed sugar water she used to hold them in place. Stretching routine complete, she met her own deep brown eyes in the mirror. Her strong jawline framed her face and made her striking. Turning to the side, she checked her profile. Blessed with a lithe and strong dancer's frame, she could accentuate or hide the feminine curves of her body depending on how she felt. It was a gift in a world where she sometimes wanted to fade into the background. She rested her hands on her tiny waist, taking deep breaths in anticipation of the night's work ahead.

A gentle bump on the elbow announced the arrival of her neighbor on the other side, Edie McCall, back from the bathroom where she normally went to change, an explosion of blue and white satin.

Grace's face lit up to see her, and seconds later she was sliding a Baby Ruth bar into Edie's small hand. It had become their routine. Grace knew how Edie loved chocolate and never bought treats for herself. Edie didn't feel comfortable accepting gifts, even from her friends, so Grace told her she got them for free from a man at a nearby bodega who always had overstocks. It was more than worth the five cents a day to see the way Edie grinned, delighted not just at the chocolate but that someone was thinking of her. Edie's life had not been easy, but she had a good heart. She had been the first girl to welcome Grace at Dominic's and show her the ropes, and in return she would always have Grace's loyalty.

Thank you, Edie mouthed silently, tearing the wrapper.

Being a performer seemed an odd choice for someone so painfully shy, but onstage Edie came to life like no one else.

"How was the big audition?" she asked around a mouthful of chocolate, wide-eyed with expectation, her voice high and fragile, her alabaster skin almost see-through.

"I was busy." Grace's voice was low and throaty in comparison. She reached for her opening-number outfit, unable to look at her friend.

"You didn't go?"

She caught a glimpse of Edie, pale and waiflike, deflating with disappointment in the mirror. No one wanted her to succeed more than Edie did. Her slim shoulders, hollowed cheeks, and legs like hairpins made her look ethereal against the dark-wood paneling of their surroundings. If Grace could, she would wrap her up and take her home to live with her, give her a proper family. Edie's huge eyes would have made even Clara Bow jealous, and she was so slim, children could learn to count using her ribs. Her beauty was undeniable, but settled on her in a haunted way, like a surface layer. She didn't inhabit it the way Betty did.

"'Course she didn't go," Betty said, pulling on the short white top with huge blue ruffled sleeves, transforming herself into a giant wrapped candy. "She never goes. What are you scared of, Gracie?" Betty was always direct, and rarely wrong. She knew these girls deserved more, but the world wasn't going to hand it to them; they had to go out and get it.

Grace yanked on her own matching top, burying her face in it so she didn't have to answer. The costumes were getting old. Not as white as they had once been, they smelled musty, of old sweat and stale cigarettes. Reaching for her perfume, she doused herself before pulling on the matching blue skirt, shorter at the front with a long, ruffled tail behind. Material puffed around their bodies so that they had to shift sideways to slip past each other. Grace took the opportunity to turn away from her friends, letting the conversation die in the chaos of girls rustling in acres of satin, pushing for mirror space to adjust their caps. One day she would make an audition for one of the big shows, but she was busy, and it was fine at Dominic's, really. There was no rush. Sure, she was twenty-one now, but there was still time. Dancing was dancing, wherever you did it.

Texas appeared at the top of the stairs in his usual black dress coat and white tie. A tall man, his black hair—the brown rule clearly didn't apply to him—was slicked down, making his head smooth as a seal. His neck overflowed from his shirt collar, and his eyes bulged, giving the impression he was being squeezed out of a tube. He took out a gold pocket watch on a chain, an affectation, and the dancers rolled their eyes.

"Line up, ladies!"

"Girls!" trilled Betty, as they jostled their way into place, making her way to the front of the line. She ran up the first two steps, stretching one leg straight up in the air past her ear in a standing split. The other dancers whooped and hollered their appreciation. "Chests out! Straight backs! Smiles on!" She transformed her own face with a dazzling smile and dipped her head back before spinning around to face them again, a glint in her eye. "Let's go make some money."

For two hours, the girls danced like their feet were on fire. They shimmied and spun, kicked and flicked, dipped their shoulders with hands on knees, batting their eyelashes for the cheering crowds. Skin glistened under hot lights as they performed chorus numbers and split into smaller groups, completing daring onstage costume changes to accompany the evening's singers. Each dancer took a small solo spot to help the men banging on the tables choose their favorites.

Draped in sequins and feathers, Grace was completely lost to the moment. Her head was clear and her body was strong. Here she could fully embody her own name and feel the grace she moved with, the thump of her heart and the beat of the music all she needed to make sense of the world. There was no sadness, no worry; she was completely herself. Onstage she was free.

Once the show was over, the dressing area was filled with the cloying smell of flowers. Gifts from their particular admirers adorned each dancer's place. Betty's flowers and trinkets spilled over onto Grace's space, but there was plenty of room. Grace didn't encourage the advances of the men, so they tended to direct their attentions elsewhere. Many of the other girls were keen to take up offers of dinner and more, but Grace just wanted to dance. Betty, though, was furious if she didn't have at least four men begging her to join them every night after the show. She said yes to most of them, rotating her admirers to keep her options open.

"Small crowd," she said, clearing a space on the bench to lean against.

Grace nodded. It was impossible not to notice the dwindling numbers, but she thought it best not to think about it. Their audiences lately were lucky to reach half of what they used to be before the Wall Street Crash the year before. Grace had only been working there three weeks before it happened, and the crowds had never been the same since.

The room cleared quickly, girls rushing out to meet the men waiting for them. It was late, and they were keen to either get home or get out on the town. The chatter died down to a gentle hum and the few remaining girls were mostly out of their costumes and in their street clothes when Texas came into the room, his heft creaking down the steps. He headed straight for Grace, Betty, and Edie, who was holding a single white rose left on her station from a stranger. The small, unbelieving smile on her face was heartbreaking.

"Good show tonight," he said with a curt nod. "Look, I want you in early tomorrow for the taxi dance next door. Be here at four." He took a cigarette from behind his ear and pulled a matchbook from his pocket.

"Ah, hell." Grace was hanging her costumes on the rack by her marker. She flopped into an old red armchair and a plume of dust puffed up out of it, making her cough.

"No thank you," Betty said, unpinning flowers from her wig. She laid them in front of the mirror, in the only small space available, bending to sniff a huge bouquet of yellow roses.

Texas struck the match against a wooden beam and lit his cigarette. "Not asking, I'm telling."

Edie was quietly tucking her dance shoes on the rack by her name, not wanting to draw attention. Texas was the boss, and if he said that was what they were doing, she would do it. She would take any money in her pocket he could give her. She would dance all day if he wanted her to.

"The men are awful," Grace said with an exaggerated shudder.

"All men are awful." Texas shrugged, taking a drag of his cigarette and blowing the smoke out into the room. He pulled at the collar of his shirt. "Get used to it."

"And are you gonna stop them from putting their hands all over us?"

Betty threw him a sharp glance and looked back to the mirror, where she was reapplying red lipstick. It stood out like spilled blood against her pale skin. "Ten cents and they think it's all for the taking."

"Anyone too handsy gets booted, you know that. You'll be looked after. They pay their money, you give 'em a spin. Charm them if you can manage that." He shot a pointed look at Betty, and she blew him a kiss.

"Can't stop them treading on our feet, though, can you?" asked Grace, standing and performing a simple rock step. She threw her hands in the air and let them fall with a clap onto thighs now covered in a blue knee-length dress, far more modest than her show costumes. "I've never seen less rhythm. I need these feet, y'know. I can't afford to keep losing toenails."

"Be here," Texas said, ignoring their complaints. His pointed finger swept the room to take in everyone who was left. "Are y'all listening? If you're here now, I want you here tomorrow."

"Sure, fine," Betty said, flicking her hand to dismiss him. "We'll be here, now can you let us change in peace? Some of us have places to be."

"With pleasure," he said, running a thumb up and down the inside of his suspenders. "Don't be late," he added as he turned and left.

"Guy's a creep." Betty raised her voice enough to ensure he heard and had to pretend he hadn't. She took off her wig and shook out her short blond hair underneath. "So what's next, ladies? I heard Greta, Mae, and Charlotte say they were heading to the Onyx Club. Vernon is playing there tonight." She gave Grace a wolfish smile.

"I've gotta get home," Edie said, slipping her arms into her fox-fur coat. Another of Betty's castoffs, Edie treated it like spun gold, even though it was at least two sizes too big and swamped her. It was also June, but she would probably wear it all summer. She was always cold. With her felt cloche hat, she looked like she was heading out on a polar expedition rather than taking the elevated to the Lower East Side.

"Okay," Betty sighed, knowing there was no point even trying to change her mind. "Are you all right to get home?"

"Sure," Edie said with a tight smile.

Grace flicked a look over at her. Edie's stockings were worn threadbare at the ankles and her shoes were scuffed. Grace knew she wasn't coming because she couldn't afford it. She also suspected that some nights Edie walked the thirty blocks home to save money. It made her heart ache that she didn't know how to help her. These were tough times for a lot of people.

"Are you sure?" she asked. "It'll be fun. We don't have to stay long."

"Not tonight." Edie started moving toward the door. "Have fun, though. I'll see you tomorrow. Goodnight."

"'Night, little bird." Betty blew her a kiss. Once Edie had left, she turned her attention back to Grace. "I love that kid. She breaks my heart. So, you're coming?"

"Well, I guess it's not far." A smirk crept across Grace's face. The club was just around the corner, and she could never resist Betty's company, or an excuse to not go home.

"When you're right, you're right." Betty slipped two cigarettes from a slim silver case and handed one to Grace. "And our best years are short. Gotta get on the merry-go-round while the music's still playing."

Although the club was close, right off Times Square, it was almost midnight by the time they finally arrived. Grace watched as Betty disappeared to the bar and came back with two tumblers full of amber liquid. Prohibition was a joke in New York City; the alcohol had never stopped flowing for a minute. She took the glass with a nod and slid into a chair, transfixed by the stage, where a beautiful Black woman, hair wrapped in a shimmering purple turban that matched her dress, was singing, glittering under the lights. Her voice dripped honey, each note effortlessly smooth and wrapped in silk. It sent shivers through Grace, as if someone were playing her spine like a piano, and the hairs rose on her arms and the back of her neck.

"*Let's do it, Let's fall in love.*" Betty was singing along softly, her eyes on the band. Grace followed her line of sight, already knowing where it would lead. Vernon. A tall man playing the trumpet onstage, looking dapper in his white dinner jacket and black bow tie. His dark skin glimmered in the soft light as he gently swayed. When he noticed Betty watching him, he couldn't help but smile.

"Looks like it's too late for that," Grace teased, eyebrows raised. Betty's mouth twitched into a smile and they both laughed as they drank.

The night drifted on, full of drinking, flirting, and conversation. Grace found herself dancing the shag with Andre, a friend of Vernon's, who had taken a break from serving drinks. Their legs moved at breakneck speed, ankles and knees flicking left to right until their swiveling shoes were almost a blur. She laughed as she twirled. They mirrored each other with progressively complicated steps until a small crowd gathered, clapping and hollering. As the music ended, the pair took a bow. Andre spun her one more time and raised her hand to his lips.

"Thank you for the dance, Miss Grace."

"The pleasure was all mine." Grace's skin was glowing under a sheen of perspiration, her eyes alive. There was nothing she loved more than to dance.

"You are a beautiful dancer," Andre said, a big grin across his face.

"You're pretty good yourself," Grace replied, leaning closer. "I'm taxi dancing at the Ivy dance hall next to Dominic's tomorrow afternoon, if you want to come along. I could do with a good partner."

Andre shook his head in disbelief. "You're too talented to taxi dance with the schmucks in this city. You should be in the big shows."

"One day." Grace smiled, gave a little shrug, and went to get another drink.

Emboldened by three drinks, on a whim she slipped off her shoes and jumped up on one of the tables, enjoying the familiar rush of surprising people with old circus tricks. To the shock and delight of her audience, she leapt from table to table as people grabbed for their drinks to make way for her well-practiced feet. Landing each time with perfect balance before springing to the next, she crossed the room to a soundtrack of disbelieving squeals and impressed chuckles.

The final table—small and circular, barely big enough to stand on—wobbled precariously as she landed, provoking gasps and shrieks from her rapt audience. The wobble serving as momentum, she used her feet to make the table rotate like a spinning top as a spotlight suddenly swung around to pick her out through the smoky atmosphere of the room. The gasps increased in volume with the speed until the table was a blur. Just before she lost control completely, she leapt to the ground, performing a perfect pirouette before taking a deep bow, reaching out to still the spinning table with one hand before it fell over.

Roaring their appreciation, the crowd sprang to their feet, the applause deafening. Men swatted each other with their hats in disbelief, eyes saucer-wide at what they had just seen.

"She was in the circus, you know," Betty said to anyone who would listen, as she barged her way across the room to reach her friend. "Spent a year swinging from rafters like a monkey." The spotlight swung away again, and Betty continued weaving between bodies, Grace's shoes in her outstretched hand. Vernon trailed behind, his work for the night finished and his bow tie undone.

"I didn't swing from anything, Betty. That's the trapeze."

"Same thing," Betty said, shrugging. "It's all a good way to break your neck. Now come on, time to go." She scooped Grace up, leading her toward the exit.

Back at street level, the bruised sky was already starting to lighten with the purple and pink streaks of the coming sunrise. The fresh air slapped Grace in the face, making her woozy, while the lingering smells from a nearby restaurant made her stomach growl. She looked up. The skeleton of the Empire State Building was already dominating the landscape. You could see it from blocks away, and they had a long way to go yet. She thought about her twin brother, Patrick, and the other men who would be up there in a few hours, crawling all over it like ants on a dropped ice cream. Better them than her. She would be sleeping in.

Betty signaled a taxi and the three of them climbed inside. "West Fifty-Seventh and Tenth," she told the driver.

Grace's head lolled against the window, melancholy feelings washing over her. The comedown from music and dancing to the misery of reality always took a bite out of her.

The city rushed by in a blur of electric lights, brickwork, and gray buildings. In no time, Vernon was jumping out of the taxi and leading her gently by the arm to the stoop of her apartment building.

"Goodnight, Grace," the big man whispered in his deep but gentle voice.

"'Night, Vernon, you're a gentleman."

"You sure you're all right now?"

Grace waved at Betty and turned to give Vernon one last lopsided smile. "Sure. I always am."

She tiptoed up the stairs to the third floor and let herself in, cursing when she knocked a tin cup off the counter with her hip, sending it bouncing across the wooden floor.

"Dammit," she hissed, stooping to pick it up. "Shh!" Admonishing herself, she heard the creak of a door opening and sighed, knowing it was too late.

"Grace." The whispered voice managed to sound disapproving, even thick with sleep.

"Patrick." Grace was already heading into her small room, not wanting any further conversation.

"Do you know the time?" He took a step toward her.

"Bedtime," Grace replied, turning to face him.

"That was hours ago." The level of annoyance started to increase on both sides as they squared up to each other in the half-light, confrontation inevitable now. "Where have you been?"

"At work, Patrick, although what concern it is of yours, I don't know, to be sure." Grace mentally kicked herself. Outside the house she sounded like an American, but at home, her Irish accent and phrasings always came back.

A thunder of footsteps clattered above, quickly followed by at least three children crying. The wailing penetrated through the thin ceiling as if it was barely there. There was no such thing as privacy in this building, and no doubt their neighbors could hear their raised voices in return.

Patrick wasn't done. "It is my concern when I have no idea where you are, Ma is worried sick, and you wake me up when you get in."

"Was it me that woke you, Patrick, or was it the Donohues' twelve children"—Grace jabbed her finger up at the ceiling—"and you just thought it was a good excuse to roar at me?"

She glared at her brother, further irritated by the fact that it was like looking at herself. They were as alike as any fraternal twins could be, with the same face shape and features. She knew her eyes were filled with anger, and she could see Patrick's flaring back at her, just the same.

"What's going on?" a small voice called out in hushed tones, before starting to cough uncontrollably.

"Now look what you've done," Patrick growled.

Their younger sister, Connie, just ten, stood in the doorway, barefoot in her nightdress, her pale face surrounded by a mess of butter-colored curls.

"Nothing, Con," Grace reassured her. "Go on back to bed."

Connie wiped her hand sleepily across her eyes and nodded, disappearing back into the dark.

"You've been acting the fool ever since Da died," Patrick hissed, shaking his head. "Do you think he would be proud?"

The words were like a punch to Grace's gut.

He turned away. "I'm going back to bed. I have to be up."

"You do that," Grace whispered, still in shock. Anger quickly took over and she clenched her fists as the screaming in the apartment above their heads intensified. "Doing my job isn't acting up, you fool," she said to his back. "And you're not him, you know that?" She wanted to hurt him as much as he had hurt her. "You never will be. You used to be fun before he died. Now, you wouldn't know how. Life is for living, Patrick," she added. "You should try it sometime."

His door closed and clicked shut. Grace padded to her own room, head swimming with alcohol; anger and sadness racing through her bloodstream. She slipped into her nightshirt and under the thin sheet. Pulling the threadbare green blanket up around her chin, she inhaled deeply, trying to believe she could still smell the faintest scent of her father on it. The grief of losing him was a wound reopened every time she walked through the door.

A couple of deep, shuddering breaths later, a half-formed thought dissolved as sleep took her quickly, a single tear drying on her face.

2

WEDNESDAY, JUNE 11, 1930

Patrick had left for work long before Grace got out of bed the following morning, her head thumping with the excesses of the previous night.

"Here she is," her mother said as Grace appeared from her room. She held out a glass of milk, which Grace took gratefully.

"I need to get clean," Grace croaked, her voice like gravel. She gulped the milk as her mother pursed her lips but said nothing.

At forty-six, Mary O'Connell had suffered a hard life already. Her past was strewn with tragedy, each loss tattooed onto her heart and turning her dark hair ever grayer, but she had proved to be tougher than all of it. She was still an attractive woman, although the skin under her eyes and chin was baggier now and lined with creases. Her hair was pulled into a bun not as neat as it once would have been, flyaway strands surrounding her face.

"How's Connie?" Grace asked. Her mother's expression immediately softened.

"Her lungs are still giving her trouble. She'll be staying in bed today."

Grace nodded, her mouth a tight line of concern. "I'm going to clean up and then I'll be out to get the shopping. What do we need?"

"Your brother needs new work gloves."

Grace scowled, turning her face away so her mother didn't see. She was planning to buy the food they needed for the day, not be her brother's lackey.

"They got burned," Mary said, shaking her head. "I don't know what I did to make all my children worry me so. Two already in the ground, three never to be born, Patrick on the steel, you out all night who knows where, and poor little Connie with lungs like wheezy bellows." She shook her head and composed herself; to speak of these grievances out loud was unlike her. "The money for the gloves is on the dresser."

Grace nodded quietly, moving to the sink. Her mother's obvious worry for Connie ignited her own and brought an acidic taste to her mouth that she fought to swallow down. She reached for the tap and it squealed in protest as water made its way through the pipes for her to rinse her glass. The stamping noise of countless feet upstairs was almost enough for her to have to raise her voice.

"They'll come through one day. We'll have a pile of Donohues on the floor!"

Mary ignored the comment. "If you could get dinner for tonight, and bread, cheese, eggs, and milk, that would be grand."

Through the thin wall, a seemingly endless number of Donohue children could be heard clattering down the stairs, screaming and shouting. Grace sighed, wondering how Mrs. Donohue could ever keep up.

"Yes, Ma, of course," she said, stepping into the bathroom to wash. Like everything in the apartment, it was small, but it was theirs and theirs alone.

As she slipped off her nightdress, she knew she was luckier than many who lived in far more squalid and cramped conditions, with a shared bathroom in the hallway. As a child, she had lived on Orchard Street on the Lower East Side, sharing rooms with cousins as her father and his brother squeezed their families in together to save money. She remembered her mother reaching out of the window to retrieve food from the lock box tied to the fire escape to keep things cold. Her uncle had hung shelves from ropes in the middle of the room to make sure no mice could get to the food. Children slept on the floor piled on top of one another, a heap of squirming limbs. Her father and uncle spent their days working hard at the docks and their evenings stopping up holes, papering cracks, and mending whatever was broken.

She would never forget the look on her father's face when they had been able to move here. Now they had five whole rooms to themselves. His pride at having the entire floor, with its three bedrooms and an ice box, was immense. The thought of his smile as he held them all close to celebrate moving in was too painful. She shut it away.

She dressed for the day, spotless in a pretty pale-blue summer dress, white shoes and white purse, hat in her hands—gifts from Betty, as many of her clothes were. The white would pick up the grime of the city in no time, but it was a beautiful warm day and she wanted to enjoy it. Her thick brown hair was set in curls that stopped between her chin and her shoulders. Placing her hat on the small table by the window, she saw a cup of coffee waiting for her and smiled. She picked it up and took it through to the room her mother shared with Connie.

"You look like a princess," Connie breathed, her eyes lighting up like flares. Grace laughed as she sat on the edge of the bed near her sister's covered legs. Their mother sat on the other side, darning socks, her arthritic fingers bent, red, and swollen. With a sideways glance she took in Grace's outfit.

"Give over," Grace said, stroking her sister's face. "Just someone else's castoffs. Princess Connie is the only princess here." The child's skin was clammy, and she was so pale she looked nearly gray, but she smiled as she rested her head back on the pillow, a halo of blond ringlets surrounding her head. Grace's teeth worried at her lower lip. Connie looked exhausted already and it was only the start of the day. She was to be protected at all costs, but there was only so much they could do. The rest was in the hands of God.

Connie was the only blond O'Connell. After the twins were born, their parents had tried for many years for more children and suffered harsh losses. The day Mary finally bore another precious child, their father had proudly held her in his arms and named her Constance. Her exhausted mother, delighted that the longed-for miracle baby had arrived healthy, agreed, not realizing until later that she had sentenced the tiny girl to the moniker Connie O'Connell. The baby of the family, she had been doted on by them all ever since.

"What would you like for dinner?" Grace asked her now. She could sense her mother listening.

"I'm not hungry, Grace," Connie sighed.

"Ach no, none of that." Grace shook her sister's leg through the cover. "So you're going to make me guess?"

Connie smiled and a little giggle escaped her.

"Hmm." Grace poked her tongue out of her mouth, screwing up her face into a grotesque mask of concentration. Connie laughed, but it quickly turned into a cough, and Grace regretted doing it.

"Hamburger?" she asked, trying to distract Connie.

The small girl shook her head.

"How about some fancy fish? For the princess."

"No," she moaned. "It smells."

"Right enough," agreed Grace. "Oh, I've got it. I know I'm right so don't even say I'm wrong." Even Mary had a small smile on her face as Grace jumped to her feet. "Pork chops! Ach yes, that's the ticket."

"Oh yes," agreed Connie, caught up in Grace's feigned excitement. She threaded her blanket backward and forward through her tiny fingers. "That would be nice, thank you."

Grace nodded, pleased with herself. "Well then, I'd better go. But I got you these yesterday to keep you going." Reaching into her purse, she pulled out a small yellow box.

"Milk Duds!" Connie tried to sit up, clapping her hands together.

"Calm down, child," Mary said, as Grace handed the box to her sister. "Ach, you spoil her, Grace."

"Well, Ma, she is a princess," Grace said with a wink. "Eat chocolates while the sun shines, I say."

"Not now," Mary warned. "They'll make you cough."

"Thank you, Gracie." Connie settled back, cuddling the yellow box to her chest. Grace picked up her purse and string shopping bag, refusing as ever to acknowledge just how scared she was about her sister's future.

Shopping done, Grace took the food home for her mother to prepare a meal she would not be there to eat, then headed out again. She had bought a peach pie at the bakery on West Forty-Eighth Street for dessert as a treat, and at least some of that would remain, whatever time she got home. As much as she didn't really enjoy the taxi dances, she was grateful for the excuse not to be at home, particularly after her argument with Patrick.

The city was bustling as always, full of people, cars, streetcars, bright colors, and a cacophony of different languages being spoken, shouted, and sung. Smoke and the sounds of construction were everywhere. Each storefront she passed had its own unique scent. The iron tang of blood from the butcher's mingled with the astringent alcohol and peppermint of the barber's. A group of boys played stickball in the middle of the street when they should have been at school. Clusters of housewives were haggling with pedal-cart sellers for everything from clothing and trinkets to vegetables. Grace had taken the Ninth Avenue Elevated from Fifty-Ninth Street down to Forty-Second, and now, on the edge of Times Square, not far from Dominic's, she realized she hadn't eaten all day and stopped at a pretzel cart enveloped in a cloud of steam.

"Three, please," she said, handing over fifteen cents in exchange for hot, doughy pretzels almost as big as her head.

"They can't all be for you!" the Puerto Rican vendor said with a smile.

"Why not?" Grace replied. "A girl's gotta eat." She flashed him a grin and heard him laughing as she walked away. Clutching her pretzels, she ducked down West Forty-Fourth Street and in the back-door entrance of Dominic's.

"Here you go," she said as she sat down between Betty and Edie, handing each a pretzel.

"Ooh, thanks, doll." Betty tore off a chunk and moaned with delight as she chewed the salty dough. "Just what I need. I had a busy night."

Grace smiled and shook her head, choosing not to comment.

"Oh, uh, thanks." Curlpapers still in her hair, Edie took the pretzel and reached for her coin purse.

Grace slapped her hand away. "Don't be silly. It's nothing, Edie. A gift."

A grin spread across Edie's face, and she mumbled her thanks as she took a bite. Grace pulled pieces off her own pretzel and ate them, running her tongue over her salty lips as thoughts tumbled around her head, fighting for room.

"Gracie?"

It took a few moments for Betty to get her attention.

"Sorry." She shook her head clear.

"Away with the clouds today," Betty said, deliberately mixing sayings to make one of her own.

"I think I'm going to wear white," Edie stated, holding up a pretty satin gown.

"That's perfect for you, baby." Betty was rifling through dresses on a rack, flicking through the rainbow of silk, chiffon, and crêpe de Chine before choosing an elegant green gown cut on the bias that would complement her figure. "Green for me."

Grace trailed her fingers through the materials and pulled out a yellow silk dress with an empire line, covered in tiny beads. The color reminded her of Connie's hair, and she smiled as she slid it off the rail. "This one."

A small contingent of the other dancers were also getting ready. The majority of girls at the taxi dance wouldn't be professionals, just pretty young women looking to have fun or in need of some cash—probably both. The number of available dancers had swelled since the economic crash, but Texas liked to have a few pros on hand to draw in the crowds. There were always eager men looking for their chance to dance with the girls they watched onstage every night. Not many of the Dominic's girls wanted to do it, but even fewer were in a position to say no.

Betty had hold of Edie's face like an overenthusiastic grandmother, cheeks squeezed between thumb and fingers as she added more makeup to her eyes. "You never wear enough," she muttered before turning her attention to fixing Edie's hair. Grace took a final look in the mirror and added some lipstick. It seemed all the girls were wearing it now, and it made her feel like Greta Garbo.

"It's time," Betty said, in charge as always. She released Edie and stepped back, happy with her work. With her eyes further accentuated, the girl looked beguiling—a heavenly being.

Betty led the group of women to the back of the room, pushing open a concealed door. They walked down a dingy corridor the length of a football field, heels clicking on the ground, before they came to a set of stairs leading up into the dance hall next door to Dominic's. Texas was waiting to greet them, along with a lineup of girls already there. The Dominic's girls moved as one, stepping out to a murmur of excitement rippling through the crowd of men impatiently waiting to pick their partners for the first dance.

The room was a gaping cavern, a big space with wooden floors and bleachers along one wall for spectators to watch. At one end, a low stage held the band, and for the next two hours as they played, people would dance and others would watch. Men began to push forward, clamoring for Betty, waving their ten-cent tickets.

"Lily! Lily!"

A broad man of around thirty, wearing an expensive double-breasted pinstripe suit, stepped forward. He held his hat in his hand, an unlit cigar in his mouth. His dark hair was swept to the side and lacquered, a thin mustache across his top lip. "Not today, fellas," he said, handing a ten-dollar bill directly to Texas. "That should take care of it."

"Howard, what a surprise!" Betty beamed, taking his hand before turning her smile on Texas to let him know it was very much not a surprise. If a girl filled every dance, she would make two dollars, half of which went to her and the other half to Texas. They all knew he wouldn't turn down the money. His jaw clenched tightly as Betty leaned in toward him. Grace just about heard her whisper, "It costs more than ten cents to dance with me."

The group of clamoring men looked crestfallen. They had come to dance with Lily Lawrence, but they could never compete with that sort of cash. Betty steered Edie forward by the elbow.

"I'm sorry, fellas, my dance card seems to be full, but this evening star is Miss Edie McCall. You've probably seen her dance with me next door at Dominic's. She's a good friend of mine and an excellent dancer. For just twenty cents, you can take a dance with her. A *professional*." She let her mouth curl around that last word and stretch it out, shooting a glance at the other girls who stood along the wall with their arms folded, looking awkward.

Edie gasped as Betty doubled her earnings, but recovered quickly, smiling and giving a twirl. As several men stepped forward waving their tickets, she looked up at Betty, her face full of gratitude. Betty just smiled. "Have fun, little bird," she whispered, leaving Edie to choose her first dance partner.

Grace watched on, a small smile twitching at the corners of her lips. Texas was at a loss, his mouth opening and closing like a Coney Island fairground game. He wanted to step in and put Betty in her place, but as she was making him more money, he said nothing, settling for scowling and looking daggers at her.

"Miss Grace."

Grace turned to the voice.

"Andre!" She heard her own surprised laugh as her dance partner from the night before reached out to take her hand. He was dressed smartly in a brown suit, white shirt, and slim brown tie. She was flooded with relief to see a friendly face.

"I'm on my break and only had twenty cents to spare, but I would be honored if you would let me be your partner for the first two dances."

"Oh Andre, the pleasure would be mine," Grace said, with heartfelt sincerity. Andre was one of the few people she believed truly loved to dance as much as she did.

"O'Connell!" Texas barked from eight feet away. "Here! Now!"

Andre bowed his head and sighed. Grace gave his hand a little squeeze before stepping away.

"What are you doing?" Texas demanded, his eyes bulging more than ever. "There are plenty of respectable men here for you to dance with."

"Andre is plenty respectable," Grace said, keeping her voice light.

Texas twitched, and his next words were forced out the side of his mouth through gritted teeth. "Do you see any other Negros here, O'Connell?"

"Why yes, sir," said Grace, gesturing over to the band musicians. "Right there on the stage." She watched as his face went from pink to scarlet and straight on through to purple.

"You don't dance with the help," he snarled.

Grace could feel her anger rising, and with it her Irish accent. "They aren't the help, to be sure, they're the talent. And Andre here is a paying customer like any other. I will dance the first two dances with him. After that, I will dance with anyone you want."

She turned on her heel, walking past Betty, who couldn't have looked more proud. Taking Andre's hand, she led him to a far corner of the hall.

"Miss McCall." Andre nodded to Edie as they passed her, and she smiled back. "You didn't have to do that," he said quietly to Grace, once they were out of earshot of anyone else. "I don't want no trouble."

"And you won't get any," Grace assured him. "It's just a dance, and we're here to dance."

She enjoyed the first two dances hugely, laughing as Andre led her around the hall in a quickstep, the only real dancing she would do all afternoon. She paid for it in misery once he left. Texas made sure she got all the very worst partners as her punishment for defying him. The lecherous ones, the sports, the old men, and the hobos looking for a pick-me-up, who chose to spend their last ten cents on a dance with a pretty girl rather than a meal. She had to put up with men who dragged her around and stamped on her feet, men who stank of alcohol, and men who tried to kiss her. Texas watched it all with vicious glee.

Grace endured. Texas going out of his way to single her out ensured she had partners for all twenty songs, earning the full two dollars, one of which would be hers. She consoled herself with the knowledge that the extra dollar would pay for the shopping she'd done that morning.

Once the taxi dance was over, the five professional dancers from Dominic's rushed back through the corridor in a rustle of fabrics to freshen up and get their ruffled outfits on, ready for the start of the main evening show. Grace's stomach rumbled. She had spent a large part of the last twenty-four hours dancing, and only eaten one pretzel. Putting hunger to one side, she fastened her shoes and went back out onstage with a smile on her face.

After the show, Grace sat in front of the mirror in her red feathered costume from the finale and took in her own pale face. She was feeling faint.

"I saw what you did with Andre," Betty said, slipping into a silver dress covered in beads and sequins even more elaborate than some of the costumes they had just danced in. She was heading up to Harlem to meet Vernon, but Grace was dreaming of nothing but peach pie and maybe grabbing something warm from a twenty-four-hour bakery on the way home.

"He's a friend." Grace shrugged.

Betty was still talking. "And what happened after. How come you can stand up for everyone except yourself, huh, Gracie? I woulda walked outta that hall and not looked back."

Before Grace could answer, or even consider the question, Texas stomped into the room. The girls groaned, knowing an after-show visit from him couldn't be anything good. Grace caught the look on his face and her breath hitched in her throat. His skin was pale and he was visibly sweating. She braced herself for whatever was coming.

He'd clearly heard Betty's remark. "Looks like you're gonna get your wish," he said, wiping a hand across his forehead.

"What's up with you?" Betty asked, all of them picking up on the feeling in the room now. The back of Grace's neck prickled with anticipation.

Texas cleared his throat to get everyone's attention. His eyes darted uncomfortably around the group, lingering for a second on Edie. He grimaced. "Listen up. This ain't good news, so I'm just gonna hit you straight." He paused for a moment before he plowed on. "We've been shut down, so I'm afraid that was our last performance."

"What?"

"You're kidding!"

"Very funny!"

"Not funny at all, I gots a baby!"

"You can't be serious!"

"Just like that?"

The voices clamored over each other.

"What is this?" Betty's voice carried above all others.

"It's not my call. The big bosses have been spooked by the crash. The racketeers are pulling the strings, and we don't make enough money for their liking. That's it. Fewer clubs keeps profit concentrated. Concentrated right into their pockets." He didn't hide his bitterness. He started to hand out brown envelopes with their names on. "Here's your pay. I slipped in an extra five for each of you. Best I could do."

"Thank you." Edie took her envelope and clutched it tightly, tears filling her eyes. Her gratitude embarrassed Betty, whose hackles were already up.

"Oh, you're all heart," she snapped as she tore her own envelope out of his hand.

"Don't be like that." Texas looked almost hurt. Anyone else would have softened, but not Betty, who carried on glaring at him, her face stony.

"Why us?" Grace asked.

Texas took a deep breath. "You've seen the crowds." He shook his head. "Nobody's here, nobody's spending. The guys with money don't come here and the other guys we used to get don't go anywhere anymore. Simple as that. Our numbers are way down. We're a casualty of our situation. This ain't the Cotton Club," he finished with a shrug.

"Don't we know it," Betty sniped.

"Looks like it's finally time to audition for the big shows," Grace said to herself, with a false optimism she hoped hid her disappointment.

Texas half laughed, half sneered. "You'll never make it, O'Connell.

No one's hiring; you've missed your chance. You'd better go back to the circus. If you haven't made it by now, you never will. You're done. We're all done."

"What a rousing speech," Betty spat, taking a drag on the cigarette she'd just fitted into a long ivory holder. "You're a real goddam ray of sunshine."

"You'll be all right," he said, looking at her. "Broads like you always are."

He glanced round the room once more before turning to leave. He hesitated, his hand on the doorframe, but didn't look back. "I'm sorry, girls, truly," he said as he disappeared.

Betty wasn't in the mood to give him the benefit of the doubt. "Thanks for nothing, Billy. Don't let the door hit you on the way out." Into the silence he left behind him, she spat the word "Greaseball."

The women started talking again in hushed tones, gathered in their smaller friendship groups for support. They were all in shock and a couple had started to cry.

"What are we gonna do?" Edie asked, her doe eyes skittering between her two friends, the huge red feathers on her shoulders trembling.

"Looks like it's time to get married," Betty said with a shrug.

"To Vernon?" Edie asked.

Betty raised an eyebrow. "Come on now, Edie. Not even you are that naïve. Vernon ain't the kind you marry, he'd need deeper pockets for that. I mean Howard. He still has some of his money. It's time to get out of here."

"But you love Vernon, not Howard."

"Love's a luxury," she said with a shrug. "And without a job, it's not one I can afford. I'll ask around, and if any of my other gentlemen friends didn't lose it all in the crash, I'll be sure to send them your way."

Edie nodded blankly, still stunned by the news. Grace knew that without a job, Edie would be homeless and starving by the end of the month, like the men they saw on the subway, or huddled under discarded newspapers in alleys.

"Here." She opened her brown envelope and handed Edie two five-dollar bills. "You're gonna need it more than me. Please take it. I'll find something, and even if I don't, Patrick's making good money on the steel."

Edie shook her head. "No, Grace, I'll be fine. I'll find a way."

"Just take it." Grace pushed the bills into her hand.

Edie hesitated, and her face colored as she nodded and took the money. "Thank you."

"Maybe I should marry your brother," Betty joked. "Although ain't you twins? I can't have a man with your face."

"I think you have enough men," Grace said, looking from one friend to the other. "You okay, Edie?"

Edie nodded, but it was unconvincing. "My mind's whirring is all. Trying to think where I can get work. You know." There was a ghost of a smile on her face. "Same for all of us."

Grace knew it wasn't, though. Edie lived in a single room in a tenement, on a floor she shared with six other girls. She had no family, and it was clear she was already running calculations on how long the money would last. It was Grace's worst nightmare, to be alone in the world like that, and her heart raced with panic as she took several deep breaths to calm herself.

"Here." Betty also handed over ten dollars, Edie fighting hard against tears.

"Oh no, I didn't mean—"

"Take it," Betty said, in a tone that would accept no protest.

"Thank you," Edie said softly, tucking her now boosted brown envelope into the pocket of her oversized fur coat. "I'll be all right," she assured them. "There are other jobs out there; there's got to be."

Grace swallowed the lump in her throat. She wanted to step forward and hug her friends but was too scared she wouldn't be able to let go again. They all stood and looked at one another in shock. Even with their help, Edie had a month at best, and they all knew it. Grace just hoped it would be long enough to find something else.

"I guess that's it, then." Grace herself was more disappointed than worried, filled with a deep sadness that she would likely never work with Betty and Edie again. She liked the job, but far worse things had happened to her than not having to see that low-life Texas ever again. She would be fine. She looked around the room one last time, suddenly not hungry anymore.

"It seems, ladies, that just like half the damn city, we are officially unemployed."

3

THURSDAY, JUNE 12, 1930

"It's not that bad, Ma," Grace said. "There'll be something."

"Have you taken a look outside recently, Grace? Families on the streets, men desperate for work, children in rags, women going through the trash looking for food. God in heaven knows we've been luckier than most so far, but with your father gone . . ." Mary paused and swallowed hard.

"I'd rather you said dead than gone. Gone sounds like he left on purpose."

The two women sat in silence. Eventually Grace got up and started to make coffee. Reality was nipping at her ankles. She wasn't ever going back to the club, and the comment Texas had made about nobody hiring rubbed against the back of her brain. She didn't want to work in a shop or scrub floors. She wasn't cut out to work in the garment district factories like her mother had.

"The salary wasn't much anyway," she reasoned, holding a cup up to her mother as a question. They both knew it was a lie. The salary had been better than most, and things would be much tighter without it. Mary shook her head and Grace put the cup back on the shelf. She filled her own and sat, ignoring the huge crack in the wall next to her. "I'll go out and look for situations vacant after this."

"I'll start taking piecework in again," Mary said. "I'll ask around."

Grace glanced at her mother's arthritic fingers. "You need to look after

Connie, Ma. We'll be fine. Let Patrick worry about the finances; he's the man of the house now, and he's earning well."

"That job isn't forever, though, and what then? When we moved here and took on a hundred-dollar-a-month rent, your father was intending to be around to pay it. And he wasn't expecting to lose the family savings when the bank closed."

"Calm yourself, Ma." Grace sipped her coffee, blocking out the truth of what she'd just heard. "Today we're fine, and that's all we have to worry about. Tomorrow can take care of itself. I have twenty dollars from my final wages you can have." She kept quiet that it should have been thirty.

"You take nothing seriously, Grace!" Standing from the table, Mary rubbed her forehead with sore hands. "Your father filled your head with dreams and let you spend time with those Ivanovs, dancing and being a clown. Learning all those circus tricks. Where did it get you?"

Grace's head dropped. "Well, up until yesterday, Ma, it got me a job." She resented being called a clown, and even if she had been, there was a great skill to it. Her time in the circus was something to be proud of. She had danced, even then, as well as walked tightropes and juggled. She could do things no one else she knew could. She raised her head; she was not ashamed. "No one was complaining the year I earned money from *those circus tricks.*"

"Why is everyone shouting?" Connie appeared behind them.

"It's nothing for you to worry about," Mary said. "Back to bed with you."

Connie looked to Grace for reassurance, as she often did, her little forehead creased with frustration. She didn't like being kept out of things.

"It's nothing, Con," Grace said, opening her arms. Connie climbed up into her lap, though she was too big now to sit there comfortably. Grace could hear her breath wheezing and held her tighter, as if she could protect her from whatever was happening in her body. She prayed every night that the infection would clear soon. "I won't be going to the club for a bit, that's all, so I'll be here in the evenings for meals, and I can read to you."

"Really?" Connie asked, excited. "That'll be grand."

"So it will," murmured Grace into her sister's hair, not believing it for a second.

With Connie safely tucked up again, Grace sat on her own narrow bed and took out her pay envelope. Not counting the twenty dollars for the family, she had six dollars left. Opening the drawer by the bed, she reached behind the stockings and pulled out a roll of small bills. She had been putting a little away ever since she started working and had around two hundred dollars. Just feeling it in her hands made her feel calmer. Things would be fine.

Putting the money back, she shut the drawer and pulled on a sweater. She tucked the six dollars into her purse and put the twenty on the table as an offering to try and calm her mother.

"That will last us awhile. And I'm still a dancer today, just like yesterday. There must be plenty of positions. People always want to be entertained. If you can do the shopping today, I'll go and ask around."

Mary curled her hands over the money and nodded, unhappy but resigned.

On Shubert Alley, off Times Square, where all the dancers, actors, and musicians gathered, an effortlessly chic group sat talking and laughing, oozing confidence, dressed to the nines. Grace heard snippets of their conversation.

"The director said he simply had to have her," a woman with angular features said with a smirk, taking a drag on her cigarette. Her black hair was poker straight and cut level with her chin, framing her face in bold lines.

"In the play? Or . . . ?" asked another woman with a slash of coral lipstick and the aura of a movie star, leaving a meaningful pause. The group laughed, loud and unashamed. A man lounged against a lamppost, his feet crossed at the ankles, radiating power. These people had star quality—they were certainly the ones to ask.

Grace approached, pulling her shoulders back and opening her mouth. Just before she reached them, she closed her mouth again and felt her posture crumble. Head down, she carried on along the sidewalk, shame burning her cheeks. It was no use, she didn't belong with them. Her own mother saw her as nothing more than a clown; what would these people think? They were rich, probably trained in fancy schools rather than by a retired Russian ballerina in a Lower East Side apartment.

A furtive look back saw a blond woman lean casually on a man's shoulder, whispering into his ear. It was like a group full of Bettys. So confident and comfortable in their skins, they knew exactly who they were. They had money and style—of course the jobs went to them, not Irish girls from the tenements. Grace would never be one of them; they would laugh at her, her clothes, her voice. Connie needed her to be ready, and she wasn't. She couldn't do it, even to keep her sister safe. The bitterness and disappointment in herself started seeping up from her feet, through her body, infecting her. Who was she kidding? Patrick was right about her. Everything he said was true.

After stumbling around torturing herself over her inability to even try and get a new job, Grace found herself at a lunch counter. Ordering a beef sandwich and a cream soda, she handed over her sixty cents, hoping a good meal would lift her mood. Maybe she would just have to be a taxi dancer anywhere that would take her. It wouldn't be as much money, but it was something, and she would be paid after every dance. You could just turn up and hope to be picked. Maybe she would be recognized from Dominic's. She could start scouting out the dance halls tomorrow.

As she chewed her sandwich, she wondered where Betty and Edie were. She missed them terribly already. They had arranged to meet up on Sunday afternoon, but it was only Thursday. She sighed deeply.

Not wanting to go home yet, she walked the streets a little longer and found herself in a basement speakeasy on Forty-Second Street. All she wanted to do was dance, and here there was music, and no one cared who she was or what she was doing. She ordered a gin and started to talk to a man at the bar with a creased shirt and a scar on his cheek. He looked like he'd seen better days. Hadn't they all in this city?

"Rough day?" he asked.

"Yes, and a long one. And it's still only three p.m."

"Don't I know it," he said, knocking back his drink, misjudging the distance to the bar and slamming his glass down harder than he intended.

She was going to miss dinner again. Connie would probably be asleep long before she got home. Images of her father danced behind her eyes, so she squeezed them shut, raising her hand for another drink to drown the pain and grief. All she ever wanted was for him to be proud of her. Standing, she dragged the guy off his stool to dance with her. He was unsteady, but it didn't matter. The voices yelling in her head faded away as she twirled under the twinkling lights. Her problems could wait until tomorrow.

4

FRIDAY, JUNE 13, 1930

Patrick O'Connell was brooding. He was struggling to concentrate, and in this job, that was deadly. Eighteen storeys up, the wind off the Hudson ruffled his shirt as he moved around the steel to set up the next scaffold platform. He gripped a column with one hand and stepped out onto a plank of wood suspended two hundred feet above street level, nothing beneath it but air. He bounced a little on the wood to check it could take the strain of two men, then looked up to check the fixings. It held, and he gave a thumbs-up to the rest of his gang as they moved into place to secure the next set of rivets.

One story below, his cousin Seamus stood on the horizontal metal ribs, at a corner where two steel beams met. In front of him a plank of wood lay diagonally, resting across both beams, with a small coke forge balanced atop it, heating rivets to a thousand degrees. With the thumbs-up given, Seamus plucked one of the glowing rivets from the forge with his three-foot-long tongs and effortlessly tossed it the fifty feet in an upward arc to the floor above. Patrick barely needed to move as he caught it in an old paint can. He retrieved the rivet with his own much smaller tongs, tapping it on the steel to remove any loose cinders and dirt before placing it into the waiting hole.

To his left and in front of him stood the two remaining members of his raising gang, Italian brothers Francesco and Giuseppe Gagliardi, otherwise known as Frank and Joe. Joe, ten years his brother's junior, stood next to Patrick, pressing his dolly bar against the rivet head with all his strength, biceps rippling with tension, while Frank stood on the opposite side of the steel with the riveting gun against the stem end of the rivet to secure it in place, sending sparks flying. As soon as they were done, the next rivet was traveling through the air.

The noise on the job was ear-shattering. The deafening sound of hammer hitting rivet ricocheted around Patrick's head. Above, steel slammed into place, and below, thousands of craftsmen were nipping at their heels. The masons, cementers, carpenters, electricians, plumbers, and painters made their own noise as they chased them ever higher into the sky.

By Friday afternoon, the physical nature of the work, paired with a week of broken sleep and the sun beating down on him, had made Patrick bone weary. His shirt was stiff with sweat, and he tilted his head to wipe his forehead with his arm without knocking off his cap. He couldn't afford to get sweat in his eyes. As he caught the next rivet, his mind started to wander again. Grace had worried, angered, and frustrated him for weeks now, gallivanting about, her selfishness increasing while he shouldered the responsibility of keeping their family together. What kind of job was dancing anyway? It amazed him that she got paid for something so frivolous; staying out half the night drinking and cavorting was about as far from hard work as he could imagine. Her hands were soft and so was she, and since their father had died, the nights had been getting later and later.

What was she up to? He'd known a few dancers in his time, and the thought of his sister acting like them was a worry he didn't need. At least she had been contributing with her wages, but it was always going to end in tears. Now she had to find another job, and the chances of that were slim. She thought she was above menial work, and as long as she had been bringing in good money with her ridiculous job, there was little he could say about it. They had needed the money since their father, God rest his soul, had been crushed in a shipping container accident on the docks just three months after the Wall Street Crash. Losing him was bad enough, but it was made even worse with his savings gone and insurance worthless, leaving nothing to help them survive without him.

Patrick glanced over the edge of the steel at the people way down below, watching them work, some of them no doubt hoping someone would fall. Even on a Friday afternoon, a group of men still remained, in the futile hope of getting any scrap of work on the site, even for an hour. Patrick pitied them. He felt the responsibility acutely of being the only thing now keeping his mother and sisters from the streets. The weight of it hung around his neck. At one dollar and ninety-two cents an hour, his wages were good, but this steel wouldn't take forever to hang, and at the rate they were moving, they would all be out of a job before Christmas. It wasn't lost on any of them that most other construction projects had stopped. None of them knew what was to come after the steel was complete, but they were all sure there would be far fewer jobs than men who needed them.

The next rivet hit the edge of his paint can and popped up into the air. The two other men drew their heads back instinctively, and Patrick moved the can in an arc to sweep the rivet in before it had a chance to go too far. Frank gave him a look and Patrick nodded: everything was under control.

"Concentrate!" Joe yelled at him as Patrick put the rivet in the hole. Patrick nodded again. They rarely spoke when they worked, having to shout to make themselves heard. They communicated mostly with nods and hand gestures. Normally it was fine, but today it just trapped Patrick inside his head with his own thoughts. There was only half an hour left of the working day; his stresses would have to wait. He couldn't afford to make a mistake.

The next rivet went smoothly. It was probably their four hundredth or so of the day, and it was hard to keep switched on through the monotony of the task if you weren't in the rhythm. *Heat, throw, catch, rivet. Heat, throw, catch, rivet.* Patrick was fighting against the flow. He couldn't relax and just wanted the day to be over.

Frank gave the signal that it was time to move. They couldn't reach any more rivet holes from where they were. Patrick stepped off the scaffold and back onto the relative safety of the beam. Looking out over the city, he felt his anger dissipate and his thoughts toward his sister soften. For a long time, until Connie was born, she had been the only daughter, and the apple of their father's eye. William O'Connell had deeply believed in the better life offered by America and all the opportunities afforded here that they wouldn't have had in Ireland. He often said that he was Irish, his children were Irish American, and their children would be Americans, the transformation complete. And he believed in taking chances, so when Grace fell in love with dancing, he encouraged it, and when he discovered that a Russian ballerina also lived on Orchard Street with her circus performer husband, he had sent Grace there two afternoons a week to learn all she could. He was determined she would be the first one of the family to have a job she loved and had been so proud of her.

A sudden bang ripped Patrick out of his thoughts, and he jumped. Spooked, standing in no-man's-land on the middle of the beam, he made the mistake of looking up. The steel swinging into place above him to make the next story was moving in one direction, while the white clouds behind were moving in the other. Woozy and disorientated, his head reeling, he lurched, balance lost completely, arms circling like windmills. With a split second to make a decision, he threw himself downward onto the relative safety of the solid beam under his feet, landing at an unnatural angle with a crack.

A dart of pain shot through his left arm, but it barely registered. Instinctively he clamped his legs around the beam, chest heaving, heart hammering, the noise reverberating through his head. His ears rang with the frantic pulsing of his own blood. He placed his forehead on the warm steel and closed his eyes. The last thing he needed was to look down. He could hear the faintest sounds of the street far below, and his stomach clenched, his throat constricting against the urge to vomit at the thought of how close he had come to falling.

"*Minchia!*" Joe cried, reacting quickly and dropping down onto Patrick's back to steady them both until the beam under them stopped bouncing. The wobble felt hugely magnified as the two men's bodies pressed together, each feeling the vibration of the other's racing heart.

Patrick's head was spinning, and he kept his eyes tightly shut until the nausea faded. He forced himself to drag in several ragged breaths. The pressure left his back as Joe stood again. Patrick sat up on the steel, straddling the beam, his legs dangling on either side.

"What the hell happened?" Joe asked, wiping his hands on his coveralls, then reaching out to help Patrick up. Patrick had to spin a hundred and eighty degrees on his backside to face him, and as he was about to grab Joe's hand, something made him pull back at the last minute and use his other arm. Despite the adrenaline coursing through him, he could feel that something was wrong.

"Everything all right up there?"

Two storeys below, on a temporary floor, Joseph Gilligan, the foreman responsible for the ironworkers, had his hand over his eyes, looking up in their direction.

"Fine," Patrick called back, hoping there was no shake in his voice.

"Good, well, then hurry up, I want this corner completed before the bell!"

Patrick gingerly took the paint can Joe was holding out to him and hurried along the steel to the next station.

"Okay?" yelled Frank, concern in his eyes.

Patrick nodded and signaled the go-ahead to Seamus, taking the tongs from the belt of his trousers, relieved to still find them there. Seamus shrugged and tossed up the next glowing rivet. Patrick caught it in the can and had to swallow a scream as the jolt caused unbearable pain to race up his arm like fire. He clenched his jaw as agony as red-hot as the rivet crept into the edges of his vision, turning sharp white and fading to black before he could see again. He felt lightheaded and swallowed down a wave of nausea.

He tapped the rivet on the steel with the tongs he held in his good hand and slid it into place. Joe and Frank both concentrated on their part of the job before staring at him in horror once the rivet was safely in. He must look as bad as he felt. He could feel the bones of his arms grating together as he moved it. It was definitely broken, but he didn't want them to know.

"Keep going," he said through gritted teeth, sweat beading on his face and prickling his scalp. He knew they had no choice.

They fixed ten more rivets before the alarm sounded at four thirty to signal the end of the working day and, thankfully, the week. Everyone downed tools, securing their equipment into labeled gang boxes before lining up to get back down to ground level.

Once in the elevator, Patrick, who by now could feel the sweat cooling on his waxy skin, tried to keep his arm close to his body and protected. When someone jostled him, it took everything he had not to cry out. He bit down so hard against the scream rising in his chest he feared he'd break his teeth. He looked at the floor, unable to meet the eye of any of his gang, not wanting to see their uneasy faces.

At ground level, he joined the line to get paid. Frank quietly stepped into place on his left in an unspoken attempt to protect his arm. Patrick could have cried with gratitude.

After a wait that left him trying hard not to sway with the pain, he eventually found himself at the front of the line.

"O'Connell, ironworker." He summoned all his strength to try and sound normal as he handed over both the aluminum ID tag he collected every morning and the brass one given out on Fridays, to be returned when they received their wages.

A small man with round wire-framed spectacles, flanked on either side by an armed guard, handed over his envelope. "Don't spend it all at once." His voice devoid of all humor, he was already looking at the next man in line. Patrick took the envelope with his good hand, smiled weakly, and tucked it into his pocket, refusing to entertain the thought that this could be the last one he collected on this job.

————

Hundreds of men poured out of the site onto Thirty-Fourth Street. Horns blared as they ambled across the road, knowing the traffic had no choice but to stop for them and let the sea of humanity pass. They laughed and joked, wiping arms across grubby foreheads and lighting longed-for cigarettes from crumpled packets as they celebrated surviving another week. Many barged through the unassuming wooden doors of a nearby hidden bar, eager to drink bad whiskey and gamble away a big chunk of the money now burning a hole in their pockets. Around a corner and out of sight, Patrick leaned against a wall, surrounded by his three workmates, and waited for the crush of people to move on.

"How bad?" Frank asked, taking his hat off and wiping a hand over his thick black hair. He was only thirty-two, but his olive skin was crinkled around the eyes from fifteen years of squinting against the sun on high buildings. He was a handsome man, or at least his wife thought so, and strong as an ox.

Patrick gritted his teeth but said nothing, watching the men flow around them. He didn't want to be overheard. Joe kicked the wall and leaned in closer, speaking under his breath, his face a slimmer, younger version of his brother's. "You know as well as I do that if you don't go up, none of us go up."

"Yes, Joe, I do." Patrick looked straight at him.

The two men stared at each other for a beat longer. Every gang of four worked closely together, forming their own team, language, and way of working. If one of them didn't work, none of them worked, meaning that each man held the future not only of his own family but of three others in his hands.

"It's bad, huh? Or you woulda gone to the infirmary," Frank said, his face clouding with a mixture of fear and concern.

"Better they don't know," Patrick said. "I don't want to give them any excuse to throw us off. I'll head to the hospital and get it checked, but it'll be fine."

"The hospital?" Joe kicked the wall again, harder this time.

"If something had to happen, it's the best time at least," Seamus added. "Friday afternoon, that's some luck." His skin was so fair that his nose was red and peeling from the sun. His green eyes darted around the group, daring anyone to disagree with him. In that moment, his need to defend his family was greater than his own worry. "Get it checked out, and then you have the whole weekend to recover."

"Yes," agreed Patrick, fighting to stop the pain from taking over.

Frank nodded slowly.

"Is it broken?" Joe hissed.

"It's not broken," Patrick said firmly, not quite able to meet Joe's eye. "I'm going to the hospital. Why don't we meet later and see what the damage is? I'll fix this, I promise. It will be fine. Just like Seamus said, I have the whole weekend. I'll be up there on Monday."

"I'll come with you," Seamus said.

Patrick looked at him and nodded. Seamus was family, and Patrick really wasn't sure he could make it to Bellevue alone. He knew the pay packet in his pocket was about to be lightened by whatever tests and treatments he needed, but he had little choice. He felt dangerously close to passing out from the pain.

He glanced at Frank. "I don't want to be overheard discussing this, so come meet me at home later. Nine should be late enough. And don't worry, I'll have it all worked out by then."

He walked away from the Italians before they could say anything else, but he caught Joe shaking his head as he went. He tried to fight down the urge to vomit, unsure if it was from the pain in his arm or the fact that he had no idea how he was going to fix this situation, despite the assurances he'd just given. An hour ago, he'd been worried about keeping a home for his mother and sisters; now, in a cruel twist of fate, not only was his worst fear about to come to pass, but he was in danger of dragging down Seamus and the whole Gagliardi family with him.

5

"One of you in for the evening and the other stays out," Mary sighed. She put Patrick's almost-cold dinner on the narrow side next to the sink to wait for him. "Will we ever all eat a meal around the same table?"

"Where is he?" Connie asked, swinging her legs and stifling a cough. She was wearing her long cotton nightdress and had bare feet. The June evening was hot, and the window was cracked open a little, just enough to let the air circulate. The aroma of fried fish and potatoes from the Donohue apartment above wafted in and mingled with the smells of their own dinner.

"Probably carousing with his buddies," Grace said, spearing some chicken on a fork and handing it to her sister, whose skin seemed to somehow be both pallid and flushed at the same time. It was a tiny victory to see her take the food—she hadn't been eating enough lately. Her eyes were dull and her hair was slick with sweat at the temples. Grace's sense of unease was getting harder to ignore. There hadn't been any improvement for days now. "He got paid today, remember. I expect he's winding down after a long week."

Connie nodded, satisfied with the answer, and chewed the chicken. With perfect timing, the door clicked open and all three of them turned to see Patrick walk in, his face pale and his arm held to his body in a muslin sling. Their cousin Seamus trailed behind, a look of devastation etched on his face.

Connie gasped and froze with the fork held in her hand like a weapon.

"Mother of God," said Mary breathlessly. She shook her head and rushed to Patrick, putting her hands on his shoulders. He winced, and she moved her hands to his face, checking he was really there in front of her. "Are you all right? What happened?"

Grace sat silently and watched the scene unfold as if she were outside her body. She knew instinctively, in an instant, what this meant. The mouthful of food she had just swallowed seemed to get stuck in her throat. It was suddenly difficult to breathe.

"I had an accident, Ma," Patrick said, his throat raw and his voice rasping with pain of more than one kind. "It's been set," he said quietly, "but it's broken."

A strange, strangled noise started to come from Mary, but she quickly balled up her fist and pressed it to her mouth to quiet herself. Grace knew it was because Connie was in the room, and her stomach lurched.

"At least he's alive," Seamus said, taking off his hat and clutching it tightly in his hand, his auburn hair mussed and his face sunburned and still grubby from the day's work. "Six weeks," he said quietly, answering an unasked question.

Patrick's eyes met Grace's identical ones, and Grace was sure she saw his heart break. She gave a barely perceptible nod, hoping he took it for the solidarity she was intending, and then turned her attention to Connie.

"Are you done with your dinner, Princess Connie?" Her tone was falsely cheerful.

"How can you work with a broken arm?" Connie asked innocently. "Do you have a cast? Can I see it? Did you go to the hospital?"

"Like this," Grace said, holding one arm behind her back and flamboyantly flipping the plates and cutlery into a pile with her free hand before lifting them in the air and taking a deep bow.

Connie laughed and coughed, clapping her hands. "Again!"

"How about a story?" Grace asked, desperate to get a closed door between Connie and the rest of the family, ignoring the fear burning at the back of her neck. How much had that arm cast cost?

It was enough of a distraction. Attention from Grace would win out over just about anything in Connie's ten-year-old mind. Grace ushered her into the bedroom. As she closed the door, she saw their mother collapse into tears, Patrick attempting to console her with his one good arm.

Connie climbed into bed and Grace settled next to her, hoping her sister wouldn't notice the pounding of her heart as she snuggled her curly head in close. Grace reached for the battered copy of *The Story of Doctor Dolittle* and read aloud to distract them both from the hushed voices on the other side of the door. With Patrick unable to work, the two hundred dollars in her underwear drawer, which had seemed like a decent buffer just that morning, suddenly felt like no cushion at all between the O'Connells and financial ruin.

She read until Connie fell asleep, then paced the three steps backward and forward that the space allowed, not wanting to head back out and see her mother's despair, but knowing she must.

"She's sleeping," she whispered as she rejoined her family.

Patrick and Mary were sitting, while Seamus was still standing by the door, hat in his hand and, by the look of it, his heart in his mouth. Her mother seemed to have shrunk in the fifteen short minutes since she'd last seen her, and Patrick clearly had the weight of the world settled firmly on his shoulders.

"I have two hundred dollars," Grace blurted, and they all looked at her. "I've been saving it. So we have another month," she finished quietly, noticing that her mother was shaking.

Her eyes traveled the room, looking from the radio to the ice box to the furniture, all bought on credit in better times, and all being paid back in installments. Her mind was in overdrive. One hundred dollars a month in rent alone, then there were Connie's medicines, which they dutifully made her inhale daily, even though they seemed to be making no difference at all. Twenty dollars a week to feed them all, plus bills, repayments, transport. She swallowed hard as she added it up.

"And you'll be back to work soon after that," she ventured, looking hopefully at Patrick. "We can get by."

Patrick's mouth was set in a grim line. He shook his head. "If we're out for six weeks, we'll never get our place back." He looked around the room at each person in turn. "I have to go back up."

"You can't work with one arm," Seamus said firmly. "As much as I'd love you to, to save all our skins, it just isn't possible. And you can't hide a cast."

Patrick looked down at the sling on his arm with disgust. Grace watched him intently, knowing his face as well as her own. She saw the despair and desperation writ large, his brain searching frantically for answers. And then the world slowed down, each second stretching before her as she literally saw the spark of an idea register on his face. His head came up slowly, and he stared at her, taking her in from head to toe as if he had never seen her before.

"What?" she asked, instantly on edge. She could recognize the look of a Patrick scheme from a mile off; their childhood had been littered with them, and a lifetime of experience told her she was in trouble.

He glanced up at their ancient clock and then looked to Seamus, his face alive with purpose. "The Gagliardis will be here in a moment; would you go down and meet them? I'll be right there."

Seamus nodded and ducked out the door. Patrick and Grace gazed at each other in silence for a moment. Then, with a sickening sense of dread, the realization hit her full in the chest, and she suddenly knew exactly what her brother was about to say.

"You could do it," he said, watching her intently. Grace felt her pulse quicken as she waited for the next words, already knowing what they would be.

"I could take your place," she whispered.

"You could take my place."

The idea fizzed around her body, the lurch of fear, the urge to run, and the smallest frisson of excitement ran up and down her arms. She could take Patrick's place.

"Ach, Patrick, don't be ridiculous," Mary said, pouring cold water on the idea. "You want to lose her in an accident like your father?"

There was a heavy silence.

"It's crazy," Grace said.

Patrick stood and grabbed her hand with his good one. He pulled her to the door, letting go of her only briefly to open it and push her out into the shabby hallway. Mary called after them, but they ignored her.

He had already dragged her down two flights of stairs before she came to her senses and snatched her hand from his. She stopped halfway down the last flight, her hand against the wall. Patrick was five steps ahead, almost at the ground. He turned to look up at her. The stairway was eerily quiet.

"Patrick, what in the name of God are you doing?" she asked. "Where are you taking me?"

"The rest of the gang will be downstairs," he said breathlessly. "Seamus and the two Italian brothers I work with every day. You need to meet them; we can make them understand. This is the way out of this mess." His eyes were shining with his own brilliance. "You had the same idea, you said it first."

"This is insane, Patrick. You're not thinking straight. I can't take your place. I know nothing about what you do."

"We'll work that out. You can do it, Grace, I swear to you. This is how I fix this."

"But it wouldn't be you fixing it, would it? It's me. You don't have to do anything at all. And you seem to think you've already decided for me, Patrick, but I have said yes to nothing."

Patrick clenched his jaw, frustration slapped across his face. He looked up at her, and once again she saw a shift in him that made her skin prickle with unease.

He took a deep breath before he said it. "Connie will die if you don't."

Hearing those words was like running into a brick wall at full tilt. Grace felt the air forced out of her lungs.

"That's not fair," she gasped.

"No, it's not," he agreed, shaking his head. "But it's the truth. The only reason she's safe is because we have managed to keep her away from other people and their sickness. We can give her medicine and keep the apartment warm, ventilated, and dry. If any of that changes, then she doesn't stand a chance."

"And if I do this, I will likely die. So you're choosing one sister over the other."

"That's not fair." Patrick echoed her own words back to her.

"No, it's not," she said, doing the same. "More than likely we'll both die."

His voice softened. "Of course I don't want you up there, but I wouldn't have suggested it unless I thought it could work. I think you'll be okay."

"You think? And how exactly am I supposed to do this? It's utterly crazy."

"I'll help you as much as I can." This was the first real tenderness she'd heard from him in a while. It brought a heavy feeling to the back of her throat, and she pinched her lips tightly together, trying to ward off tears. He reached out to touch her, and she flinched. She was staring hard at his now useless plastered arm, hanging against his body, wrapped in a sling.

"Will you at least see what they say?" He gestured with his head down toward the street, where Seamus and the Italians were waiting.

"I'll see."

As she carried on down the stairs, Grace could feel her whole body shaking. Her legs were wobbling and her entire being was screaming at her to stop, hide, run away. Her heart hammered so hard it felt like it was choking her. She had never been so scared in all her life.

Outside, the light was fading but the street was still busy with people. Grace spotted Seamus standing half in the shadows, smoke drifting up from the end of a cigarette drooping from his bottom lip. With him were two dark-haired men with similar features. The older brother looked like he could be a boxer. The younger one had a more compact and athletic build. Grace was intrigued, and despite herself couldn't help but notice how attractive he was. He looked like he could be a good dancer, if he stood up straight instead of slouching against the wall. These men in their working clothes, with strong arms and dirt on their faces, were nothing like the men she was used to seeing at Dominic's or the taxi dances. They were a different type altogether—strong and rough with a realness and vitality that no man in a suit could match. They scared her a little.

When they heard footsteps approaching, they both turned their heads. The younger brother's face turned to anger when he saw the sling on Patrick's arm. He threw his hands in the air before launching into an impassioned speech in hissed Italian. His brother's response was hushed and intense. The younger man fell silent, watching warily from under thick, dark eyebrows as the O'Connells drew closer.

"I'm sorry about your arm, Patrick," the older brother said, sadness in his voice.

"I'm sorry that we will all starve on the streets," the younger one added bitterly. "You said it wasn't broken. You know my brother here is about to have a fourth child?"

"Giuseppe," the older man warned.

But the young man seemed unwilling or unable to stop the emotion pouring from him. "What about Bruno, eh?" He spun back around to Patrick, and his eye caught Grace for the first time. "And who is this?"

"Fairly obvious, I would say," Seamus offered.

"Why do you bring your sister?" the angry young man asked. His voice had a singsong quality, and Grace noted with interest that her family weren't the only ones whose natural accent seemed to make an appearance when emotions were running high.

"Because, Joe, if you'll just can it for a minute, I will explain. I told you I would fix this situation and I have." Grace bristled as Patrick pointed at her with his good hand. "This," he said, "is Grace. We're twins, in case you hadn't noticed."

The older Italian man stepped forward, tipped his cap, and offered his hand with a little bow of his head. "Francesco Gagliardi. But please call me Frank—everyone does except my mother and my brother here. Pleased to meet you, Miss O'Connell." His hand was rough and thick with calluses, and Grace had to stop herself from pulling her own back in alarm. She had never felt anything like it. She smiled a little to show her gratitude at his kindness toward her, but she had lost all powers of speech. The younger brother was now regarding her with barely disguised hostility, and she decided her earlier assessment was wrong: there was nothing at all attractive about this man.

Patrick continued. "Brother and sister twins rarely look this alike, but we do, and it's a lucky thing for all of us. This is the solution to our problem." He put his hand on Grace's shoulder. She was so on edge, she jumped at the unexpected contact.

The older Italian's eyes went wide with realization, and his mouth fell open a little in shock as he tried to understand what Patrick was saying. Joe was still scowling. What his Irish workmate was alluding to was lost on him, but not on Seamus, who froze, cigarette halfway to his mouth.

"Sweet Jesus," he said, his eyes flitting from Patrick to Grace and back again, incredulous. "You want us to take a woman up on the steel."

6

"*Vaffanculo!* This is insane! *È pazzo?* Francesco, tell them! *Idea stupida!*" Words had been exploding from Joe in alternating English and Italian for nearly a full minute before Frank managed to calm him down. He grabbed him by both arms, speaking in hushed Italian no one else could understand, until Joe's breathing eventually slowed, his body heaving.

"I don't think he likes your idea, Paddy." Seamus was deadpan as ever.

"I can see that," Patrick agreed.

Grace stood awkwardly and watched, an outsider in this world, her cheeks burning. Oh, how she wished for the familiarity of the Dominic's dressing area, with Betty on one side of her and Edie on the other. She might not like the idea, but she liked even less how this man had decided without knowing a thing about her that she couldn't do her brother's job.

"I see what you're saying, Patrick," Frank said, stroking his chin. "But there must be a better option for replacing you in the gang. You have a brother, don't you, Seamus?"

"Ha!" Seamus barked out a laugh and started to light his next cigarette from the remains of his last. "Sean? He's a barber. Terrified of heights. He'd be shaking like a dog in the rain up there. He'd curl up and cry, so he would."

"And a girl wouldn't?" chipped in Joe as if Grace wasn't even there. "She'd be scared at the top of a ladder!" He shook his head, adamant.

"Patrick himself nearly killed me today. If I hadn't seen him going down, the bounce would have thrown me over. And that's after two years of working together. I'm not putting my life in the hands of a woman who knows nothing about steel."

"How about another guy?" Frank asked. "I'm sure we can find one. It's not as if this city is short of men looking for work."

"No." Patrick shook his head. "You know Gilligan would rather take on a whole new gang who already work together. It's too risky. You think those Indians who drive the twelve hours back and forth from Canada every weekend don't have another four men just waiting to get on the steel? And anyway, that would be fine for you, but what about me? I've got a family to look after too. The point is, we're not replacing me. I will be there on Monday morning, same as always. Or at least that's what everyone will think." He glanced at Grace, and she could barely believe he was serious. How did he expect her to just step into his life? Joe Gagliardi might be obnoxious, but he was also right—this was madness.

"You really think it can work, Patrick?" Frank was assessing him carefully. The idea was stupid, but his wife, Maria, was going to have another baby in a matter of weeks, and he trusted Patrick's judgment. If there was any possible solution to this mess, he was going to take it.

"Of course not!" said Joe. "You know it, Francesco. Don't listen to this madness. He is a fool. Of course she can't do it!"

"Yes, I can." The words were out of Grace's mouth before she even knew she had said them. She turned and walked away. "How hard can it be," she mumbled to herself under her breath, "if this idiot can do it?"

"Grace!" Patrick tried to call her back, but she wasn't leaving. She wasn't going far at all. The stupid Italian, the situation, the fear, the thought of Connie cold and hungry, her anger and disappointment at losing her job, and Texas's jowly face all spread through her mind like wildfire. Adrenaline raced through her veins. She stopped at the nearest fire escape and pulled against it to check it was secure. Seconds later, she was scaling the outside of it, pulling herself up in her dress and Spanish-heeled shoes. Her work as a dancer had left her body fit and strong, and her fury pushed her ever upward as she climbed, hand over foot, all the way to the top. The only person who was going to decide if she could do this was her.

In no time, she was on the roof of the four-story building. She walked along the very edge like she was strolling through the park, before lying down, leaning out headfirst, the top half of her body hanging over the edge. She heard the gasp from her brother below but ignored everything except the task at hand. The air was dead and there was no wind at all, not even the slightest breeze.

"What is she doing?" Seamus asked.

"Someone stop her! Don't jump!" a stranger shouted up, but Grace was focused. She didn't even hear them.

She reached down as far as she could to a washing line strung between this building and the one opposite, and tugged on it to test how taut it was and the strength of the pulley holding it to the wall. There was no crumbling brick, and it was a double line that could be pulled from above to send the washing out across the street and then pulled back in again. The fixings were strong and the line was thick. Good enough. From this end at least.

She sat back up on the edge of the roof with her legs dangling and took her shoes off. Rolling her stockings tightly, she pushed them deep into her shoes, then, with just a quick look to check it was clear below, tossed the shoes over the side of the building. They made a dull thud as they landed on the street four storeys below and bounced. She heard a collective gasp, and Seamus darted forward to pick them up.

Without thinking about it, Grace took a deep breath and stepped down onto the washing line, feeling it cut into the soft soles of her feet.

The busy street had stopped to watch her, and an eerie quiet filled the air. People murmured and gasped. The gap between the buildings was easily fifty feet. As she let go of the wall, Patrick looked away, before forcing himself to turn back and watch. He was furious at her for doing something so reckless, but he knew he was in no small part responsible for it.

After a couple of tentative steps to find her balance, she held her arms out wide, turned her feet out slightly and walked confidently across the makeshift tightrope. The double line made it easier than other ropes she had walked, even if this was higher and she hadn't properly prepared. Her anger and frustration fueled her. Faces appeared in the windows of both buildings, and she had time to be grateful that their own apartment had no windows on this side, so there was no chance her mother would see. Halfway across, she wished she hadn't been so impulsive. She had no idea if the line was secure at the other end. If it came away from the wall, there would be nothing she could do to save herself.

The line creaked. The light was fading fast, the rope getting harder to see. If she fell now, she would die just trying to prove a point. If she was going to die, it should be because she was trying to save her family. But there was nothing to be gained by regretting her decision now; she had no choice but to keep going. She never looked down, so she didn't see the white faces of four terrified men watching from below, or the growing crowd witnessing a woman risk her life for no apparent reason on a Friday night in June.

She reached the other side and pulled herself onto the roof of the building. After a second of stunned silence, the gathered crowd erupted into applause. Although they didn't understand it, they knew they had just seen something extraordinary.

She stood and made her way to the nearest fire escape, climbing down ladders and steps, her calm actions belying the raging of her heart. Adrenaline thrummed in her as if fired from an arrow now ricocheting around inside her body. It felt good. It had been more than a year since she had walked a rope like that. She'd left the circus when they'd decided to tour the country, the prospect of adventure outweighed by her desire to stay near her family, but sometimes she missed the excitement.

At the lowest balcony, she hopped up onto the railings and swung her legs over, carefully placing her bare feet on the edge and swinging herself down onto the ground, where she stood and held out her hands for her shoes. Seamus crossed the street to give them to her amid the hushed whispers of her confused audience.

Grace took pains to look calm on the outside, but inside she was fizzing with the rush of what she had just done and the huge sense of relief that she'd gotten away with it. Her mind flashed back to performing in front of crowds: the height, the thrill, the smell of popcorn and sawdust, and that feeling of doing something others couldn't. She took her time putting her shoes back on, pushing her stockings into the pocket of her dress before walking across the street, daring Joe Gagliardi to look at her. Frank's jaw seemed to have become unhinged, and his mouth hung open in utter shock at what he had just witnessed.

"Fifteen years hanging steel," he muttered, "and never would I dream." He shook his head in disbelief.

"So you're not scared of heights," Seamus said.

"That is the most stupid and dangerous thing I have ever seen anyone do." Joe shook his head.

"I agree," Patrick said, emotions chasing each other across his face. He was clearly annoyed that she had taken such a risk, but Grace could see other things there too. Satisfaction, relief, even pride. He looked back to his friends. "But I told you she could do it. I'm not crazy."

"Your sister, however . . ." Frank shrugged, looking at Grace.

"Oh, great," said Joe. "Real helpful. That's just what we need. A nutjob. Some crazy girl playing with red-hot steel."

"What we do isn't performing for an audience," Seamus said quietly, serious for once. "Showing off will get you killed."

"You wouldn't listen." Grace was defiant. "I had to show you."

The men were silent now; they couldn't argue. None of them would have believed for a second that Grace was capable of what they had just witnessed if they hadn't seen it with their own eyes.

"This really could work," Patrick said, daring them to disagree.

They stood in silence. They all knew the decision would be down to

Frank, as the oldest and most experienced; the unofficial leader of their group. They watched him as he studied Grace intently.

"I can do it," she said, meeting his gaze.

"Okay, I'm in," Frank said eventually. "We have a weekend to teach you everything you need to know."

Joe huffed all the air out of his lungs and shook his head, but he wouldn't go against his brother. Instead, he looked at Grace. "You do realize the Empire State Building is already five times higher than this," he said, jabbing with his thumb at the block behind him, deliberately unimpressed by what he had seen her do. "And that's just where you would start from. It goes higher every single day."

"I know." Grace's stomach clenched at the thought, panic rising as she understood instinctively, as the others did, that this was Joe's deeply grudging way of accepting the plan. There was no turning back now.

"Then we're agreed," Patrick said gravely, looking at his sister with a mixture of gratitude and admiration she had never seen from him before.

Frank gave one sharp nod. "Welcome to the gang, Grace. There is much to do."

7

SATURDAY, JUNE 14, 1930

G race tossed and turned for most of the night, wondering what she
had done. Her temper had gotten the better of her, and now she
had to face the reality of what she'd agreed to. The task was enormous
and threatened to swallow her whole. As she lay in bed, she reached
her hand out and placed her palm on the wall separating her from her
sleeping sister. The walls were so thin, she almost imagined she could
hear Connie breathing, with the distinctive wheeze she had developed
over the past month proof enough that there was no choice—she had
to take Patrick's place on the steel. No other job she could possibly get
would make even half of what they needed. Even then, things would still
be tight without her pay from Dominic's. Having neither was unthinkable, and there was no way he could carry on with a broken arm. As
impossible as it seemed, their only option was for her to become Patrick.

As soon as the decision had been made the previous night, Seamus,
Patrick, and the Italians had wasted no time discussing how to teach her
everything she needed to know in one weekend. As Grace had retired to
bed, her thoughts racing like a stampede, she had promised she would be
up at sunrise to start her training and transformation. Patrick had barely
looked up from the table where he was writing, sketching diagrams on
a jumble of loose papers, a man possessed. A cup placed on the papers
stopped them moving without the use of his left hand to steady them. At
least it wasn't his dominant right arm he had broken, a small mercy to be

thankful for. They had agreed not to make a final decision or say anything to their mother until after Saturday's training, but Grace already knew. They both did. She was going up on the building on Monday morning no matter what. The dread she felt in her stomach was a writhing pool of acid threatening to burn her alive from the inside out.

Staring at the ceiling, with its small damp patch in the corner, wasn't helping any with her jangling nerves, so Grace got up. Her father had always told her that action was the enemy of fear, and she resolved to spend the day one step ahead of her swirling thoughts. It was barely five a.m., but it was clear that all the sleep she would be getting to prepare for the day ahead had already come and gone. Slipping out of her room to the bathroom, she saw her twin slumped asleep at the tiny wooden table, still dressed. He had been there all night. She watched his chest rhythmically rise and fall. She might be the one who had agreed to risk her life, but Patrick carried a heavy burden too. If she died up there, he would have to bear that guilt, and still be left with no income to save the rest of his family. Things were on a knife's edge whichever way she looked at it, and she'd spent pretty much the whole night doing nothing else.

As she tiptoed past Patrick, she pondered how just a few short days ago they were doing fine, and now everything had collapsed around them. It made her think of all the people she saw on the streets and gave her a new understanding of how it might have happened through no fault of their own. It had never occurred to her until her father died that she would ever be anything other than loved, safe, and secure. It was a hard lesson to learn that no one was ever really safe. Each person was just one piece of bad luck away from a completely different life.

When Grace emerged from the bathroom, Patrick was gone from the table. The sound of running water from the wailing pipes must have woken him. Back in her room, she stopped and stared at her narrow cot bed. On it were a pair of his work pants, a belt, and a shirt. She gulped as a finger of trepidation trailed down her spine. This was really happening.

She dressed quickly, feeling strange wearing the pants. They were at least a size too big, and even on the last notch the belt was no use. She temporarily swapped it for a silk scarf Betty had given her, forcing it through the belt loops and tying it tight in a knot just to keep them up. She slid on her flattest shoes. They still had a heel, but only two inches. The shirt ballooned around her, and she looked ridiculous. Snatching the belt up, she headed out to find Patrick making coffee.

"Too big," she said, holding it out to him as he paused to take in her new look.

He nodded, taking the belt from her and turning it over in his hands. "Nothing a hammer and nail can't fix. I'll put a new hole in."

Grace took the coffee he held out in exchange and wondered how he would manage that with just one arm. She sipped the hot, bitter liquid.

"We should get moving soon," he said in a low voice. He gestured at a folded piece of paper on the desk. "I've left a note for Ma, saying we're following up some work leads."

Grace nodded. They had to be sure they were going ahead before they told her. She cleared her throat. "There are a lot of things we need to work out. I can ape your voice well enough if I lower mine, and I can work on matching my face, but I'm slimmer than you, shorter than you, my hands are smaller. I can wear your clothes over mine to bulk myself out a bit and bind my chest to keep it flat, but your shoes will be too big." The certainty in her voice increased. "I need to have shoes that fit, to have any hope of balancing up there. I can't wear yours."

Patrick looked at her and swallowed, as if seeing his twin in a new light. "Write a list," he said, pushing a notepad and a small, chewed fragment of pencil toward her and taking the belt away to punch new holes in it.

Forty minutes later, Grace and Patrick arrived at what seemed to be a randomly chosen corner on Franklin Street in the Lower East Side. The dawn sky was streaked pink and orange. Five-story tenement blocks in a worse state of disrepair than their own stretched up either side of the street, each building decked with cluttered fire escapes, washing lines, and crowded stoops. The area had the squalid look of a ghetto, and despite it being early morning on a Saturday, it was busy with people going to work, coming home, or escaping the ill-ventilated buildings. Half-naked children played in the streets, and the noise of industry and the multiple languages of the immigrant community filled Grace's ears. A nearby factory pumped out smoke, and the sweet tang of death and iron on the air from a nearby slaughterhouse or tannery made her gag. It was a terrible smell she didn't remember from when she'd lived on this side of town as a child, although she knew it was amazing what you grew used to given time.

"A beautiful morn." The voice made her jump, and she turned to see Seamus approaching behind them, swinging an empty paint can.

"It is that," she agreed, her eyes fixed on the sky, swallowing the rising fear in her throat.

"You two look a picture." A small smile of disbelief crossed Seamus's face. "Already you're two sides of the same coin."

Grace glanced down at herself and then across at Patrick. He had given her a newsboy flat cap, into which she had tucked her hair. Save for her shoes and underwear, she was now dressed head to toe in her brother's clothes. She had helped him button his clean shirt and retied the sling, aware that they had never looked so similar in their lives.

"There's work to do," Patrick said, looking up from the sheaf of papers in his hand. "But it's a good start. Most of the people working on the site don't know us well, and they definitely have no idea I have a twin. They will see what they expect to see."

The two Italians, dressed in dirty blue overalls with grubby shirts underneath, turned the corner, walking toward them. Frank had a heavy burlap sack thrown over his shoulder, and Joe was carrying a lunch pail brimming with food.

Frank nodded approvingly at them, dropping the heavy sack onto the sidewalk with a clank of metal. "Good morning, my Irish friends," he said with a warm smile. Grace liked the man already. Despite his youth, he reminded her of her father. "Patrick, get your sister some overalls. I have only been here two minutes and she has pulled up those slacks three times. Overalls will fix the problem."

"Okay, good idea. I have some." Patrick nodded.

Joe was looking intently at Grace, flicking his eyes to Patrick and then back again, comparing them. "You really think this is gonna work?" he asked, still unconvinced.

"Morning, Joe," Patrick said by way of response. "Only one way to find out."

"Excuse me, sir." A boy pushed past Grace, weaving between the group on his way down the road. Seamus laughed, and Frank tilted his head to the side, jutting his lower lip out and nodding his head as if impressed.

"Well, we've convinced one sucker," Seamus said, reaching into his pocket and pulling out a cigarette.

"I'll have one of those." Grace held out her hand. The men stared at her. "I have to rough up my voice some more." She looked down at the floor before forcing herself to raise her eyes, gaze steady. She couldn't afford to feel intimidated.

"Makes sense." Seamus struck a match to light both cigarettes in his mouth before taking one out and flipping his hand over to pass it to her. Grace placed it between her lips. She had already decided she should say as little as possible. With a reasonably deep voice for a woman, she could impersonate her brother with some accuracy. The added gravel and rasp from the smoke would be a help when she had to keep it up all day.

"We don't talk much up there anyway," Seamus said. "It's a lot of this." He jerked his thumb upward and then raised his hand toward her, palm out.

"Up and stop?" Grace asked.

Frank clapped his hands. "She's sharp, boys, we'll have this nailed in no time."

"A thumb can mean yes. Most often it means we're ready to go or we're done," Patrick said. "But it's always a good thing." He tried to shuffle through his notes one-handed, but couldn't manage, so he passed them to Joe.

"What's this?" Joe said, cracking his first smile of the day. "Looks like a child did them. Is it your writing hand that's busted?" Seamus and Frank laughed, and Grace watched carefully the way the men reacted to one another. She would have to convince everyone that these strangers were her friends and she knew them well. She already knew that men ribbed each other in a way women didn't, and she had to get used to that.

"Forget your scratchings," Frank said, waving his hand. "Why do you think we brought you here? The only way to learn is to do. We can't get on the building, but we can get on *a* building." He pointed to the fire escapes. "You've already shown you can climb these pretty well, and today they're going to be our steel for some practice."

"I don't understand." Grace could feel her cheeks coloring. "These are already built."

Joe sniggered a little and she wanted to kick him. How was she supposed to trust this man with her life when she didn't even like him? The feeling was clearly mutual.

"*Bella.*" Frank's lilting voice was gentle. Grace could imagine him saying the same to his small children. He was obviously the father figure of the group, even though only a decade separated them all. "There are four of us, and we each have our own job. Very lucky for us, Patrick's is probably the easiest for you to learn. It is more skill than strength. He catches, and today, *you* will catch."

Seamus handed Grace the empty paint can, and she looked at it blankly.

"That's what you catch with," Joe said, speaking slowly as if she was stupid.

"Giuseppe Alfonso Gagliardi!" barked Frank. Joe's head snapped round to look at his brother, whose face was red with anger. "You will stop this now! This girl is helping us! She is trying to make sure we have food on our table. That our mother and brother have a roof to sleep under, and your nieces and nephews have clothes to wear. She does not have to do this for us!"

Grace dropped her head. She did have to do it, for her own family. She was doing this for Connie, not out of the goodness of her heart. She didn't want to be here at all. If she thought there was any other way out of this, she would have taken it.

"Could you do what she did last night on the building? No. Could you do another person's job without being shown how?" Frank pointed a finger at his brother, jabbing it toward his chest. "Enough! The first day you walked on steel you were carrying water for the workers, and you went from the ground up. The first day this girl steps out, she will already be up high and have to do far more. And she has to be someone else at the same time. A man, no less, in a world she does not know." He shook his head in disbelief. "I couldn't do it. She is brave and you should show some respect. We must help her. She will only be as good as we make her, and we are all in danger if we don't teach her well. You understand me, Giuseppe? Be kind. What would Mamma say?"

Joe scuffed his feet on the floor, like a naughty child rather than a grown man, before looking up at his brother and nodding, suitably chastised.

"I apologize," he said stiffly to Grace. She looked into his brown eyes and saw fear. She could at least relate to that. She took a deep drag on her cigarette as he continued to speak, with far less attitude than before. "Seamus heats the rivets and throws them up. You catch them in the can." He pointed at the paint can. "You take out the rivet with tongs and tap the cinders off. Then you put it in the hole. I hold it in place and Frank secures it with the riveting gun."

"And that's pretty much it," Patrick added. "The same simple process. Over and over."

"Two hundred feet in the air," Seamus added helpfully. "And rising."

"Is that all?" Grace asked, imitating Patrick's voice for the first time. Patrick looked shocked, and the other three men laughed.

"That's very good." Frank smiled. "Your sister, Patrick, she has many talents."

"But is catching one of them?" Seamus asked.

———

Nearly two hours passed with the street waking up around them as they sat huddled together on the sidewalk. The men walked Grace through each aspect of the construction world she would be stepping into, speaking over each other to add every little detail they could think of. Grace's mind whirled with the information; from the width of the beams to the stages of construction, to what the thousands of men on-site did. A picture was painted for her of what she would see, what she would need to do, and who she would speak to. From the delivery of the materials, arriving like clockwork and so efficiently that the steel was sometimes still warm, to the narrow-gauge railway inside the building taking everything where it needed to go. The inspectors who would check both the work and the workers, the young rivet punks who would keep them supplied with bolts, and the water boys who made sure they were all hydrated. She tried to take it all in. They told her of the bets made between gangs about who could hang the most steel in the quickest time and what to expect from the wind.

"The weather is our biggest enemy up there." Frank was solemn. "We're lucky it's summer now, but the wind doesn't blow straight, it curls around the building and strikes like a snake. You need to get to know it, feel it, and predict what it will do next."

Grace nodded, doing her best to keep up.

"If it rains, we stop. If there is a storm, we get the hell out of the way," Seamus added.

"In the sun it gets hot," Joe said. "Be ready for that. If you faint, you die."

She wasn't sure how she could be ready for that, but she nodded again, looking down at the papers in her hand where Patrick had tried to give her step-by-step instructions about how to be him, complete with maps and diagrams.

There was a deluge of information to absorb, and yet she didn't feel overwhelmed. She stood, and the men watched her as she marked the steps as they spoke, the way she would learn the choreography for a new dance. She measured her stride, practiced where to put each foot, counting in her head, feeling the timing of when to move, letting her body guide her, as she always did.

"Face the other direction," Frank said, twirling his finger in the air, picking up on the way she would learn best. "Imagine an L shape on the floor, then stand at the corner. Now one step to the right. That's it."

Grace looked at him and their eyes met. Frank nodded. "Twist your body to the right."

She followed his instructions, memorizing the new body position so she would remember how it felt when she got it right.

Each bit of information was an additional piece of armor to keep her safe, another thing to occupy her mind and stop her from worrying about the danger of what she was doing, or the distance down to the street below. The work itself sounded easy, far less complicated than the twelve routines and four costume changes her dancing job had called for. Her panic was easing by the minute.

"And now we catch," said Frank, who had clearly had enough of talking and was itching for action. "You cannot talk your way into knowing what to do or how it will feel. You must *do*." He reached for his burlap sack. "When Seamus throws the rivets, he is on the floor below, more than fifty feet away."

Grace gulped. That sounded an awfully long way.

"So, you need to practice." He turned and pointed to the black metal fire escapes snaking up the outside of the buildings. "Up there."

"Up there," she repeated quietly, as Frank pulled a metal bolt out of his sack.

"These aren't rivets, but they are the nearest thing I could find at short notice. A rivet is an inch and a bit long; these are close to that. I've screwed the nut onto each one to make it heavier. It's not the same, but it'll do for practice." He held it up to show Grace.

"Take your paint can and go up there," he pointed to the building on the left, "all the way to the top floor. We'll start with just the catching.

You'll have nothing to bang it against and no hole to put it in. I don't even have any tongs, so you'll hold this in your other hand, just so you don't rely on both hands." He handed her a spoon from the lunch pail. "You'll feel foolish, but it will work. On the steel, Giuseppe will be standing next to you, so he'll go up too."

Grace flicked her eyes toward Joe. He was listening to his brother, and while he was far from friendly, he wasn't as hostile as he'd been before. Still, she wished it was any of the other men she would be with.

"Seamus will be over on that fire escape." Frank pointed to the building on his right, across the street. "On the third floor. He'll toss a bolt up to you. He doesn't have his tongs either, so it's not quite the same, but it should at least give you a sense of what you'll be dealing with. The size, the distance."

"This is a grand idea." Patrick slapped Frank on the back and looked at Grace. Grace knew her twin well enough to know he was anxious. This was the moment when they found out if there was any chance at all she could actually do this and take his place.

"Keep the can out in front of your body," he told her. "Around chest height. Keep your eye on the bolt at all times, and just guide it into the can. Seamus will do the work for you. He'll get it in the right place. You just need to catch it. That's all." He almost whispered the last two words. They were full of more hope than Grace could bear.

"I got it. Let's go." She sounded braver than she felt.

"I know all these people, don't worry." Frank waved a hand in the direction of the street. "They won't say nothing, and they don't mind us using their escapes."

Grace followed Joe, climbing up the fire escape in silence, paint can in one hand. She stepped over jugs, barrels, and boxes strewn across the landings on every floor. Washing hung on ladders reaching up the walls and on every conceivable surface, and was strung in zigzag lines across the street. Frank had chosen the one area where there was a clear line of sight from one building to the next, and she wondered if he was responsible for that. A couple of quarters was probably more than enough to convince people to keep their washing confined to the escape for a day.

Once they reached the top floor, she turned and looked across the street, to where her cousin was already waiting on the opposite building, two floors below, the sack of bolts at his feet. She could feel the panic swirling in her chest. The height wasn't a problem, but the distance was greater than she'd imagined. Seamus seemed mighty far away, and she had no confidence at all in her ability to catch from this distance.

"Ready?" he called. Grace glanced down. There were children playing in the street and she didn't want metal bolts raining down on their heads.

"They'll soon move if they have to," Joe said, following her eyes and speaking for the first time since they'd been on their own. "The idea is that they *don't* have to."

Grace looked at the young man's face and tried to imagine standing with him high up above the city, but she couldn't do it.

"There will be men below you on the steel, too," he said. "And what you'll be catching there will be about the hottest thing you can imagine. It will be far more dangerous," he added helpfully. Pep talks were clearly not Giuseppe Gagliardi's strong point.

Grace took a deep breath. She set herself square, facing Seamus, the paint can in one hand at chest height as she had been instructed, spoon in the other in lieu of the tongs. She looked to Joe next to her and he gave a curt nod. She was used to an audience, but only for things she was good at. Having Joe breathing down her neck only increased the nerves.

"Go!" he shouted across the street.

Grace felt incredibly exposed and unbearably aware that her twin and Frank were standing below, their eyes fixed on her, necks craning upward to watch. The whole building suddenly shook and shuddered as the elevated train rumbled by. Something else she would have to contend with. Seamus reached into the sack and took out a bolt, then in one smooth movement tossed it across the street in a soaring arc, up toward Grace and Joe.

Grace watched the dull gray missile turning end over end as it crossed the street and sped toward her. She jerked the paint can up to try and meet it. At the last minute, Joe grabbed her, pulling her toward him. The bolt sailed over her shoulder and smacked into the wall behind them, right where her face had been a split second before. She gasped and watched it fall to the floor of the escape with a heavy clink. Her eyes went wide as she looked at Joe, his hand still on her arm. He jerked away, and she suppressed a shiver at the contact and the closeness of their bodies.

"It was going to hit you," he mumbled.

"Sorry!" called Seamus. "Terrible throw!" He barked out a little laugh of embarrassment and held up a hand in apology. The kids on the street were now sitting lined up along the curb, fascinated by what they were watching. They had never seen adults play games before. No doubt this would become a new favorite for them to try, as soon as they had the street to themselves again.

"I normally have three feet of tongs to throw with," Seamus shouted. "I never do it by hand. Just got to get my eye in."

"*Coglione*," Joe muttered under his breath. Grace had no idea what it meant but could tell it wasn't anything good. Mercifully, it wasn't directed at her for once. She could still feel the imprint of his fingers around her arm where he'd grabbed her. The shock of him touching her resonated on her skin. At least he hadn't let it hit her in the face.

"Okay, again!" Frank shouted from below, curving his hands around his mouth like a megaphone.

Grace gave Seamus a thumbs-up and he threw another one. This time, she watched the bolt moving toward her and took a step back, catching it neatly in the can. Pleased with herself, she turned to Joe, foolishly expecting praise. Her face fell instantly when she saw him glowering.

"You just stepped back off the beam and fell to your death," he said flatly. "No step back." He shook his head, then made a whistling noise that Grace took to be his impression of her body hurtling through the sky as it made its imaginary fall to earth. He clapped his hands together. "Splat! O'Connell tomato sauce. Scrape it up from Thirty-Fourth Street and put it in a jar."

"Okay, okay." She scowled at him. "I get it."

"Again!" called Frank.

The third bolt came flying up and Grace got the paint can ready. She misjudged it slightly but resisted the urge to step back, and it hit her in the center of the chest before bouncing off. She caught it on the rebound in the can and couldn't help but be pleased at the rattling sound it made. Joe tutted loudly beside her, shaking his head.

"What now?" she asked, annoyed.

"The rivet, it is one thousand degrees! Glowing red-hot. You cannot catch it with your body! You put your body behind it, you will burn. You catch out in front of you." He grabbed the can in her hands and jerked it to where she should be holding it, the rest of her body following like a rag doll. He didn't even pause before raising his voice to shout "Next!"

Grace snapped her attention back to Seamus, no time to even digest what had just been said. The next bolt came flying through the air and she reached out with the paint can. The bolt hit the edge of the can and bounced off, falling to the street below.

"Heads up!" Joe, Seamus, Patrick, and Frank all shouted as one. The chorus of voices made Grace jump, her heart thumping in her chest. She looked over the fire escape and saw the bolt had fallen safely. One of the street kids rushed over to pick it up, a scavenged souvenir, like a baseball sent into the crowd. He shoved it into his pocket and held on to it there so none of the others could get it.

"Sorry," Grace said, her hands starting to shake a little.

"Again!" shouted Joe, and before she had a chance to think, another metal missile was looping through the air.

This time she reached out and caught the bolt smoothly. She could hardly believe it, but there it was, safely landed in the paint can.

"Yes!" called Frank from the street. "Well done!"

Grace looked down to Patrick. He gave a short, silent nod and his tense shoulders seemed to drop a little.

"One out of five," Joe said beside her. "At that rate we will have hot rivets raining down on the men below and we might get the building frame done in five years. Although we will of course be fired and kicked off the site long before then."

Grace felt anger rising inside her. She was here, wasn't she? And she was trying. She had never done this before. She'd only had five goes, and now she knew what it felt like to get it right. She tipped the bolt out of the can onto the fire escape and without saying a word to Joe turned back to Seamus.

"Again!" she shouted. She would be the one to call from now on.

The decision finally came from Frank that it was time for lunch. Grace rolled her aching shoulders as she reached street level again, closely followed by Joe, who still had the look of a sulky child, annoyed that his Saturday was being spoiled. He seemed to cheer up a little when he dumped the can full of bolts on the sidewalk, flopped down beside it, and reached into his lunch pail. The Irish contingent hadn't brought any food, so Seamus went to buy some from a nearby market while Grace sat with her back against the wall, resting her weary body. Patrick had disappeared for the time being and she didn't think to ask where he had gone.

"You are doing well," Frank said, taking a jar from the pail. He unscrewed the top, offering it to Grace. Inside were sundried tomatoes in olive oil and she took one gratefully, popping it into her mouth. She had no idea whether it was because she was so hungry, or if it really was the greatest thing she had ever eaten, but the sweet, oily tomato slid down her throat and made her sigh with happiness.

"You cannot beat Italian food," Frank said, unwrapping a ceramic dish that seemed to be full of rolls of pasta filled with more tomatoes and ricotta cheese. The smell made Grace's stomach yawn for food. "Made by my wife, Maria." He took a mouthful and moaned in delight. Joe was eating a parcel of folded fluffy dough cooked to a perfect brown crisp, stuffed with meats, olives, and cheese. Grace was envious and couldn't wait for Seamus to return.

"You catch more than you drop now," Frank observed. It was meant to be a compliment, but Grace was frustrated by her slow progress. She wanted their approval, wanted to be good, but her body was complaining at the unfamiliar movements, and she felt weak.

"It's harder than I thought," she said quietly, with a whole new respect for what her brother did all day.

"Of course," Frank agreed cheerfully. "What isn't? But with practice it will become like breathing air; you will do it without even thinking about it."

Grace nodded, taking another tomato when it was offered. She savored its flavor as she looked up at the now blue sky. People walked past on the sidewalk and barely noticed the group in scruffy work clothes eating lunch. They were already as much a part of the scene as the rumble of the elevated trains. Most of the children who had been watching had grown bored and scattered, but the few that remained crept ever closer to the group now they were eating. As Grace glanced over at Joe, she saw him tear a corner from his dough parcel and hand it to a scrawny girl in rags, who took it gratefully, shoving it into her mouth as if scared someone would take it from her. Joe looked into the pail again to see what else he could give away, and Grace smiled to herself. At least he wasn't all bad.

Seamus returned with a large bucket of water and offered around small cardboard cups. Grace dipped her cup and drank gratefully. He also handed her a hot dog, still steaming, wrapped in a paper napkin. The smell of onions made her mouth water, and she couldn't remember a time when she'd felt hungrier. He pulled an apple from his pocket and handed that over too. He had the same meal for himself.

She ate most of the hot dog in four bites, watched by a dirt-streaked boy with eyes as wide as cartwheels. She thought he might cry when she gave him the final piece. He cradled it carefully, pulling tiny pieces of bread off, chewing them slowly to savor every mouthful. It broke her heart to see, even more so to imagine Connie ever being that hungry.

Seamus took a small knife from his pocket and cut slices off his apple, giving away every other one. When he'd finished, Grace borrowed the knife and did the same before drinking another two cups of water. Satisfied, she sat back against the wall and closed her eyes, the sun on her face. A few moments later, a shadow fell across her and she opened her eyes with a start. Patrick stood above her, holding out a brown paper bag. She took it, Patrick sliding down the wall to sit next to her, careful to protect his broken arm.

"What's this?"

"Open it and find out."

Unrolling the top and looking in, she pulled out two pairs of work socks, a packet of cigarettes, and some battered secondhand work boots.

"They might still be a little big," he said. "Best I could do."

"Thanks." She took off her shoes, placing them in the bag and handing it to Patrick. "Look after these." She pulled on both pairs of socks and then the boots, standing to stamp her feet and check the fit. The four men looked at her expectantly.

"A little big," she said with a grimace. "But I can wear them."

"Are you sure you will be safe?" Frank asked. "Balance and knowing where your feet are is so important up on the steel." His thick eyebrows twitched with worry.

"They'll be fine. I can do it."

"Great, because this afternoon no one goes home until you make ten perfect catches in a row."

Joe groaned. "You want us to sleep out here?"

Frank shot him a look and Joe raised his hands in surrender. Grace suspected that as much as he didn't want to be there, Joe would delight in calling her out on every mistake she made, taking the count back down to zero so they would have to start again. She sighed and nodded. Frank knew what he was doing.

They said nothing as they stood, ready to get back to work, but each of them knew it was going to be a long afternoon.

8

SUNDAY, JUNE 15, 1930

G race's whole body ached, and her shoulders were on fire. She had woken feeling stiff but also satisfied, as if the hard work was somehow purifying. Relieved to be back in her own clothes, she sat cradling a cup of hot coffee, watching her mother fuss around, fixing her hat with pins. Mary had been on edge ever since Patrick explained the detail of their plan. As her twin children had walked through the door, she and Connie had been sitting at the table, playing cards.

Connie had burst out laughing to see them. Her voice was still weak and raspy, but hearing the joy in it made Grace's heart soar, as did seeing her up and out of bed. "Gracie! Why are you dressed like Pat?"

Mary frowned at them in confusion for a second before the truth dawned on her and she sat in stern silence. Grace went to change, leaving Patrick to explain. By the time she returned, her mother's incredulous fury had given way to grudging acceptance, paired with anxious worry.

"Are you sure about this?" Mary had asked, Connie banished once again to the bedroom.

"If Patrick can do it, so can I."

"I'm sure. But the work isn't designed for women, Grace. And Patrick was trained on the job over time. He wasn't pretending he knew it all right from the start, and he wasn't trying to be someone else at the same time."

Grace didn't need to be reminded of everything that was against her. "What choice do I have, Ma? It's the only way."

Mary had given a single nod and hadn't said another word about it, but as she got ready for church now, Grace could feel the tension rolling off her in waves.

"All of you are coming to church today," she said tersely. "We need all the help we can get."

"Ma," Patrick and Grace both protested at once.

"I'm not hearing any arguments. Connie hasn't been out of these rooms for a week. She needs to sit in church where the Lord can see her, and we all need to pray to keep you safe." She shot a look at Grace.

Grace frowned. "Is Connie well enough?"

"Connie is having a good morning," Mary said firmly. "And we are going to make the most of it."

Patrick shook his head. "We have more work to do."

"Well then, it's lucky church doesn't take all day, isn't it?"

"Patrick can't go," Grace said. "What if someone sees his arm? You know most people only go to church to spy on their neighbors."

"Keep your arm inside your coat," Mary said.

"But it's hot, Ma."

"We'll sit at the back."

The twins shared a knowing look. It was obvious there was to be no arguing with their mother on this, even though their whole plan could be ruined if anyone from the construction site saw them. Grace was angry; she didn't want to do all this work and have it be for nothing. She also wasn't sure she wanted to be seen by God right now. Pretending to be another person to claim their wages wasn't very Christian. Even if she did plan on doing the work, it was still a sin, and she knew she would feel shame to sit in his house with the truth in her heart on display. But then, what kind of God sat by and watched a whole country go hungry? He had his own explaining to do.

"How do I look?"

All three adults turned to look at Connie, dressed for the first time in what seemed like weeks. She was wearing a pretty green dress with a collar, her blond curls as unruly as ever. The dress hung off her and

Grace realized her sister was even more frail than she'd thought. She had lost a lot of weight and was now all bony angles and pale skin, with dark circles under her eyes. She coughed, recovered, then gave them all a dazzling smile.

"Like a princess, to be sure." Grace reached for her hand. "Would you like to borrow one of my hats?"

"Oh yes, please!" cried Connie, her eyes dancing. Grace nodded and went to her room, glad to be out of sight to compose herself. She saw her brother's clothes carefully folded at the end of her bed. Her stomach was rolling and dipping at the thought of what she had to do the next day, but she would have to put up with it. She would do anything for that girl in the green dress.

The service had been going on forever when Mary finally took Connie with her to the front of the church to receive the Eucharist and Patrick and Grace managed to slip out of the doors onto the street.

"I'll see you later," Grace said as they left the church, the bells ringing behind them.

"Where are you going?" Patrick stepped closer and lowered his voice. "We've already lost the morning." He was irritated and had fidgeted all through the service, shuffling and tapping his feet, uneasy and agitated, his eyes constantly scanning for anyone he might recognize.

"I'm meeting my friends. It's been arranged for days. I won't be long."

Patrick reached for her arm. "We don't have time." There was panic in his eyes.

"Patrick," she said firmly, shaking him off. "What more can we do?" She stepped away from the flow of people leaving the church and tucked herself into the wall, her brother following. "My body aches. If I do any more, I won't be able to move tomorrow. I need to rest. You've talked me through it, and I made fourteen catches in a row." She took a deep breath before she continued, whispering now. "And if I'm to be you, I'm not going to be able to see my friends anytime soon, am I?" Her eyes flashed as she added, "If at all. I might die, remember? I have a lot to think about. For the next few hours, you need to let me be."

Patrick took off his hat, brushing his hand through his dark hair before replacing it. Grace saw the struggle playing out on his face. "Fine." He took a step back. "But no one's going to die."

"I wasn't asking your permission," Grace mumbled under her breath as she walked away, heading for the subway station. She was grateful to be stepping back into her own life, however briefly. She always worried about Connie, but it was a very different feeling now that she was responsible for her.

As she walked down West Forty-Fourth Street, through the milling crowds of people, she was able to at least temporarily put her problems to the back of her mind as she anticipated seeing Betty and Edie. It had only been a few days since they last danced together, but it felt like a lifetime ago.

Stepping through the doors of Ruthie's, one of countless lunchrooms in Manhattan, she scanned the long counter down one side of the room and the small tables on the other. Families and couples who were still able to scrape together the money for a meal out were scattered around. Grace's eye was drawn to a small woman with telltale hunched shoulders and a gray felt cloche hat, sitting alone at a corner table by the window, a glass of water in front of her. She recognized Edie immediately.

"Edie," she called, and Edie stood to receive the hug Grace gave her, arms wrapped tight around each other.

"Hello, Grace," Edie whispered into her shoulder. "It's good to see you."

"Room for one more?" boomed a familiar voice, making sure everyone in the place heard and would turn to look.

Edie and Grace pulled apart, turning to greet Betty, her blond hair set in perfect finger waves framing her face. She wore bright red lipstick and a white dress with feathers across the shoulders. Endless necklaces of pearls and beads draped around her neck, every bit the glamorous movie star, rather than a woman meeting her friends for a dollar lunch on a Sunday afternoon.

"You look beautiful," Edie said in wonder, accepting the air-kiss Betty gave her, turning her cheek so as not to smudge her lipstick.

"Thanks, doll." Betty sat down. "*You* look hungry." She swept her eyes across Edie, who glanced down at the table and blushed. "Let's eat," Betty declared, raising a menu like she was reading a book.

Edie picked hers up nervously, and Grace knew in an instant why she had arrived first. She'd already studied it and decided what she could afford. "I'm going to have the salad," she said with a small smile. "Looks good," she added unconvincingly.

"You are not," Betty said.

Grace looked down at the menu herself, unsure of what she wanted.

"You're going to have a beef sandwich," Betty told Edie. "With pickles and French fries and cobbler for afters."

"But—" Edie started to object.

"And you're not going to complain unless it's to tell me you would rather have turkey. You need meat, and warm food, and Howard is paying for it." Betty tapped her purse. "So order whatever you want."

Edie looked back down at the menu with wide eyes, so many more options now available to her.

"You too, Irish," Betty said. "What's the point in shacking up with Howard if I don't get a few perks?"

Grace smiled. "Things are going well, then?"

"He's moved me out to his place in Jersey," Betty said. "Well, our place now. We got married." She said it flippantly, waving her left hand in the air to briefly show her ring.

Edie squealed. "You got *married*?"

"And you didn't tell us?" Grace added with a raised eyebrow. "We saw you three days ago, and now you're married?"

"Ah, get over it. I didn't tell no one except my sister. It was no big deal, and no one's in the mood for a big wedding. His mother would've had a fit if he was living in sin, and I want Howard's money where I can see it. And use it. Everybody wins."

"So romantic," Grace said, rolling her eyes, and they all laughed.

"Ain't the time for romance, O'Connell, and you know it. I'm one of the lucky ones. Do you two have new jobs yet?"

Edie's face colored again, and she shook her head slightly. "I'm working on it. It's hard out there, but one of the girls I live with says she might have something for me. A hat-check job at the Empire on Thirty-Ninth."

"That's good." Betty patted her hand encouragingly. "You'll find something."

They both turned their attention to Grace, who opened and closed her mouth without speaking. She should have prepared for this, but her mind had been so full she hadn't thought ahead to how she would answer the question. She knew she couldn't tell them the truth, even if they were her best friends.

"I'm . . ." She paused. "I'm starting something new tomorrow." She nodded. "It's not dancing. My brother got me the position, and I'm not sure it will work out, but I'm going to give it a try."

"Good for you," Betty said, Edie nodding in agreement, a small smile on her face. Grace knew Edie was happy for her, even though her own situation was desperate.

"If I hear of anything, I'll let you know," she added, feeling guilty.

"Thank you, Gracie." Edie looked back down at the menu. "I can't decide whether to have the steak sandwich or the omelette," she said with excitement.

"Hell, you're having both." Betty took the menu away. "Grace?"

"I'll have the roast chicken sandwich and a lemonade," Grace decided. It was her favorite, and she intended to enjoy it. It might be her last one. This time tomorrow, she would be no more than a tiny speck up in the sky above the city.

Grace waved her friends off, tucking into her pocket the napkin Betty had scribbled her new address and telephone number on, already missing them before they were even out of sight. She was buoyed by seeing them, but with each step farther away, the dread crept back in. She decided to walk home, using the opportunity to smoke the cigarettes Patrick had bought her the previous day. If she hadn't been so nervous, it would have been a pleasant walk through the city, but under the circumstances, she couldn't enjoy her surroundings.

Reaching home, she had to climb over a hockey team's worth of Donohues playing on the second-floor stairs.

"Good afternoon, Miss O'Connell," one of the children said from under a mop of thick dark hair. A boy of about ten pulled one of his toddling siblings onto his lap and out of Grace's way. They were all remarkably clean; Sunday was bath day.

"Good afternoon, Connor," Grace said, taking a stab at his name.

"Ciaran," he said with a shrug, as if it was unimportant and happened a lot.

"Sorry, Ciaran." She corrected herself with a kind smile.

"No bother. Connor is out with Da."

"Right. Have a good afternoon." Grace disappeared up the stairs. She had no idea how the Donohues even attempted to feed so many mouths every day. Families with ten to twelve children were the norm with the Irish Catholics. Two of her older brothers had died as babies before she and Patrick were born, and her mother had miscarried many times before having Connie. It felt awful, but Grace couldn't help but be grateful things had turned out the way they had. Trying to keep just the four of them solvent was proving hard enough; the thought of them tripled in number sent a shiver up her back. God worked in mysterious ways.

She heard voices as she opened the front door and was greeted by a sight that made her stop in the doorway. Four adults and Connie all crowded into the small living space.

"Hello, Gracie." In front of her was the familiar smiling face of a man a few years older than her. He was dressed smartly and had clearly been to Sunday Mass. "It's been a while, so it has."

"Sean." Grace took in the green cloth spread across their small wooden table and the scissors set upon it. No one had discussed this with her, but the meaning of it and the inevitability hit her instantly.

"I thought me brother could be of some use to you, Grace," said Seamus.

Grace stepped inside and closed the door. Leaning against the wall, she reached up and took off her hat. Her other hand went to her hair and lingered there.

"You've told him?" she asked in Seamus's and Patrick's vague direction. Patrick nodded.

"Sean's family," Mary said, changed now from her Sunday best back into her house clothes, her hair a fuzzy halo around her head.

"Handy having a barber in the family," added Seamus.

Grace nodded. She supposed it was true. She had always known it would have to happen, she just hadn't let herself think about it. And at least Sean wasn't someone they would have to bribe to keep quiet.

"This will be a first for me," Sean said, beaming. "Never cut a woman's hair before." He spun two chairs around and signaled to Grace and Patrick.

"You here, Paddy." He patted one chair, indicating with his eyes for Grace to take the other. "Just so I can make sure I do it the same."

"What are you doing?" Connie asked.

The adults all looked at each other.

"She'll have to know," Patrick said to their mother. Mary hesitated before reluctantly nodding.

"I need to look like Patrick for a while, Con," Grace told her. "You can help me later and I'll explain it all."

"Okay." Connie nodded, accepting the situation unquestioningly. She sat quietly on their only small armchair, a book in her lap, watching intently, tired from her trip out to church.

"Ma'am." Sean bowed deeply, the scissors now in his hand.

"All right," muttered Grace, sitting next to her brother. "Don't make a fuss."

She reached up and tentatively took out her hairpins, clutching them tightly in her hand. Before she could say a word, a big hank of her shiny brown hair fell into her lap. She tensed at the shock of it, pressing her lips together so as not to cry out. She heard Connie gasp, and closed her eyes, not wanting to look. She willed herself not to cry. Of everything she had done so far, this was by far the worst. She knew it was stupid and vain, but she felt her identity fall away with every snip, her head feeling lighter by the second.

Once her hair was short, Sean wetted it and began to cut it into the same close style as Patrick's, short at the back and sides, longer on the top. Grace felt the comb sweep across her head, the journey finishing far sooner than it should have done. It was only hair, but it was her hair. There was no going back now; the sacrifice had been made.

"Great snakes!" Seamus cried when his brother took a step back to admire his work, giving the others their first view of the transformation. Sean moved forward and made a final adjustment before stepping back again.

"And you're done," he said.

Grace opened her eyes and looked around the room, taking in the expressions on the faces of her cousins, her brother, and her mother before her gaze fell on Connie, who was staring with interest.

"How do I look?" she asked softly.

Connie's brow furrowed as she considered her sister carefully. "Like Pat," she said, nodding solemnly. "It worked. You look just like a boy. It's . . . strange."

Grace brushed at her shoulders and Sean stepped forward to help her. Mary had a hand over her mouth, and Grace could feel a lump forming at the back of her throat as she tried to ignore the remnants of her hair lying on the floor. She turned and looked at Patrick, still sitting next to her. He met her gaze straight on, and Seamus laughed.

"Like looking in the mirror!" he said. "Good work, Brother."

There was a sadness in Patrick's eyes, a realization finally of what he was asking of her. Grace couldn't hold his gaze for long. Silently she got up and went to the small bathroom.

It took her a while before she was brave enough to look at herself in the mirror. Arms braced against the sink, she stared down into it, then took a deep breath and raised her chin. She gasped. Patrick stared back at her. She turned one way and then the other, running her hand over the back of her head, her hair so short there that it felt like a nailbrush under her fingers. Her hair was gone, and what little remained was styled exactly like her brother's. She knew this was a good thing, a big step closer to their plan working, but she couldn't fight the sense of loss. Her shoulders caved in and sobs racked her body.

A few minutes later, she splashed water on her face and composed herself. She left the bathroom with a plastered-on smile that wouldn't have been out of place at a Dominic's performance.

"Ach, Sean," she said. "You've done a wonderful job, thank you. I didn't recognize meself." Everyone must have heard her crying—the apartment was small and the walls were thin—but they did her the kindness of pretending they hadn't.

"What about the scar?" Connie asked, running her finger under her own eye to demonstrate.

The adults all looked to each other. She was right. Patrick had a small scar under his left eye. Grace went to perch on the edge of the armchair.

"This is why I need your help, Princess Connie. What else are we missing?"

Grace sat on her bed, peering into her mirror, unhooked from its nail on the wall and now balanced on the chest of drawers. Connie was sitting next to her. Grace had dabbed some lipstick under her eye and smudged it with her finger to create a passable copy of her brother's small crescent scar. Luckily it was from childhood and was smooth and somewhat faded, rather than angry and puckered, which would have been harder to replicate.

"How do I look?" she asked.

Connie tilted her sister's head toward her, her cool little hand resting gently on Grace's chin. She leaned in and peered intently at her face.

"I think it's perfect," she decided. "And I also think it's a good thing Pat doesn't have a beard."

Grace found herself laughing, a momentary relief from the pit of snakes squirming in her stomach. Taking one final look in the mirror, she turned back to her sister.

"Con, you understand it's important that no one knows about this, don't you? You can't tell anyone what we're doing."

"Who would I tell?" Connie grumbled. "I don't see anybody."

Grace nodded. "I'm not proud of deceiving people. I wouldn't be doing it if we had any other choice, so can you promise me you won't tell? I have to go to Patrick's work and pretend to be him, because he can't work for a while with his bad arm and we need the money. We could all get in trouble. Not just me and Pat, but Seamus and their friends, too, if anyone ever finds out."

"Of course." Connie got up onto her knees on the bed, reaching over to give her sister an awkward hug. "I won't tell." She rested her head on Grace's shoulder. "I think you're brave going all the way up there. It's our secret, Gracie," she added. "I will never tell. Not ever. For my whole life."

"Thank you, darling." Grace turned her head to kiss her sister on the forehead, hoping that Connie's whole life would be an incredibly long and happy one.

"Are you all right in here?" Mary opened the door and Grace looked past her, trying to see where everyone was.

"They're all gone," Mary said, leaning against the doorframe. "Patrick can't take the nerves of it, so they've gone to get themselves a drink."

"Oh." Grace's voice was quiet.

"That's the way of it." Mary straightened the front of her skirt. "Same when babies are born. The women are the ones doing all the work and the men do all the fretting. No time for fretting when you're just getting on with things."

The three of them were silent for a moment, before Mary stepped forward and gently ran her swollen hand over Grace's newly shorn head.

"You're a good girl, Grace," she said softly, her only concession to the situation. "Now, Connie, back into bed and get some rest while we get dinner started. It'll be corned beef hash tonight."

9

MONDAY, JUNE 16, 1930

There was no window in Grace's room, so she couldn't wake with the sunrise, but the clanging of pots and pans in the kitchenette jolted her awake just as effectively. As soon as her eyes cracked open, a wave of anxiety crashed over her, pinning her to the bed, sweat prickling the back of her neck.

The night before, after fitfully tossing and turning for an hour, feeling the panic rise, she'd found herself on her knees, reaching under the bed for her purses. Checking each one, she finally found what she was looking for: a small metal flask that still held a measure of whiskey. It seemed like a relic from another life, and she downed it gratefully. There was no way she could face what lay ahead without sleep. It had done the trick, and she'd slept soundly for the next few hours.

"I may die today," she whispered out loud to herself, grimacing as she heard the words spoken. She closed her eyes and concentrated on dissolving the thought as she sat up, hands gripping her sheets tightly. Then her eyes flew open and her hands went to her head, heart pounding. She had momentarily forgotten her new haircut, and for a split second foolishly thought she'd been scalped in the night. Taking deep, calming breaths, she swung her feet onto the cool floorboards.

As she emerged from her room in her pink cotton pajamas, her hand was still running over the novelty of spiky hair at the back of her neck. Things were eerily quiet from the apartment above, with only the faintest shuffling audible. The smell of breakfast assaulted her nostrils as she took in the spread of coffee, bacon, eggs, and toast her mother was preparing, her own way of combating the fear and using her nervous energy. The sight turned Grace's fretful stomach, and she clenched her jaw against the nausea.

"There you are. Did you sleep?" her mother asked, eyes searching her face anxiously.

Grace took a seat at the table. She would normally bathe and dress before eating, but today was no normal day, and she wanted to put off for as long as possible the moment when she had to don her brother's clothes.

"A little." She took the plate her mother offered her. The last thing she wanted to do was eat, particularly anything greasy, but she knew she shouldn't leave with an empty stomach. She raised a piece of toast to her mouth and nibbled a corner, trying to force herself to believe this was a morning like any other.

Patrick came out of his room on hearing their voices, deep purple circles under his eyes; it seemed Grace hadn't been the only one who had found sleep hard to come by. He was already dressed, but had clearly struggled with only one working arm, and his buttons were haphazardly done. Over his good arm was draped a pair of dirty blue overalls, and in his hand his own work gloves and flat cap. The pained look on his face made it obvious that handing them over was proving difficult.

"Just a few short weeks," Mary said to both of them. "Then things will be back to normal."

Back in her room, with breakfast sitting uneasily in her unsettled stomach, Grace started to dress. She put on her own underwear, then took the long strip of bandages her mother had given her and bound her chest until it was flat, fastening the binding with two safety pins. She took a deep breath to make sure she still could, and found the constriction oddly comforting, like being in a tight and reassuring embrace. She glanced at herself in the mirror, adding the scar under her eye, holding one hand with the other to steady it as she applied the makeup. For the first morning in many years, her hair needed no pins or setting.

Next, she pulled on her brother's white vest and his shirt, rolling up the sleeves. Both were too big, but not by enough to look ridiculous. She added two pairs of socks and put on the overalls. The boots and the cap were the final touches, with the gloves safely stowed and poking out of a pocket. When she looked in the mirror, she gave a little gasp to find her twin staring back at her. In looks at least she would pass for Patrick. If only that was all that was needed.

When she left her room, Patrick was sitting at the table with their mother, his leg jigging up and down. They both turned as the creak in the floorboards signaled her arrival. Mary's eyes went wide, and Patrick took a big gulping swallow. Grace's hand flew to her throat.

"Adam's apple," she said, a hint of panic in her voice.

"I don't think anyone will notice," said Mary.

"Me neither, but better to be safe. Do you have a bandana I can use as a scarf?"

Patrick shook his head. "It's June, too hot. And I never wear one. It'll draw more attention. No one will be looking that closely; everyone will be busy doing their own job. Just tilt your chin down to your chest if you need to, but I doubt anyone will be getting that close."

Grace nodded, more nervous now. What else had they overlooked?

"But . . ." In two steps he was in front of her, reaching with his good arm to unroll her sleeves and cover her arms. Grace looked down and saw his hairy wrists. The hairs on her own arms were much fairer, her wrists far more delicate. "That's better. Fine once you're up on the steel to roll them back if you get hot, and you'll have gloves on by then too. Just for now, better to be as covered as you can. And remember, you might feel like you have a flashing sign on your forehead telling everyone who you are, but no one else knows, and no one will suspect anything out of the ordinary. For them, it's just another day."

"Just another day," Grace repeated back to her brother in his own voice. He smiled.

"You're going to do fine," he said quietly, glancing at the clock. "Seamus will meet you down on the street. Just for today. For moral support." He stepped forward and grabbed her in a spontaneous hug. It was over as soon as it began, and he stepped back, jaw clenched. Grace felt a surge of warmth for him.

"Good luck." Mary struggled to look at her daughter but forced herself to. It was unsaid between all of them that no one was going to say goodbye. Grace nodded and headed for the door. She took a final look back. Seeing the fear in her brother's eyes and catching her mother cross herself, she wished she hadn't.

Down on the street, she felt uneasy. From now on, she had to be Patrick completely, and her skin was crawling at the thought of making a mistake. One slipup and three families would be in danger. The pressure was enormous. She took a deep breath and looked around, noticing that everything seemed brighter and sharper than normal: the brownstone, the red brick, the asphalt. The risk of not seeing out the day certainly made her appreciate the world around her.

"Morning, Mr. O'Connell," called one of the Donohue children as he rushed down the stairs, bookbag bouncing. It was the same boy Grace had seen the day before.

"Morning, Ciaran." She took the opportunity to practice Patrick's voice.

The boy spun back around with a huge grin on his face, a gap where one of his front teeth had not long ago been. "You got it right!" he said. "Thanks, Mr. O'Connell!"

Grace would have smiled, but Patrick wouldn't, so she made a gruff noise in the back of her throat instead. Already she was second-guessing herself. Patrick probably didn't know Ciaran's name; what if he saw him later? They hadn't thought of the neighbors. They could easily see both Grace and Patrick in the same day, one with a sling and one without, and wouldn't they wonder where Grace was? The back of her throat grew tight. There were so many ways this could go wrong, so many opportunities to be caught out. She looked up at the building and felt the urge to run back inside. Surely there was no way they could pull this off.

"Patrick!" The familiar voice came from behind her, followed by a hissed, "Where is she?"

She turned around to face her cousin. Seamus stopped walking and took in the person in front of him. Grace could see the confusion on his face and the cogs whirring in his brain. When his eyes fell on her arm and he saw that not only was it not in a sling, but there was no plaster cast, he seemed to realize it was Grace standing in front of him, not Patrick, but he still wasn't quite sure.

"Where's Grace?" he asked cautiously.

"Still in bed most likely," Grace said in Patrick's voice. Seamus rubbed his hand across his mouth. "Got a cigarette for me?" she asked, and he nodded, reaching into his pocket.

"You had me fooled," he said with a big grin on his face. "And I've known you my whole life."

"I don't know what you're talking about," Grace growled as they set off down the road. She was secretly pleased. If she could fool Seamus, she knew her disguise was convincing enough to fool anyone. She was in character now, and it felt safer to stay that way.

When they reached the entrance to the site, Grace wanted to stop, look up and catch her breath. She burned to take in all the chaos of noise and motion, but Patrick wouldn't, so she kept walking. This would be nothing more than a normal day for him, and so it had to be for her. She had to keep her face neutral despite the onslaught to her senses. Smoke already hung in the air, cranes swung, engines roared, and huge crowds of men were pouring in, talking and laughing, jostling her, catching up with colleagues and telling tales of the weekend. Trucks thundered by, and Grace tried not to flinch at the overwhelmingly deafening clang of metal and thwack of wood as materials were unloaded.

Seamus nudged her gently in the direction of the office where they had to sign in for the day, and she joined the line. For her first mistake, she found herself in front of Seamus, with no room in the crowd of bodies to maneuver herself behind him. She would have preferred to watch what he did first. Instead, she focused on the men ahead of her, filtering out the other noise to listen to their conversations. Before she had any real confidence in the situation, she was in front of a big oak desk, where a man with round wire-rimmed spectacles glanced up briefly.

"Patrick O'Connell," she said confidently in her brother's voice, silently rejoicing that the nerves she felt weren't evident in her speech and she had said the right name.

The man cocked an eyebrow, clearly waiting for something else. Grace heard "Callaghan, carpenter" from the adjacent line. She kicked herself for giving a first name. It was a job title the man was waiting for. Her mind went blank, nothing but an expanse of white, a snowstorm at the North Pole. Steelworker? No, she remembered that much. Although it seemed like it would be the right answer, it was actually a completely different job. Even though they worked with steel, they were ironworkers. Or should it be more specific? Should she say catcher? Her mind was buzzing with interference, but no words would come. She stood with her mouth open for what felt like hours but was really only a couple of seconds. Was she going to ruin everything before even getting on-site?

"Riveter," she blurted out of nowhere. She heard Seamus exhale heavily behind her.

The man gave her a slightly quizzical look but handed over an aluminum tag with a worker identification number on. Grace knew that someone would be making rounds twice during the day to check them, to make sure everyone who was meant to be on the site was there. She would also need to hand the disc back at the end of the day. She tucked it into her pocket and was tempted to keep her hands there; they were the thing most likely to give her away. Moving away from the office, she made the decision to put her gloves on, even though no one else had yet. Having her small hands exposed just seemed too risky.

She waited for Seamus by the elevators, spotting the Gagliardis approaching. Even Joe looked grudgingly impressed at her disguise.

"You're keen, O'Connell," a man said, walking by, gesturing to the gloves. He was tall, with dark hair and droopy skin under his eyes. He had a faint Irish accent and a dark, bushy mustache. Grace had no idea who he was, but he looked important. This was confirmed as she felt the other three men tense around her. She decided to stick to the plan and say as little as possible.

"Yessir," she replied with a little tilt of her head in a perfect impersonation of her brother.

"Always keen, Mr. Gilligan," Seamus said, saving Grace from having to speak further and letting her know who he was. The foreman. They had told her about him. He was the one man they had to make sure didn't find out what had happened to Patrick. She had been on the site for only minutes and she was already being tested.

"Better head up, then," said Gilligan, gesturing toward the elevator shafts. "The aim is for four floors this week."

"I think we'll do five," Joe countered boldly. Gilligan chuckled as he turned away, and they all breathed a little easier.

"You're in," Seamus whispered as they headed into the elevator cage that would take them to the top of the structure. Connectors were already up there waiting for cranes to send up the first delivery of steel. They were the only people who worked higher than Grace was going, receiving the steel and temporarily fixing it in place, ready for the riveters to come along behind and secure it properly. They would be creating the twenty-first floor of the building.

"Don't look down," Joe mumbled into Grace's ear.

The elevator started to rise at the same time her stomach began to drop. The ground fell away and she quickly found herself on an upward trajectory to the moment she'd been dreading. When the cage stopped, she made sure she was behind the rest of her gang this time, in position to follow them, copying everything they did.

She stepped out onto a temporary floor on the eighteenth story and watched men climb onto unconnected steel beams suspended between cables. Her knees were rubber and her throat started to constrict as she felt the wind push against her. Men gestured to the crane operators, who swung them into the air, and she watched, eyes wide, as they stepped off onto the bare steel beams even higher up. Looking out over the city, her breath caught in her throat. She had never been anywhere close to this high in her life. The buildings in the distance by the river looked to be the size of matchboxes, the details impossible to make out. The street traffic below was so far away it sounded muffled, and panic started to creep up her spine and tickle the back of her neck. She shook it away.

"Eh, Gagliardi!" A man in his forties, with a trilby hat and well-worn overalls over a shirt and tie, shouted over. Grace was shocked; she hadn't expected to see any workers wearing ties, but as she looked around, she realized that a large number of the men, particularly the older ones, were dressed almost as if they were heading to the office. "You fancy a little wager for the week?" He wiggled his thick, dark eyebrows.

"What are you thinking?" Joe answered, just a couple of steps ahead of Grace.

"Two dollars says we raise more steel than you this week."

Joe's eyes momentarily flicked to Grace, and a grimace crossed his face. He recovered quickly; no one else would have noticed it, but Grace did. "Sure thing," he said, reaching over and shaking the man's hand. "I look forward to taking your money from you, Marco."

The man laughed and headed off in a different direction. Joe moved toward the equipment box and Grace followed.

"That's two dollars I'll never see again," he mumbled under his breath, so only she could hear.

"Here, Patrick." Seamus handed her a foot-long pair of tongs and a can. It was the first time Grace had ever seen the tongs, and as she took them in her hand, their weight surprised her. She turned them over and flexed her fingers to test them. The can was also smaller than the one she had practiced with. Her stomach hit the floor. How was she meant to catch with this? Her chest started to heave, her breathing heavy and labored. A hand on her arm pulled her back to reality.

"You can do this," Joe said, his tone matter-of-fact, before he moved away.

"Are you ready?" Seamus asked right by her ear, and she nodded. The noise was already increasing as more people started work. It was frightening how isolated and alone it made her feel to be separated from the others by a wall of sound. Seamus gestured to where their starting position for the day was, on the nineteenth floor, soon to be moving to the twentieth, and Grace followed Joe's movements exactly to get herself up onto the beam, silently begging her legs not to give way.

The sight of the steel frame teeming with men, moving all over it like insects, made her head spin. Vertigo gripped her and panic detonated in her body, reverberating in her limbs, her legs suddenly boneless and wobbling dangerously. Her heart jogged desperately between tight ribs as she forced air into lungs that suddenly seemed three sizes smaller than they had the day before. Her head felt light, and she was terrified of getting dizzy. She gripped hold of the steel column in front of her so tightly she wasn't sure she would be able to let go long enough to catch anything.

Joe seemed to be ignoring her, busy with his own preparations, but Frank was watching her like a hawk. They were in position now, no one else within earshot, but the noise of the site had kicked up even further and was louder than anything Grace had ever known. Frank tapped her gloved hand with his to get her attention and raised two fingers to point at his own eyes, gesturing that she should look at him.

"Just like we practiced," he said, raising his voice as far as he dared and speaking the words carefully so she could read his lips.

Grace nodded, but her heart was pounding like a steam engine, and the power of it alone seemed enough to knock her off the beam. She needed to shuffle her feet and find her balance. The others instinctively knew the width of the beam and where they were on it through years of repetition, but she couldn't possibly know. She had no choice but to look down. Her plan was to glance at the beam directly below her and the position of her feet, but she couldn't help but see straight down to the ground, an impossibly long way away. The design of the building was tapered, and the workers were high enough that the steel had already recessed inward, so she tried to imagine the flat area she could see below her as a floor, not too far away. Unfortunately, her eyes were more interested in the real street level, where little blobs were moving. She looked again and realized they were people. Her head whirled. The shock of it made her swoon slightly, her knees going weak. Her breakfast churned in her stomach, making her feel queasy. She closed her eyes, but understood immediately that only made it worse, and quickly opened them again.

"Come on!" Joe shouted at her. "Don't think, work. Give yourself no time to think."

With a monumental effort, Grace managed to pry her hands away from the column. She stood on the beam and searched for Seamus. It made her calmer to look into the building, where there was a structure and something substantial rather than empty air. She took a deep breath, noticing he was already heating rivets in the forge as they were getting into place. She thought back to her circus days, a fearless teenager performing precision moves with an audience watching her. This was just the same, she told herself. She cleared her mind and blocked out all other noise, movement, and distractions, concentrating on the beat of her heart until she could slow it down. The rest of the world melted away and all she could see was Seamus.

"Ready?" she heard someone shout but wasn't sure who. With the paint can poised in front of her chest and the unfamiliar tongs in her other hand, she raised her thumb. She was ready.

Grace had never in her life seen anything so hot it glowed red, until the moment the first rivet was spinning through the air toward her—a comet in a shower of sparks. It was equal parts self-preservation and skill that guided her paint can into the right place to receive it. Seamus had aimed it perfectly, and it fell easily into the can. There was no time for any kind of celebration or self-congratulation as she took the tongs and lifted the rivet out, trying to ignore the constant movement around her threatening to distract her. She could feel the heat of the rivet on her face.

"Wrong way!" Joe hissed in her ear. She was holding the rivet upside down. She let it go and picked it up again the right way, terrified of dropping it, then timidly tapped it on the steel.

"Harder!"

She could barely make out what was being yelled at her through the cacophony of hundreds of other people doing their jobs. She banged the rivet again and saw cinders and dirt drop off, the orange glow already starting to fade.

"Quickly!" Joe motioned for her to put the rivet in the hole he pointed to. It was harder than she thought it would be, the fit necessarily tight, but she managed, and Joe immediately pushed his dolly bar against it to hold it in place. Frank lifted the rivet gun and set it to the exposed end of the rivet, sparks flying. Grace tried her best not to flinch. The noise was extraordinary, and she was sure she would be deaf by the end of the day.

Despite warnings, it still took her by surprise that along with the rivet gun, everything was jumping and shuddering. The steel was shaking and her bones were rattling in her body. She clamped her teeth together to stop them chattering against each other, fighting the strange sensation of seasickness as she was jiggled around like she was on the worst streetcar ride of her life. It was terrifying, the height was nauseating, and her body and brain were overloaded by unfamiliar sensations, but she had completed her first rivet. She tried to tell herself they would get easier from now on, refusing to think that the process would need to be repeated hundreds of times more before the day was out.

Seamus sent the next rivet up and she caught it neatly again. It was clear that this was far more natural for him than what they had been trying to do on Saturday, throwing by hand. Grace felt the muscles in her back relax a little with the knowledge that every throw to her would be a good one. She moved quicker this time, picking up the rivet the correct way, tapping it harder and finding the hole. She hadn't anticipated just how quickly the rivet cooled and lost its glow. The hotter it was when it went into the steel, the more malleable it was and easier to fix in place. Frank gave her a beaming smile, and Grace hadn't felt pride like it since she was a child.

It wasn't until the eighth rivet that she missed one. She watched it fall harmlessly, landing in an empty wheelbarrow on the floor below. She carried on. The hot cinders and sparks landed on her regularly, and more than once she had to pat at her shirtsleeves with her gloved hand to dislodge the burning fragments. She felt the tiny burns prick her skin, but there was no time to think about it. She had never concentrated so hard in all her life, and it seemed as if both years and mere minutes had passed when midday came around and Frank lowered the gun.

"Lunch!" he said, and relief flowed like warm, soothing water through her veins. Her ears were ringing, and she was starving. Scrambling down to the relative safety of the floor below, her body relaxed slightly as her feet finally hit something wider than a plank of wood. This was a new way of using her body, and the physicality of keeping her balance for such a long period of time was astonishing. Her muscles ached and objected already to the thought of getting back into position, even though the day was only half done.

Joe and Frank had brought their lunch with them, dishes of pasta and jars of artichokes and olives. As they began to unwrap their meals, the scent of tomato and parmesan filled the air and hunger clawed at Grace's stomach. Not only had she not brought any lunch, but she also had no money. In fact, she had nothing with her. She had been so distracted that morning she hadn't thought to put anything in her pockets.

"I'm heading down to the cafeteria on ninth," Seamus said. "Coming?"

She looked down to the streets, trying to orientate herself and see which direction that was.

"Ninth floor." He sidled up beside her and whispered in her ear.

"Oh." Trying not to blush, she nodded. As they started walking, she tugged his sleeve. "I don't have any money," she said out of the corner of her mouth, in her own voice.

"No bother," said Seamus, reaching into his pocket and handing her a dollar.

"Thanks," Grace said, using Patrick's voice as they joined the crowd of men waiting for the elevator.

The cafeteria was a revelation. It was like a regular lunch counter, but temporarily set up on the ninth floor of the uncompleted building. Grace heard men around her saying that a new one would soon be built higher up because it was getting to be a long way to come down. They only had thirty minutes for lunch, not long enough to get down to the street and back. The choice was good, and she scanned the counter and the board before making her order: two chicken sandwiches, a coffee, and a slice of apple pie, all for forty cents. Taking her cup and her wrapped food, she was planning to head back up to the Italians when an open hand smacked her on the back, sending her stumbling forward a couple of steps.

"Since when were you such a weakling, O'Connell?" a voice asked with a hint of confusion.

Grace turned to see a young man, taller than her, with huge arms, his broad shoulders covered in a dirty shirt. Dirt was smeared across his face, too, and she suspected she probably looked the same. He had fair hair and a lot of big teeth. His neck was so thick he seemed not to have one, giving the illusion that his body was made up of a series of boxes.

"Bergmann," Seamus said, arriving at Grace's shoulder and once again letting her know who she was talking to. The broad man ignored him entirely and turned his attention back to Grace. She knew she had to get out of the situation quickly; the longer she stood in front of someone, the more likely she was to give herself away.

Bergmann took a sip of his coffee. "So, what happened with that Nancy broad? Are you ready to pass her over to me yet?"

Grace froze. She had no idea who or what he was talking about.

"Or how about that Greek dame from Fourteenth Street? Has she given you a bounce yet?"

She had no real idea how groups of men spoke together, but she already knew she didn't like it. Feeling uncomfortable, it dawned on her that she didn't really know her brother either, not the version of him these men knew. His apparent womanizing was a revelation.

"A gentleman never tells," she said, trying to add some humor and shrug it off.

"That's never stopped you before!" Bergmann laughed. A small crowd had started to gather around them, and Grace felt panic rising, her skin tight with it. She had to get out of there.

"Just too many to keep up with," she said, her stomach turning.

"Ain't that the truth," another man agreed. "All the women in New York, and ain't nothing to make their drawers drop quicker than telling them you're up here every day, risking your life."

"You're a *hero*," someone else said, mimicking a female voice. "So *brave*."

"Brave men deserve rewards." Bergmann lifted his coffee cup toward the men, as if in salute.

"Just a shame that not one of them has low enough standards to sleep with a Kraut like you," Seamus said, steering Grace out of the cafeteria and toward the open doors of the elevator cage that was just about to depart.

"What?" Bergmann called, fury in his eyes. "You'll regret that, you filthy Mick!"

Seamus waved as the elevator started to rise, leaving Bergmann red-faced.

"He seems nice," Grace said, shooting a sideways look at her cousin.

"Sorry about that." Seamus's pale skin was coloring, and it wasn't completely from the sun. When they stepped out of the elevator and were alone again, he added, "Not the place for a lady. Probably best to steer clear of that one. Nothing but trouble."

Grace remained silent, nodding to show she understood, her lunch clasped in her hands.

"Jealous of your brother's good looks, I would say," Seamus said with a grin. "And who can blame him, when he has a head like a block of concrete." He frowned for just a second. "He's always a little too inter-ested in what Patrick is up to, Lord knows why. We should have thought about that."

Grace filed the note away in her memory. Bergmann—nothing but trouble. Just what she needed.

When they reached the Gagliardis, Frank, who was sitting with his back against a steel column, moved to make room for her. "You've done very well," he said as she sat and unwrapped her sandwich. He was eating his dessert of tiramisu and waved a spoon as he spoke. "We are a little behind where we would normally be, of course, but not enough for anyone to notice. This is very, very good. Better than I even dared to hope. I don't think any of us got much sleep last night."

Grace nodded, her mouth full of sandwich, proud of herself but not willing to show it.

"When we move, make sure you stay on the inside of Giuseppe. It saves you having to shift position on the steel."

"Right."

If that was the only note, Grace would take it. She found herself distracted by the conversation she had just unwillingly been part of. She wasn't sure she liked the sound of who her brother was up here, but wasn't she herself different when she was dancing at Dominic's compared with the Grace at home? She looked like Patrick, and she was quickly learning she was capable of catching rivets like him, and that would have to be enough.

"Your brother still doesn't want me here," she said. She jutted her chin in Joe's direction, where he sat in the discarded wheelbarrow where her first dropped rivet had fallen that morning. He was frowning, looking out over the city as he ate.

"*Bella*, none of us want you here," Frank said.

Grace glared at him, but his eyes were kind and he was smiling.

"Of course we don't. It is dangerous for everyone, particularly you. None of us want to put you in this situation. What Giuseppe is feeling is fear, and guilt. He just doesn't know how to deal with these things."

Maybe Frank was right. She swung her legs around, dangling them over the edge of the steel. Frank chuckled behind her.

"Day one and you already sit looking out to the sky rather than into the building, where it is normal and safe."

"I've never been one for normal and safe." Grace's tone was wistful. "And I figure I'd best enjoy it while I can. When am I going to get views like this again?"

"Whenever you like, once we've finished," Frank teased. "But from the safety of inside the building. We are gifting this view to the world."

He stashed away his lunch pail and Grace thought about Joe as she took the last bite of her pie and crumpled the paper. Maybe he wasn't heartless after all.

"Back to it," Frank said, and she pulled herself to her feet.

"Repetition is the mother of skill," Irina Ivanova used to say, as Grace practiced dance moves and circus skills over and over again in their musty Orchard Street rooms. And so it proved to be. At the end of the first day, Grace had caught close to four hundred rivets. She had missed or dropped around twenty. She knew the gang were a little frustrated to be moving slower than normal, but it hadn't been noticed by the foreman, and they were all glad to be earning money for every hour she spent up there. When the end of the day came, it was a relief to everyone. After handing in their ID tags, they were more than ready to go home.

"Good work today," Frank said, as they left the site with hundreds of other workers. There was nothing else he could say, surrounded by so many people, but to Grace, it was enough. She caught his eye, nodded her thanks, and used what was left of the money Seamus had loaned her to treat herself to a taxi home. Her body was battered, and she was spent; she couldn't face public transport. She sank into the seat and tried to calm the thrumming of adrenaline still coursing through her body. She had survived the first day.

Arriving home, she remembered her key was in her purse and had to knock. Her mother and brother greeted her, relief on their faces. Grace felt strangely empty, as if the day had wrung everything out of her and left her hollow.

"How did it go?" Patrick asked, taking in her dirty clothes and face. He looked like a caged animal, and Grace imagined he had been pacing up and down the small room all day. If he hadn't been off with Nancy or the Greek girl, of course. Whoever she was.

"Fine. Where's Connie?"

"In bed, sleeping. She had a rough day."

Grace nodded. She wasn't the only one.

"Tell me about it," Patrick said. "What happened? Did it all go right? Were there problems?"

Grace was overwhelmed, with no idea how to explain any of what she was feeling. "I did it," she said quietly. "I'm going to take a lie-down." She closed the door to her room behind her. The day had gone well by anyone's standards, but still, when she sat on her brass bed to take her brother's clothes off, she found herself shaking uncontrollably.

An hour later, once Grace had examined the little burns on her arms and wiped as much of the dirt from her face as she could, she lay on her bed in her pink pajamas, looking at the damp mold stain on the ceiling but not really seeing it. She didn't understand what was happening to her, but she felt more terror now than she had during her first moments on the steel. The day was a trauma survived, but at a cost. The thought of repeating it felt impossible. There was a knock at the door, and she was too tired to even turn her head to see who it was. She was expecting her mother, but instead it was Patrick, holding a tray in his one usable hand. He had two hot-water bottles under his arm.

"Here," he said, setting the tray down. It was vegetable soup and a hunk of bread. He handed one of the bottles to her. "Put this on your shoulder, it will help with the stiffness."

Grace took the bottle and eyed the other.

"And that one?"

Patrick sat on the edge of the narrow bed. He pulled a glass from his sling, unscrewed the bottle top, poured out a clear liquid and handed it over. Grace took it and sniffed. Her nose wrinkled. All she could smell was the rubber from the bottle. She took a sip.

"Gin."

He nodded. "I thought you could do with it. For the shock." His brown eyes were full of concern.

"Where's it from? Bad bathtub gin and gut rot is all I need right now."

She took a gulp and coughed, her throat on fire. "Strong," she managed, her eyes streaming.

"Just something to take the edge off." He held the bottle between his knees to put the stopper back in, then picked up the bowl of soup and handed it to her.

"I spoke to Seamus; he said you did really well."

"I can't go back up there," Grace said, her hands shaking so much she had to set the bowl down. She hadn't meant for the words to leave her mouth. "I can't." Her face was wet and warm and she realized she was crying.

"You can," Patrick said firmly. "You've done the worst day; every one will be better now."

She shook her head in disagreement. "Yesterday I was scared, but I didn't really know what I was scared of. Now I do." She felt a resentment rise in her. Patrick had known. He had known what it was like up there and had sent her anyway. Her eyes stung with the betrayal.

"I'm sorry," he said, as if he could read her thoughts. "For all of it. But you know you have to." With that, he got up and left the room, leaving Grace alone with her soup and her terror.

She knew he was right. She screwed her eyes shut and longed for her old life of dancing and feathers. One day down, but there were still twenty-nine to go until the nightmare would be over.

10

THURSDAY, JUNE 19, 1930

Grace left the apartment for the fourth morning in a row with her body screaming at her to go back inside. She had picked up the job quickly, and she ached a little less as her muscles grew accustomed to the task, but the fear was still there. The three previous days had gone well, with only a couple of mishaps. On Tuesday, her footing had slipped when she was climbing up to a new position, but not enough to put her in danger. On Wednesday afternoon, a rivet had hit her on the head, singeing her cap and hair, but they'd laughed it off. Frank had beamed at her at the end of the day and told her she was a real riveter now.

As she approached the site gates for her fourth day, a young woman walked toward her with purpose, head held high, ignoring the catcalls and admiring glances of the men flowing in the other direction. She was unfazed by the attention; in fact, Grace suspected she was enjoying it. She had dark hair, a rosebud mouth, and a look on her face that said she knew more about everything than you did.

"Patrick."

"Hello," Grace replied, keeping her face neutral despite the panic rising in her chest. She had absolutely no idea who this girl was, and this time there was no Seamus around to help her. Was she Nancy? She definitely didn't look Greek. If Grace had to guess, she would say this woman was Irish too.

"That building gets taller every time I'm here."

"That's the idea."

The woman laughed. "I've just taken some lunch to me da."

Definitely Irish, Grace thought. Her father must work on the site and be someone Patrick knew, but this still wasn't much to go on, so she just nodded. It was her main form of communication these days, but fitting for her brother. He didn't tend to waste words.

"You live in Hell's Kitchen, dontcha, Patrick?"

"I do."

"I'm heading there now. I'm helping out in one of the soup kitchens up there today."

"Right, well, good for you." Grace glanced pointedly at the stream of men heading into the site around them. Through necessity, she was becoming an expert at extracting herself from awkward situations. "Have a good day. I don't want to be late." She knew she looked least like her brother when she smiled, so she pressed her lips together and tipped her cap, already moving to get on with the day, the woman instantly forgotten.

"Today, we are going to match the others rivet for rivet," Frank said as they got into position. "I can feel it."

Despite her body's protestations, Grace had to admit she felt calmer on the precarious beams. Her feet now placed themselves without her having to think about it. She knew how to ride the wind that blew in off the Hudson, and how to position herself to make sure she was as useful as possible to Joe and Frank. She might still hate it, and she couldn't take a single movement for granted, but she was definitely getting better. She wasn't as confident as Frank that this was the day she could match any man on the steel, but she felt more than able to try.

For two hours, everything went perfectly. There wasn't a rivet missed or dropped; they worked like four parts of a well-oiled machine. Seamus glanced around at the other teams and grinned as he sent the next rivet up. They were keeping pace with every gang. Things were going well, as they so often did before suddenly they didn't. Heavy gray clouds began to move in like a sickness, throwing gloom across the site and taking everyone by surprise. It was unusual for a June day, but the weather was one thing they could never control. It was the only element of the project that didn't stick to the strict schedule made by the pencil-pushers down on the ground. Frank pointed upward just as Grace felt a fat raindrop fall on the peak of her cap, followed by several others.

"Shall we go in?" he shouted, just as Grace tapped off the latest rivet and slid it into place.

"Not yet!" shouted Joe, holding the dolly bar against the steel as Frank used the rivet gun to seal it in place. "We are never the first ones to go, it will look suspicious!"

Frank nodded in agreement. Grace was already watching the next glowing missile flying through the air toward her. She caught it neatly, not sure what difference the rain would make to what she was doing. She guessed that any water getting on the rivet would cool it quicker, so she grabbed it with the tongs and tapped off the cinders as swiftly as she could.

They had completed two more rivets when the rain started to pelt down. The first raising gangs were already storing their tools and heading inside until the shower passed. Mr. Gilligan was visible on a half-finished floor below, his face upturned to the sky, his mustache twitching. He needed to keep the men safe, but they all knew he also needed to keep on schedule and couldn't afford any unwelcome delays.

"I'm calling it," Frank said. "We're done."

"One more," Joe said, gesturing at the steel. It was the last one to complete in this area. If they did that one, they could restart on a fresh set, rather than coming back. It would just take a few seconds. Frank hesitated, flicking his eyes to the cloud before nodding. Grace signaled to Seamus, and the rivet arrived safely and was secured in place without a problem. Section complete, they were ready to get out of the rain.

Frank was already on his way down to the floor below, and Grace had just secured her tongs to her belt when she saw Joe slip on the wet beam, his feet flying out from underneath him. Without thinking, she lunged forward, threading her arm around the column to grab him. Her hand closed on his arm, and she squeezed so tightly she had to bite back the pain as she looked down into his terrified eyes, all her weight against the steel pillar. She had no idea how she'd done it, but she'd caught him. He dangled in the air for a split second as she clung on with all her strength. The weight of him almost dragged her from the beam, but her arm around the column steadied her, providing the leverage she needed as she braced her boots on the edge of the beam and heaved back with all her might to help pull him back up to safety.

His reactions were lightning fast. Almost as soon as she had hold of him, his foot was swinging back up onto the steel. Grace adjusted her position to make sure she didn't disappear backward herself with the momentum. It was over in seconds. They were both breathing heavily, their faces so close she could see his pulse jumping in his neck, matching her own racing heart, beat for beat, as the rain continued to fall, soaking them. The look they shared was so intense she had to glance away.

"Gagliardi! O'Connell! Get down!" Gilligan's voice reached them, and Joe raised his hand in acknowledgment, grateful that his slip hadn't been seen. Frank's face had drained of color to a sallow gray, and Seamus seemed frozen in time. Grace's breath sounded like a rivet gun in her ears. Her chest was rising and falling so hard she was sure her binding was going to explode open.

It wasn't until she was sure Joe had both feet back on the steel that she even felt the searing pain in her arm. Her first thought was that she had broken it, and terror seized her. Her imitation of Patrick was definitely not meant to stretch as far as sustaining the same injury. When she looked down, she saw there was a black-edged hole in her shirtsleeve, and a bright red circular burn on her forearm, with cotton fibers sealed into it, caused by pressing her arm against the column. A permanent reminder of what she had just done. The rivets might cool rapidly in terms of being able to manipulate them, but Grace had just had her full weight against a bolt that a minute before had been nestled in Seamus's forge. She hadn't even felt it. The reaction to the situation in front of her had been pure instinct. By the time she'd realized what she was doing, the adrenaline was already coursing around her body.

They scrambled down to safety, Frank pulling his little brother to him in a hug, tears in his eyes. Seamus was still wide-eyed. When he saw Grace cradling her arm, he took a look.

"Nasty," he said. "The infirmary will patch that up."

"I can't go there, can I?" growled Grace, still with the presence of mind to use Patrick's voice. Seamus nodded grimly and fetched some water. She wasn't sure whether she was meant to drink it or pour it on the burn, so she just held it.

"Great catch," another riveter shouted over, having seen the incident. "You should sign for the Yankees, O'Connell!"

Grace tipped her cap in acknowledgment but said nothing. Satisfied that Joe was fine, Frank practically ran at her and pulled her into a hug.

"Grace," he said, loud enough for people to hear, now that no one was working. His emotions had overtaken him, and Grace froze in his arms. He must have felt it, because he pulled back, horror in his eyes for half a second before he saved himself. "Grace of God! Patrick O'Connell, you saved my brother. I thank you."

"No worries, Frank. He'd do the same for me." She glanced over at Joe and saw from the way he looked back at her, with gratitude and a newfound respect, that it was true. She had saved his life. He would never doubt her again.

When the rain stopped, they went straight back to work. If his near-death experience had spooked Joe, he didn't show it, but it was clearly playing on Frank's mind. Every now and again he would shake his head in disbelief, and a couple of times Grace saw him raise the back of his gloved hand to his eye to wipe away a tear. She was just glad she had been there. Instead of terrifying her, as perhaps it should have, the incident had oddly reassured her. To know that a slip didn't have to end in death made her move a little easier around the steel. It was no doubt false confidence, but it was getting her through the day.

As she caught the next rivet and tipped it out, she sucked air in through her gritted teeth against the throbbing pain of the burn on her arm. It was ugly and would scar. She didn't let herself feel the sadness at the periphery of her mind that told her she would never look the same again. There was no time; she had to concentrate. Besides, it was worth it to still have Joe standing next to her.

11

Patrick O'Connell couldn't stand being in the apartment. He had worked every weekday of the last six years; not being able to do so now and provide for his family dented his pride and made him agitated with the need to move. He had spent Grace's first day pacing around, driving himself crazy as he imagined every little thing that would be happening, everything that could be going wrong.

If there had been any chance of him picking up other work, he would have taken it. Somewhere far away, where there was no danger of anyone he knew seeing him. But there were plenty of men with two working arms who couldn't find a position, and he knew his chances were almost zero. Instead, he had decided that he would study. The accident had been a wake-up call. He knew the job was dangerous, but he was just twenty-one, and had no intention of dying. He enjoyed the work at times, and the money was good, but he saw the other men on the steel: old at forty, mostly deaf, and many of them alcoholics, needing more and more liquid courage to stop the shakes, numb their minds, and get them up into the sky. Then there was Patrick's own father. He had given his life to the docks, and the job had repaid him by killing him. Patrick wanted more than that. He was getting off the steel.

For the last couple of days, he had headed to the New York Public Library, making his way up the steps between Patience and Fortitude, the marble lions that guarded the entrance, hoping to absorb both traits from their namesakes. He had spent all day poring over texts, leaving at four in the afternoon and getting home just before Grace did. His sister wasn't the only one who could dare to dream and make their father proud.

As he'd run down the steps of his apartment block early that morning, he'd noticed his buttons were done up wrong yet again because of his useless arm. His head was down as he inspected the rest of himself.

"Oh!" A woman's voice split the air as he rounded the corner and crashed right into her.

"Sorry, ma'am, my mistake." He looked up, to be greeted by a familiar face. One that had suddenly drained of all color. "Florence. Long time no see. Sorry about that, are you hurt?"

The pretty woman with the dark hair and eyes the same shade as cherry wood opened and closed her rosebud mouth, no sound coming out.

"You look like you've seen a ghost." Still there was no response. "What are you doing in Hell's Kitchen? Don't you work at the hospital?"

Florence's face crumpled in confusion. She looked over her shoulder, down the street and back again. "But you know why I'm here, I've just told you that. You were going into work . . . how are you here?" Her eyes traveled down his body. "And what happened to your arm in the last fifteen minutes? It was fine before."

Realization settled on Patrick like a heavy quilt.

"Shit," he muttered under his breath. His mind whirred, trying to come up with a plausible explanation, but it wasn't agile enough. Florence was recovering quickly from her shock. She now had her arms crossed at her chest and a frown on her face.

"Patrick O'Connell, you tell me right now what is going on here."

"Well," he said slowly. "I have a twin."

Understanding dawned on Florence's face, and she nodded. "And he's pretending to be you."

Patrick hesitated. A male twin would be a far more palatable situation. "Yes."

"Because of your arm?" She gestured at the sling as a group of pedestrians jostled to get past, tutting and muttering. It was a busy morning and the sidewalks were heaving. Florence took a step closer to the road to get out of their way, never taking her eyes off Patrick.

"Yes."

"And I'm guessing my father doesn't know?"

He shook his head. He took a deep breath and thought about what to say next. Of all the people to bump into who could find out about their plan, Florence Gilligan, the foreman's daughter, was undoubtedly the worst.

"My kid sister is sick and my father is dead. When I broke my arm, we had to find a way for me to keep my job and keep the money coming in."

"By telling lies and putting everyone else in danger? You have an untrained person up there, in a situation that my father is responsible for, no less!"

Patrick sighed. It would be too much to ask for Florence to be the quiet type who wouldn't get involved. He only knew her through a friend; they had all gone as a group to Coney Island one weekend a couple of months ago. He hadn't thought twice about her since. She owed him no loyalty and was clearly not in the mood to be generous.

"Well, she is trained now," Patrick snapped, his frustration getting the better of him. "The gang have taught—"

"*She?*" Florence cut in. Her eyes were so wide and bulging they were practically on stalks. "Your twin is a *woman*?"

He threw his head back, cursing himself, and kicked a nearby bag of trash in frustration. "Well, I never said she wasn't, you just assumed."

"But . . . how? I just met her." Florence shook her head in disbelief. "I have to tell my father." She turned on her heel to go. "Right now."

Patrick reached out and grabbed her arm. "Please don't. Have mercy. Think of my sister." He refused to beg, but the image of Connie pushed him close to it.

"That's exactly what I am doing," Florence said, indignant. "Someone has to. That poor girl, working up there on that noisy, filthy steel. It's so dangerous. And if anything happens to her, it's my father who will take the blame. How could you?" Her face screwed up with disgust and her cheeks flushed with anger as the color leached from Patrick's. Grace wasn't the sister he had meant.

Florence turned and stepped into the road, straight into the path of an oncoming car. The driver blared his horn and Patrick moved before he even knew he had, grabbing her with his one good arm and dragging her back onto the sidewalk, where he spun around, turning his back to the road, curling around her like a shield. If the car was going to hit anyone now, it would be him. He braced for impact, certain he was going to get clipped, but a draft of air told him the car had passed, with nothing but a "Watch where you're going, lady!" from the driver.

He let her go and stood back, breathing heavily, a dull ache in his broken arm where he had twisted it to pull Florence against him. She was panting and shivering. Her knees buckled and he caught her again.

"Okay, you're okay, just come with me, we'll get you some sweet tea. Good for shock." He bundled her through the door of a nearby coffee-house.

They sat opposite each other at a small wooden table. A large Turkish man with a beard and an impeccably clean white apron tied around his waist served them. They nodded their thanks and sat in awkward silence for a moment.

"You saved my life."

Patrick probed his teeth with his tongue and looked away, unable to hold her gaze. "Guess so."

"You didn't have to." Florence nervously rolled a sugar dispenser around in her hands. "I mean, I'd just told you I was going to ruin you. If you'd let me get hit, it would have solved your problem." Her bottom lip wobbled as she blinked furiously to stop herself from crying.

"You honestly believe that?" Patrick shook his head. "For one, I didn't have time to think of anything, I just did it, and anyway, do you really imagine I'd have let you die?" He made a "pfft" noise, forcing air through his lips. "I'm not a monster."

"No, of course not." She placed the sugar down and took up her tea-cup. "I just mean . . . Oh, I don't know what I mean. Except thank you."

Patrick said nothing, drinking his own coffee and wishing he'd left home five minutes later and missed her altogether.

"I just can't stop thinking about Anne, and how sad she would be if I'd died. I keep imagining someone pulling her out of lessons and her face as they told her. She's my little sister." Florence dabbed her eyes with a handkerchief.

Patrick nodded. He pulled out his wallet and removed a folded black-and-white photograph of his family, taken the year before. He handed it to Florence, tapping the girl with the blond curls and the huge smile in the middle of the picture, sitting on her father's lap.

"That there is Connie."

"She's very pretty," Florence said, studying the photo closely before handing it back.

"That she is, a regular china doll, but her lungs are bad. Been nearly two months since she was at school. It's a constant worry. That's why my other sister is up on that steel, to keep a roof over her head. The only reason. We ain't greedy; we're desperate."

"I understand," Florence said quietly. "I'm just trying to keep my own family safe too. If something happens and my father gets fired, Anne will be the one out on the streets." She looked up at him, their eyes meeting across the table.

"I get that," Patrick said. "Family is family."

"But I guess I owe you now."

He shook his head. "You don't owe me anything. You have to make your own decision. One you can live with."

She finished her tea and set down the cup. "Can I think about it?"

"That's all I'm asking."

She nodded, considering him for a second. "I need some time. Meet me tomorrow, at one o'clock, under the clock at Grand Central."

12

FRIDAY, JUNE 20, 1930

Patrick stood at the circular information booth in the middle of Grand Central and looked up at the clock, tapping his foot nervously on the marble floor. People flowed around him in all directions, a mass of humanity like a living carpet. There was never a time when this cavernous place wasn't busy. Shafts of sunlight poured in through the seventy-five-foot-tall windows, creating a holy, church-like feel. He took a moment to ponder how it had been built, how they had managed to maneuver so much heavy marble. Steel was hard enough.

Florence appeared in front of him from nowhere, like a magic trick.

"Afternoon," Patrick said, tipping his hat and offering his hand.

She laughed. Not the small, tinkling laugh of girls who thought they were cute, but a real, throaty laugh. "Come on now, Patrick, you saved my life, I think we're beyond that." She grabbed his outstretched hand and dragged him off into the crowd.

Trying his best to protect his arm from the masses, he followed her red-heeled shoes as they clicked across the floor, vibrant in a sea of brown and black leather. She wore a white dress patterned with cherries, and her purse and belt matched her shoes. He had never seen anything like it. He also didn't fail to notice that today her lips were red, whereas the day before they had not been. Her hair was set in the same waves he had previously seen Grace take great care to create. If Patrick knew anything about women, and he was sure that he did, she was trying to impress someone, and he wondered if it was him. He smiled a little to himself. He knew he was an attractive man. Women liked him, and he liked them. Florence was a nice enough girl, and if his jawline and strong arms were a help in getting her to keep his secrets, he was fine with that.

The two of them seemed to be fighting against the tide of people, until Florence steered them off the main concourse, toward the many interconnected underground tunnels of the terminal. They passed all kinds of stores selling items the traveler might need, from food and liquor to flowers and theater tickets. She swept past newspaper stands, shoe-shine kiosks, and a soda fountain with a line three-people-deep, until she found a quieter counter, tucked away, manned by an older man with white whiskers and a hat like an upturned paper boat.

"Let's have ice cream," she said, perching on one of the stools at the counter, swiveling around to face Patrick.

"Well, okay." He wasn't used to being told what to do by a woman, but he couldn't say he minded.

"Good afternoon, kids," the old man said. "I'm Walter, and this is my stall. Been making my own ice cream since '89."

"I hear you're the best, Walter," Florence said with a winning smile.

"Well, I ain't bad, miss. I've got ice cream sodas, sundaes, banana splits, and eight different flavors."

Patrick took a look at the hand-written markers: vanilla, chocolate, strawberry, mint, lemon, cherry, coconut, and caramel.

"Well, *you* should have cherry," he said, gesturing at Florence's dress.

She laughed again, and he noticed that hearing it made him happy. "Then you should definitely have vanilla," she said, teasing, taking in his plain white shirt under a gray vest. "I'm going to have chocolate, of course. Two scoops, please, Walter."

"Right you are," said Walter, placing the dish in front of her almost before she had finished ordering.

"I think I'll take a banana split," Patrick decided.

"Now that's a good choice, son." Walter moved with a blur of speed that belied his age as he scooped ice cream, peeled the banana, took cherries out of a glass jar, and sprinkled nuts and chocolate sauce seemingly all at once. He added the spoon to the dish with a flourish and spun it around so that it landed neatly right in front of his customer.

"Now that's the work of a real craftsman," Patrick said as he slid two dimes across the counter, paying for them both.

"Thank you kindly. I'll leave you kids alone. I'll just be over here." Walter moved to the other end of the counter, where a well-dressed mother had arrived with three very excited children.

It struck Patrick that he was having fun, and suddenly his shoulders tensed. This was no date. The woman with the easy laugh could be about to destroy his family.

Florence flicked her eyes over him. "So, I guess you want my decision," she said, reading his body language. She ate a full spoonful of ice cream, not the dainty amount Patrick would expect from a woman. Hell, most of the girls he knew wouldn't touch ice cream for fear of it being messy or ruining their figure.

"It's why we're here, after all," he replied, annoyed at the slight tremble he heard in his voice.

Florence's eyes flashed up at him, and he had the feeling he'd said the wrong thing, but she just nodded and ate another spoonful.

"I've thought about it. Done nothing else, if I'm honest." She paused again. "I came here ready to tell you I'm sorry but I have to tell my father." She watched his face and patted her lips gently with a napkin.

Patrick's stomach fell through the floor. He looked down, clenched his jaw and nodded once.

"But now," she continued, getting his attention again, "seeing you here, with that look on your face, I just don't know." She sighed heavily. "I don't think it's a good idea, Patrick." Her voice was softer now.

"I know that," he said. "Don't you think I hate it?" He studied his ice cream with fierce concentration.

"Maybe it's not my business," Florence reasoned. "If my da hasn't realized it's not you up there, then this sister of yours must be doing a pretty good job. And why wouldn't she? Women are just as capable as men, as I keep telling the doctors at the hospital, not that they listen. They think I'm just a nurse. Well, a trainee nurse, but I still know what I'm doing." She waved her spoon at him fiercely to emphasize the point. "Anyway, this situation, it's only until your arm heals, right?"

Patrick nodded, his ice cream melting in the dish. He was too nervous to eat.

"But on the other hand," she said, raising her hands like the scales of justice, momentarily distracting him with how dainty her fingers were, "if something goes wrong—" She stopped abruptly, and he didn't have anything to offer her. He knew the risks better than anyone.

"We're just trying to get by." His shoulders slumped, defeated.

Florence was watching him closely, nodding. "I still don't know," she said honestly. "I thought I did, but I don't. I need to decide what to do about this, but . . . not today. I need a bit more time."

"Okay." The tension running through him eased just slightly. He wanted to shake her, cry, beg, but given the position she had started from, this was the best he could hope for. "Thank you, Florence, honestly, thank you."

She shrugged. "You did save my life. And it's the weekend tomorrow. I can give you that at least. No one is in danger over the weekend. I still think this is too dangerous; the question is whether I can pretend I know nothing about it, or if my conscience compels me to step in. I need to pray on it. I will have an answer by Monday." In an instant, her demeanor changed, as if they weren't having the most important conversation of Patrick's life. She tapped the counter by his dish. "Now hurry up and eat your ice cream. Walter doesn't create these masterpieces for you to waste them."

Patrick did as he was told. There was nothing else he could do for now, so he ate a hearty scoop, although he would have been lying if he'd said he tasted it. Florence was watching him, taking in every feature of his face. In return, he did the same, his eyes drawn down to the dip at her throat and the rise of her chest under her cherry dress. It was a real shame this woman could be the reason he might end up homeless. He was starting to like her.

"I would say I still owe you a thank you, for saving my life," she offered, putting her spoon in her mouth to lick the final remnants of her ice cream before dropping it into her dish with a clatter.

"Keeping quiet would be the perfect thank you," Patrick suggested, and Florence raised an eyebrow. "It was worth a try." He shrugged.

"It's nothing personal," she said, reaching out and touching his hand. "You know that, dontcha?"

A wry smile crept across his face. "How can it not be?"

Her face softened. "I'm sorry."

"Me too." He sighed, pausing for a moment before turning his face toward her. "But I'm not sorry I got to see you again."

He couldn't help but like this girl. She wasn't like the others. Even with her decision still hanging over his head, he couldn't ignore the spark of something in his chest. He pulled a pencil from his pocket and reached for a fresh napkin, writing on the back of it.

"Here's my address. You can come and tell me your decision on Monday. But I won't be available until six p.m., I'm afraid."

Florence scowled. "You want me to come to you?"

"I'm trying to keep a low profile," he said, indicating his cast.

"You think I don't know you're buying an extra day with this?" She took the napkin.

"Just the one." He met her gaze. "Give us Monday, at least. Please."

She ran her tongue quickly over her lips as she thought, and he pretended not to notice. "That's fair. You can have Monday."

"Thank you, Florence." He moved as if to take her hand in his, then thought better of it and gave her a rare Patrick O'Connell smile instead. He'd bought them at least one more day.

Grace stood on the twenty-fifth floor of the Empire State Building, triumphant. She had made it through a whole week, and Joe had been right, they had managed five storeys and were now another fifty feet up. The height was dizzying—she could hardly believe they were only a quarter of the way done. This building was truly going to be like nothing else the world had ever seen.

Men continued to gather at the gates looking for work, the building a symbol of hope after such a devastating economic crash. If something such as this could still be built, things must be going to get better soon. More and more apple vendors crowded the streets as Grace walked from the station to the site each morning. The sidewalk was full of desperate people doing whatever they could to make ends meet. Seeing them reminded her of Edie, and she made a mental note to check in with her friend soon. She bought two apples every morning, each time from a different seller, hoping the few cents was enough to guarantee them at least a meal. At any moment she could be caught out in her deception, regretting all the coins that had spilled from her pockets, but for now, she was in a better situation than her fellow New Yorkers and felt compelled to help.

"Stop smiling," Joe told her, but not unkindly.

Grace brought her face back into a normal expression, her mouth a straight line.

"You don't look like him when you smile," Joe said under his breath, as if the idea fascinated him.

"You're right."

"You're far prettier than he is," he added, turning his back on her to climb onto the scaffolding platform he had just secured to the edge of the building.

A little laugh almost escaped her, but she clamped her mouth shut and swallowed it. If she didn't look like Patrick when she smiled, she certainly didn't sound like him when she laughed. Her cheeks pinked as she rolled what Joe had said around in her head before dismissing it. Things had been different since his slip, and he didn't snap at her anymore, which made everything seem a little easier.

She climbed onto the scaffolding beside him, while below, Seamus tipped rivets into his forge like he was manning a Fourth of July barbecue.

"Let's go!" Grace called. Her brother's voice was now so familiar in her mouth that she sometimes even used it at home without meaning to, much to Connie's delight.

Rivets flew all around her, like little orange meteors shooting across the sky. It still awed her that it was these tiny pieces that held together the behemoth structure. The day was hot, and sweat soaked their backs. The binding on her chest chafed against her damp skin, but for the first time since she had stepped into her brother's life, she was almost happy. She was working hard, earning good money, and helping her family. It sent a fizz of pride and excitement through her veins as she swapped her brass disc at the end of the day for a brown envelope containing eighty dollars.

"I think we should celebrate," Seamus said when they were back down on the ground. He gestured to the unremarkable wooden doors of a bar that hundreds of men seemed to be flocking through.

"Not for me," Grace said with a shake of her head. She saw Bergmann walk past them, slapping his friends on the back with his giant paddle hands, and turned away from him so he didn't see her. "And I would say you should probably give it a miss yourself."

"Ah, come on," Seamus insisted.

"I'm going home to see Connie." Grace tapped the envelope in her hand. "Rent money, Seamus, not beer money. Besides," she moved closer and whispered in his ear, "I can't drink if I can't use the facilities." The toilet situation had been proving an issue all week. There was no ladies' toilet and she couldn't have used it even if there was. Obviously a urinal was out of the question, and so she just had to hold it. It was yet another small way that her life was harder than the others'.

She patted her cousin on the shoulder, said goodbye to the Italians, and slipped into a lunch counter to pick up a dime's worth of doughnuts for the walk home in the sunshine. She had developed a newfound hunger from her exertions all day. She tried to eat all the doughnuts in a race against the grease making its way through the paper bag to her fingers. When the last one was finished, she crumpled the bag and tossed it in the trash, her stomach happily full of sugared, fried dough. Once she was sure she was out of sight of the building and there was no one around who might know her brother, she let the smile she had been hiding all day take over her face.

She and Patrick arrived home at the same time. She spotted him in the street, and it jolted her, like unexpectedly catching your reflection in a shop window. She froze, unsure what to do. The street was busy with people, but no one seemed to have noticed anything out of the ordinary. They were wearing different clothes, and a lot of men walked along here; no one was paying enough attention to notice that two of them had the same face. She scampered up the stairs to the apartment block and could sense Patrick not far behind her. They both hurdled over a couple of bemused Donohues and found themselves laughing together at the ridiculousness of it, like they hadn't done since they were kids. As they reached the third floor, she pulled the brown wages envelope out of her pocket and handed it to him.

"It's got your name on it."

Patrick shook his head, refusing to take it. "But you earned it."

He didn't tell her it might be the last one she got.

13

SUNDAY, JUNE 22, 1930

Patrick had been tapping his fork against the table with his good hand for thirty seconds, a faraway look in his eyes.

"Patrick?" Mary said, reaching out to still his hand. "What is it, Son?"

"Nothing, Ma." He shook his head to clear it, looking at his mother and sisters around the table. He had avoided church and was struggling to contain his nervous energy as he did endless sums in his head. If the next day was Grace's last on the steel, the money they had wouldn't keep them very long. Right on cue, Connie had a coughing fit and Grace immediately pushed her chair back to kneel in front of her and comfort her, rubbing her back in gentle circles.

"Are you all right, Con?"

Connie nodded, her face red, eyes streaming. Patrick held his breath. She was so brave. They both were. He was filled with pride, and an equal amount of frustration that he could do nothing to help them.

Grace caught his eye. "It will be okay," she said with a wide smile he almost believed. "I've done a week already. Only five more. It's really going to work."

He nodded but couldn't bring himself to smile back. He had an urge to tell her about Florence, but he couldn't. She couldn't go up on the steel worried about that. If she was only to have one more day, it ought to be a good one.

Mary moved to the sink, and Patrick joined her to help get Connie's next round of medicine ready. The little girl coughed until she retched, and Grace cooed soothing words into her ear.

"Are you going to be sick, Connie?" Mary asked, and Connie shook her head. "Good girl. Hold on, and we'll get this to you. Deep breaths, if you can."

Patrick put his hand on his mother's back to comfort her, but she carried on moving, not catching his eye as she put some fresh water on to boil. There was no time to feel sorry for themselves. He looked down at his broken arm and a sad certainty settled over him. Grace being able to keep working was their only hope. If Florence told her father and got his gang kicked off the steel, he would never be able to forgive her.

14

MONDAY, JUNE 23, 1930

Grace arrived at the construction site on Monday morning tired and distracted. It had been a tough couple of days for Connie, and Patrick had been in a strange mood all weekend. Her body ached, and while she put everything aside to focus on the job, she wasn't really there, and never once felt the sparks from Frank's rivet gun as they landed all over her arms. She turned herself into an automaton to do what she needed to do, until the moment she could drop her tools and go.

At the end of the day, she stepped into an elevator ahead of her gang, not realizing until she turned around that she had left them behind. There was no room for them; they would need to get the next one. She gave an apologetic shrug in Frank's direction as the door shut. An unsettling prickle raced over her skin, and as she turned her head, she found she was standing next to Bergmann. Her stomach sank with the elevator; she should have paid more attention. She had no backup, and there was no escape. She felt his eyes on her and braced for whatever was coming.

"Have you shrunk, O'Connell?" Bergmann asked, looking down at her.

"Maybe you've grown," she replied with forced joviality.

He narrowed his eyes and studied her. She could feel his gaze boring into her and tipped her head down and away from him, doing her best to disappear. She shuffled backward, farther into the crowd of men, her neck prickling with the fear of discovery.

"You look small," he said, half to himself.

"Do you spend a lot of time looking at other men?" someone else asked, causing everyone to laugh. Grace could have kissed him, so grateful was she for the intervention. With Bergmann's attention now elsewhere, she skipped out of the elevator cage and away as soon as it hit the ground, without looking back. Another lucky escape.

At home, Grace was greeted by her flustered mother. She had the windows open, a pile of towels on the table and a pan of water boiling on the stove. It was clear she had been crying. Fear shot through Grace's body.

"Ma?"

Patrick came out of Mary's bedroom, his shirtsleeves rolled to his elbows, his face a picture of concern. On seeing Grace, he pursed his lips before meeting her frantic eyes.

"Connie's taken a turn."

Grace's heart sank with his words, her blood immediately replaced with ice.

"Let me see her," she said, forgetting she was filthy from her day on the steel. She went to the door to look in. "Connie," she whispered, tears immediately springing to her eyes to see her sister shivering under her blankets, face so pale her lips looked blue as she moaned in her restless sleep.

Patrick's hand was on her shoulder. "Go and wash."

Grace glanced behind him to check their mother wouldn't hear her. "What do we do, Patrick?" she whispered. Even hushed, there was no disguising the fear in her voice.

"What we're doing already," he replied.

"She needs a doctor."

Patrick bit his lip and shook his head. "Not yet."

"What do you mean, not yet?" Grace hissed. "Is this not bad enough?"

"Give her the night to see if she can shake it off. She's done it before."

"And what if she can't?" Grace swallowed hard as she said out loud what she knew they all must be thinking. "She's not getting better, Patrick." She was beside herself.

"We can't afford it." His voice was quiet. "Not right now. And you know Ma doesn't trust hospitals. She's never been inside one in her life."

"And look where that's got her," Grace snapped, before instantly wishing she could take back her words.

"Grace," Patrick said, his tone firm, "go and get clean. Please. For Con. The last thing we need is her breathing in more dirt."

Grace had rarely bathed quicker. When she raced back, there was no change. She crouched down, holding her sister's hand, while Mary pressed flannels to Connie's forehead, trying to encourage her to sip water as her body fought its invisible enemy.

When a knock came at the door, Grace pulled herself to her feet, but Patrick was already there, slipping outside to meet their guest. When he didn't come straight back, curiosity propelled Grace to the open crack of the door, where she stood and listened.

"Do what you have to do," she heard her brother say, trying to keep his impatience in check. "I have bigger problems to deal with right now, I'm sorry."

"What could be bigger than this?" asked a female voice.

"My sister isn't well. I have to go."

Grace was too caught up in trying to piece together who he might be talking with to notice the door opening. She wasn't expecting Patrick to step back inside at just that moment, and didn't have time to move out of the way. She was caught in full view, her hand flying up to her short hair in panic at being seen.

"You." She found herself staring at a mass of neatly pinned dark hair, big brown eyes, and a rosebud mouth she recognized.

Patrick sighed heavily, a defeated man. "Grace, this is Florence. Florence Gilligan."

"We've met," Grace said, her body rigid with terror, remembering their very brief encounter the week before. This was the woman she'd bumped into. Grace had forgotten all about her, but now she was at their home.

Florence was wide-eyed as she glanced from one twin to the other. "Gosh, you really do look alike."

Panic made Grace leap to the worst scenario she could imagine. "Are you here to blackmail us?"

A small grimace crossed Florence's mouth. "No."

Grace couldn't understand what was going on. She had never told Patrick about meeting this woman. And why hadn't Florence looked more surprised? Then another thing filtered through her consciousness, and her heart began to pound in her throat.

"Gilligan?"

Patrick nodded, and the reality hit Grace in the chest as all the pieces slotted into place. When they'd met, Florence had said she'd been taking lunch to her father. This woman was the foreman's daughter.

The words fell from her lips like stones into a lake. "You're going to tell your father."

At that moment, there was another moan from the bedroom and their mother called out. "Grace? Patrick?"

Both of them turned as one to go to her, finding Connie writhing under the covers.

"Connie?" Grace cried, putting a hand on her sister's forehead. Her blond curls were slicked to her head with sweat. "Can you hear me?"

"Sit her up." The voice shocked them all, and they turned to see Florence in the bedroom, pushing her way past them to the bed. Rather than waiting at the threshold, or leaving, she had boldly followed them into the apartment. She was all business, taking control as she folded back Connie's blankets and rested a hand on her chest, cocking her head to the side in concentration. "Do you have a nebulizer?"

"Who are you?" Mary asked.

"Ma, this is Florence," Patrick interjected. "She's a nurse."

"You are?" Grace asked.

Florence just nodded, giving no further explanation. "Mrs. O'Connell, what medicines have you been giving her? Do you have an adrenaline chloride solution?"

Patrick grabbed Grace by the elbow and steered her outside the doorway to give Florence some room. She was reluctant to go, fighting against her brother to get back in. Patrick held her tight.

"Do you trust her?" she asked him in a hissed whisper, her eyes wild.

"Yes," he said firmly. "You said she needed a doctor, Grace. This is the next best thing. Let her help."

Hours passed as Florence tended to Connie, the O'Connells helping where they could. As the night started to draw in and it got dark outside, she came out of the room, wiping her face with a clean handkerchief from her pocket.

"Do you have a telephone?"

"Out in the corridor," Patrick replied. "Why?"

"I need to tell my family I won't be home tonight."

"Florence, you don't have to do that. You've done enough, thank you." He placed his hand on her arm for a second and then removed it quickly, as if unsure whether he had overstepped.

"I'll stay with her." She was adamant. She looked to Grace. "That way you can get some rest."

"I'm not leaving her." Grace shook her head.

Florence leveled a cool gaze at her. "It's getting late. If you're going back up on that steel tomorrow, you sure as anything aren't doing it with no sleep. Now go and get some rest before I change my mind."

Patrick and Grace looked at each other as Florence stepped outside to use the telephone.

"Go," Patrick whispered, putting a gentle hand on Grace's shoulder, tears of pure relief in his eyes. "You need to look after yourself, too."

Grace nodded but still didn't move. She looked intently at the closed door her sister was behind, as if she could will her to get better.

"I mean it." He swallowed hard. "You should keep a distance. We still don't know what it is. You can't get sick."

Grace nodded. She knew that. But still she didn't move.

"Go to bed," he said, his voice more insistent now. She heard him as if snapping out of a trance. "You have work tomorrow."

Grace didn't believe she would be able to sleep, consumed as she was by such dread and terror, but the moment she stepped into her own room, exhaustion covered her like a blanket. She was barely able to get her clothes off before her eyelids drooped, and she was asleep before her head hit the pillow.

15

TUESDAY, JUNE 24, 1930

G race woke with a start early in the morning and rushed to the next
room to check on Connie, her heart in her mouth and her pulse
pounding in her ears. *Please be okay.*

She found her mother sleeping fully clothed on one side of the bed
and Connie on the other, looking far more peaceful now. Florence sat
beside the bed, holding Connie's hand. She glanced up with the smallest of smiles as Grace came in. Her curls were limp and flat now after
a long night, and she was visibly weary, her eyelids heavy, but to Grace
she looked like an angel.

"Morning," she whispered. "She's doing a little better now."

"Oh, thank the Lord," Grace whispered back. "She looks a lot better.
Thank you." She looked around the room. The apartment was silent.
"Where's Patrick?"

"He's gone out to get some supplies, went as soon as the store opened."

Grace nodded. "Do you know what's wrong with her?" She knelt
awkwardly on the floor beside Florence, this stranger in her home, and
rested a hand on her sleeping sister.

"A bad case of bronchitis would be my guess," Florence said. "She
might get better now, but there's no guarantee. If she gets worse again,
she really needs to see a doctor."

"I know." Grace nodded. "It's the money."

Florence pursed her lips, considering her words carefully. "I think you're incredibly brave," she said, her voice even, her gaze pinning Grace in place like a butterfly on a board. "I know what you're doing, and I know why. I bumped into Patrick just after I saw you the other morning. He explained your situation. I'm just worried about my own. If something goes wrong up there, it will be my family without a home."

A lump had formed in Grace's throat. "I understand. I can't ask you to lie. I won't, and I'm sure Patrick wouldn't either. But what else can we do? If there was another way, we'd take it."

Both women sat in silence, watching Connie. Grace had seen the way Patrick had looked at Florence last night. With what she now knew about his romantic habits, it wasn't surprising he was sweet on her, but it was an added danger. Even if Florence could be convinced to turn a blind eye for now, how long would it last? Having anyone know their secret was another thing to worry about. The list was getting long.

She braced herself to say something, but Florence got there first. "I have no desire to harm your family, Grace, I promise you. I have a little sister myself."

Grace bit the inside of her cheek and nodded.

"I think what you're doing is incredibly stupid and dangerous," Florence carried on, stroking Connie's curls away from her forehead, not looking at Grace. Grace started to lean forward, with an intense urge to push the other woman's hand away, but Florence reached for her wrist, holding it gently. She looked straight into Grace's eyes. "And it is also the greatest act of love I've ever heard of."

Tears filled Grace's eyes, but she blinked them away. She couldn't deny the relief of having this woman at least acknowledge her sacrifice. Someone understood. The belief that maybe Florence really wouldn't harm their family started to bloom in her chest.

"Anyone would do it," she said.

"They might want to," Florence replied, "but not many could even try."

Grace stroked Connie's arm, and the small girl murmured and groaned, kicking her legs a little, movement coming back to her body. The two women looked at each other, and a small smile crept onto Grace's face to see it.

Florence sighed. "You're a hell of a woman, Grace O'Connell. You put your sister in my hands, and I think I'm going to have to put mine in yours. We're just going to have to trust each other. I don't think we have any other choice."

The number of lives Grace was responsible for up on the steel continued to grow.

16

WEDNESDAY, JUNE 25, 1930

Another long day done, Grace arrived home, followed five minutes later by Patrick, coming back from wherever it was he spent his days now. She was looking forward to a calm evening at last, but it was clear something was on their mother's mind. Grace's first thought was Connie, but when she went in to see her, the little girl was warm-skinned and sleeping. Grace smiled, placing a kiss on her sister's forehead. She wasn't out of the woods yet, but there finally might be a horizon up ahead. She closed the door quietly, returning to where her brother sat at the table, her mother wringing her hands as she paced the small room.

What now? Grace thought, but she didn't have the energy to say the words. What else was left to go wrong? She wanted to call Betty and Edie, to catch up with her friends, and yet here she was, faced with another problem.

"Ma, will you just spill it," Patrick said. "You're making me nervous."

Mary took a deep breath. "The rent collector has been around." There was a solemn look on her face. "He says the rent is going up. Five dollars a week."

"Five dollars a week!" The chair Patrick had been sitting on squealed across the floor with the force of him standing. "How can he justify that? People are struggling as it is."

Grace sat in silence, a weight like a stone settling in her stomach.

She closed her eyes against all these problems as if she could keep them out of her mind and soul. She was tired of it. When would it end? She heard screaming and laughing coming from above and thought of the Donohues. There was no way they could find an extra twenty dollars a month. She just hoped her own family could.

"He said the rich people who lost their money and had to move out of their big mansions are looking for places to live. He said he can afford to put the rent up and drive out the likes of us to get a better quality of tenant." Mary swallowed hard.

"What a bastard!" The words exploded from Patrick, and he knocked over the chair.

"Patrick, please," Mary hissed. "Connie."

That was enough to silence Patrick, but he was clearly seething. Without another word, he grabbed his coat and hat and disappeared out the door.

"We'll be all right, Ma." Grace offered a small smile that didn't reach the rest of her face. She looked down at her bare arms, covered in burns and bruises, and knew her dreams of dancing again were gone. Four more weeks until Patrick was healed, and she didn't dare imagine what she would look like by then, or what she would do for work when this was all over. Anything more than surviving seemed too much to ask for. "We can cope."

"For now."

Her mother's words sent a shiver through her.

Grace struggled for sleep. She could hear Mrs. Donohue's sobbing above her head as if she was in the bed beside her. Earlier, as they'd gathered in her mother's room, listening to the radio, the crying had stopped, replaced by the rhythmic banging of the bedstead against the wall.

"What are they doing?" Connie asked weakly, her face still sleepy.

"Moving furniture, I would think," Mary answered quickly, reaching over to turn up the volume on the wireless. The adults shot each other a look over Connie's head. It sounded much more like they were making another Donohue, as if that would solve their problems. Soon afterward, Grace had gone to bed, and as she lay there, the crying above her had started again. She pulled her thin pillow over her head and breathed into it, wondering how much more any of them could take.

17

THURSDAY, JUNE 26, 1930

G race was exhausted. As she started her ninth day, she found she had become used to the ache in her body, but the tax on her brain of the last few days was something else entirely. Standing on a beam, she was laying planks of wood down from one part of the steel to another. By putting three next to each other, you could create a walkway far wider than anything else they had to stand on. This was one of her favorite parts of the job; it came naturally to her. She felt far safer walking across the steel with a plank in hand. By now she understood how the wind worked, and it reminded her of the tightrope, but easier.

"It's much harder to fall with something like this in your hands," she told Joe.

"Until the wind takes you."

"If you put a weight on either end, it would be almost impossible to fall; it would bring your center of gravity below the beams."

"Very clever," he said, preferring to crouch and slide his plank across between two beams without holding it up in the air. "Where did you learn that, *Patrick?*"

Grace felt herself blush. Joe was smiling, teasing her, but he was right, she was becoming more comfortable on the steel, and when she was tired, she found herself being a bit too much Grace and not enough Patrick. Just that morning, Joe had pulled a face when he first saw her.

"What?" she'd asked.

"You look different."

She'd shrugged her shoulders; she didn't know what he was talking about. He kept glancing at her as they placed rivets, until his eyes lit up when he finally worked it out. He took his glove off and wiped his finger along the dirty steel where she had been tapping the cinders off, then smeared the ash across her cheek. Her face was just forming into an indignant scowl when he leaned his mouth to her ear and whispered, "No scar." She lifted her hand to her cheek and then looked away, knowing he was right. Little slips were becoming more frequent the more tired she got, and she had forgotten to draw it on that morning. She was fairly sure no one else would have noticed, but Joe seemed to spend a lot of time looking at her face. She caught him watching her sometimes, and when his eyes met hers, her mouth went dry and she had to look away.

"Seamus!" Frank called down. Seamus was talking to another man, but quickly turned his attention to the job at hand.

Grace readied her new conical catcher. Earlier, she'd noticed a man across the beams using one, and had asked Frank if she could give it a try. He'd smiled at her.

"The tools are the preference of the worker; you choose for yourself. You're a proper ironworker now."

She grasped the cone by its handle and turned it one way then the other in her hand, testing the shape, size, and weight of it, like a giant ice cream cone. It felt comfortable, but her heart fluttered in her chest. She had been the one to suggest the change, so if it didn't work, it would be her fault if they fell behind. She turned to Seamus and gave him a nod. He sent the first rivet up and it pinged neatly into the cone, where the tapered end trapped it, sitting upright, making it much easier to grab. She darted her tongs in, tapped the rivet off and had it in place for Joe in record time. She bit her bottom lip to stop herself from smiling. She would definitely be quicker now.

And with that, the paint can was retired to their box of equipment, ready for Patrick to pick back up when he was healed. Each day, Grace was getting closer to becoming as good a catcher as her twin.

Lunchtime came, and she was glad to stop working. She headed straight down to the temporary floor below and curled up.

Seamus laughed at her. "No lunch?"

"No, I just need sleep."

"Come now," said Frank, pulling her up. "You must eat. And thirty minutes' sleep will just make you feel more tired. What is the problem?" He looked concerned. "Your sister?"

Grace reluctantly took the sandwich Seamus handed her and nodded. "It's been a long few days." The weight of the rent increase had settled in the back of her throat and the pit of her stomach. Just another worry to carry. She could feel the tension throughout her body and longed for a time when she could relax. She tilted her face up toward the sun and closed her eyes for a moment before taking a deep breath and unwrapping her lunch.

Two hours later, they were just contemplating stopping for a ten-minute coffee break when a messenger boy clambered up on the steel near them and waved his hands to get their attention. Grace felt cold all over, fearing the worst. It had to be bad news; it had been the week for it. Messages didn't get passed along unless they were serious. *Connie.*

"Mr. Gagliardi?" the boy called out, mangling the name. He looked around at all the heads that had turned to hear him, waiting for someone to claim it. Grace only felt momentary relief that the message was not for her before she replaced it with worry for her friends.

"Which one?" Joe asked.

"Uh, F?" The boy looked down at the dirty note in his hand.

"That'd be me, kid." Frank raised his hand.

"It says here your wife has had a baby, sir."

A cheer went up from all the workers, and they banged their tongs against the steel in celebration. Grace flinched at the cacophony, not expecting it, before raising her own tongs and joining in. Joe reached across and embraced his brother, and when the noise died down and they let go of each other, Grace saw tears in Frank's eyes.

"Does it say whether it's a boy or a girl?" he called down, but the boy shook his head.

"What's with the noise?" Joseph Gilligan appeared below, summoned by the disturbance. Grace froze to see him, still chilled by the power this man's daughter held over her life, and the knowledge that she could decide to tell him at any time. Trusting a near stranger with her biggest secret did not come easily. Gilligan took the dirty note from the messenger boy and read it, smoothing down his mustache. Then he looked up at Frank, shielding his eyes from the sun. His face softened. "Congratulations, Gagliardi."

"Thank you, sir."

The foreman looked at his watch. "You're done, the four of you, go down. Gagliardi, go and meet your baby." He nodded, and Grace wondered if he was remembering what it felt like to first hold Florence in his arms. They all knew the decision was partly made for fear of Frank losing concentration and causing an accident, but Gilligan was also a good man and fair.

None of them needed telling twice, and they were in the elevator on their way down to the ground in no time, handing in their ID discs. The timekeeper made a note of their early leaving time, but none of them cared. Seamus disappeared almost instantly in case Gilligan changed his mind. No doubt there was a girl somewhere he was on his way to meet.

At the street corner where they were set to separate, Grace pulled Frank into a hug. "Congratulations, Papa," she whispered in her own voice.

"*Grazie, bella.*"

When she let go, she turned to Joe and punched him lightly on the arm. "Congratulations, Uncle Joe." His lips curved upward, and she was pleased with herself for getting a smile out of him.

The Italians headed off toward the Lower East Side with their arms around each other to meet the newest Gagliardi, and Grace felt almost euphoric to find herself on her way home early with her feet back on solid ground. Another day done.

———

As Grace's key turned in the lock, Mary jumped up from the table. She had been leaning toward the light of the window to see better as she darned one of her own dresses. Her graying hair frizzed around her head, her fingers red and swollen.

"Grace, oh Lord, what's wrong? No, not now, please."

"Shh, Ma," Grace said, taking her mother's sore hands in her own. "It's fine. It's nothing bad, I swear." They had all become so used to expecting the worst that they were braced for more bad news at every turn.

"Oh, thank God." Mary put a hand to her chest to try and calm her hammering heart. With the news of the rent increase, Grace knew the pressure on her was even greater than before.

"Sorry to worry you," she said, pulling her mother into an awkward hug and releasing her quickly. "We got to leave early today is all."

Mary sat down again and went back to her dress. "You scared me, Grace," she said, puffing out her fear.

"Sorry. How's Connie?"

"Sleeping," Mary replied, her lips pursed tightly.

Grace nodded, too tired to ask anymore. "I'm heading to bed. When Patrick gets in, tell him that Frank's wife had the baby."

She headed to her room and dove under the covers, certain that the much-needed sleep was worth every cent of the three dollars that would be docked from her wages at the end of the week.

18

FRIDAY, JUNE 27, 1930

"He is beautiful!" Frank said, for roughly the four hundredth time that day. After almost every rivet, the beaming father had reminded them how wondrous his baby boy was. Grace chuckled. His joy was infectious.

"Really?" she asked, and Joe shot her a look that told her not to encourage him, which only made her laugh more, grateful that no one else could hear her. After a decent sleep, she felt much better able to cope with everything being thrown at her, literally and figuratively. Plus, it was Friday, she had a job, and Connie had eaten a whole piece of toast for breakfast.

"He has eyes like a wise man," Frank said, waving his rivet gun around as he spoke.

"Eh! Concentrate!" shouted his brother. "How would you know, anyway? He hasn't even opened his eyes yet." Joe rolled his own brown eyes and Grace tried to hide her smile.

"And he has thick hair, like his papa."

Grace was impressed with the amount of time Frank had been able to spend talking about his new son, given that he had only known him for a few hours.

"If this is what he's like with baby number four, I can't imagine what the first one was like," she said to Joe.

"Oh, he started talking about her and never stopped."

"Two of each, Giuseppe!" Frank cried. "Two strong boys and two beautiful girls."

Grace caught the next rivet and slotted it in the hole. It turned out to be the last one of the day, the whistle letting them know it was half past four. The hours had flown by, and with it came the end of Grace's second week on the job. She was a third of the way through.

She had learned many things, not least of which was how to go all day without relieving herself, and she was looking forward to getting back to ground level to rectify that particular situation.

As they stood in line to receive their pay packets, Grace bouncing on the balls of her feet, desperate to visit the nearest water closet, Frank climbed up on an overturned box.

"Everyone! Please join me for a drink to wet the head of baby Mateo Giuseppe Gagliardi!"

A cheer went up again, and Grace noted that not many of these men needed an excuse or encouragement to take a drink. It wouldn't have surprised her at all if the bar next to the site was owned by their employers, with many of the workers collecting their pay only to hand it straight back again. When it came to her turn, she took her wages envelope and slipped it into the pocket of her overalls.

"Hey, where do you think you're going?" She flinched as Joe grabbed her arm. "You think he's going to let you get away with not coming?"

"Joe—"

"*Patrick*," he said, with an emphasis that reminded her that her brother would definitely have gone along for a drink. He was right, of course. Sometimes she hated him.

"All right, all right," she said. "I'll be there in a minute. I've just got something to . . . attend to."

"You'd better be," Joe said, "or I will come and find you. You can't disrespect the Gagliardi family name."

Grace racked her brains to think of somewhere nearby that had a unisex toilet she could use without arousing suspicion. Eventually she remembered a small twenty-four-hour grocery store with a convenience.

Rushing there and back, she felt uncomfortable having so much money just sitting there in her pocket. The one thing she couldn't get used to in her new life as a man was not carrying a purse.

Men were still pouring out of the site on Thirty-Fourth Street. Thousands were working on the building now, and a big chunk of them were heading through the wooden doors into the bar. Grace followed them, as if it was something she did all the time, trying not to let her mouth fall open in shock once she got inside and saw the sheer size of the place.

The bar was a vast, yawning space with dark wood paneling everywhere. It reminded her of a dance hall, if you replaced the bleachers with a huge bar and crammed the dance floor with tables. The only difference was the wooden staircases up to a mezzanine level, where a row of doors led to private rooms. Half the tables were tall, with men standing around them, and the other half looked as if they were made from huge cable reels, with men sitting, playing cards. The place was heaving with bodies and noise.

As Grace looked around, she saw that the workers were largely staying with their own kind: ironworkers with ironworkers, plumbers with plumbers, electricians and carpenters with electricians and carpenters. She decided the place must be owned by gangsters, or at least under the protection of a racket. The bar wasn't in any way hidden; any raid would have left the police in no doubt what was going on here.

She found the group of ironworkers and sidled her way through, avoiding Bergmann and keeping her head down, conversing with as few people as possible. Frank was holding court, telling yet more tales of fatherhood. Joe tilted his glass in her direction, and she bit her lip to hide a smile when she realized he was pleased she was there.

"Here you go." Seamus handed her a lit cigarette and a whiskey.

Grace took them, nodding her thanks. She smoked the cigarette but held the drink in her hand without touching it. When she was dancing, she used to drink a lot, partly to mask the grief for her father that threatened to drown her, but since she had been on the steel, she hadn't touched alcohol. Not since Patrick had visited her with the hot-water bottle on that first night. She preferred to keep a clear head these days. Her brain was too full of the here and now to have time to dwell too much anymore.

The atmosphere in the bar was overwhelming. She had never been in a place like this before, and she couldn't help looking around and taking in the scene. Hundreds of men were celebrating the end of the week and making it through another day relatively unscathed. This was their church, and they came here to worship the holy trinity of friendship, alcohol, and gambling. She watched men arm wrestle each other for money, play cards, throw back drinks, and play the fool. One walked on his hands across the floor, empty glasses balanced on the soles of his feet, while everyone cheered. When he stumbled and the glasses fell, they just cheered louder and kicked the broken glass away. A boy with a broom scampered around them as he tried to sweep up the mess. They could only have been here for an hour, but that was long enough for many of them to be drunk.

It took Grace by surprise when music started, to raucous cheering. Joe caught her eye from across the table and grimaced an apology, before looking away and suddenly finding his shoes the most interesting things in the world. She didn't understand until she felt the rolling wave of men moving as one to create a space in the middle of the floor. Accompanying the music came two rows of women in tight gold dresses held on with only the thinnest of straps across their backs. Shining gold headpieces sat snug on their heads like swimming caps. Grace's eyebrows rose up her forehead. It seemed there was one other thing the men came here for.

There must have been close to thirty women in each line, and they danced together, three simple steps, waving their arms in the air and then posing to blow kisses to the men. They did this round in a circle, allowing everyone to get a good look at them. The men punched each other in jest and pulled caps down over their friends' eyes as they pointed out their favorites. Grace watched, mesmerized and sickened in equal measure. The girls were all beautiful and smiling widely, trying to sell how much fun they were having, but she could almost smell the desperation that had led them to this moment. She knew their smiles were fake, and that behind them, these girls were scared. Her stomach lurched to think that if things had gone differently, she might be one of them.

The bar was like a cattle market, and in a few short minutes these women were about to get ripped limb from limb by feral dogs. They were there purely to entertain the men, and there didn't seem to be anyone around to stop things from getting out of hand. They shimmied out of line and then back, looping their arms over their neighbors' shoulders to start spinning as an outward-facing circle, performing cancan kicks, each one receiving a huge cheer from the men. And then, with the next rotation around, through the crowd of heads in front of her, Grace could see a girl shorter and paler than the others, skinnier but just as beautiful. She jostled forward, moving from side to side, trying to get a better view. Surely not, no. Her stomach fell through the floor when another glimpse confirmed it. Right there in front of her, like a shimmering gold angel, was Edie.

She pushed through the crowd of men, following the circle, trying to keep Edie in her sightline, until the scrum became too dense.

"Back off, O'Connell!"

"Yeah, wait your turn!"

Someone pushed her shoulder, and she stumbled into other men, who shoved her in the back. She felt like a cork bobbing on the ocean and looked for her gang. She could see them, but they were far away now and barely even paying attention to what was happening in the rest of the room. Out of the corner of her eye, she saw the boy with the broom slip his hand into a drunk man's pocket, stealing his money. He noticed her watching him and disappeared into the crowd as if he'd dissolved into thin air. Grace's body flushed with the heat of panic and her hand went instantly to her own pocket to check her money was still there, breathing a sigh of relief to feel the reassuring thickness of the brown envelope. She pushed it even deeper. Her heart was thrashing in her chest. She hadn't spent all week risking her life to have nothing to show for it.

The golden girls had finished their dance and the crowd whooped and cheered. Men waved fans of cash at them as they surged forward as one, trying to take the hand of the girl they wanted. Grace lunged through the crowd desperately, searching for Edie among the identically dressed women. She saw her and reached for her at the same time as a huge hand settled on Edie's arm. Grace turned her head to see Bergmann trying to lead the tiny girl away. Of course it was him. Of all the thousands of men working on the building, he was the very last one she wanted to draw the attention of, or see with his hands on her friend. She couldn't let it happen.

"Hey," she called. "Not this time, Bergmann." She knocked his hand away and spun Edie away from him. "I know this girl."

Bergmann turned and laughed. "Of course you do, O'Connell. You can't have all the ladies. Leave some for the rest of us."

"Just this one," Grace said, taking Edie's hand.

Bergmann frowned, and his tone went dark. "You always get what you want, huh, O'Connell?" He stared at her, and a muscle twitched in his jaw. "It's all so easy for Patrick." His voice was mocking. He paused for a second and licked his lips. "What if I said I'll fight you for her?"

Panic started to rise through Grace, but she refused to let it show on her face. It dawned on her that for whatever reason, this guy really hated her brother. She didn't know what to do. Bergmann was enormous. In the end, she didn't have to do anything. He was just posturing, toying with her. He started to laugh, although there was still malice in his eyes. "She's not worth it anyway." He shrugged, and with a benevolent smile grabbed another of the gold-clad women and threw her over his shoulder. The girl played her part and squealed, beating her fists on his back.

"Oh, aren't you strong!" she shrieked. The lipsticked smile on her face was as wide as the Holland Tunnel, but Grace could see the fear in her eyes and had to look away. She hated it, but she could only save one girl that night, and it had to be Edie.

She hadn't even looked at her friend yet as she grabbed her by the wrist and pulled her up the stairs and into one of the private rooms, slamming the door behind them and pretending not to hear the cheer from the men below. She hoped to God her brother had never taken one of those girls into a room like this. Seamus and the Gagliardis had hardly even looked up when the dancing had started. She didn't know if it was because she was there or not, but either way, she was grateful for it.

Inside the room, there was nothing but a brass bed with a red cover thrown over the sheets, and a small bedside cabinet with a jug of water and two glasses on top. Grace sagged with relief, glad to be away from everyone else. She reached for the key in the door and locked it.

"Sir, I'm sorry, I . . ." Edie's wide eyes were brimming with tears and her lip wobbled as she wrung her hands in front of her, a quaver in her voice.

"Edie," Grace said gently.

This forced Edie to blink away her tears. "How do you know my name? Oh!" She gasped, and her hand covered her mouth as she finally took a good look at her companion. "You're Grace's brother, you must be. Boy, you look alike." She screwed up her face in concentration, trying to remember. "Patrick!" Her eyes burned brightly with the triumph of her recollection. "Oh, I'm glad it's you."

Grace took her cap off and threw it on the bed, running her hands through her far-too-short hair. She used her own voice but kept it low. "Edie, it's *me*, Grace."

"Gracie?" Edie's voice was hushed as she stepped toward her friend, her hands held out to tentatively touch her face. "Is it really you?"

"It's me," Grace said, pulling her into a hug. "It's really me."

They sat on the edge of the bed, staring at each other, clasping each other's hands.

"What's going on, Grace? Your hair!"

"I could ask you the same thing. What are you doing here?"

"It's a job." Edie shrugged.

"You don't belong in a place like this, Edie McCall."

Edie's narrow shoulders started to shake as she cried silently, and Grace scooted closer to comfort her. "Oh, Edie."

"It's been hard, Grace, but I'm trying. I didn't really know where I was coming to. I've just been taking every dancing job I can get. I'm so glad you were here. I was so scared."

"Me too. Jeez, Edie, you can't just go off somewhere like that, not in this city, it's not safe. You could have ended up in real trouble." Grace thought of the wages in her pocket. The temptation to give her friend as much as she needed to never do a job like this again was strong, but she knew her own family needed the money, and Edie wouldn't take it anyway.

Edie changed the subject. "What's going on? Why are you dressed like a man?"

"Shh!" Grace put a finger to her lips. She thought they were safe in the room, but she couldn't risk anyone overhearing. The men were childish, particularly when it came to women, and she wouldn't put it past one of Bergmann's idiots to be listening at the door. "We've gotta be quiet." She kept one eye on the door as she whispered her explanation. "You know how I told you in the lunchroom that I was starting a job my brother got for me? Well, it *is* my brother's job. He broke his arm the day after we got fired at Dominic's and so we had no choice but for me to take his place."

Edie's eyes were so wide they were like two headlights shining out from her face. "You're pretending to be your brother? Doing his job and everything? Oh, Grace, and you tell me to be careful! That dancing in a place like this isn't safe. At least my feet are on the ground."

"Trust me, they wouldn't have been if Bergmann had got hold of you. Look, I know it's not ideal, but even you didn't recognize me. It's working, and it's just until Patrick's arm has healed. He's out of the sling already; there's only another month before the cast is off and he can go back to work."

"A month is a long time."

"I'm just taking it one day at a time."

"Well, I certainly know that you have to do what you have to do at the moment for the money." Edie's face was so sad that it near enough broke Grace's heart in two.

"Have you seen Betty?" she asked.

Edie nodded. "A couple of times. She wants to help, but I need to look after myself, you know? I think she's lonely out there in Jersey."

Grace ached for the company of her friends. "Where are your clothes?"

"In a bag, hidden out back."

"Let's get them, and get you changed. You're coming home with me for dinner."

"Oh no, I couldn't."

"You want to stay here, do you? With those men downstairs? How much are you set to make tonight?"

"A couple of dollars," Edie mumbled, looking at the floor.

"Edie, please. Wouldn't you rather leave this place and come with me? You can eat a chicken dinner and stay the night. I've missed you. I have a whole load of Betty's things I need to get rid of. I don't have the room. You can take anything you want with you. Surely an evening with me, free food, and new clothes is worth a couple of dollars?" Grace nudged her friend gently and Edie nodded, a slow smile spreading across her face.

"Thank you, Gracie."

Grace gave her another hug and put the newsboy cap back on her head. She rolled her shoulders, visibly stiffened her neck, and stood up on her toes to get herself back into the feel of being in her brother's body rather than her own. Edie watched in fascination.

"Let's go." She led Edie out of the room. As they walked down the stairs, she put her arm around her friend to protect her, and when they reached the bottom, they were greeted by a leering man Grace vaguely recognized as one of the stonemasons from the site.

"Hand her over. My turn," he slurred, bad beer riding high on his breath. He made a grabbing motion for Edie.

"Don't think so, pal." Grace's voice was as much of a growl as had ever come from her mouth.

"She ain't yours," the man said, shoving her in the shoulder. Out of nowhere, Grace felt a rage rising in her chest she had never felt before, and knew the anger was only partly for this man. It was a dangerous cocktail of fury at the situation and how helpless the world made her feel. She had felt fear when Bergmann challenged her, but as her chest swelled and her heart quickened, she knew with a certainty as clear as the liquor being poured behind the bar that if she needed to, she was going to fight this man.

The drunk squared up to her and people started to clear a little circle around them. Edie pulled on her arm, but Grace was staring at the man, trying to get him to focus on her. Suddenly there was a body between her and the drunk, pushing the man away. "Go home, Leary, you're drunk." Joe Gagliardi stood firm, his arms tensing as he flexed his hands into fists and unclenched them again rhythmically by his sides. Then he took a step back and stood shoulder to shoulder with Grace.

The man snorted and turned away, looking Edie up and down. "She's a scrawny one anyway. Ain't worth the hassle."

"Thanks, Joe, but I had it covered." Grace patted him on the back as she thought Patrick would have done, as if his intervention was no big deal. It burned in her that she was unable to tell him how deeply grateful she was that he had stepped in. Resisting the urge to leave her hand resting there, she gestured to her side. "This here is Edie, a friend of mine, and I'm going to make sure she gets home safely."

Joe tipped his chin up in acknowledgment, his eyes searching Grace's face to make sure she was okay.

"Tell Frank to have a drink for me," she said.

"I think Frank is having a drink for everyone in this place," Joe responded wryly.

Grace laughed despite herself, adrenaline charging around her body. The laugh started as her own, so she turned it into a cough so as not to give herself away.

"Thanks again," she said, holding his gaze and hoping he knew that she truly meant it. She was lucky he had seen what was happening. Lucky he had been looking out for her, checking where she was. She wanted to hug him, but she knew she couldn't. She put aside her thoughts about that, to examine later. As much as she had felt ready to fight in that moment, in reality she was no match for a man. She wouldn't have had a clue what to do.

She tipped her hat and let Edie lead her through the crowd to the back room. Edie slipped inside and came out a few moments later with the cap removed from her head and her fur coat pulled over the gold dress.

"A fur in June, in New York?" Grace asked, a smile stretching across her face. She'd forgotten already that Edie always wore this coat. "I'm surprised you're not just a puddle of sweat." Edie didn't answer, and Grace grabbed her hand, both to show she was just teasing and because it would look more normal if they left hand in hand. She couldn't deny that the skin-on-skin contact was comforting as they made their way outside and hailed a taxi.

"And who is this?" Mary said with a welcoming smile as Grace shepherded Edie into the apartment.

"This is Edie, Ma."

"Another dancer," Mary said. "I've heard a lot about you."

"You have?" asked Edie, who was shrinking into her coat.

"Only good things." Mary was clearly tired, but fussing over Edie was a welcome distraction from her problems.

"I don't want to intrude," Edie said, trying not to look longingly at the food spread across the small table. Grace was glad it was Friday. They were cutting back during the week, but each pay packet was cause for a small celebration in the O'Connell home, and that meant good food. The smell of roast chicken filled the apartment and was making her mouth water.

"Nonsense! Please." Mary gestured for her to take a seat.

"Edie's just going to change real quick, Ma," Grace said, showing her friend into her bedroom. "How's Connie?" It was her most asked question.

"Why don't you go and see if she's up to joining us?"

Grace nodded and went into Mary's bedroom, where Connie was lying in bed with a book on her lap, her face pale. She looked tired, but smiled when she saw Grace, before a huge racking cough took over her small body.

"Hello, princess," Grace said, stroking her sister's hair. "How are you feeling?"

"Fine." Her stubborn bravery nearly brought a lump to Grace's throat.

"I have a friend here, would you like to meet her? Do you think you're up to joining us for dinner, or should I bring you a tray?"

"I said I'm fine, Gracie," Connie said, her little voice annoyed. She swung her skinny legs out of the bed, and Grace wrapped her in a blanket before they headed to the table.

Mary put the plates down, laying places for all four of them, just as their guest emerged from Grace's bedroom. Edie had her arm across her body, her right hand fiddling with a hole at the elbow of her left sweater sleeve.

"Good heavens," Mary said. "Now you're out of that coat, I can see that you're nothing but skin and bones. Sit yourself down." She was already piling a plate high with food. "Let's see what we can do about that, child."

"Connie, this is Edie."

They grinned at each other, both so pale and thin they looked dangerously like ghosts.

Grace slipped into her room to change, returning to her seat at the table moments later and handing her wages envelope to her mother with a small amount removed for herself. Patrick was out for the evening with their cousin Sean and his friends. She bathed in the joy of having Edie next to her on one side and her sister on the other, as they ate and laughed and joked together. Here with her favorite people, she could finally be herself again, albeit herself with her brother's hairstyle.

Mary kept filling Edie's plate with chicken, potatoes, and green beans until Edie begged for mercy, saying she couldn't possibly eat any more. Grace smiled to herself around her fork, certain this was the first time Edie's belly had been truly full in a while. Even Connie had eaten more than a couple of bites. Despite protesting, Edie still accepted a huge slab of cherry pie for dessert, and ate it with one hand on her ever-expanding stomach.

"Ach, don't make her sick, Ma," Grace chided.

Her friend talked animatedly about her plans and the next gig she had lined up. Grace listened intently, trying to work out how much of her excitement was genuine and how much was her trying to convince everyone, herself included, that her life was just fine.

"It's a dance competition," Edie said. "You dance in pairs and that's it. You just dance and dance and dance, doesn't that sound great? And it can take a long time to find a winner, so you sort of live there, and they give you meals and people can come and watch, and you just keep dancing. And the last ones left win the prize. Doesn't it just sound perfect?"

"Perfect," agreed Connie. "What's the prize?"

"It's five hundred dollars! Each!"

Mary coughed in surprise. "Five hundred dollars?"

Grace took a careful sip from her bottle of cream soda, a treat to herself, not saying anything.

"Yes, can you imagine?" Edie's fork hovered halfway to her mouth as she went all glassy-eyed, clearly thinking about what she could do with five hundred dollars. Even at Patrick's good rate of pay, that was more than six weeks' wages. Grace was chewing silently. She had heard about these dance marathons, and she wasn't sure they were as great as Edie was making out, but it was surely better than dancing in bars, and at least Grace would know where she was.

"Sounds just great, Edie," she said. "When does it start?"

"Sunday. So this meal will really help fuel me up. Thanks again, Mrs. O'Connell."

"You're very welcome." Mary smiled. "Such a lovely girl," she added quietly, just to herself.

"I'll come and watch you dance," Grace promised.

"Can I come too?" Connie asked, a tiny bite of cherry pie on her fork.

Grace smiled and reached over to stroke her sister's hand. She had barely made it from the bedroom to the table; it was far too soon to be planning trips across town. "Maybe. We'll see," and with that, Mary changed the subject.

Grace, however, continued to brood. She was worried about Edie. She really needed to call Betty. Now she was married, she had more time on her hands than Grace; maybe she could try again to help. Edie's prominent cheekbones and collarbones were all too apparent. She didn't look like a girl who could dance for days on end, but she seemed excited to be fixing her own problems, and that was all Grace wanted, to see her happy.

After dinner, Edie was too stuffed to move, so she stayed in her seat while at Connie's request, Grace performed for them, acting out her favorite bits from the latest book she was reading. Connie nodded along, Edie laughed and clapped in all the right places, and Grace's heart was full.

Later, once the dishes were done and they had listened to the radio awhile, Mary reached into the back of the cupboard and took out a tin, blowing the dust off the top. Muttering about special occasions, she made them all mugs of hot chocolate, even though it was a hot June night. Connie's face lit up, and Grace dissolved in giggles when she looked over and saw the exact same expression on Edie's face.

With Connie sleeping, after some argument, Grace eventually convinced Edie to take her bed and gave her a white nightgown to wear. When Edie slid under the sheets, she looked so content that Grace smiled, pleased that for one night at least, her friend had a family. Grace laid a blanket and cushion on the floor and pulled another blanket on top of her. It wasn't a cold night, and she was more than warm enough.

"Are you sure you're all right down there?" Edie asked. "I feel terrible taking your bed. It should be me on the floor."

"I'm perfectly fine, thank you," said Grace. "More than happy. I'm just so glad I saw you when I did. I've missed you."

"Me too." Edie's words swept out of her mouth on an exhaling breath. "I've had just the best evening. Your family is so lovely." Her voice cracked a little on the last word. "Thank you for letting me stay."

"You're always welcome here, Edie," Grace said, reaching up from the floor for Edie's hand. They lay like that, holding hands, until they fell asleep.

19

SATURDAY, JUNE 28, 1930

As Patrick rounded the corner to the subway station, he was whistling a bright tune, a smile on his face and the sun on his back. Grace had made it through two weeks on the steel, Connie was holding steady, his mother seemed calmer, and he had a whole day ahead of him to spend with Florence. Things were looking up for Patrick O'Connell.

The smile on his face got even bigger as he saw Florence waiting for him in a yellow sundress. He had asked her if he could take her out for lunch to say thank you for helping Connie, and she had accepted. Sadly, the happy feeling lasted only briefly as he took in the sight of her hands on her hips, and noticed that her narrowed eyes did not look in any way pleased to see him. Before he could even say a word in greeting, she was pointing at him.

"Patrick O'Connell," she said, in what was dangerously close to a snarl.

"Florence?"

Her nostrils flared. He had never seen her angry before. It made her look even more beautiful, but it was also terrifying, particularly when her anger seemed to be directed at him.

"Please correct me if I'm wrong, but I was under the impression, after what you said that morning when we sat and held your sick sister's hand together, that you might be interested in getting to know me better."

"Of course," Patrick said, brow furrowed in confusion. He'd never known a girl speak to him like this before, and it would have been oddly thrilling if the stakes weren't so high. "I'm here, aren't I?"

Florence's eyes flashed dark with anger. "Just tell me. Are you stepping out on me?"

The streets, as always, were busy with people, and a couple gasped and sucked in their breath as they heard the public accusation. One man patted Patrick on the back as he disappeared into the subway station, saying, "You're in trouble, brother." Patrick was too shocked by the question to even be annoyed.

"No, o' course not."

"Because after everything I've done for you," Florence said, lowering her voice, "and am continuing to do, it would not make a girl feel like keeping secrets to find out you were."

Patrick gulped. Here it was. Whatever was going on here, this was the moment when Florence changed her mind and ran home to spill her guts to her father.

"I don't know what you're saying, Florence, honestly. I've done nothing wrong."

"Then why," said Florence, taking a step closer to him and hissing her words out through her teeth, "am I hearing that you were with another girl last night, when you told me you were with your cousin? Left the bar with her and everything, so I hear! You do remember who my father is? I hear things, you know, and I've heard all about your reputation. You can't just fool me like I'm one of your harem of clueless girls. How dare you!"

"What? You've heard what? From who?" Patrick screwed up his face, bewildered. "What are you talking about?" He thought back to the night before. It was a little hazy, but he was sure there hadn't been any women in the bar, and he certainly never left with one.

Florence turned on her heel and began to stalk off down the sidewalk. Patrick raced after her, reaching for her arm.

"Wait!" His blood was pounding. He hated that his family's future was being held in Florence's angry little hands, especially when he didn't even know what he was supposed to have done wrong.

Florence turned to look at him. "Are you lying to me, Patrick O'Connell?"

"No." Patrick was exasperated. He was fighting for his life now, trying his best to stay calm so they could fix this. "I have no idea what you're talking about. I wasn't with no other woman. I don't want no other woman. You're the one for me, I knew it from the moment I saw you eat that ice cream!" The words were out of his mouth before he even knew he was thinking them, let alone going to say them.

Florence's face registered her shock for just a second, before she carried on with her tirade, poking him in the chest. "Don't you dare think you can talk yourself out of this one by saying whatever you think will help your cause, just so I keep my mouth shut. I—"

"Wait," Patrick said, cutting her off. The ambush had taken him by surprise, but as his thoughts finally filtered through, he didn't have to look far for an answer to his confusion. Just an hour ago, he had sat next to a tiny slip of a girl at his breakfast table who had been dipping toast into her egg with the excitement of a child. Grace had introduced them, and the girl had flushed red—with shyness or embarrassment, he wasn't sure which. He felt his mouth start to twitch with the start of a smile, and he couldn't help but laugh.

"What exactly is funny? Lord help me, Patrick O'Connell, I am going to—"

He grabbed Florence by the shoulders and whispered in her ear between his chuckles, "It was Grace."

"What?" Florence pulled back from him to look at his face. "You were with Grace?"

"No," Patrick said, the truth still tickling his funny bone. "It *was* Grace. Not me." He mouthed the last two words even though no one was paying any attention to them anymore. "Grace bumped into her friend and brought her home. But obviously she was . . ."

"Dressed like you," Florence finished quietly.

"Yes," said Patrick. "I met her friend for the first time this morning at breakfast; she seemed nice enough." He was teasing her now. "As if I would take any girl back to my mother's home from a bar." He laughed again.

Florence's own mouth twitched, and he watched her calming herself down, falling for her a little more by the minute, particularly when she tilted her head back and burst out laughing. Patrick was secretly pleased that she was jealous at the thought of him being with someone else.

"Of course," she said, wiping her eyes. "I can't believe I didn't think of that."

"You can trust me," Patrick said.

She looked up at him from under her dark eyelashes, their faces impossibly close together. "Can I? Did you mean what you said?"

"Yes." It was the simplest thing in the world. He knew it without a doubt. He'd thought breaking his arm was the worst thing that could have happened to him, but without it, he might never have had that ice cream with Florence Gilligan.

Florence nodded and started to walk again. Patrick moved to the other side of her so he could grab her by the hand with his good arm. After a few steps, Florence said, in an offhand way, "I wouldn't have told my father, you know." She paused before continuing. "I like your sisters too much."

He grinned and kissed her on the top of the head.

20

WEDNESDAY, JULY 2, 1930

It was a glorious day, and Grace turned her face to the sun as she ate her lunch on the beam, enjoying the view in easy silence, Joe beside her. When it was time to move again, she jumped to her feet with a spring in her step and turned to look for Frank.

"Come on, old man!" she called to him. "You're slow today."

"Eh! You try and sleep with a baby in the house!" he called back, and Grace smiled. Twelve Donohues above her head was probably just as bad.

Everyone was in position, and Grace was just about to signal to Seamus for the first rivet, when a bizarre feeling came over her, the hairs rising on the back of her neck and along her arms. She caught the movement from the corner of her eye, her head snapping around.

A man fell from above them.

Grace didn't know what had happened, but he fell straight past her, lying flat on his back as if on a bed full of pillows, and just kept going. Joe grabbed for her, pinning her hands to her sides to keep her safe, although the man seemed to be falling a few feet out from the building and had no chance of knocking anyone else off on his way down. And he was way past them now.

"Don't look," Joe said, but it was too late. Grace had already seen too much. She didn't need to see the man hit the ground to know it was going to happen. It had probably already happened by now.

Her body was frozen. Her insides a tight corkscrew. She hoped no

166 · GEMMA TIZZARD

one on the ground had been hurt. Other than the poor man who had just fallen three hundred feet through the sky, of course. Inside her head, she was screaming, but in reality, she wasn't making a sound; no one was. The site had become eerily silent. Plenty of them had seen what had happened, and word soon spread to those who hadn't. Everyone stopped work, downed tools, and stood still where they were, hats in their hands as a sign of respect. Grace tried to reach up and wrench her own cap off, but Joe was still holding her as tight as a straitjacket. She could feel his chest heaving against her back and his breath in her ear. The falling man had been close, so close that she had seen the shock on his face. She would see it for the rest of her life. Their eyes had met for just a split second; his mouth had been open, but if he was screaming, Grace couldn't remember hearing it.

"You have to pull yourself together. Right now, *Patrick*," Joe hissed urgently in her ear, in a sharp voice she hadn't heard from him in a while. She realized she was leaning into him and stood back up, taking her own weight again, but her body was rigid with terror. She could see the concern on Frank's face, but she couldn't register anything. She'd locked away her emotions in the only way she could and completely shut down.

Less than five minutes after the man fell, Gilligan was making rounds to talk to people. Grace thought he might be checking everyone was safe to carry on, but that appeared to be assumed and expected. The main feeling from the others seemed to be relief that it wasn't them. Within ten minutes, they were all back at work. What else could they do?

"It's a tragedy," Gilligan said, and Grace saw he meant it. "But we can't stop or we'll never start again. We'll figure out a way to pay our respects, but for now, we can only go on."

Grace's eyes went wide as she tried to take this in. She looked down at the tongs in her hand as if she had never seen them before. But she also knew there were thousands of men on this site; they couldn't stop because just one of them had died. Died. The man had died. Of course. He was alive when she saw him falling past her. At that moment she was witnessing his last few seconds of life.

She carried on with her job, forcing her hands not to shake, reminding her lungs to breathe in and out. She bullied herself into thinking of Connie's face, to get her through the day, stopping every few rivets, swallowing hard as she saw over and over again the man falling through the air. It sickened her—more than once she thought she was going to vomit. She marveled at the fact that everyone around her could carry on as if nothing had happened. She glanced down at one point and saw the tiny speck of an ambulance below. From this height there couldn't have been a body for them to collect. Not a whole one, at least. She pulled her eyes away and blinked hard to make sure her tears didn't obscure her view as the next rivet came flying toward her. Her toes curled inside her boots as if she could grip on to the steel tighter that way, but the truth was, it could happen to anyone, at any moment.

The man's name started to be whispered around the site. Lukasz. Lukasz Kowalski. A connector, doing the most dangerous job on the site. Grace kept hearing more snippets of information, even over the noise, even though she didn't want to know. The name would haunt her dreams. On a coffee break, men solemnly toasted sandwiches in their forges. She wondered how they could even think of eating. Lukasz Kowalski. Polish. He was thirty-nine. He had six children. She was being force-fed the information, swallowing against it as it stuck in her throat. No more, please. She sat, her eyes staring but not seeing. She didn't know if anyone had tried to talk to her. Her body was on the steel, but she had locked the most important part of herself somewhere far away, to stop herself from crying or screaming. She couldn't scream, because if she started, she might never stop. She went back to work and caught rivets until the clock told her she could rest.

On her way down to ground level, she felt increasingly sick, dreading what she might see. Had they taken him away by now? She imagined a sheet covering a mangled, broken body, limbs clearly pointing the wrong way even under the cover. Or what if the impact had obliterated him entirely? Would there be blood staining the ground? Her breathing started to labor, and she fought to get air into her body. Her skin was slick with sweat, and she turned her identification tag over and over in her clammy hand. Was that what it was really for? In case you fell and it was the only bit of you that survived?

She held her breath as she stepped out of the elevator, expecting to see chaos. What she saw was nothing. Nothing at all out of the ordinary compared to any other day. There was no sign of what had happened. No sign of Lukasz Kowalski. He had already been cleaned up, taken away, erased, as if he had never been. She expected to feel relief, but in some ways, this was far, far worse. A man held a paint can, calling out, "Collection for Lukasz, for his widow." Already he was calling her a widow. She might not even know yet. Grace reached into her pocket and stuffed some bills in the can, hoping the money would make it to the family.

Joe caught up with her, walking beside her. "You okay?" he whispered, and Grace nodded, even though it was a lie. Without a word to anyone, she handed in her tag and drifted away from the building site, a ghost.

When Grace got home, she went straight into her mother's bedroom. Connie was propped up on pillows, resting.

"Gracie," she said quietly, frowning when she saw Grace's expression. "What's wrong?"

"Bad day, Con" was all Grace could manage before she kissed her sister's hand and went into her own room, closing the door. She lay down on her bed, expecting to cry, but her eyes were dry and her mind was empty except for one thought. *Every time things start to get better, they get worse.*

Her mother left her alone, but she heard hushed voices when Patrick came home. Not long afterward, he knocked and came in.

"Bad day," he said. It was a statement, not a question.

Grace looked to see if her brother had brought alcohol with him this time. He hadn't, which was a shame. "Someone died."

Patrick sucked air in through his teeth. They sat in silence for a moment. "Who?"

Grace remembered that these were Patrick's people, not hers. "Lukasz

Kowalski." The name sounded thick in her mouth, as if her tongue was too big, but she was pleased to have said it out loud.

"Didn't know him," Patrick said, the relief in his voice unmistakable.

"That's all right, then," Grace retorted with a hint of bitterness. She felt as if she was floating outside her body. *She* knew him. She did now, anyway. She knew what his face looked like in the second he realized he was about to die. She knew him in a way nobody else ever would.

"I didn't mean that." Patrick's cheeks flushed red.

A wave of heat and anger crashed over her. "It's relentless," she whispered, her eyes burning. "I lose my dancing and my friends, I have to do this god-awful job, Connie gets sick, the rent goes up, and now this. I don't know how much more I can take. Every time we take the tiniest step forward, life kicks us back down the stairs. What's next?"

"I'm sorry." He knew the words weren't nearly enough. His twin was broken in front of him, and he had no idea how to put the pieces back together. He stared at her helplessly.

There was a knock at the front door, and Patrick left the room to answer it.

"Frank," Grace heard her brother say in surprise, followed by hushed voices. A few moments later, there was a knock at her bedroom door. She got up to open it.

"*Bella*." It was strange to see Frank in her home. His normally dancing eyes were sad and subdued. "It has been a terrible day. I have come to invite you to dinner tonight with my family. Really it was Giuseppe's idea." He smiled at her. "He is at home, getting things ready. Please say you will come."

Grace wanted to say no, she wasn't feeling up to company, but she also had a strange desire to be with Frank and Joe. At least they understood. Frank had come all the way from the Lower East Side to see her. It would be rude to send him away. And above all of this, she knew that she desperately needed the distraction or she was just going to lie on her bed and drive herself insane.

"I know you love my wife's cooking," Frank teased. "Your eyes are always on my lunch! Are you going to pass up the opportunity to eat at her table?"

Grace wasn't hungry, not even for delicious Italian food, but she didn't want to disappoint Frank, particularly the part of him that reminded her of her father.

"Who could turn down such an offer?" She forced a small smile. "Thank you."

He clapped his hands in triumph. "You are all welcome," he said with a beaming smile, turning to the others.

Patrick had been watching Grace closely. "Another time."

"Another time," Frank agreed. "Come, *bella*, tonight we will feast."

Grace didn't think she would be eating anything, but she nodded none the less.

Grace stared at her clothing options in her small room as if they had an answer for her. Unsure whether to dress as herself or Patrick, in the end she decided to wear the slacks he had given her for her first day of training, suspenders holding them up over a clean shirt. It would make no sense for Frank to be seen with Grace. As far as the world knew, they had never met, so she decided to dress like her brother, but she was looking forward to at least using her own voice for a change, once they were safely inside.

"I cannot wait for you to meet everybody," Frank said, sounding more like Connie in his excitement than a grown man as they rounded a corner onto the busy street in the Lower East Side. It was old and crumbling, but spotlessly clean, strung with electric lights and red, white, and green streamers to create possibly the most inviting place in New York.

"What's the occasion?" Grace asked, gesturing to the decorations.

"We are Italian," he said by way of explanation. "We don't need one. But there is always something to celebrate. Always a birthday or a baby, a marriage, or a religious festival. We just keep them up all year to save time. They make people happy, and it is impossible to have too much joy, *bella*."

Grace smiled, and for the first time since Lukasz had fallen past her, she felt something. It was a small flicker in her empty shell of a body, but it felt a little like coming back to life.

"This is the one," said Frank, leading her up the stoop of a brownstone.

"Oh my," Grace breathed, when Frank opened the door to his second-floor apartment. The room was a riot of color, activity, voices, and the smell of freshly baked dough and tomatoes. In the middle was a large table taking up almost all the available space, with what seemed to be hundreds of chattering people standing around it.

"Papa!" Two dark-haired, olive-skinned children barreled into Frank's legs and he easily lifted one in each arm, planting kisses on their faces. "*Bambini!*" He tilted the children toward Grace to make introductions. "This is my friend Grace. Grace, this is Carlotta and Giovanni."

"Nice to meet you," Grace said. The children were beautiful, with mussed hair and huge dark eyes that stared at her in wonder and confusion. Carlotta seemed to be around six, with Giovanni only slightly younger. Grace had already seen at least three other small children in the room.

"Are you a boy or a girl?" Carlotta asked.

Frank laughed, and Grace smiled. "Sometimes I'm both. I'm a girl who sometimes dresses like a boy. It's complicated."

"Doesn't sound complicated to me," said Giovanni, puffing out his little chest.

"Ai, Gio, that is because you are very clever!" said Frank, kissing each child again and placing them back on the ground. "My beautiful Nicolette is over there"—he waved toward a pile of small children climbing all over each other on a chair—"and of course you must meet Mateo!" His face broke into a wide smile.

Grace hadn't even made it beyond the doorway before she found herself being greeted with kisses on both cheeks by all sorts of family members, who chattered to each other in rapid Italian and spoke to her in English of variable fluency. Frank was calling out names but giving no indication of who these people might be. "Sophia! Marco! Little Enzo and Big Enzo! Frankie! Big Giovanni, call him Gio!" She was swallowed by a sea of people, all grinning and greeting her like a long-lost family member.

"This way, *bella*!" Frank called, pulling on her hand as she slowly made her way around the table. A beautiful woman with long dark curls came from the kitchen with a tiny mewling baby in her arms and a cloth thrown over one shoulder. She looked effortlessly glamorous in a red dress covered by a white apron. "Here she is!" said Frank. "My Maria! Meet Grace! And this, this beautiful boy is Mateo!" Grace was welcomed with kisses by Maria, who then thrust the tiny baby into her arms and turned back into the small kitchen, which seemed to be bursting at the seams with yet more people.

"Mamma!" called Frank, bringing forward a slightly hunched lady wrapped in a beautiful black shawl. Her gray hair was tied back behind her head in a bun, and when she looked up, Grace saw Joe's eyes staring back at her. "This is Grace!" Frank swooped in and took Mateo from Grace's arms so they could greet each other properly.

"Grace," said the woman, taking both her hands and pulling her down to kiss her cheeks. "Thank you, my darling, *grazie mille*, for all you have done for my family." Grace felt a lump rise in her throat, and all she could do was smile.

"Here's someone you know!" said Frank, and Grace's breath caught as Joe came out of the kitchen. Seeing him here was completely different from seeing him at work, and she found herself studying him with new eyes. "Get Grace a drink, Giuseppe! It is so hot in here! Marco, throw open another window! What do you mean, they are all open? Make some more!" Frank laughed and handed Mateo to another beautiful woman as he went off to follow someone Grace assumed was another brother.

Joe beckoned to her, and she found herself squeezing around people and into the tiny kitchen, where the intensified smell of cooking was almost too much to take. Despite the fact that she didn't think she was hungry, her mouth was watering as she caught sight of bowls full of glistening olives and tomatoes, milky mozzarella, pink ham, and white-topped mushrooms.

Maria was spreading homemade tomato sauce over fresh dough with the back of a ladle. "I bet you have never had proper Italian pizza before," she said as she worked. "You will never be the same again!" Grace didn't doubt her.

Joe was watching the scene with interest, a softness in his eyes that made Grace feel warm. "I'm glad you came," he said softly, and she swallowed hard and nodded, trying to tell herself she wasn't disappointed he hadn't pulled her into a hug like the other members of his family had. "Wine?" he asked, holding up a bottle of red.

"A little, please."

"Yes please!" cried a joyful voice, and Grace looked around for where it had come from.

Joe laughed as he poured and handed her a glass. She had rarely heard him laugh, and she wanted to catch hold of it like a butterfly and keep it. "Not for you!" he said, reaching for someone and bringing them through the crowd. "This is our friend Grace," he added, and Grace felt a fizz of pleasure at the description. "Grace, this is my brother Bruno."

The man who stood in front of her was so large, she couldn't believe she hadn't seen him until that moment. He was tall and broad, bigger even than Frank, and he had the same dark hair and skin as his family. He was also good-looking like the rest of them, but the way his eyes roamed the room loosely and his mouth was a little turned down and slack made it obvious to Grace there was something different about him.

"Hello, Bruno. A pleasure to meet you." She held out her hand and he grabbed at it with both of his and said, "Kiss!" She laughed and leaned forward, kissing him on both cheeks.

"She's pretty, Joe!" Bruno said, and Joe looked embarrassed for a moment before he nodded.

"Very pretty."

Grace blushed.

"Can I sit next to you at dinner?" Bruno asked.

"Why, of course," she said. "It would be an honor."

Joe looked at her and held her gaze for a second longer than he needed to before he looked away. If Grace were to guess, she would say that Bruno was around twenty-five, but his way was more like that of a child. She thought back to the first night she had met the Gagliardis. One of the first things Joe had said when he'd thought they were losing their jobs was "What about Bruno?" Grace wasn't the only one working to provide for a sibling. She knew Joe was protective of his brother and she had been given a gift by being allowed into their private space to meet him.

Looking around the room, she tried to count the number of people, but everyone was moving and changing positions and the family resemblance was so strong she gave up at twenty. However many people there were, it made the Donohues look like they weren't really trying.

"Seats, please!" Maria called, and everyone started to scramble to the table. It was heaving with plates, cutlery, glassware and even candles, despite it not yet being dark. The whole family were now speaking in English for Grace's benefit. She hovered at the edge of the picture, unsure where to go, until Bruno wrapped his huge hand around hers and led her to a seat.

"You sit there, Grace," he said, pushing down on her shoulder.

"Easy, Bruno," said Joe. "Be gentle." Joe sat on the other side of Bruno, and Grace felt the tiniest pang of disappointment that he wasn't sitting next to her. There wasn't much time to think about it, though, as a small child scrambled up, settling herself on Grace's lap. She was only a toddler and had a ragged doll clutched in her fist.

"Ah!" said Frank, sitting himself down opposite. "I see you have met Nicolette!"

Frank and Joe's mother, who Grace had picked up from conversations was called Giulia, sat on Grace's other side and placed a hand over hers, giving her a warm smile.

"I hear something bad happened today," she said quietly in her heavily accented English, her voice lost amid the hubbub of the table. Grace was ashamed to realize she had temporarily forgotten about Lukasz. She nodded. Giulia squeezed her hand. "We celebrate life by living it for those who cannot." She tapped Grace's hand before placing her own back in her lap. "And we eat." She gave a little shrug. "We are Italian."

Maria and two other women swept around the table laying out huge dishes of pasta and plates piled high with slices from pizzas the size of sewer covers. Grace had no idea how they had cooked them in their tiny kitchen, and raised her eyebrows in Joe's direction. *How?* she mouthed.

He laughed, and mouthed back, *Magic.* Then he winked, and butterflies took flight in Grace's stomach. He beckoned her closer, and they leaned toward each other in front of Bruno, their heads almost touching. "There's a brick oven on the roof," he said, placing a finger over his lips. Grace smiled, relishing the feeling of sharing a secret with him.

The table was heaving with food. The second Maria was seated, Frank said a few words, looking at his wife with so much love in his eyes, Grace thought he might burst. Then he turned to his mother.

"*Mangiamo!*" Giulia declared, adding in English for Grace's benefit, "Eat!"

Grace had never tasted such food. Bruno kept looking at her and laughing at the faces she was making as she tried one dish after another. For someone who had just hours ago sworn she would never eat again, she was doing a pretty good impression of a starving woman.

"Joe, she's funny!" he said, clapping his hands in delight when Grace closed her eyes with pleasure as she sucked spaghetti into her mouth. "Haven't you had food before?" he asked, and the whole table laughed.

"Not like this, no," she admitted, picking up a slice of pizza and supporting the narrow end of the triangle with her fingers as she sank her teeth into the dough.

Joe was cutting Bruno's pizza into squares and spearing each morsel on a fork before handing it over to his brother, his own plate untouched, food going cold.

"I'll do that." Grace reached over to take charge of Bruno's plate. "I've certainly had enough. Eat, Joe." Joe looked at her as if he was about to protest, but then nodded. Grace caught Frank smiling at his wife out of the corner of her eye as she handed the fork to Bruno, who was trying to talk with his mouth full.

"One thing at a time, Bruno," Frank said. "Eat, then talk. One, then the other."

Watching the Gagliardis with their family filled Grace with warmth and love. She had a strange ache in her chest; meals hadn't been like this in her own family since her father died.

"This food is just incredible, thank you so much," she said, handing Bruno his next mouthful.

"You are welcome here any time," said Giulia. "You are the reason there is food on this table."

Grace looked down, embarrassed.

"It's not cheap to keep an Italian family fed!" Frank caught her eye and smiled at her.

In her mind, she saw Frank standing across from her on the beam, rivet gun in his hand, and imagined that each sealed rivet paid for another olive, or tomato, or mushroom for his wife to weave her magic upon.

"No," she said. "I don't imagine it is."

When the meal was finished, Grace got up to help with the dishes but was pushed back into her seat. "No, no, you stay."

"How was it?" Joe asked, his chin resting on his hand, dark eyes trained on her.

"Perfect," Grace said, smiling at him before taking another sip of her wine.

Frank went to the corner of the room and put on some music. "Mamma, Grace is a dancer," he announced.

Giulia clapped her hands together. "You must show us!"

"Oh, um . . ." Grace looked around. "Well, there isn't much room."

"Everybody move!" shouted Frank, who was already trying to push the table against the wall. "Grace is going to dance."

"She is?" Grace murmured to herself, and heard Joe snort a laugh. She shot him a pleading look, and he raised his hands in surrender, shaking his head, a smile tugging at the corner of his lips. He wasn't going to help her.

The music was a gorgeous piece, but it was being sung in Italian, so she had no idea what it was about. She assumed it was a love story—after all, most music was. "Okay, well, first I need a partner." She looked around the room, as if seeking a person to dance with, but there was only ever one choice. "Bruno, will you dance with me?"

"Me?" Bruno's eyes went wide.

A flicker of panic crossed Joe's face as she took Bruno's huge hand, bringing him to his feet, and she gave a little nod to reassure him that everything would be fine. As they stood under the yellow glow of the electric lights, Bruno was too excited to listen to her instructions, so she just placed his hands where they should be and did the leading, sweeping him around the room in circles as the rest of the family cheered. Bruno relaxed and his once stiff movements became loose. Grace whispered, "Ready?" and then executed a little spin, careful not to make him dizzy. He held her with a tenderness that made her heart ache, and he didn't step on her toes once, which was far more than could be said for many of her dance partners. When they finished, Bruno was beaming and at least a couple of the family were crying.

"And that," Grace said, "is how you dance."

A spontaneous burst of applause came from the family, led by Frank, who cheered and whistled, joined by others. Grace looked around the room, filled with a swell of warmth for these people. As her eyes settled on Joe, she thought of how he fed Bruno, the same way she fed Connie. He looked completely different here; all his hard edges had relaxed into soft curves. He was gentle and kind. His eyes shone in the candlelight and he was beautiful.

She suddenly realized with a jolt what had been terrifying her. It wasn't the thought of falling off the steel and dying; it was the thought of having to watch it happen to Seamus, or Frank, or—she gulped as her mind fought to let her even think it—Joe. The panic and fear from earlier in the day came back with a vengeance. It was rising like the tide, and she grabbed at the neck of her shirt. It was far too hot in the Gagliardi apartment; there were too many people. She had to get out. She gritted her teeth to try and control her breathing and plastered a Dominic's smile on her face.

"Thank you for a wonderful evening," she announced to the whole room. "It has been a pleasure to spend time with you in your home, but I really must be going now."

"I will walk you," Joe said.

"I live on the other side of town," Grace said. "You don't have to go all the way there and come all the way back. I'll be fine, it isn't late."

"Just let the boy walk you, *bella*," Frank said, wrapping her into a hug and giving her a kiss on each cheek.

"Fine, fine." Grace didn't protest too much as she circled the room, saying her goodbyes as fast as she could. As much as she needed to get out, she also wasn't ready for the evening to end. Here, she had been wrapped in warmth and love, and been able to momentarily escape some of her problems. At home waiting for her was a small girl who couldn't seem to get better, and a family worried sick about whether they would make it through all this.

Out on the street, Grace took several deep breaths, trying to calm her racing mind. The evening air was still warm, but the breeze off the river swept up the streets to keep them cool as they walked.

"Is everything all right?" Joe asked. "You looked like you were having fun, and then suddenly you want to leave. Did Bruno say something . . . ?" His voice trailed away.

"No, nothing like that. Your family is just great."

"They are crazy, but I love them."

"Bruno is a sweetheart, and, might I add, in my professional opinion, a most excellent dancer."

Joe laughed. "He loved it, thank you."

"The pleasure was all mine," Grace said, and meant it. "It's hard to find a good dance partner in this city, and I haven't been able to dance for a while now." She went quiet, thinking about how much she missed it and how much safer it was as a career choice. In all her years dancing, she had never once had to watch anyone die. Even in the circus, the worst she had witnessed was a broken leg. "Do you mind me asking . . ." She paused, unsure how to phrase the question. She didn't have to. Joe knew. It probably wasn't the first time he'd had the conversation.

"It was a difficult birth," he said, kicking a stone along the sidewalk. "They said he didn't get enough air and his brain was damaged. That was all." He shrugged. "It could have happened to any of us."

"Yes." Her stomach full of Italian food clenched and she fought against the nausea. She was thinking of the falling man again. *It could have happened to any of us.* "It isn't fair."

"No," said Joe. "It isn't fair. But we can waste our time being angry and cry about it and try to fight the world, or we can accept it and enjoy what we have. At least Bruno is still here. He is happy every single day of his life. Who else can say that? How can I be mad about that?" He shrugged again. "Maybe he is the lucky one."

"Maybe." Grace felt the word on her lips, but it hardly made a sound. The man who had fallen was definitely not the lucky one. "I'm sorry, Joe," she blurted. "I thank you all for your hospitality tonight, but I don't think I can go back up on the steel again." The words were tumbling out of her. "You hear them talk about the men who lose their nerve—well, that's me, it's gone. It's like my brain has suddenly realized what I'm doing every day and has said no thank you, no more."

Joe listened carefully as they continued to walk, side by side. They passed the subway station, but they both needed the fresh air, and there would be another one soon enough. "I understand," he said. "I do. It was a horrible thing, but you have to see, he made a mistake. *We* don't make mistakes."

"Everyone makes mistakes." Grace's voice was grave. She was thinking of her first week on the steel, when Joe had slipped and nearly fallen himself. The thought alone was enough to make her knees weak. She cared too much now to risk seeing that again, even more so now she had met the whole family.

"Not working will not bring him back. And what happened to him doesn't make it more likely to happen to anyone else. We are as safe as we were before because we look after each other. Seamus, he is your cousin; it is like another brother, no? And Francesco and I will never let anything bad happen."

"I'm sure Lukasz's friends felt the same." Grace couldn't stop her body from shaking. "You can't promise against accidents, Joe."

"Nothing has changed." A thin thread of the old, angrier Joe had crept into his voice, and she felt her own anger rise in her to match it.

"Except *everything* has changed. It's all I can see. I'm shaking just thinking about it, down here on the ground. He just keeps falling, again and again and again. And it . . . it took so long." Her voice broke on the last word and the tears came. Joe reached for her hand, holding it in his. Earlier in the evening, Grace would have been thrilled to have his skin touching hers, but now there was no comfort in it at all.

"I'm sorry you saw that, but we must not think about it."

"I guess this is why they don't let women do this job. Maybe we are too emotional. I can't just carry on, Joe. Maybe you can, but I don't feel like it will all be okay, and I can't pretend that nothing has changed. I can't just not think about it." Grace stopped walking, and Joe turned to face her.

"Please." She could tell that this was costing him everything, and she cried harder to hear the desperation in his voice. "I promise I will keep you safe." He tilted her chin up so she was forced to look at him, tears streaming down her cheeks. She wanted to look away, didn't want him to see her like this, but he wouldn't let her go.

"We can't do it without you. I wish we could. I know it isn't fair to ask you to go back up there. It was never fair for you to be up there in the first place, for even one day, but you saw tonight why we do it. And you have come so far. I don't even worry anymore; you have done the hard work and you are one of us. You know how to be on the steel. Please."

He paused, and Grace willed him not to go on. One thing had jarred her ears as he spoke. *You saw tonight why we do it.* Her stomach plunged to her feet. That was why she was here. The Gagliardis had wanted to show her why she needed to go back on the steel and who she was hurting if she didn't. So many people. What she'd thought was just an offer of friendship had been emotional blackmail, and it had been Joe's idea. She felt sick.

"Carry on, please." Joe was still speaking. "See this through. Or just give it two more days, until the end of the week, and then think about it again at the weekend. Not for me, or Francesco, or Patrick." He held her gaze, and she knew what was coming. She watched him rip the next words out from deep inside himself, knowing they would hurt both of them; break both their hearts. "Do it for Bruno and Connie and Mateo."

The Gagliardis had done what they had to do. Grace understood that, and she didn't blame either of them, but she was still hurt, reeling from the relentless emotional toll of the day. She cried harder than ever, and when Joe tried to hug her, she pushed him away. Neither of them had any idea what the tears meant, or if she would ever set foot on the steel again.

Joe grabbed her hand. "You are my family now. I had to show you. I'm sorry. But I will keep you safe, I promise."

At the beginning of the evening, this was all Grace would have wanted to hear him say, but now the words felt hollow and meaningless. Nothing could keep her safe hundreds of feet in the sky, and no one could protect her from these feelings.

THURSDAY, JULY 3, 1930

Grace sat on the staircase outside her apartment early in the morning, a thin sweater on over her pajamas and a silk scarf covering her lack of hair. She hadn't slept and the apartment was too stuffy, so she had gone outside to sit on the landing, ignoring the stale smell of fried fish and potatoes that always seemed to linger. It must have permeated the walls. She leaned her head against the cool metal railings. It looked like she was in jail, and it felt that way too. She had been there for a while now. Her thoughts pinned her in place, and she was staring off into the middle distance when she heard someone light-footed descending the stairs above.

"Good morning, Miss O'Connell. What are you doing there?" The oldest Donohue boy, who could be no more than fourteen, sat down next to her.

"Morning—"

"Connor," he supplied, before she even had a chance to try.

"Connor," she repeated. "You're keen for school."

"I'm not going to school, miss, not no more." Grace turned her head to look at him. "I'm going to find a job."

"Are you now," she said with interest. "And what sort of job are you going to find?"

The boy had a sprinkling of freckles across his nose and his hair was too long; he had to keep brushing it out of his eyes. "They've put the rent up."

"I know."

"So I've got to bring some money in. I like school, but"—he shrugged his shoulders—"I like having a home more."

"To be sure," Grace muttered as the boy stood up again and headed down a couple more steps until their heads were level. For some reason he reminded her of Betty, and she felt a pang of missing her friends, telling herself yet again that she needed to find the time to check in with them.

"I'm hoping to find something in a restaurant. I'm hungry all the time," he said in hushed tones, as if it were a secret or an insult to his mother. "I'm hoping I can do something that gets me some extra food."

Grace nodded. "You're a growing boy."

"I am," he agreed. "And I always give a bit of mine to the little 'uns. They don't understand when there's no more."

Grace felt emotion clog her throat. "You're a good boy, Connor. I hope you find something."

"Me too. Have a nice day, Miss O'Connell." And with that, he was gone, down the stairs and out of sight. Grace closed her eyes and sighed. So that was why she was sitting out here, so she could be schooled by a teenage boy. He was only a few years older than Connie, and here he was putting what he wanted aside for the sake of his family. She thought about Joe's words to her the night before, and how strange it had been to see him get emotional. *You have come so far.*

Tracing her hand over the wooden floor, careful not to get splinters in her fingers, she thought of Connie, her mother, and Patrick. She thought of Seamus, and the look on his face the day he brought Patrick home with a broken arm. She thought of Florence and the burden of the secret she was keeping. She thought of Frank's children—Carlotta, Giovanni, Nicolette, and brand-new Mateo—and imagined each of their faces. She thought of Giulia, who had welcomed her into their home and thanked her so earnestly for helping her family. She thought of Bruno and the smile on his face as they'd danced, and she thought of Joe. She couldn't let any of them down. She would take the lesson that Connor Donohue had just unknowingly offered her. It wasn't about her; it was bigger than that. She couldn't allow her fear to hold her back. With another sigh, she pushed herself up off the steps and slipped back inside the apartment. It was time to get ready for work.

Grace was only a couple of minutes late as she reached the site. Most of the men were already on their way up. Her feet didn't want to take her any farther, but she had overcome her fears before and she could do it again. She had to. Waiting at the gate, she saw the rest of her gang, despair on their faces. They hadn't seen her yet and it was clear they didn't think she was coming. Honestly, if she hadn't seen Connor Donohue, she might not have. From about fifteen feet away, she whistled to get their attention. All three men turned to look in her direction, pure relief flooding their faces.

"Come on, or we'll be late," she said, in a perfect impression of her brother. Joe closed his eyes and tilted his head up to the sky, either offering a silent prayer, or grateful that one had been answered. Every molecule of Grace's being told her she didn't want to go up on that steel, but confusingly, also that she wanted to be wherever Giuseppe Gagliardi was.

"Good morning, *Patrick*," he said, in that way of his. Grace didn't trust herself to speak, so she just nodded in response.

Once they were in the elevator, Frank couldn't control his emotions any longer and threw his arms around Grace's neck. "Thank you," he whispered in her ear. "I have nothing to give you but my gratitude, love, and respect, and you have it."

"And pizza," Grace added, much to Frank's delight.

"Let's get to work," Seamus said, pulling open the cage door and stepping out onto the thirtieth floor of the building. Terror snatched at Grace's legs, threatening to freeze them, but she forced herself to head out with the others.

"Just like before," Frank whispered to her. "We do it just like before."

As she reached into the gang box to pick up her catching cone, Grace felt someone looking at her. When she turned her head, Bergmann, the big blond German, was staring. He held her gaze for a moment before looking away. Grace felt a shiver race up and down her spine. She didn't know why, but she knew she didn't like it.

As Joe reached down and helped her up onto the beam, she took a deep breath in and out. *Just like before.* She tried to settle herself into position and take comfort from the proximity of Frank and Joe, but as she prepared to catch the first rivet of the day, two words chugged through her brain in time with her pulse pounding in her ears: *Lukasz Kowalski, Lukasz Kowalski.* They sounded like a train passing through her head, clouding everything else. *Lukasz Kowalski, Lukasz Kowalski.*

She missed the first rivet and it landed on Joe's leg. He hissed as the material of his coveralls did the same, and kicked away the rivet, gritting his teeth, clearly burned.

"I'm sorry," whispered Grace, in her own voice, too upset to remember to pretend. He nodded, his jaw clenched.

"It's okay," said Frank. "It's no big deal. We'll try again."

She caught the next one, and slowly her confidence and rhythm returned, but the joy she'd experienced the day before was gone and wouldn't be coming back. Lukasz Kowalski's death had destroyed her love of being up high, and she was sure she would never enjoy another day on the steel again.

When lunchtime arrived, Grace felt more exhausted than ever before. Even the very first day hadn't been as tough. She was constantly fighting against her tense body, and it made every movement ten times harder. The Italians were both patient and kind, grateful to be up there at all, but Grace knew she had to pull herself together soon, before people started to notice.

"Here." Joe handed Grace a wrapped parcel. "I brought you lunch today."

"Really?" She was touched by his kindness. He had obviously had faith she was going to turn up. It was more than Grace herself had had.

Frank was smiling. "Well, we know how you love the Italian food."

"It's a calzone," Joe said. "And it is delicious."

"I'm sure." Grace sat beside him on the safety of a temporary floor to eat.

"What the hell?" a gruff voice called over. Grace looked up and saw Bergmann, like a free-standing wall, tongs swinging in one hand, an expression of disgust on his face. "What's with you two looking all goo-goo at each other? It's making my skin crawl."

"What are you talking about?" Joe said, his voice fierce.

"Obviously you are mistaken, friend," Frank said, trying to placate the mountain of a man. "What you see is friendship."

"You wouldn't know about that, though," Seamus said, suddenly appearing. Grace was sure he had a sense for danger and was always compelled to be right in the middle of it.

"I know what I saw." Bergmann pointed his tongs in the direction of Grace and Joe. "And"—he shook his head—"it doesn't make any sense. You a fairy now, O'Connell? Since when? There's something not right about you."

"Back off, Bergmann," Joe snarled. "I brought Patrick some lunch, so fucking what?"

"He's just jealous," said Seamus, taking a bite of his sandwich without a care in the world.

"I've had enough of you!" roared Bergmann. He took a swing at Seamus with his tongs. Seamus easily ducked out of the way, but the shock was written all over his face. He had never thought Bergmann would actually try and hurt him.

"*Hey!*" shouted Frank. "What the hell is the matter with you? A man died here yesterday, or did you forget? And yet you do something so dangerous? You dare threaten anyone on this steel again, Bergmann, and I will end this myself. Now go, before I report you!" His face was red with fury. Grace had never seen him so angry before, hadn't believed him capable of it.

Bergmann waved his hand dismissively and turned away, but not before he glared at Grace, his lip curled. It was a look that chilled her.

"Well, that was more than your average Thursday," Seamus said as he went back to his sandwich.

As delicious as Grace's calzone was, she couldn't enjoy it now that she had yet more danger buzzing in her head. What was Bergmann's problem? She vowed to keep her distance from Joe. She hadn't forced herself back up here just to blow her cover by acting in ways her brother never would.

"Bathroom break," Joe announced, standing. Frank went with him. Normally they would have shot Grace an apologetic look, but they were all more wary now.

"Rivet run." Seamus gestured with his thumb as he went off to collect more bolts for his forge.

Grace was left alone. She finished her lunch and stood, one hand on the steel column as she looked out over the city and practiced breathing deeply. She had told herself she wasn't ever coming back up here, but here she was. Again. As she turned, she found Bergmann towering in front of her. He certainly moved quietly for a big man. She managed to fight her instincts and didn't react.

"Did you shrink, O'Connell?" he asked, leering down, forcing her back into the column.

"Get out of my face," Grace growled. "What is your problem?"

Instead, he moved closer, until he was just inches away, and studied her. Grace refused to flinch.

"My problem is that you swan around this steel and this city like you own it. You're no better than the rest of us, Patrick." He spat the name out like it was poison. "Far from it." His eyes drilled into hers, then went wide with the briefest flicker of recognition. Grace held her breath, convinced he was close to working it out. Then he moved his head back a little so that they were no longer sharing the same breath of air. "There's something going on here, and I intend to find out what it is."

"Well, let me know when you do," she retorted, with far more humor and bravery than she was feeling.

"Oh, I will," he said, stepping away and spitting over the side of the building. "I'll let everyone know."

Her stomach dropped. They weren't even three weeks through yet, and Bergmann suspected something. And if he thought something wasn't right, he was going to tell anyone who would listen so they could all look out for it too. She closed her eyes, and the images of the falling man played again in her mind, but this time it wasn't Lukasz Kowalski, it was Bergmann. She snapped her eyes open. This was silly, there was no reason to panic. Bergmann didn't know anything. She would just keep her head down and hope he went away.

"All okay?" Frank asked as he came back into view.

"Grand." She climbed back up into position, Joe not far behind. They didn't need the extra worry. Frank nodded and picked up his rivet gun, grateful for another afternoon of work.

22

SATURDAY, JULY 12, 1930

Florence linked her arm through Patrick's just above his cast as they strolled through Central Park, the sun shining down on the city. He carried a small picnic basket with his good hand as they searched for somewhere to sit.

"How about here?" She pointed to a free patch of grass. Families played nearby, children doing cartwheels, running and jumping, couples strolling on the path. It was hard not to notice the strain on the faces of the adults—financial worries didn't take the weekend off—but everyone was trying to make the best of the day, and the park was free at least.

Patrick nodded and reached into the basket for a blanket, letting Florence spread it on the ground. He knew it probably wasn't the smartest move to come here on a busy Saturday, but he also knew that love made people do reckless things – or at least, he did now. He had never been in love before Florence Gilligan had threatened his family and stepped in front of a car, nearly getting herself killed. Since then, it felt like he was the one who had been hit by a car, and he had a sneaking suspicion that if love was anything, it might be this.

Florence kicked off her shoes, tucking her feet under her as she sat before immediately switching positions, stretching her legs out in front of her and leaning back on her elbows, face turned to the sky to soak up the sun. Patrick sat awkwardly, scanning the horizon, and she nudged him.

"Relax a little," she said, reaching into the picnic basket and handing him an apple.

They sat for a while contentedly sipping lemonade, until Florence noticed the clouds passing across Patrick's face.

"Out with it," she said, scooting next to him and leaning against his shoulder. She knew instinctively he would find it easier to talk if he didn't have to look at her face.

"It's nothing," he said, plucking a stem of grass from the ground and using it to draw circles on the back of her hand. They sat in silence for a little longer until he finally spoke the words that had taken an hour to surface. "It feels a little easier at the weekends."

"What does?"

"The guilt." He looked away, toward the trees.

"You don't have any reason to feel guilty," Florence assured him. "You got hurt. It happens."

"Once my father died, it was my job to look after the family, and I couldn't. I hate that I wasn't the man he expected me to be. I thought I was the strong one, but it was Grace all along."

She turned to look at him. "It isn't a competition, you know. It's a family. You look out for each other, and you do a good job of it. And that's how it should be." She tutted, nudging his shoulder playfully. "You'll soon get tired carrying the weight of the world around on your shoulders, Patrick O'Connell."

"She shouldn't be up there, Florence, you said it yourself."

"It's a temporary solution to a temporary problem." She reached for his arm, and gently knocked on the plaster cast. "In my professional opinion, you'll be good as new in no time."

Patrick nodded, but couldn't quite bring himself to smile. He knew Florence didn't think he was any less of a man for not being able to work, but that didn't change the way he felt about himself. He blew out his cheeks and huffed all the air out of his lungs in a heavy sigh. "All this lurching from disaster to disaster, waiting for the moment when we can't keep going and the money runs out. I have sleepless nights wondering what will happen to them, you know. If we can't stay together."

"Things are tough now, to be sure, but I'm willing to bet that you O'Connells are tougher. Things won't be like this forever." Florence waited until he looked at her before she continued. "You're a good man, Patrick."

Patrick gazed into her eyes and his chest tightened. As he looked away, over her shoulder, panic crept up his neck. "Wait," he said. "Is that …?"

Florence twisted her head to see where he was looking, her eyes going headlamp wide. "My father? Yes, it is."

Not very far away, Florence's whole family were taking a stroll in the park. She scrambled to her feet and started to run toward the safety of the nearby trees, before doubling back to pick up her shoes.

"Hurry!" she hissed, as Patrick tried to shove the blanket back into the picnic basket. She grabbed the blanket and threw it over her shoulder, then darted out of sight, Patrick right behind her.

They dropped everything on the ground once they reached safety, peering out between branches, breathing heavily, as they watched the Gilligans walk by, oblivious.

"Phew." Florence collapsed back against a tree, her chest heaving. Patrick leaned his good arm on the bark above her head, facing her, his heart racing. They were so close their bodies were almost touching.

He grimaced. "You shouldn't have to lie and hide from your family because of me."

"Are you kidding?" she said with a gleeful laugh and a glint of mischief in her eye. "That was exhilarating."

Something came over Patrick then, with the sunlight dappling their skin through the trees and their blood charging through their veins. He boldly ducked his head down toward her, hesitating for a moment until she tilted her face up to meet his, unable to stop smiling as their lips met. When he pulled back, they were both grinning and his heart was almost bursting from his chest.

"I shouldn't have done that. Your father is just over there."

"He's not over here, though," Florence said, placing both her hands on his shirt front, where Patrick was convinced she must be able to feel the pounding of his heart.

"One day, Florence Gilligan," he said, slightly breathless, "I'm going to marry you."

Florence's eyes danced. "Kiss me like that again, and I might just let you."

23

SUNDAY, JULY 13, 1930

"Ladies and gentlemen, take your seats as our stars dance for you! Pick your favorites and watch these couples dance, dance, dance! Our heroes have been dancing for . . . now, let me check . . ." The man onstage wore a black suit and had gray hair swept back from his face. He turned to looked at the huge board with hanging numbers under a date and a clock. "Three hundred and thirty-four hours! Isn't that something? Show them your appreciation! And don't forget, you can sponsor your favorites!" He swept his arm across the dance floor in front of him, where around thirty tired-looking couples dragged their feet, hardly moving, just shuffling enough not to get disqualified.

Grace had hated the place from the moment she walked in. The hall was stuffy, and the smell of stale sweat and desperation hung in the air. She had paid twenty-five cents to enter and had been told that she could stay as long as she wanted. "Days if you want; there's a couple of homeless who sleep here."

She couldn't believe Edie was still there. A sign told her they had started out with two hundred couples, and now, two weeks later, they were down to thirty-three. As Grace sat herself down on the wooden bleachers, she was immediately offered the chance to buy popcorn, sandwiches, soda, coffee, or hot dogs to add to her viewing pleasure. She said no to everything. She wasn't here to enjoy the show, because the show was her friend, and it was awful.

When she'd first caught sight of Edie, she was shuffling to the slow dirge that was playing, her head on the chest of her dance partner, a man Grace had never seen before. As they twirled slowly around the large room, Grace tried to get a good look at her face, but Edie kept moving her head, as if she were twitching during a bad dream, which didn't seem that far off the truth. She wore an oversized sweater over her dress that had CLARK'S GENERAL STORE embroidered across it, and her partner wore a vest emblazoned with the same. They both wore the number eighty-nine pinned to their backs.

"Come on, sixty-three!" yelled a middle-aged woman with frantic red hair next to Grace. "Move your feet! Are you asleep or what?" She turned to Grace. "They play the slow stuff to make them sleepy. They gotta stay awake!"

"When's the next break?" Grace asked. She had to speak to Edie and get her out of here.

"Not for an hour," the woman said, flipping popcorn into her mouth. "I doubt these are all gonna make it. Exciting, ain't it? Who's your favorite? I got a sponsor on sixty-three. COME ON, SIXTY-THREE! KEEP IT MOVING!"

"That's my friend," Grace said, pointing out Edie, hoping for some information. It seemed like this woman had been here for a while.

"Eighty-nine? Oh, she's a good dancer. I have no idea how she's still going, though, there's nothing to her. I doubt she'll make another speed round."

"Speed round?"

"Ah, you'll see," said the woman, eating another handful of popcorn and offering Grace the box. She shook her head. "Here we go!" said the woman as the emcee stepped out onto the stage again.

"Who's ready for a special performance?" the man asked, throwing his arms out wide to greet the response.

"Yeah!" shouted the crowd, stamping their feet and waving sweaters in the air.

"Good!" said the emcee. "Because this one is fabulous. You may have seen her before over the last two weeks, but once is never enough! Will you welcome to the stage, Miss Edith McCall!"

"Edie?" Grace half rose to her feet until people behind her shouted for her to sit down. Edie let go of her partner and dragged her tired body to stand in front of the stage.

"It's your friend!" said the woman, nudging Grace and moving closer to her on the seat as if she were famous by association. Grace couldn't breathe.

"Is this a speed round?" she asked.

The woman laughed. "No. You really don't know anything, do ya? Have you never been before?" Grace shook her head. "Shame on you, your friend has been here two weeks!" The comment stung.

"I've been at work."

The woman shrugged. "This is a special performance, a solo dance."

Grace's eyes went back to the stage, where the band was starting up with a higher-tempo number. Edie's partner shuffled off to the side while someone with a clipboard watched him carefully to make sure he didn't stop moving.

From some deep reserve of strength Grace had no idea she had, Edie pulled herself up straight, smiled, and started a solo tap routine. Grace watched with a mixture of amazement and horror as the crowd all cheered. The dance lasted a minute, and although Edie was obviously exhausted and her limbs were heavy, she was still good. At the end, she made a little bow, and it looked as if it took all the strength in her body to pull herself upright again.

"Miss Edith McCall, ladies and gentlemen." The emcee was back. "What a gal. Now let's show our appreciation and give her a little silver shower, shall we?"

Amid more cheering, people started throwing nickels and the occasional dime in Edie's direction. Grace gasped. It reminded her of the rivets coming at her all day. Edie scrabbled around on the floor for the coins like she was trying to get to the last lifeboat on the *Titanic*.

"Oh, Edie," said Grace under her breath, as her friend made the humiliating crawl across the floor.

A buzzer sounded.

"That means she's got thirty seconds and then she has to be dancing with her partner again. Any coins she can't get will be swept away and kept by the house," the woman said.

Grace closed her eyes. This was horrible to watch, like dancing bears, no better than animals in a zoo. But watch she did, as yet more minutes dragged by and the couples continued to shuffle across the wooden floor. Some took it in turns to sleep while their partner supported their weight; others just stepped from foot to foot.

"This is getting boring!" yelled a man near the front, and people started to boo.

"Boring, you say?" The slick emcee was back onstage in a moment, back in control. "Who says we speed things up a little, then?"

The cheers from the crowd were loud, not least from the woman beside Grace. Grace watched with a sort of horrified fascination as three men came out and laid a huge oval piece of carpet in the middle of the floor, with a black-and-white checkered section halfway around. It looked like a racetrack.

"Pardon me?" said Grace. "How is this a dance competition?"

The competitors all heaved themselves to the black-and-white squares. Bandages were handed out so the couples could tie their hands and forearms together to make sure they didn't get separated.

"You've seen it before, but now, ladies and gentlemen, it's time for another speed round!"

The cheering was beating against Grace's ears. The people in the room were escaping from their own tough lives for a while, taking their entertainment in the form of watching others who were worse off than themselves.

"When I blow my whistle, the couples will run around the track for three minutes, and the last couple to cross the line will be eliminated. Dancers, are you ready?" They looked like they could barely stand, let alone run.

The emcee blew his whistle, and the couples set off, baring their teeth and elbowing each other, men dragging their female partners around by the wrists.

"Dear God, this is barbaric," Grace said under her breath. She instinctively got up and moved down the bleachers to the front, where people were leaning over the railing to shout for their favorites. She just wanted to reach Edie and pull her out of this place. The three minutes seemed to last a lifetime, and she couldn't help but feel disappointed when Edie survived the cull through sheer determination and some other poor couple got dragged off the floor, heels scraping. Grace felt sick.

Moments later, the emcee was back. "And that's time, ladies and gentlemen. Our dancers now have a ten-minute break. That's ten minutes. See you all back here in TEN MINUTES!"

To the side of the room, trestle tables heaved with food and drink. About half of the dancers headed there, while the other half disappeared off to bathrooms or to change their clothes and shoes. As Grace thought she would, Edie made for the food. Grace pushed through the crowd to get to her, much as she had two weeks ago in the bar. The situation was just as dangerous.

"Edie!" she called and waved her arms. Edie spotted her and came over, a paper cup in one hand and a sandwich in the other.

"Grace, you came!" Her face was haggard, the deep hollows under her eyes as dark as if someone had punched her full in the face.

"Edie. For the love of Christ, you look . . ." Grace hesitated. "Tired."

Edie laughed and took another bite of her sandwich. "Look at all this food, can you believe it? Six meals a *day*, Grace!"

"Keep moving, eighty-nine!" a man with a clipboard shouted.

"Oops," said Edie, shuffling from foot to foot. Grace looked around. Even on the break, the dancers had to keep moving, swaying as they choked down chicken sandwiches and hunks of dry cake.

"Edie, you need to get out of here. Come with me."

"Oh no." Edie was determined. "What are you talking about? I'm doing *good*, Gracie, can't you see?" She gestured around her at the reduced number of couples. "I've got a sponsor, too." She pointed to the lettering across her chest. "It means they *like* me. I get two dollars a week and all the socks I could want. Plus, all this food." She walked to the table and came back with another sandwich. When she looked at Grace, her eyes were rolling around in her head.

"Jesus," Grace said under her breath. "Edie, are you on something? Have you taken something?"

"Shh!" hissed Edie. "Of course not! Don't you dare get me disqualified, Grace! You should be happy for me! I'm gonna win! Five hundred dollars!"

"You're delirious," Grace said. "Please, let's just go, right now. Get out of this place. Come home with me."

"Grace, I'm fixing things, getting my life back on track, and I'm doing it by myself. I needed a job, so I got one. I needed money, and now I have it." Edie shrugged. "I can look after myself. We all have to do things that are hard. You know that." She shot Grace a look, then turned her back on her. "Thanks for coming, Gracie," she called over her shoulder, and with that, she moved away, disappearing through the curtains to the backstage area. Two minutes later, the buzzer went to signal the end of the break.

"Let's get back to it!" the sleazy emcee said, wearing a silver jacket now. "We'll kick things off with a little dance from Mabel Samson!" A tired woman who looked to be in her forties dragged herself to the front of the stage. Grace couldn't watch. She buried her head in her hands. She couldn't leave, either. She knew she had to try again, so she went outside to get some air, resigned to staying for hours more just for another shot at speaking to Edie. She wished Betty was with her. Betty would have just dragged Edie out of there, she was sure. But Betty could maybe offer an alternative. Grace couldn't really help Edie with money, and what if she really did win the five hundred dollars?

The two hours she waited were torturous, but eventually the next break was signaled, and Grace was there, shouting for Edie. She was exhausted herself—she'd only been here for three hours, and only watching; she couldn't begin to imagine what two weeks in this place would do to you.

Edie came a few steps closer, squinting to focus. "Grace? You're still here? How lovely."

"Edie, come and speak to me, please!"

"I'm sorry, Grace," Edie said, her words light as air. "I need to get some sleep now. Ten minutes should do it." And with that, she disappeared through the curtain, where Grace couldn't follow.

Grace kicked a wooden board in frustration, but there was nothing she could do. She had tried. If this was what Edie wanted to do, she couldn't stop her. It was getting late and she had her own problems to worry about; she was going back to work the next day. Edie's words floated through her mind and she spoke them out loud: "We all have to do things that are hard." If Edie had tried to stop her from going up on the steel, would she have listened? She knew she wouldn't. She couldn't make her friend's decisions for her; she just had to hope this would be over soon.

Grace's shoulders were slumped when she got home, and she sat at the table with a meal of ham and eggs in front of her, chasing the yolk around the plate with her fork.

"How was it?" Connie asked when Grace went in to see her. "Can I come next time?"

"No." Grace shook her head. "Absolutely not. It was a horrible place."

"Oh," said Connie, disappointed.

"Come on now, Connie." Mary's eyes lingered on Grace. "Try and get some sleep."

Grace slipped out into the hallway, a scrap of paper in her hand. Pleased to see there wasn't a line for the telephone, she dialed the number Betty had given her at the lunch counter, what seemed like years ago.

"Betty? It's Grace."

"Grace, doll, it's nice to hear your voice."

"Have you seen Edie recently?" Grace jumped in, she didn't have the time or money for a long chat, as much as she longed for it.

"Yeah," sighed Betty. "She's competing at one of those crazy dance competitions. Honestly, Gracie, it's a bad business."

"I went to see her today, tried to convince her to leave."

"Me too." Grace could imagine Betty nodding, sitting in some fancy parlor in her new home. "A few days ago. She's not gonna listen. You know what her life's been like, Grace. She doesn't trust anyone to help her, even us. She wants to do it on her own."

"I know," Grace said with a sigh. "But she has no one else, Betty, we have to look out for her."

"Oh I've tried. I've lost count of the times I've offered her money, or tried to take her to dinner. She's only agreed once. I even told her to come and stay with me here, but she didn't want to leave the city. What more can we do? We all have our own problems, Irish."

Grace had kept her eye on the clock, and knowing she couldn't afford another minute, she hurried her goodbye. "I know you're trying, that's all we can do. I've gotta go, but let's see each other soon, put our heads together. There must be a way we can get her to listen." As she hung up, she realized they had only spoken about Edie; she hadn't even had a chance to hear how Betty was.

She went to her room, too many things on her mind. She had hoped for a fun weekend to forget her problems, but it had turned out to be far from relaxing, and now she had to face another week catching rivets. After forcing herself back up there, she had to see it through. She retired to bed with a glass of water and a headache, hoping for a few hours of respite, but even unconscious, her problems still bothered her. As she slept, she was haunted by fitful dreams of dancing on steel beams with Edie as Seamus threw rivets at them and the woman from the dance marathon pelted them with popcorn. When Grace finally caught Edie's eye, she watched helplessly as her friend's exhausted body took a step backward off the steel and disappeared. Grace screamed and leaned over, expecting to see Edie fall like Lukasz, but she was so light she was floating down like a feather, before she turned into a little brown bird and flew away.

24

TUESDAY, JULY 15, 1930

"Nine days to go," Grace muttered to herself as she fished yet another rivet out of the catching cone and slotted it into place for Joe. It was her new mantra and it was giving her strength. Now they were into single figures, it all seemed a little more manageable. The countdown was on, and in less than two weeks, Patrick would be back up here and she would not. What she would do instead, she had no idea, but she would have completed the task, done what had been asked of her and kept her family safe. By then she would have caught more than twelve thousand rivets. It was enough.

"Everything all right, Patrick?" Frank yelled over the noise of his rivet gun. Grace gave him a thumbs-up. For now, it was. Bergmann was lurking and Grace had been doing her best to stay out of his way, but whenever he saw her, he shot her menacing looks, frustrated that he hadn't yet cracked the mystery. He showed no sign of giving up trying to work out her secret, and the precarious nature of her position made the hairs on the back of her neck stand on end. Just nine more days.

The sun was hot and they stopped to take a drink as the water boy reached them. The inspector arrived at the same time to check their ID tags. Grace took hers from her pocket and showed it to him. He nodded and left. If only it could all be that easy.

"You're quiet." Joe flicked his eyes in her direction.

"Just want to get on and get it done," Grace replied, barely even looking at him. If Bergmann had noticed something wasn't quite right about Patrick O'Connell these days, then so could anyone else. She had been particularly embarrassed when he had picked up on the way she and Joe had been looking at each other. She had to play things safe and keep her distance. For the next few days, she was going to do nothing but catch rivets and keep her mouth shut. And once this was all over, she was going to help Edie. She couldn't believe the awful dance marathon could possibly last another two weeks. The thought of Edie there even now made her flesh creep. As soon as she could, she was going to find her friend, and they would go up to stay with Betty in Jersey for a few days and talk about what they should do next. Everything was going to work out fine. Just nine more days.

25

THURSDAY, JULY 17, 1930

G race sat alone and exhausted, her back against a beam, for once grateful for the wind that rushed around her, cooling her hot skin. Seamus was down at his forge heating up the first rivets after lunch, Frank and Joe on a bathroom break. All at once she felt the air around her change, suddenly charged with menace. Her body tensed.

"O'Connell." Bergmann's bulk was making its way toward her.

"No, no, no," Grace mumbled under her breath. There were only six and a half days to go; she would be damned if he was going to ruin it now. "What do you want?" she called out in her brother's voice. "I'm busy."

"You don't look busy."

"Patrick!" Seamus called out from his forge; he'd noticed what was happening but was far too far away to do anything. Hardly anyone was back from lunch yet. Grace was stranded. "Come here for a moment, will ya?"

"Gotta go," Grace said, ducking under Bergmann's arm just as he moved to trap her in place. She skipped across two planks of wood and onto a different beam.

"You don't move right," Bergmann called after her, and she cringed. Dammit. There'd definitely been too much circus Grace in that getaway. "Come back here! Let me look at you!"

"Get back to work!" Seamus shouted across. "You have a worrying obsession with my cousin, Bergmann! It's not normal."

Bergmann scowled at them both and Grace's heart jackhammered in her chest. That had been too close. He was going to work it out soon, she was sure of it. When she reached Seamus, her cheeks were aflame before she got anywhere near the forge.

"We're in trouble here," she growled, watching Bergmann turn away shaking his head.

"If he was smart, maybe." Seamus shoveled rivets around with his tongs. "But he's not."

"Smart enough to know something is wrong."

"But he'll never figure it out," Seamus said with a grin. "How could he? No one would guess. It will just drive him insane the harder he tries."

"I wish I found this as funny as you." Grace rolled her eyes.

"One more week, Cousin," Seamus said, slapping her on the back.

"Hey, Patrick!" Frank called, back in position. "What are you doing down there? Come on! *Fretta!*"

"*Fretta!*" Seamus repeated to Grace, gesturing at her with his tongs to get moving.

"What does that mean?" Grace asked.

He laughed. "I've no idea."

26

FRIDAY, JULY 18, 1930

Grace curled her fist around her pay packet. She had made it to five weeks and completed twenty-five long, hot days as a riveter. She took out a handkerchief and wiped the sweat from the back of her neck. Her hair had grown out a little and was a bit too long, but with just one week to go, she was reluctant to get it cut again. She pulled her cap over it and hoped no one would care enough to notice.

As she'd stepped down from the steel at the end of another week, they had reached the thirty-eighth floor. Just thinking about it made her brain hurt. She was working eighteen floors higher in the air than she had on her first day. The structure had nearly doubled in size. The building Patrick would be returning to would bear little resemblance to the one he had left. He had never been that high before, and Grace knew it would be an adjustment for him. Until that time came, she was the O'Connell who had worked on the highest steel. The thought made her smile to herself.

"Here." Frank exited the office and handed her a large ceramic dish. "Lillian in the office kept this safe for me today. It is for you."

"What is it?" Grace asked, having to take the dish in two arms it was so big.

"Cannelloni," he said, as if everyone should know that. "A gift from Maria, from my family to yours." He leaned forward and whispered, "To celebrate another week of this." He waved his brown wages envelope.

Grace would have thrown her arms around him in thanks, but Patrick wouldn't, and besides, her arms were now full.

"Well, thank you," she said instead. "Much appreciated."

"Will you be able to get home all right?" Frank asked, before remembering he was asking the question of a grown man. "Without eating it all?" he added in case anyone had been listening. No one was; they were all heading home or into the bar. Grace looked at the wooden doors and felt a shudder run through her body at the thought of the place.

Her arms were easily as strong as Patrick's now, after five weeks of manual labor—more so, in fact. Patrick's broken arm would be weak once the cast came off. He would need to spend some time strengthening it again. She hoped that wouldn't mean more days for her on the steel, but they would cross that beam when they got to it. For now, she was tired and had nothing to prove.

"I'm going to get a taxi," she said, a little treat she saved for herself on pay day.

"*Molto bene.*" Frank nodded his approval.

"Unless you want to come and join us?" She gestured at the huge dish. "Help us eat this?"

"Another time, my friend. I have my own at home." He laughed to himself, and Grace found her eyes drawn again to the wooden doors of the bar.

"He's not in there," Frank told her with a kind smile. "He is taking Bruno swimming."

"Right," she said, surprised by the relief she felt. "See you on Monday, Frank."

He held up his hand in a wave.

A couple of hours later, the O'Connell apartment smelled better than it ever had as the whole family huddled around the table.

"Delicious," Connie said, taking small bites and swinging her legs.

Grace smiled at her. "And after this, you need an early night, to get plenty of rest for tomorrow."

"But I'm excited!" Connie said. "How will I sleep?" She coughed into her hand and the adults tensed, three faces turning her way. "I'm fine," she said, rolling her eyes.

"Mary, Mother of God," Patrick exclaimed, finishing his final mouthful, his mother hitting him on the back of the hand with a spoon for his blasphemy. "The Gagliardis are sent from heaven itself."

Grace couldn't argue. The cannelloni was delicious, and there was so much left that she took it upstairs and gave it to the Donohues. Mrs. Donohue accepted with tearful eyes as her children fell upon the food like savages. Grace laughed, and was certain that Mamma Giulia and Maria would have approved of their enthusiasm.

27

SATURDAY, JULY 19, 1930

"**I**T'S MY BIRTHDAY!"

Grace was woken by a curly-headed tornado diving onto her bed and trying to wriggle under the covers. Connie put her head close to Grace's ear and shouted again. "Wake up, Gracie, it's my birthday!"

Grace groaned, pulling the covers up over her head. "What time is it?" she asked, her eyes still closed.

"Birthday time!" Connie said, bouncing to her knees and tugging at the blanket.

"Ach, you're a nuisance," said Grace through a smile. Connie dragged back the covers and squealed at her success.

"Birthday time, birthday time!" She would have kept going if she hadn't had to stop to cough.

"Urgh," Grace grumbled. "Calm down. Take it easy, Con, don't overdo it. You're a beast, waking me this early." She grabbed her sister, pulling her into a hug. "Happy birthday, you little beast." She kissed her on the top of her head.

"I'm not a beast." Connie giggled. "I'm a princess!"

"That you are," said Grace. "Now, what time is it?"

"It's late," said Connie sagely. "Nearly seven."

Grace groaned again, falling back onto her pillow. "On a Saturday? Please."

"I want to enjoy every single second of my birthday!"

Grace opened one eye and Connie laughed at her.

"Right you are." She was just grateful that her sister was still with them to have an eleventh birthday, after how ill she'd been only a couple of weeks before. Seeing her so excited filled Grace with joy. She swung her feet out of bed and onto the floor. "In that case, you know what's next?" She cocked an eyebrow at her sister before they gave their answer together.

"Birthday pancakes!"

"Did someone say birthday pancakes?" Patrick stuck his head around the door.

"It's my birthday, Pat!"

"I heard that rumor." Their brother nodded. "That must be why there are presents on the table. Lucky you told me, I thought they were for me. Nearly opened them all."

Connie was out of Grace's room so fast she was a blur, leaving her siblings in her dust.

"Go slow!" they called in unison, turning to laugh at each other. It'd been a while since they'd been in tune enough for that to happen.

Once they were all dressed, Mary made the best pancakes any of them had ever eaten.

"Mmm, those were delicious, Ma." Patrick rubbed his stomach.

"Fit for a princess," Grace agreed.

"Can I open another present please, Ma?" Connie asked, her little face flushed with color.

"Go ahead." Out of habit, Mary reached over and put her hand on her daughter's forehead to feel her temperature. Connie ducked away.

"This is from Frank and Joe," Grace said, handing over a package wrapped in red paper and tied with string.

"Really? The Italian man who came here?"

"That's right. They know all about you."

Connie wasn't one for tearing off paper. She undid the string and rolled it up neatly before carefully unwrapping the parcel. "It's a book!" she said, holding it up for everyone to see.

"How lovely," said Mary. "Thank them for us, Grace."

"Of course," said Grace, picking up on the tense set of Patrick's jaw. She forgot sometimes that the Gagliardis were his friends and she was just borrowing them.

"Well, this is from Florence," Patrick said, handing over a small square box. Grace caught her mother's quick raised eyebrows but didn't think Patrick had seen. Patrick had never had a girl before. Not one they knew about, at least. And definitely not one who bought his little sister birthday presents. "She's sorry she can't come today. She's working at the hospital."

"That's okay," said Connie, the magnanimous dictator, without even looking up.

Grace craned her neck to see what Florence had given her. Connie held out her palm, on which lay a little gold-and-brown brooch in the shape of a monkey. "It's so pretty."

"It is," agreed Grace with a smile.

"Can I wear it on my dress, Ma?"

"I should think so," Mary said, clearing plates and cutlery away. Patrick started to help with his good hand. Grace watched with interest. He never would have thought to do that before. Now that he wasn't working, it was as if he felt the need to prove his worth to the family at every opportunity. It wouldn't be long before he could take back his rightful place, and Grace was more than happy to give it to him. She had managed to fight her way through five weeks on the steel now; just one more to go, her hard work rewarded by them having just enough money to treat Connie for her birthday, which made it all worthwhile.

"These are the best presents ever," Connie said, hugging her haul to her chest. Patrick had bought her a parasol, Mary had spent a long time forcing her fingers to cooperate as she sewed a beautiful new summer dress in pale green cotton, and Grace had given her a little white purse. Connie didn't really have anything to put in it, so Grace had slipped her fifty cents in change and a lipstick, on a promise that she wouldn't tell their mother.

"What are you most excited about seeing, Con?" Patrick asked.

"I can't choose. All of it! Turtles and jellyfish and sea lions!" Connie's face was so full of life, it seemed impossible that this was the same girl who had floated around the apartment like a ghost for the last couple of months. Grace sent up a silent prayer for that at least. Everything seemed a little more manageable when Connie was out of bed.

"The aquarium was an excellent idea for a birthday treat," she said as she bent to put on her shoes. It was going to be a hot day, and she was relieved to be out of coveralls and wearing a sundress. She accompanied it with a wide-brimmed hat that covered the back of her neck and made it look possible that her hair was just neatly pinned up underneath, rather than not there at all. She also put on a sweater, despite the heat, to cover her now scarred arms, which would have made her sad if she'd let herself think about it, so she didn't.

"Are we ready?" Mary asked, with a hint of a smile threatening when she saw Connie bobbing up and down, raring to go.

The New York Aquarium at Battery Park was a distinctive circular building, and Connie started vibrating with excitement as soon as she saw it. Grace studied the two gilded sea horses carved above the main doorway; it had been a long time since the family had done something fun together.

Inside, Connie flitted about in awe of everything she saw, her eyes wide as if she could take in more that way. She was reading every sign she came to, and Grace had to try not to laugh at how earnest she was.

"There are seven large floor pools, eighty-eight glass-fronted tanks, and eighty-three small tanks," she gushed. "Gosh, that's a lot. How on earth will we see it all?" She stopped to cough, and the adults paused.

"Are you sure you're feeling okay, Con?" Grace asked, stroking her sister's hair back from her face.

"Calm down, child," Mary said, taking her hat off and holding it against her body. "You have plenty of time."

The tension of the last few weeks melted from Grace's shoulders as she wandered idly around the aquarium with her family, marveling at the exhibits. From turtles and the barking sea lions to the huge heft of alligators and brightly colored fish of blue, green and orange, there were hundreds of things to see in the enormous tanks.

"Penguins!" Connie cried as she rushed to one exhibit. "How big is this one?" she said, as she darted back to another to point out an enormous two-hundred-pound grouper.

"Look, Grace, look, it's lighting the bulb!" She was entranced by the electric eels, generating enough current to light a bulb above the tank. "How do they do that?"

"I'm not sure, princess, it's a clever thing," Grace said, clutching Connie's new parasol under her arm for safe-keeping.

Connie ran off again and Mary trailed dutifully behind. Grace was just about to follow when her brother went rigid beside her. Instantly she was on alert. She turned to look and saw a huge blond head bobbing toward them. And just like that, their good day was over.

"Bergmann," she muttered in disbelief, and then caught herself. *Grace* had never met this man.

Of all the places for him to be! For some reason that wasn't clear, the giant German was also spending his Saturday morning at the aquarium. There was no time for Grace and Patrick to speak to each other or form any sort of plan. Grace thought about heading straight off with her head down to follow her mother and sister, but it was too late; they had already been seen and she couldn't leave Patrick alone to flounder. Patrick didn't know about her confrontation with Bergmann, or anything that had happened between them on the steel, which was going to be very awkward in about three seconds' time when Bergmann started speaking to him. Grace didn't even have time to panic; they were caught like deer in headlights and there was nothing they could do.

"O'Connell!" Bergmann took a step closer to them, and Patrick casually slid his broken arm behind his back in the hope that it wouldn't be seen.

"Bergmann," he said, and his cool tone told Grace that their dislike for each other was mutual.

216 · GEMMA TIZZARD

"And who is this? Yet another lady friend?"

Grace turned her face defiantly toward him from under her hat and saw the shock register as he looked from one of them to the other. It often happened when people met them for the first time, but never before had it felt so sinister.

"My sister," Patrick said, as if there had never been two words in the world he had been less happy to utter. Grace flicked her eyes over to her mother and Connie, who were blissfully unaware of the situation, watching a tank of scuttling orange crabs in fascination.

Despite what Seamus thought, Bergmann was not stupid, and it didn't take long for the tumblers to click into place in his mind, despite the conclusion being most unlikely.

"Nice to meet you, miss," he said, holding out his hand and playing his cards close to his chest. Grace knew her arms were covered, but she was still worried he would notice the telltale signs of the work he knew well when she offered him her no longer smooth hand. She took it back as quickly as possible.

"Nice to meet you too," she said in a voice she didn't even recognize as her own. She had made it higher, to try and differentiate it from Patrick's as much as possible. Bergmann's face was like stone.

"You know what I was saying to you yesterday, O'Connell, about the Yankees?" Grace wanted to pinch her brother, but he would have no idea what that meant anyway, so she clenched her jaw and waited for the inevitable outcome.

"Sure," said Patrick lightly, and she felt a single bead of sweat slide down the back of her neck. "That Lou Gehrig home run was—"

"That's funny," said Bergmann, speaking over him. Here it comes, thought Grace. "Because I didn't talk to you yesterday. In fact . . ." He paused, as if he were the best detective in the world. "I think it's been even longer than that." His eyes fell on Grace with a dark malevolence.

"Wait, I can explain," a hint of panic leached into Patrick's voice.

"Show me your arm." Bergmann held out his hand.

"Get away from me." Patrick took a step back, his panic replaced with anger, but he didn't raise his voice.

Bergmann chuckled to himself; then, in one quick movement, he reached forward and flicked Grace's hat so it fell off her head.

"I knew it," he said, punching one hand into the other, delighted to have his proof. "I knew there was something wrong with you. It can't be, but it is. It felt wrong because it wasn't you at all." He smirked. "Well, at least that explains Gagliardi."

Patrick either didn't hear or ignored the last comment. "This is nothing to do with you, Bergmann," he said, taking a step forward again so he could speak in a hushed voice and not alert anyone else to what was going on.

Bergmann was shaking his head. "Perfect Patrick. Well, not this time."

"What does that even mean?" Patrick asked, exasperated.

"You have it so easy, don't you? Any woman you like, no concerns in the world. Even something like this, which should lose you your job, you think you can just squirm out of it. Well, I've had enough." Bergmann flicked his eyes to Grace. "And you, you're just as bad. The arrogance to think you can just do a job that takes years to learn." Nonchalantly he picked something out of his teeth before he continued, his attention back on Patrick. He was a shark, circling, toying with them. "You think you're so clever. Sending a woman up on my steel, as if she can do what we do."

"She is doing it, though," Patrick argued.

Bergmann shook his head, then stopped as if something had clicked into place. "She doesn't hold a catcher right. *That* was what was bothering me. Not to mention the fact that she's too small, and blank-faced in conversations, like you'd had your brain removed." He smirked at Patrick. "I can't believe you thought you would get away with this. Neither of you is ever going to catch a rivet again."

Grace said nothing. It was over. She'd made it so far, and now it was all for nothing.

Or at least it was until their savior came into view. A small girl of around five ran up to Bergmann and took his hand, her blond hair pulled into braids at the sides of her head. Behind her came two slightly older tow-headed boys and a plump blond woman, looking slightly disheveled and out of breath, balancing a bald baby on her hip.

"There you are!" she said, the unmistakable hint of a German accent in her voice.

"Come see the penguins, Papa!" the little girl said, tugging on her father's massive hand.

Papa.

Despite the gravity of the conversation they were having, Bergmann's attention went straight to his daughter. He turned to her and placed his free hand softly on the top of her head. The action was so out of character for the man Grace knew.

"In a moment, my love." The tenderness in his voice was nothing the O'Connells had ever heard from him before. Grace's mind whirred at all this new information.

"Oh, hello," said the woman. "I'm Clara, nice to meet you."

"Hello, Clara, it really is lovely to meet you too." Grace meant every word. She turned to Bergmann to make sure her assumption was correct. "Is this your wife?"

Bergmann scowled, could only nod in response. Clara, however, was more than happy to provide the information.

"*Ja*, Johan and I have been married for seven years now. These are our children, Karl, Friedrich, and Hilde, and this"—she joggled the baby on her hip—"is Hans, named after my grandfather."

"How lovely," said Grace.

"How do you know Johan?" Clara asked, with genuine interest.

"My brother Patrick here works with him," Grace said, taking control of the situation. This revelation seemed to be of little consequence to Clara, who was being pestered by the children.

"Mother, please can we look at the penguins?"

"Please?"

"The penguins!"

"Oh, on the Empire State Building?" she said, distracted. "I don't like it; so dangerous, but I suppose in these times you cannot be ungrateful for a job. Okay, children, okay, take me to the penguins."

"I'll be right there," Bergmann assured his daughter, slipping his hand gently from hers.

Clara smiled and excused herself, leading the children away as fast as they had arrived, but their appearance had been the stroke of luck the O'Connells had deserved for a while now, and it had just changed everything.

"What a lovely family," Grace said, her voice flat and sarcastic, in her best impression of Betty.

"You're *married*?" Patrick seemed more shocked by this revelation than Bergmann had been that a woman was impersonating a man to rivet steel hundreds of feet in the air. "You have *children*?"

"It's none of your business," Bergmann spat, his whole head now bright red.

"Exactly," said Grace. "It isn't." Her stomach turned to even look at the poor excuse for a man, but this was her only chance to make her argument, and it had to stick. "Now, Clara looks like a lovely lady, and from a very upstanding family, I'm sure." She had no idea if this was true, but from the way Bergmann was squirming in his shoes in front of her, she was pretty sure she was on the right lines. "And wouldn't it be such a shame if she had to find out what a cheating, lying horror her husband really is? I imagine your horsing around with every woman in the five boroughs wouldn't be quite so much fun without a wife to go home to who cooks and cleans and looks after you. Or how about without ever seeing your children again when she ups and leaves you?"

"And what makes you think she would believe you?" spat Bergmann.

Grace paused to check her words were sinking in. It was a dangerous game, but this was the only hand she had to play. Bergmann opened his mouth to continue, but she carried on, taking a step closer to him.

"Do you really want to risk it? Your daughter growing up knowing exactly what kind of man her beloved father is?"

A muscle twitched in his jaw. Grace wasn't convinced a man like this cared anything for his wife; how could he if he betrayed her relentlessly? But you couldn't mistake the look he had given his daughter.

"Now, of course that doesn't have to happen. You keep our secret and we'll keep yours. And unlike you, we aren't hurting anybody. Patrick will be back on the steel in no time, so all you need to do is pretend that none of us ever saw each other here today. What do you say, *Johan?*"

For a second, Grace was sure he was going to tear her limb from limb and feed her to the alligator just a few yards away. "You wouldn't," was all he said.

"Oh, I would," she assured him. "And I'm fairly sure I could find a whole heap of girls to line up around the corner and take it in turns to tell Clara just what kind of man her husband is—maybe even take out an ad or two in the *New York Times.*"

Bergmann glared at Patrick. "So you need your sister to do everything for you, huh? Not just your job."

Patrick shrugged, refusing to rise to it. "You must admit, she's pretty good at it."

He and Grace smiled at each other, a perfect team. Grace looked back at Bergmann.

"This is a short-term deal, I'm afraid," she added. "Truth is, you have more to lose than we do. It might be hard to find another job, but it would be harder to find another wife, and . . ." She paused again to make sure he was looking at her. ". . . impossible to replace your children when they want nothing to do with you. They obviously adore their mother; it's just a shame that you don't."

She braced herself. She thought of Bergmann taking a swing at Seamus with the tongs. Men like him didn't respect women, and he would resent being spoken to as she had done. She was certain he was going to hit her. She saw him think about it. Then he looked over to where his daughter was copying the penguins, trying to walk like one. His face softened.

"This isn't over," he said quietly, not looking at either of the O'Connells.

"But you stay out of my way and I'll stay out of yours." And with that, he stalked off to join his family.

All the air was punched out of Grace's body, and it took her a few seconds to register that Patrick was hugging her, more tightly than he ever had before. Too tightly, in fact.

"Can't. Breathe."

"You were incredible," he said, letting her go.

Grace put her hat back on her head. "Don't celebrate yet. That didn't sound like an agreement to me, but it gives him something to think about. Let's just hope it's enough."

Patrick seemed instantly at ease, as if nothing had happened, but Grace was distracted for the rest of the day. She stood against the big tanks and let the cool glass soothe her skin. She had slithered out of yet another problem, but she knew that men like Bergmann hated losing, particularly to a woman. She had another week to survive on the steel, and she wasn't convinced he would keep quiet that long.

"Don't they move funny?" Connie said as they watched the jellyfish propel themselves around a tank. "It's like they're falling, rather than swimming." She was quiet now; she had tired herself out and looked pale again.

"Come on, Con, let's get you home." Grace pulled her sister close. Images of a body falling through the sky were back in her head, but this time it was Grace herself that was falling, and the last thing she saw was Bergmann's grinning face as he pushed her.

28

MONDAY, JULY 21, 1930

"Just five more days," Grace said to herself. She heard the words vibrate in her chest as she spoke them, but the noise of the site was too loud for anyone else to hear her. That was how she wanted it. The message was just for her. She said it after almost every rivet now, a new ritual.

She had made it to the final week, and it was Monday afternoon already. Patrick's cast was all set to come off on Friday, and this time next week, it would be her brother standing up here under the beating sun, with sweat pooling in the hollow of his throat, and Grace would have her feet firmly on the ground. They would be beyond the fortieth floor by then, edging toward halfway. She wouldn't be sad to say goodbye to this job, but as she looked out across the city and watched it sparkle from every reflective surface the sun hit, she had to admit she would miss the views.

Catching the next rivet, she glanced down at her sunburned arms and saw a galaxy of marks and scars forming their constellations across her once pale skin. Black marks, scratches, and silvery white lines crisscrossed like shooting stars, each one orbiting the bold red circle, the sun in the middle, where she had burned herself saving Joe. She would never regret that one.

Suddenly there was an enormous bang. Everybody instinctively covered their heads or grabbed for the nearest solid thing they could reach, as the beams shook and the whole structure seemed to judder beneath them.

It was instantly clear there was something wrong, but with all the noise, yelling, and people scurrying around, it was impossible to know what.

"Up," Frank said, gesturing with a gloved hand as he set down the rivet gun.

The three of them stared up to the next floor, cranes everywhere they looked, where the connectors were still building. The men who normally flew through the sky to meet hoisted beams were making their way back to safety, jumping off headache balls and shimmying down thick cables, getting their feet firmly planted back on beams and planks. Everyone was grounded in the face of the problem. Grace's gang followed the crowd toward a group standing around one of the cranes, Seamus hot on their heels.

"It's got stuck!" a man yelled to Frank and gestured in front of them. "Snarl-up with the cable or some such."

Grace peered over Frank's shoulder, expecting to see a couple of men working on fixing a crane snag, but instead she saw a whole line of men on a beam, lined up like birds on a wire, pointing and shouting. Nearby, the Mohawk ironworkers, who kept to themselves, had all stopped working and were looking on with interest. A terrified crane operator was staring out in front of him, where his crane held a horizontal beam by steel cables at either end. It was suspended three hundred and fifty feet in the air, way out from the building, paused on its journey up to its place in this giant jigsaw. And on that beam of steel, about as stuck as anyone could possibly be, stood a man. Grace sucked her breath in through her teeth.

"Oh boy," said Frank, flicking his eyes over his shoulder to check his little brother was still where he could see him.

"You ever come across this before?" Seamus asked, as work all around them ground to a halt.

A huge cry echoed in the silence as men crawling over the crane did something and the cable on the right-hand side jolted, tilting the beam like a seesaw and tipping the man on it toward that end.

"STOP!" Gilligan forced his way to the front of the crowd. "Everyone stop! Don't touch anything! Not until we figure this out."

Grace took in the scene. All the other cranes were still, everyone watching the one operator still in position, sweating as he tried not to do anything that would cause a colleague to plunge to his death. The man on the beam was now lying down in the middle of it, arms and legs hugging it like his life depended on it—which of course it did. It sounded like he was softly crying, and there wasn't a man among them who blamed him.

He'd seemed unconcerned when the beam got stuck, even by the jolt when it stopped moving. He'd seen it all before and had shouted across to his friends, laughing and joking about getting a break. Connectors were the toughest guys around. They had to ride steel beams into the sky and make them stay there, creating something solid where there had been nothing but air before. But that last bump, and the fact that the beam was now hanging at a slight tilt, was enough for even the most hardened of men. And that was before you took into account the fact that one of their own had already fallen that month. What had seemed like a joke just a moment before now seemed anything but.

"He's got to stay still," Frank whispered to Grace. "He has to balance. If he moves any farther back, he will slide down that beam and end up resting his full weight against the cable. It should hold, but that is not a place anyone would ever want to be."

Grace watched intently, and could see not only that Frank was right, but the connector knew it. She had liquid knees at the thought.

"I don't wanna die out here." The man's wailing voice cut through the air. The other men were silent. No one spoke. No one seemed to know what to do. They knew this was bad. Everyone up here had to share in the delusion that they would be fine. To have it spoken aloud how precarious the situation was for all of them could send a ripple of panic and fear through everyone like a contagion.

"Let me think!" Gilligan was running a handkerchief over his forehead, new beads of sweat breaking out seconds after the last had been collected.

"He's gone," Grace heard someone say, and her heart leapt, thinking he meant the man had fallen. She couldn't watch that again. "His head's gone," he went on, with a shake of his own. He had a toothpick in the corner of his mouth. "Sad to see it," he added, his tone sorrowful.

A gust of wind took hold of the steel beam as if it were a swing, and gently rocked it backward and forward.

"Arrrghhhh!" The connector's scream was bloodcurdling. "Get me offa here!" The words were strangled in his throat. The only thing they heard from him after that was whimpering, and some crazed humming in an effort to calm himself.

Grace edged closer to the group gathered at the base of the crane. Gilligan was issuing hushed instructions, and her belly flipped when she heard him sending men down to the ground to warn people and clear the area, just in case. The rest of the workers stood along the edge of the building, looking out toward the problem, or around them at the masses of equipment at their disposal, each with their own ideas.

"He can't get back in," said a stocky older man with a dirty face and a cigarette hanging from his bottom lip. "If the crane don't move, he don't move."

"We can't leave him out there," argued a Polish man with a crazed look in his eyes, and Grace guessed he might be a friend of Lukasz Kowalski.

"Someone needs to swing out and get him," said the smoker, taking a drag on his cigarette.

"Don't be crazy, you old drunk," someone else hissed. "Ain't nobody can get out there."

The smoker shrugged. "Okay, so we leave him. Soon enough he won't be able to take it anymore and he'll throw himself over. I've seen it before. Once the crazy sets in, you ain't got long before it takes you."

"Oh Jesus," said another man, taking off his hat and grabbing it as if trying to tear it in two with his bare hands.

"Can we send someone out on another crane? How about a ladder?"

"It won't reach."

"Headache ball?"

"You wouldn't get him onto it. Not in that state."

"What about the loop?"

Grace turned her head and saw a man holding up a big strop of brown leather attached to the crane like a life belt.

"We can throw it to him."

"As if he's in any position to be catching," the smoker said, looking back out to where their stranded colleague was still hugging the beam.

"Mick!" someone called. "Y'all right, Mick? We're gonna get you, fella, just hold on."

A couple of nervous titters went around the workers.

"I don't think you need to tell him to hold on," one muttered.

"How do we get the loop to him if we can't throw it? The only thing connecting where he is to where we are is the arm of the crane."

Until this point, Grace and her gang had been quiet observers. Grace hadn't been around this many other men in all the previous five weeks. She was trying to keep herself back in the crowd and unnoticed, but the sight of the poor man hanging on for dear life was too much for her.

"We take it to him," she said in Patrick's voice. A whole host of faces turned to look at her.

"What are you talking about?"

"How are you going to get it over there?" The man with the loop in his hand held it up as if to show her how ridiculous she was being.

"*Patrick.*" Grace heard the warning tone behind her.

"Just an idea," she mumbled, stepping back into the crowd.

A huge creak took all their attention, and the beam slipped another inch or two at one end. The connector opened his lungs and screamed. Joseph Gilligan took a step closer to the edge of the building.

"Just hold on, Mick, we're working things out."

Grace couldn't contain herself any longer; they didn't have time. "You take the loop to him," she repeated, stepping forward. "Someone climbs the crane, then walks along the top of the arm." She pointed, tracing the route with her finger. "They climb down the cable onto the beam, then wrap the loop around him and he gets lifted to safety."

A rumble of voices, opinions, and objections exploded around her.

"No one's going to do that!"

"What if the cable breaks?"

"Sounds to me like a good way to kill two people instead of one."

"And drop a steel beam three hundred and fifty to the floor."

"And then we'll be one short."

"Everything will be off."

"Enough!" shouted Gilligan. "We need ideas that could actually work. Even if someone was mad enough to try it, a grown man is too heavy to risk it, and I'm not sending a boy out on a suicide mission."

"*Patrick.*" Joe's voice was a hiss this time and came with his hand clamped like a claw on her shoulder. Grace couldn't turn and look at him or she knew it was over. One glance at his face and she would step back and decide this wasn't her problem. She wasn't even meant to be here. She looked around the group of men and locked eyes with Bergmann. He was staring at her. She knew what he was about to do, but it didn't matter, because she had already made her decision.

"You could do it," he said, his voice flat.

Grace had never believed it was over between them; she'd known he was just waiting for the moment to expose her, and it had come sooner than he'd imagined, practically gift-wrapped. But the strangest thing was, it didn't feel like that. There was no malice in his face, or his voice; he was saying it with a grudging respect, to encourage her. He didn't know anything about her circus training and the fact that there was a chance she really could do it. He just meant she was light enough, brave enough. And she was. She knew she was.

Another gust of wind came in and ruffled their clothes, soothing Grace's rapidly heating face as the reality of the situation settled on her.

"No," Frank said in her ear.

"Get me a ladder," she said to no one in particular.

Joseph Gilligan looked from the terrified man gently swinging on the beam to the group of men watching helplessly. Grace felt sorry for him. This situation couldn't have been in the training manual, and he didn't know what to do. But she did, and she was going to do it.

The ladder appeared and was set against the side of the crane. She probably could have clambered up the metalwork of the crane itself like a fire escape, but the ritual of climbing a ladder, each step measured and even, was calming.

"This is pure madness," the man with the cigarette said.

Grace shot an apologetic look at the stricken faces of Frank, Joe, and Seamus. She had wanted to hang back, let someone else deal with this, but it was clear no one else could. And she just couldn't watch another man die. She couldn't. She reached down and pulled off her boots and socks.

"What the hell are you doing?"

She started to take off her coveralls. They were too big and would act like a sail in the wind; she needed them gone.

"She can do it," Bergmann said.

"*She?*" cried a chorus of men as Grace dropped the coveralls to the ground and tore her shirt off over her head, along with her hat.

"Grace!" Joe cried out.

"*Grace?*" the men shouted.

"What the hell is this?"

"What's going on?"

"I don't understand."

Grace was a sight as she stood there in a white vest and the old-fashioned white underclothes she had taken to wearing under her coveralls to make her body look bigger. They were almost bloomers, white and knee-length, held in place with frilly elastic. She still had her big workmen's gloves on her hands.

"Patrick O'Connell is a cross-dresser?"

"A fairy?"

"But I know him, that can't be right!"

"No, Patrick O'Connell is a *woman!*"

The noise around her was deafening, but she was already blocking it out, concentrating on her breathing. Joe pushed his way to the front of the crowd and grabbed her arm. "You can't do this."

Grace didn't want to look at him, didn't want anything to distract her, but she also knew this might be the last time she saw his face. She turned to him, saw him shaking his head with a look of pure terror.

"No, please. You can't do this."

She smiled and reached her hand out to rest for a moment on his cheek. "Yes, I can." Then she turned away, reaching for the leather loop, as the man holding it handed it over wordlessly.

"Stop!" Mr. Gilligan put his hands over Grace's at the bottom of the ladder she was preparing to climb. "Stop immediately! I don't even know who the hell you are! And you most definitely cannot do this!"

She pulled her hands free, looked him dead in the eye and spoke in her own voice. "I'm Grace O'Connell."

In the stunned silence that followed, she started to climb the ladder with the leather ring looped over one arm. She couldn't look at anyone; she had to clear her mind, find that quiet place the Ivanovs had taught her and keep moving forward. As she neared the top, she realized it had been five weeks since the last time she had done something this reckless and stupid, but this time she had a better reason. The Gagliardis had doubted her then, and she had proved herself by walking a tightrope between the buildings.

Joe had dared to scoff at her and say that a woman would be scared at the top of a ladder. As it turned out, he was right. When she reached the final rung and steadied herself to step onto the crane arm, she was definitely scared. But given that the ladder was three hundred and fifty feet in the air at the top of an unfinished building, a little fear was justified.

She stood up straight, holding her hands out for balance, the leather loop on her right arm, focusing on the beat of her heart until she could feel it slowing. She looked out to the horizon, where blue sky met blue water. What a view. The crowd of men behind her were still silent, and she pretended they were her audience. The only sound was Mick's muffled cries as he sobbed into his shirt, and that was what would lead her to him.

Apart from the monumental height, which threatened to turn her inside out, this was the easiest tightrope she had ever faced. The crane arm was as wide as her bare foot, so if she walked from heel to toe, she would always have something solid beneath her. As long as it didn't move and the wind wasn't too bad, it was a straightforward walk, just twenty-five steps or so. The metal had been warmed by the sun, so she didn't even have to worry about the shock of it feeling cold against her skin, but it wasn't too hot either. She also had the lifeline of the loop on her arm, attached to the crane. Even if she fell, there was a good chance she could hold on to it and swing herself back to safety using it as a trapeze. Maybe. And at least she would have tried, which was more than anyone else was willing to do.

She took a deep breath. The height made her knees weak, and she wanted to gag. Her stomach lunged and her bowels cramped in complaint. She had never been this high up before, but neither had many other people on the planet. She thought it was a safe bet that none of them had walked along a crane arm.

She evened out her breathing and found the clear space in her mind. Though she had only been standing on the arm for a couple of seconds, it felt much longer. Her aim was to get down onto the beam with Mick before the next big gust of wind. She started to walk.

The first couple of steps out from relative safety were always the worst. Once you were beyond that, you were committed and there was nowhere to go but forward. Nothing sharpened the mind like having no other options. Grace pretended she was on a beam like any other, walking confidently to the point where the first cable was. She couldn't afford to look down, or the dizzying height would throw her off-balance, so she crouched carefully, feeling for the metal beneath her, and sat on the end of the arm, dangling her feet over the edge as if she was just sitting on a park bench. She knew she had to do this next bit very carefully so as not to rattle Mick. Any panic from him now and they would both be on a one-way trip to the ground.

It was the most dangerous thing she had ever done in her life, edging her weight forward and flipping her body over so her belly was against the crane arm, her legs dangling by the cable. She heard distant murmurs from the watching men, but she ignored them. This was the part where she had the smallest amount of her body on something solid, and therefore it was the most risky. She felt for the cable with her feet. Barefoot had been the best way to walk along the crane arm, but it wasn't the best thing now. She caught the cable gently with her covered knees, doing her best not to rock the beam, and lowered herself down to hold it in her gloved hands. She swapped the leather loop from one hand to the other, making sure it didn't get caught on the jib, and hung there like she was climbing a rope in gym class. There was nothing but sky all around, and she couldn't have been more aware of it. Mick had started to scream with the inevitable movement of the beam.

"It's okay, Mick," she called out in her own voice. This was too tricky for her to pretend to be anyone else, and besides, it was too late now.

She started to lower herself down the cable. She slipped down a little quicker than she'd expected, and grunted with pain, which made Mick scream louder. Her bare arm felt aflame where stray wire strands from the cable had sliced into her flesh. She looked down, expecting to see blood everywhere, which wouldn't help anyone, but instead there were just several long metal splinters the length of a finger lodged under her skin like dark gray darts. Painful as it was, it was by far the better option in this situation. Blood would have made everything so much worse.

A few more seconds and her feet were on the end of the beam.

The cables were now taking her full weight along with Mick's and that of the steel. They made an unsettling creaking noise, and she knew she needed to move quickly. She lowered herself until she was straddling the beam, forcing herself not to look down. It was one thing being high up on the building, but suspended over thin air was a different beast. The fine hairs on her arm stood to attention, and she sensed another gust of wind was coming their way.

"Hold on, Mick!" She put her head down and clung on tight, mirroring Mick's position as the wind hit them on the left side. The beam moved less with her on it, and settled again quicker. "Let's get you off this fairground ride," she said, scooting toward him with the longest, smoothest movements she could manage.

She glanced back to the building for the first time and was shocked by just how far away it looked. Fear gurgled up in her throat, and she switched her attention to the crane, checking that the operator was still there and ready to lift them to safety. When she'd first had the idea, she thought the loop would take Mick and she would go back the way she'd come, but there was no way she could climb back up the cable, and she could already tell that getting him off this beam was not going to be easy. As she got nearer, she could see that his whole body was rock-solid with tension. His eyes were screwed tightly shut, and he was alternating between deathly silence and screaming.

When she reached him, she was careful to lean back slightly so they didn't tip the balance of the beam and slide down to the end. She didn't fancy that little jaunt at all.

"Mick?" If he could hear her, he showed no sign of it. She couldn't get the loop over him without him sitting up; she needed it to go under his arms. "Mick?" she tried again. "Can you look at me?"

He started making a droning noise to drown her out. After a moment or two, Grace realized she recognized the tune. It was "Ain't Misbehavin'." A wry smile played on her face. Someone somewhere was definitely messing with her. The last time she had heard this song, she'd been with Betty. This was a far cry from the Onyx Club.

"Oh, I like that one," she said softly, and ever so quietly she began to sing to Mick. "*No one to talk with, All by myself, No one to walk with, But I'm happy on the shelf*. . ." Even in the perilous position she was in, she had to stop herself from laughing out loud at the absurdity of it, and how appropriate the lyrics were. "I'm not happy on *this* shelf, Mick, truth be told," she whispered under her breath.

Slowly she lowered her hand to his back. He screamed, then instantly started to calm. The human contact seemed to break through his fear. He wasn't alone anymore. Grace moved her hands until they were on his shoulders.

"Can you sit up for me, Mick? Nice and slow. Keep your eyes closed if you like. Feel for my arms and then just gently, ever so gently, come up to meet me."

Mick seemed to be hypnotized by her voice. He started to move, inch by inch, his eyes still screwed tight.

"That's it," Grace whispered. "That's the way."

When he was finally sitting upright on the beam, facing her as if they were on a date, Grace scooted a little closer—as close as their knees would allow. "You're doing great, Mick," she said, studying the man's grizzled face. By the looks of him, he had been on the steel for years, infinitely longer than Grace herself. But only one of them was in any position to be in charge of this situation. "I'm going to loop you now, Mick," she said, raising the leather and slipping her own torso inside it first. "If you feel anything touch you, that's all it is."

She opened the loop up and managed to slip it over his head, lifting his arms up and over so it settled around his middle like a life preserver, both of them safely inside. All she had to do was tighten it and they were ready to be rescued. Thank God.

"You're safe," she said. "You're in the loop. Do you want to open your eyes now?"

When his eyes finally opened, they were just inches from Grace's own. Calm brown met terrified blue.

"You're a girl," he whispered. She was amazed he hadn't worked that out already. He took in her white attire. "An angel."

"Ach, well, not quite." She tightened the loop. "Are you ready?"

He suddenly jolted with the realization of where they were, and threw his arms around her, holding her tight.

"Okay, then," Grace managed through a squeezed chest. She signaled to the crane, and nearly screamed herself when they were lifted into the air. As they left the beam, the movement was both terrifying and disorienting. Having nothing at all beneath her feet caused Grace's lunch to make a definite bid for freedom, and she swallowed hard, her feet dancing on air. Mick was whimpering like a kicked dog.

"You're okay, Mick," she said, closing her eyes and trying to convince herself as much as him. She was sure she could feel the loop loosening, and eyed the edge of the building hungrily as they moved toward it. She hadn't come this far to fail. Seconds later, Mick's feet hit the steel beam at the outermost edge of the building, and Grace let out an enormous sigh of relief.

She was sure the plan had been to swing them onto the safety of the floor, away from the edge, but Mick had been so desperate to reach solid ground, he had stopped still, as if frozen again, as soon as his feet made contact with something he could stand on. Behind him, Grace stretched forward with her toes, keen to get herself back to safety too. She was so close.

And then disaster struck. Whether it was pure relief, or a reflex, or Mick had assumed she was on the beam too, it was impossible to tell. It also didn't matter, as with all three options, the outcome was the same. Mick, who had been clutching her so tightly as he was dragged to safety by the men on the beams, did something utterly unexpected. He let go of her. At the same time, he tried to wrench the loop of leather holding them together off over his head.

Grace felt hands grab for her, but unlike the moment she had saved Joe, she evaded the grasp of those trying to help her and fell out of the bottom of the loop, with nothing but three hundred feet of air beneath her. She had been Mick's angel, and now she was going to fly.

29

So this is what it feels like. She heard a collective scream from the men, but they sounded hundreds of miles away, down a tunnel. She saw the beams she had been standing on yesterday disappear above her, and realized it was going to take a long time to fall to the ground. She was so close to the building, she hoped the people down there would have time to move—she didn't want to hurt anyone. She'd thought her life would flash before her eyes, or that she would see Connie, but instead she saw Lukasz Kowalski, falling next to her. She reached out, wanting to hold his hand, but of course there was no one there.

She had fallen almost four storeys when a gust of wind darted inward through the open steel latticework of the building and took her with it. Her body was pummeled, jarred violently as she was buffeted into the edge of the structure. By some impossible stroke of luck, and the reactions of a circus performer, she grabbed a beam with her flailing arm, landing hard with it jammed up under her armpit. She hadn't even registered what was happening until she felt an almighty jolt go through her body as it stopped falling. Acting purely on reflex and survival instinct, and aided by the strength she had built up over the last five weeks, she threw a leg up and clutched at the steel with her other hand, and with an almighty heave, dragged herself to safety, collapsing face down onto the beam, breathing heavily.

The steel was warm from the sun. Her legs were wrapped so tightly around the beam she was sure she had fused herself to it. She had no idea how similar she looked to her brother, whose own brush with death had left him in exactly the same position with a broken arm. The only difference was that Grace hadn't just brushed death; she had grabbed it by the lapels and kissed it on the lips before sending it away again like a spurned lover.

The fact that Grace didn't weigh much, and that the floor was fully riveted—by her own gang, no less—meant the beam hardly wobbled, and everything was eerily still. She was winded, and her shoulder already ached, but it wasn't dislocated, and a few tentative breaths convinced her no ribs had been broken. A calmness traveled through her that could only be a manifestation of shock. She found herself looking over the edge of the steel to where she should still be falling. Just one floor below where she now lay, the building was already fully enclosed and cladded. If she had fallen that far, the wind would have done nothing except maybe throw her into a concrete wall. A second earlier, and she would have been tossed into the beam at head height, which would have either knocked her unconscious or dashed her brains out. In a hundred other scenarios, Grace O'Connell would be dead by now, but in this one, she had danced on the head of a pin and survived.

Her moment of contemplation was rudely interrupted when the steel started to vibrate with the movement of men surging toward her.

"Can you move?"

"Can you get down?"

"Now we gotta rescue the rescuer!"

"Well, it'll be a damned sight easier than getting hold of Mick."

"Are you all right?"

"That's about the damnedest thing I ever did see!"

"I don't know how you did it, but you did!"

"You must have been a cat in another life, kid; you've got nine lives, all right!"

Grace scooted along the beam and started to climb down to the solid floor where people were gathering.

"Not a scratch on you!"

"Well, I'll be damned!"

"That was one hell of a thing you did."

"Jesus, Mary, and Joseph, if my hair ain't all white by this evening, that'll be something. Scared me outta my goddam mind."

"Can you believe what we're seeing? That's a *woman*."

Grace was suddenly very aware of being in her underwear, and was desperately looking around for faces she knew. It was Frank who reached her first and pulled her into a hug so fierce he was in danger of causing her far more damage than the fall had.

"My ribs," she gasped, as he choked all the air from her body and refused to let go. Eventually he held her at arm's length.

"Did you see that?" he asked her, and then turned to the people around him like a preacher addressing a congregation. "Did you see that? That was the hand of God! We witnessed a miracle here today! You saved a life and so he saved yours! He lifted you onto that beam! *Mamma mia.*" He shook his head. "We have witnessed the grace of God!"

Several men voiced their agreement, and Grace saw some of them cross themselves, but she could think of it as nothing but dumb luck. She caught sight of Seamus coming toward her and pushed herself through the mass of bodies on unsteady legs to hug him. He had her clothes and boots in his hands, and she scrambled into them gratefully, looking around desperately for the one other person she needed to see.

She eventually spotted him behind the crowd of men, crouching on the floor with his arms covering his head. When she got closer, he looked up at her, and she saw the tears in his eyes. His face was so full of conflicting emotions, she thought he might spontaneously combust. One of those emotions was without doubt absolute fury. She backed away, but he jumped up and threw his arms around her neck, tears cascading down his cheeks as he spoke in rapid Italian. Grace had no idea what he was saying, but she could feel the relief flooding through his body. It was only once Joe's arms were around her that she finally started to shake.

Mr. Gilligan strode through the crowd and the men started to scatter.

"Back to work." The three words were enough to disperse the gathering, leaving just Grace's gang and a few stubborn spectators.

"Where do I even begin?" The foreman's mustache was twitching as if it was a creature with a life of its own.

"How about a thank you for saving a man's life?" Seamus asked. He rested his hand on Gilligan's shoulder. Gilligan glanced down at it with disgust, and Seamus moved it. "No one died," he tried again, "and that"—he pointed at the steel beam still swinging gently at the end of its jib—"can be fixed, I'm sure. We haven't dropped a single piece of steel so far, and I'm sure we never will."

"Shut your trap, Flaherty!" Gilligan snapped.

"Yes, of course, you're right, sir. I talk when I'm nervous. See, I'm doing it again, can't stop." A withering glare was enough, and Seamus pinched his lips together, tight as a drum.

"I have no idea what to say about this." Gilligan looked at the three men. "And you should all be ashamed of yourselves for going along with it. Can you imagine what would have happened if a *woman* had just dropped out of the sky? If a *woman* had died on my steel?" He shook his head as if the very notion was unthinkable, which of course it was. He moved his gaze to Grace. "Of course, it's just as much my fault for missing it. *How* could I have missed it? And while I'm grateful that you saved a life, you should never have been here in the first place. I can't imagine how I'm going to explain this to Mr. Bowser."

Joe stepped forward. "She's been as good as any man," he said, his voice quivering with emotion. His appeal fell on deaf ears.

"It goes without saying that you are all fired. Please remove yourselves from my steel. Now."

Not even Seamus had a smart answer for that. Grace closed her eyes and felt the burden of every decision she had made that day seep into her bones to be weighed and measured.

Frank put his arm around her, and they headed toward the elevators. When they were a few steps away from the cage, Grace heard clapping coming from overhead. She squinted and looked up. Three storeys above her, with one foot balanced on a giant winch cable, was the massive figure of Bergmann, clapping his gloved hands. At first she thought it was a taunt, but she soon realized it wasn't. Several others joined in, and as she stepped into the elevator cage to descend, she was accompanied by the sound of applause.

The journey to the ground was silent as the four of them contemplated their lost livelihoods. Grace silently rued the quirk of fate that had made the whole thing possible. Their entire lives, people had told her and Patrick how alike they looked. She had never thought much about it until this ruse had started. She had managed to step in and save their family, keeping money coming in, but it had also cost her so much. Her body was battered and ruined, and she had experienced things she would never forget, however hard she tried. She had nearly died, and all because of the face she had been born with.

As surreal and mundane a task as it was after what had just happened, they had to go to the office and hand in their ID tags. The man there glanced up and held his hand out. Grace took in the surroundings of the office for the last time. The wood paneling, the papers and schedules tacked to the walls, the row of pencils neatly lined up at the head of the desk.

"They modeled this building on the pencil, you know," the man had said to her one morning, holding one upright, point in the air, to demonstrate. "Yours is a damn sight easier to sharpen," Grace had said, and they had laughed together. She wasn't sure if this man knew who she was now, and what had just happened, or if it hadn't filtered down to the ground yet. His face gave nothing away. Perhaps he didn't care. His job was to keep the records straight and check each worker in and out, making sure not to pay anyone a cent more than they deserved.

As he took their tags, he made a note in his ledger and read it out loud to them. "Flaherty, S., Gagliardi, F., Gagliardi, G., O'Connell, P. Ironworkers. Clocking out Monday, July twenty-first, two forty-one p.m."

That was the moment they would stop getting paid. They had come so far, but it was over. Grace's cover was blown and she wouldn't be going back up to catch any more rivets. She was four days short.

———

When Patrick came out of the New York Public Library, he caught a flash of dark hair and a nurse's uniform in the crowd at the bottom of the stairs and knew instantly it was Florence. This ability to pick her out made his heart swell, and he knew he would be doing it for the rest of his life. The sun was shining and she must have decided to pop by and see him on her way to the hospital.

Halfway down the steps, he registered that she was running toward him, dodging around people. At first he thought she was just excited to see him, but her frantic movements told another story. Patrick's face crumpled and he wanted to turn and walk away into the crowd. There was an urgency about her that he didn't like at all, and if he didn't speak to her, he didn't have to find out why.

"Patrick," she said, flinging herself into his arms. She was out of breath, gulping in air like a fish on the dockside.

"What is it? What's wrong?"

"There was an accident," she gasped. "On the site."

"Grace." Patrick's entire body went cold, and he was already moving. Florence grabbed him by the arm to stop him.

"No. Well, yes, but no. She's okay."

He tried his best to stay calm and not be irritated by her lack of coherence. Now that he was facing whatever the problem was, he wanted all the information far quicker than she was able to give it to him. He held her by the shoulders and looked straight into her eyes. "What do you know? Tell me."

"My father called my mother, just as I was leaving," Florence gabbled. "He never does that. He was telling her he would be late for dinner because of some incident with a crane. I only heard my mother's side of the conversation, but it was definitely about Grace. I think she saved someone's life." Her chest was still heaving with exertion. "But now everyone knows who she is."

Patrick tried to take it in, but the words that pounded in his head were the only ones that mattered. *She's alive, she's alive, she's alive.*

"She's a hero." Florence's speech was finally returning to a more normal cadence. "But they've been thrown off the site. All four of them."

Patrick nodded. He knew this was terrible news, but he couldn't bring himself to care when just seconds before he had been convinced his twin was dead.

"I need to see her," he said, struggling to focus.

"Of course." Florence nodded. "You go and see her. I've got to go to work, but I'm going to speak to my father as soon as I can. It isn't fair. He can't do this. She saved someone's life!"

He hugged her to him. "It's all right. It'll be all right." But he had no idea if what he said was true. They had been riding their luck for weeks; it had to run out sooner or later. They had been so close, but a part of him was singing with relief that his sister would never again have to set foot on the steel. It was over.

"I'll fix this," Florence whispered, reaching up to kiss him on the cheek. "I promise."

Patrick nodded, but he had no expectation of her being able to do anything. In fact, it would be better if she stayed out of it, he realized a second too late. If anyone was going to speak to Mr. Gilligan it should be him. He didn't want her fighting with her father over him and his family. But for now, as they headed in opposite directions, he had to let her go. The only thing he could think about was seeing Grace with his own eyes.

30

"Grace, *bella*, please, just sit down!" Frank Gagliardi was in the O'Connell apartment with his brother and Seamus, trying to get Grace to stop moving.

"I can't, Frank, don't you see?" She pulled up the sleeve of her shirt and worried at the metal splinters under her skin, only stopping her pacing when Joe gently caught her arm and took over, taking great care to slide them out without hurting her. She looked down at her arm, relieved to see no blood, then nodded once at Joe in thanks, pulled down her sleeve, and started moving again.

Mary had been in her bedroom when Seamus had led Grace and the two Italians into the apartment. Now she emerged, her face already drawn and pale with worry. She knew instantly that whatever had happened wasn't good.

"They know," Seamus said simply. Mary closed her eyes and gripped the back of the chair until her swollen red knuckles went a deathly white.

"Grace saved a man's life!" Joe was quick to add.

"It wasn't enough, though. I'm still not a man myself."

"It shouldn't matter!" Seamus said. "No man could have done it!"

"But it does," said Grace. "I need to go back out."

"Grace, *bella*, please, just sit down! Let us calm down and think about this."

"What's to think about?" Grace said. "Everyone has lost their jobs because of me. I tried to do something good, but it backfired. You were right, I should have stayed out of it."

"What you did," Seamus said, "was nothing short of a miracle."

"An expensive miracle." Grace's eyes drifted to the daily shopping, which for some reason was still on the table.

"Grace!" None of them had heard the door open. Patrick strode in and swept his sister into his arms. It wasn't normal for the two of them to touch each other at all. The hug was unexpected, but Grace hardly registered it. "Florence told me you were in an accident."

"An accident?" This was the first time Mary had heard anyone use the word.

"I'm fine." Grace shrugged him off. "And I'm sorry I ruined it all."

"What happened?" Patrick asked.

"Someone tell him," Grace said. "I need to get ready." She slipped out of his grasp and into her room.

"What do you mean, get ready?" her mother called after her. "Get ready for what?"

Grace ignored her. Nothing anyone could say would make a difference now.

She flew around her small bedroom, tearing her clothes off, kicking off her boots and looking for something appropriate to wear. She ran her hands through her hair, fluffing it up as much as possible, then pulled on a white spaghetti-strapped dress and hurriedly applied dark red lipstick in her small cracked mirror. Her arm was red from Joe's splinter removal, but there was no time to worry about that. She grabbed her dance shoes from under her bed, dragging a coat on over her outfit and tipping coins, lipstick, and key into her pocketbook. Her heart was pounding, a euphoric mixture of feelings flooding her nervous system. She had been saved by the wind on the building so that she was still alive to save them all. She was sure of it.

Opening her bedroom door, she was met by a host of faces who couldn't be more shocked to see her dressed as if she was heading out for a night on the town.

"It's all okay," she reassured them. "No one worry; I'm going to fix this."

"Grace, please." Patrick reached out for her. "It's all right, just sit down. This isn't your fault."

She waved him away. "I won't be long. I know exactly what to do." She was frustrated by the worried looks on their faces. Why didn't they understand? "This is how it's meant to be," she said, nodding vigorously. She found Joe's face in the crowd of people. "For Bruno, and Connie, and Mateo? Yes?" Before anyone had a chance to say anything, she ran to the door, clattered down the stairs as fast as she could, and hurried into the street.

"What do we do?" Patrick asked, stricken. The others had filled him in on the events of the day. "Do I follow her, Ma? She's not right."

"She's in shock. She needs to work her way through it," Mary said, her mind elsewhere. "Besides, there are other things to worry about." Patrick didn't register this enough to ask what she meant.

"I'll go after her," Joe said. "It's not safe." He headed for the door, followed by his brother.

"Go home," Patrick told them. "I'll let you know when she's back."

Frank had his hat clutched in his hands. "This is our fault," he said. "We made her do it. Time and again we pushed and pushed. And now . . ."

"Grace doesn't do anything she doesn't want to," Mary said. "Never has. Don't blame yourselves. You need to go home and work out how to feed your families. And we need to do the same."

Grace was at Shubert Alley. She saw the group of creative types standing on the corner chatting and walked right up to them.

"Hi, hello there, how you doing?" Every head turned to look at her. She had no reason to be intimidated by these people anymore. She had riveted steel, she had danced on air, and she had faced death. Nothing would ever scare her again.

"Can we help you?" A woman with blond hair cut in a sharp line at her jaw took a step toward her. She wore a stylish green dress with white brocade and looked at Grace along an aquiline nose.

"Have you heard of any auditions taking place around here? I'm a dancer mainly, looking for a spot in a show."

The woman said nothing for a beat.

"You're in luck," said a guy with a fedora tipped down low over his eyes. The blond shot him a look. Don't I know it, thought Grace, still riding high on her near-death experience. "I heard there's an audition on this very afternoon up at Mulroney's on West Thirty-Ninth Street." He gestured with a finger. "You might be too late, but"—he shrugged—"only one way to find out."

Grace thanked him and set off, determined, her feet skipping over the sidewalk into a trot when walking wasn't fast enough. By now it was late afternoon and she just had to get there in time. She dodged cars and streetcars, children in line on the corner waiting for a shaved ice, and men with cigars in their mouths and newspapers folded under their arms. She hurried past a pretzel vendor, his basket of goods balanced on a Lucky Strike carton, and waved away a man trying to sell her flowers.

Her eyes darted back and forth as she got closer to her destination. She was on the right street now and saw an unlit sign for Mulroney's above a big brown door, a piece of paper tacked to it. She didn't let herself believe it would be bad news, and when she got close enough to read it, she saw the hand-scrawled notice said: *OPEN AUDITIONS, USE BACK ENTRANCE.* Delighted to be in the right place, she ran to the edge of the building and straight down the alley, kicking trash out of her way to get to the stage door, her dance shoes still swinging from her hand. She arrived just in time to see a young man wearing a white shirt with black suspenders and a purple cravat reaching to close the door.

"Stop!" she called, running toward him with her hand out. "I'm here to audition. I want to audition!"

The man looked her up and down. "You do?" He glanced at his watch. "You're late."

"I didn't know," she said, trying to keep her breathing under control. "I went to the front. I just saw your sign."

He nodded. He had red hair slicked tight to his head and wore gray trousers that looked a size too big. "Well, I'm just the door guy, but the last group is just about to go in. What's your name?"

"Grace O'Connell."

He nodded and gestured with his head for her to go in. "I'll put you on the list."

Grace entered the building and followed the sound of voices until she saw a group of around ten women getting ready to go through a door. She just had time to register that she had her outfit all wrong, but there was no time to worry about that. Throwing off her coat, she dropped her purse on top, hopping on one foot as she pulled on her dance shoes. Following the other women straight into a harshly lit room, she didn't even have time to brush the soles of her shoes. They would have to do.

Two women and two men stood at the front of the room, watching as the dancers came in. A sophisticated woman in a white shirt and pale gray skirt stepped forward. Her curled black hair was so shiny and moved so little that it looked carved from marble. When she spoke, she had an English accent.

"Thank you for coming, ladies. Can you line up in three rows of four, please?" The girls shuffled into place. Grace joined the back row, making them five.

"Oh, sorry, dear," the woman said as the red-haired man put a list into her hand. She scanned it. "Miss O'Connell, is it?" Grace nodded, and the woman took in her white tasseled dress. She didn't look impressed until her eyes reached the floor and she saw Grace's shoes. Then she nodded, to acknowledge that she was at least looking at a dancer, and with the flick of a wrist handed the man a crumpled number. It was only then Grace noticed that the other girls had numbers pinned to their more appropriate outfits of tights and tops.

"Thirteen," said the woman, as the doorman hurried over and pinned the number to Grace's dress.

"Unlucky for some," the girl next to Grace said with a sideways glance, stretching out, her hand reaching over her head.

One of the men stepped forward. He looked like a film star, his tight white undershirt tucked into beige trousers, a flat cap turned backward on his head. His biceps bulged.

"Right, girls, we're going to do a simple Charleston. I'll show you first and then you copy the second time. If you get tapped on the shoulder, thank you for your time but you're not for us and you are free to leave."

As the music started, Grace had a sudden realization of where she was. She hadn't stopped to think about what she was doing. It hit her hard that less than three hours before, she had been three hundred and fifty feet in the air with Mick. Her head spun at the thought, but the instructor was already moving and she had to concentrate. He was calling the steps out as he did them and she watched intently, muttering the sequence under her breath. The routine looked easy enough and she relaxed.

"Your turn! Go!" he shouted, clapping his hands, and the girls picked up the beat of the music.

Grace hadn't danced properly in weeks, and her body was aching from her fall, but it felt incredible to be moving again. The mixture of her new strength and the adrenaline coursing through her made her steps effortless. The four people at the front of the room started to walk forward between the rows of girls, their eyes scanning from side to side. When the dancers came to the end of the short routine, the Englishwoman shouted, "Again, please!" She walked close to Grace, who plastered a smile on her face even though the woman was watching her feet. A girl to her right was tapped on the shoulder. She immediately stopped dancing, turned and left. Grace kept going.

They went through the routine four times before they were told to stop. Grace looked around the room. There were only eight girls left.

"Thank you," said the man in the backward cap. The second woman stepped forward. She had gray hair but a smooth, unlined face. She wore a pea-green dress.

"New steps. As before. Watch me, and then copy."

Grace replicated the movements, flicking and kicking her legs with perfect balance and sharp retractions. After another round of cuts, she was one of only four girls left when the music stopped.

Now the second man stepped forward. He was older and looked like a scrunched-up tissue, with a puckered mouth and squinting eyes. His features were too small and were all crammed into the middle of his face.

"Line up, please, but give yourselves some space," he said in a voice like the rasp of a saw on wood. One of the four audition judges stood in front of each girl. Grace got the Englishwoman with the rock-solid hair. "Congratulations for making it this far. We only need two dancers, and as you will have seen, four of you remain. For the next section, you need to combine the moves from both dances, in any order or sequence you wish. Put together your own routine. Music from the start, please."

The red-headed man nodded and restarted the record, giving them no chance to even think. A couple of the women stood there for a few seconds, looking bewildered, but Grace wasn't concerned. All they wanted her to do was dance, and she loved to dance. She lost herself in the music and didn't register anything else in the room, her brain blissfully clear until the music ended. When her feet stopped moving, her body ached, but she was certain she had done well.

She stood in silence. The thought flitted across her mind that if she had died at the Empire State Building earlier that day, she never would have danced again. The idea of it raised the hairs on her arms as she waited for the verdict. The four judges converged around her. She was to be the first dancer to learn her fate.

"I just don't understand you," the woman with black marble hair said. "Can't make it out."

Not the best start imaginable. Grace kept her expression neutral.

"Best Charleston of the day," the gray-haired woman said, and Grace nodded her head slightly in thanks. That was better.

"You turn up looking like this," the Englishwoman went on, gesturing at Grace's outfit, "and then you dance like *that*."

"You're good." Backwards Flat Cap nodded, his arms flexing. "No denying it."

"But there is more to this than dancing," the man with the scrunched face said. This was news to Grace. "You've gotta look the part, and you,

Miss O'Connell, don't. You dance like a dream, but your hair is a disgrace, and you have the shoulders of a linebacker." He looked with disgust at Grace's muscular shoulders and the thin strap of her dress draped across their width. "We need slim, dainty girls. And what"—he stepped forward and lifted one of her arms at the wrist—"is all this? How can I put a girl on my stage who looks like she spends her days as a welder at a shipbuilder's yard? What on earth?" He dropped her arm as if frightened he might catch a disease.

"I—" started Grace.

"*I*," he interrupted, putting emphasis on the word, making it clear that his was the only voice that needed to be heard, "did not ask you to speak, thank you, number thirteen."

The Englishwoman pursed her lips a little, as if disappointed, and then stepped forward and placed her hand on Grace's linebacker shoulder. Grace just stood there for a moment, frozen to the spot.

"That means you can go. Thank you," said the man with the cap.

She turned and shuffled out of the room before they started their appraisal of the next girl. When she reached the door, the man with the purple cravat was holding her coat for her to slip her arms into.

"That's too bad," he said. "Close, too."

No. This can't be happening, thought Grace as she picked up her purse and stumbled out the back door into the light.

"I was meant to get it," she mumbled to herself, her only audience a big black rat rummaging in some discarded newspapers by the wall. "I had to get it."

She was in a daze, unaware of her surroundings, sleepwalking her way down to the subway to pay her nickel fare and step onto the train. In the carriage, a man slept slumped across two seats with his feet on the floor at an awkward angle and his fedora over his face. Grace sat in silence. Across from her a homeless man with a dirty face and a coat full of holes watched her with rheumy eyes.

"You look awful," he said.

"Thanks," she replied.

31

"There you are!" As Grace opened the door and walked into the apartment, Mary jumped to her feet. "Where have you been?" She looked wretched, her eyes flicking nervously to her bedroom door.

"Out." Grace slumped into the nearest chair at the table.

"Your friends are out looking for you. That Italian boy looked worried sick."

"He's worried about Bruno. Worried about his family."

"If I know anything, he's worried about more than that."

"I went to an audition," Grace offered, ignoring her mother's comment. The last thing she could think about right now was Joe. "Didn't get it."

Mary nodded as if she had thought as much, which seemed an odd response. "Something will turn up," she said, rubbing Grace's hand. "Now listen . . ."

But Grace was in no mood to listen. "I thought I was meant to go," she said, staring straight ahead. "What happened this afternoon, I thought it was trying to tell me I was ready, and I could do it now. But if that's not it, what is?" She was wringing her hands in her lap without even knowing she was doing it. The comments of those judges were clawing at her. They had ripped her confidence to shreds. She knew that working on the steel had changed her body, but they had looked at her in disgust, where people used to gaze at her with envy. "What am I meant to do?" she asked the universe, but it was only her mother who heard.

Before Mary could even offer an answer, Patrick appeared from his mother's bedroom with a grim look on his face. Finally picking up on the silence and tension in the room, Grace jumped to her feet with a new sense of urgency, panic sparking in her spine as she noticed what was missing.

"Where's Connie?" she asked, her voice filled with horror.

"Grace," Patrick said, taking a step forward and placing his hands on her shoulders. "We think she overdid it yesterday." He paused for a second that felt to Grace like an eon. "She's got a fever."

Grace ripped his hands away and stumbled into the bedroom, where Connie lay burning up, her skin red and angry. Cool flannels had been laid across her forehead and legs, but she was unresponsive beneath them, sheets soaked through with sweat.

"No," Grace whispered. She said it again, "No, no," volume rising until she was wailing, all the day's emotion pouring out of her. "NOOO!" She crumpled and Patrick caught her, holding her until she was ready to stand again. Then she fell on her sister, trying to open her eyes, shaking her to wake up. Fevers took O'Connell children; it had happened before.

"Grace!" Patrick grabbed her, and Grace stood there in her stupid white dress, her face wet with tears. Mary was crying now too.

"Where's Florence?" Grace asked, searching the room as if she might be hiding under the bed.

"She's at the hospital," Patrick said calmly.

"Grand, that's perfect, let's take Connie there." She rushed into her own room, tearing her dress off and putting on more sensible clothes. *What does one wear for a crisis?* a detached voice she didn't recognize taunted in her head. Pulling her coveralls back on, she squared up to Patrick in the living area. "Come on! Why aren't you *doing* something?"

"Grace." Patrick swallowed hard. "We can't take her to the hospital. What if she needs to stay for weeks? It's five dollars a day on a ward, not to mention all the tests and medicines."

Grace looked to Mary, who gazed at the floor and sobbed quietly.

Grace shook her head, tears glimmering in her eyes. "You can't be serious?" She disappeared back into her room, dragging open her top drawer, throwing things out until she found the money at the back. She shoved the roll of bills into Patrick's chest, eyes blazing. "There!"

"Grace," Mary said quietly. "We'll need that for the rent." Her voice became harder. "Connie will need somewhere to live. We have to just trust she'll get better. She has every time so far."

"No!" Grace cried. "You can see how sick she is! We can't just *hope* this time, Ma. She won't need anywhere to live if she's dead!"

Mary's head jerked back as if Grace had slapped her, and they stood in the silent aftermath of the word they had all danced around for months but never uttered.

Grace turned back to Patrick. "It's my money. This is what it's for. Take half out for next month's rent, and we'll use what's left. Or we'll sell everything if we need to, move from here into one room and sleep on top of one another like we did as kids. Whatever it takes." She dashed away the tears that were now streaming down her cheeks. "Have I not already done whatever it takes, Patrick? Have I not given enough? How can you just stand there? She's our baby sister. We can't lose her." Her voice cracked. "What was it all for, if not for her?"

Patrick blinked hard, looking from his sister to his mother and back again, gulping down the emotion gathering in the back of his throat. He nodded once.

"Go and flag a taxi. I'll bring her down."

32

W hen Patrick carried his little sister into Gotham Hospital, her skin was so hot it was burning his chest where her head lolled against him.

"Can you help us, please?" he asked the first ward sister he saw, who beckoned him to follow her, a shell-shocked Mary and Grace trailing behind.

"Put her here." The woman gestured to a trolley as she called over a doctor in a white coat. He was tall, with white hair swept across the crown of his head, and as he strode forward, he polished his glasses on his tie. He was just putting them back on when Florence appeared from around the corner, stopping mid-step when she saw the O'Connells.

"Patrick!" she said, her eyes going to his arm first before she noticed Connie. Her eyes widened slightly before she rearranged her face into neutral professionalism.

"Patient's name?" the doctor asked.

"Constance—"

"Gilligan," Florence butted in. "Constance Gilligan." She held Patrick's eye as she added, "This is my sister," and although he didn't know what she was doing or why, he trusted her.

"That's right," he agreed.

The doctor looked up and fixed his gaze on Florence, who was staring back defiantly. "Is that so?" he asked.

"Yes, sir, Dr. Armstrong."

There was a moment of silence, broken by a painful gasp from Connie. "Right," Dr. Armstrong said, making a decision to concede. "Constance Gilligan it is. Age?"

"Eleven," Patrick said, as Mary and Grace clung to each other behind him, Mary praying furiously under her breath.

"She's been unwell for a while," Florence chipped in. "Suspected bronchitis."

"I see." The doctor took another look at the distraught family. "I need to run some tests. She will have to be admitted to a ward. The hospital administrator will speak to you about fees."

"Do whatever you need to," Grace said, her face blazing. "We can pay."

Dr. Armstrong's expression softened. He took in Mary's shabby clothes, and the cast on Patrick's arm. "I will do what I can."

He signaled to the ward sister, who had been watching and listening, and they started to wheel the trolley away. The family moved as one to follow, but the doctor held up a hand.

"You need to wait here." He looked at the clock on the wall. "In fact, you need to leave. It's late, come back tomorrow morning," and with that, Connie was whisked away out of their sight.

Mary let out a gasp of pain, while Grace hopped from foot to foot, desperate to follow.

Florence stepped forward and put her hand on Patrick's arm. "Nurses and their families get discounted treatment," she whispered to him.

Patrick's breath hitched in his chest and his love for this woman bloomed. "Thank you," he whispered back. All he wanted was to bury his face in her hair and breathe her in; to pretend none of this was happening.

"You really should go home," she said gently. "It will be a while yet before there's any news. I'll be here all night."

Grace was shaking her head, adamant. "I'm not leaving this building until Connie walks out beside me."

Patrick knew better than to argue. He turned to his mother, who was trembling now, her eyes unfocused. She had lost children before, and he could hardly bear to think that it might be about to happen again. "Shall I take you to Aunt Frances, Ma?" he suggested gently. "We can all go to church." He gulped. "I don't want to leave her either, but they can look after her better here than we can."

As he gently steered her toward the exit, Mary turned back and grabbed both of Grace's hands in her own. Her voice was hoarse. "Whatever happens, Grace, promise me you'll bring her home to me."

Grace's bottom lip wobbled as she pulled her mother into an embrace, breathing in her familiar scent. Those two small words, *whatever happens*, had chiseled a crack down the center of Patrick's heart. He knew his twin would have a matching one.

"I promise, Ma. I won't come home without her."

Mary nodded furiously and let Patrick lead her away.

"Come on," Florence said gently, steering Grace by the elbow. "You've had a helluva day. Let's find you somewhere to wait."

33

TUESDAY, JULY 22, 1930

Grace was so tired she was almost delirious when Florence touched her shoulder, sending a jolt of alarm through her, almost causing her to fall off the extremely uncomfortable iron chair she had spent the night on. Every muscle in her body burned like fire, and the bone-deep ache of fatigue was making her feel intoxicated, but she jumped to her feet in an instant.

"Connie." The word was a reflex; saying it out loud felt like water on her dry lips. "Where is she?"

"She's on the ward," Florence said gently. "Grace, she has pneumonia."

Grace's eyes rolled wildly in her head before they settled back on Florence and she started to sob. "No." She shook her head. She knew how dangerous pneumonia was. "A lot of people die from that." She didn't even realize she had voiced her thought out loud until she felt Florence squeezing her hand.

"And a lot of people don't," Florence said in her best soothing voice. She was a good nurse. "There's a treatment, a serum, I've seen it work. The doctor is looking after her, and you know Connie is strong."

"Let me see her, please," Grace choked out. "And call Patrick."

Florence nodded and led Grace to her sister. When she pulled back the curtain, Connie looked so small in the hospital bed. She was less distressed than the night before, but she was still unconscious and sweating, her skin glowing red like a beacon.

"Can you bring me my chair?" Grace asked, already using all her remaining energy to keep breathing and blinking.

"Grace," Florence chided, "you're no use to anyone like this. You had such a stressful day yesterday. Go home and get some rest. You don't want to end up in the bed beside her."

Grace took her literally. "Can I do that? Get in beside her?"

"No," Florence said, shaking her head.

"Then I'll have a chair, please."

34

WEDNESDAY, JULY 23, 1930

At three p.m. the next day, Grace was flopped face down against the hospital bed when she felt a tickling sensation by her ear. She shook her head, but it persisted, and when she finally turned to look, there was a tiny hand resting there. She froze, as if scared the moment would melt away like a mirage. Inch by inch she raised her head and looked up the bed to see her sister's big eyes looking back at her.

"Connie," she breathed.

"This isn't my bed," Connie croaked.

"No, it's not," Grace agreed.

"Can I go home now?" Connie asked with a frustrated sigh, and Grace's face opened like a sunflower, transforming into one giant smile. She stood, reaching over to kiss the little girl on the forehead. "Let me find out," she said, as she hurried off to find Dr. Armstrong.

After another round of tests and an examination, it was decided that the best thing for Connie now was rest in her own bed, and the doctor agreed she could go home. Patrick looked an odd shade of green as he paid the hospital bill—twenty dollars even with Florence's discount—but Grace would have paid three times that and more to know her sister had finally had some proper medical treatment. She'd handed him the notes and told him to pay it in full rather than have yet another payment plan hanging over their heads. There would be a way to find work, there had to be.

As Patrick carried Connie into the bedroom, in a much better state than when he had carried her out, Grace couldn't help but feel happy. There was no price they could put on Connie's health and having their family together.

"You should get yourself to bed too," Mary said, stroking her arm. "Get some rest." Grace wasn't the only one; Mary had deep, dark circles under her eyes.

Grace was nodding her agreement when her attention was caught by a white envelope addressed to her, propped up against the water jug on the table.

"What's this?" she asked, lifting the envelope as if she had never seen one before. She very rarely received any mail.

"It came for you this morning," Mary replied.

"Maybe it's good news at last," Grace said with a hint of hope, turning the envelope over in her hands.

"As far as I can see, there's only one way to find out."

She tore open the envelope and slid out the folded paper.

"It's from Betty. She's upstate with Howard." But the warm glow she felt at seeing the familiar handwriting was short-lived.

Throughout her life, Grace often thought of the watershed moments. The ones just before something big happened. Those few seconds before your life was changed in irrevocable ways. She was worried all through her time sitting in the hospital that one was coming. As it turned out, she was right; it just wasn't the one she thought.

As her eyes crawled across the words on the page, her stricken face lost all color.

"No, no, no, please no," she muttered as her knees gave way.

"What is it? Grace, what's wrong?"

She squeezed the tiny word out through her rapidly constricting throat. "Edie." Her wild eyes searched for her mother. "Edie's dead."

Then she collapsed to the floor.

———

Grace was curled up on the floor, crying. She had been there for fifteen minutes, and Mary had lowered herself down beside her, lifting her daughter's head gently onto her lap. What had started as an ordinary week had driven a tornado through Grace O'Connell's life and bent it out of all recognizable shape.

"She's gone," she said quietly, her voice thick with tears. It wasn't the first time she had said it. Edie hadn't won the dance marathon. She and her partner had exited the competition on the twenty-second day of dancing when they had collapsed from exhaustion, unable to get back up within the thirty seconds they were allowed. When they'd left the floor, there were still three couples dancing. Although no one was really dancing by then.

A distraught and delirious Edie had made it home, only to find that she no longer had a home. She had been gone for three weeks and her room was being rented out to a new tenant. One of the girls in the rooming house had taken pity on her and said she could stay for one night in her room while she went out to work. When she returned, her generosity had been repaid in the form of an unresponsive Edie in her bed. It was too late to help her. Betty said in her letter that it was a mixture of exhaustion, drugs, and alcohol that had done it, but no one was sure if it was an accident or not. The question would haunt Grace for the rest of her life.

Betty's details had been found in the scant belongings Edie had kept in her one small, battered valise; she was contacted as the closest thing to a next of kin and was taking care of all the arrangements. The funeral was on Monday. Grace's heart was in a thousand pieces.

"I tried," she croaked to her mother. "I tried to get her out of there, I really did."

"You were a good friend to that girl, Grace. You know you were. This is a tragedy, but not one of your making."

"I could have saved her."

"No," said Mary firmly. "Only the Lord could have done that, and he decided to call her home. It was her time to go, Grace."

"She was so young." Grace immediately regretted her words. Mary had lost children far younger. Her own babies, held swaddled in blankets, their tiny bodies destined to grow no bigger. And they had come so close to losing Connie, who even now was lying in the next room with Patrick watching over her. "Sorry," she whispered.

"No loss hurts any less than another." Mary stroked her daughter's hair.

"I can't live through another day like today." Grace's tears cascaded silently over her nose and down onto her mother's skirt, where they made a dark patch on the fabric.

"You can," said Mary. "Because you must." She took a deep breath. "I've known every kind of pain. The kind that wants to strangle you, drown you, and bury you. The kind that clings to your back and the kind that claws at your throat. And believe me, I know what it feels like to consider letting it win." She rubbed her hand across Grace's back, something she hadn't done for many years.

"But you are strong, Grace O'Connell, maybe more so than any of us. And you will find a way to pick up that pain and carry it with you. The next time, and the next. And your arms will get stronger. On some rare days you will find that pain fits in your pocket and you barely notice it, and other days it's a huge trunk that threatens to topple you under its weight, but it is never more than you can manage. Even if you have to put it down and drag it along behind you for a while, you just keep moving. You have to. And when your arms are stronger, you'll pick it up again."

"I can't."

"You will." Mary's voice was calm and certain. "The Lord never gives you more than you can manage."

Grace took in a couple of huge, shuddering breaths and then sat up, facing her mother.

"Edie is pretty heavy for someone who weighed so little."

Mary gave her daughter a closed-lip smile. She cupped Grace's cheek in her palm, wiping away the tears with her thumb. "All the best ones are, my girl. The weight is your love for them that has nowhere else to go."

Grace closed her eyes, more tears falling over her mother's fingers. When she opened them, the tears had washed them clear.

"I have to go out again."

"Grace, no, you need to stay here. You're upset, you've had an awful day."

"Just look after Connie. I can't be here right now. I need to get some air. I'll be fine, I promise."

Mary stared at her, and Grace felt an understanding pass between them.

"Be careful," her mother said. "And come back to me soon."

Grace nodded, and stood on wobbly legs for her first attempt at carrying her new grief.

After what felt like hours of aimless wandering that evening, trying to get the movement of her body to overpower the thoughts in her head, Grace was both surprised and not surprised at all when she found herself with her hands on giant locked iron gates, looking up.

Up close, other than its height, there wasn't anything that impressive about the Empire State Building. Just a huge, unassuming edifice of gray shooting into the sky so high that from this angle you could barely see the top, even with your neck craned back. Grace gazed into the early-evening summer sky and saw, way above her head, the steel beam she had lowered herself onto to save Mick. It was still there. They clearly hadn't managed to fix the crane yet and move it to its proper place. It looked like no more than a matchstick. The height was staggering, and yet Grace had been standing right there, the only one willing to climb out and save a man's life.

She gripped the bars of the gates and thought about how the Gagliardi family had lost two salaries, and how she had no idea when she would ever be able to buy her little sister Milk Duds again. That was the price of Mick being at home with his family tonight. And even though Grace had risked her life, refused to leave her sister's side, and would freely hand over the money she had worked so hard to save to help her family, none of it had been enough to stop Edie from being found cold and pale in a mess of sheets in a Lower East Side tenement.

Grace screamed. She held the iron bars and screamed and screamed until there was nothing left in her body. Many people came to take a look at the progress of the Empire State Building or stopped to glance up on their way past. The street was always busy, but crazy things happened in New York, and no one approached her while she yelled. They all just took a step back and left her to it. God knows they had enough problems of their own and reasons to howl. The night watchmen in their office, playing cards, didn't even move. Unless someone was about to die, it wasn't their problem. What they didn't realize was that someone already had.

When Grace's throat was raw and her body had used up all its fury, she sagged her forehead against the gates. "Edie, meet Lukasz," she muttered under her breath, then turned and walked away without looking back.

She kept going through the city. She remembered from her father's death the feeling of disbelief and anger at people carrying on with their lives as if nothing had happened. The truth was, for them nothing had, and that just made things worse. She let her feet carry her to Forty-Second Street, where she headed to the familiar backstage entrance of Dominic's. The door was boarded shut and there was a plank of wood nailed haphazardly across the second-floor window. She climbed the pipes and ledges until she was level with it. Still in her coveralls, she used the strength in her new linebacker shoulders to rip it away. It was shoddy work, and she imagined Texas himself doing it as a half-hearted attempt to secure the property when he left. Either way, the wood and the bent nails were both dropped to the floor, and she contorted and squeezed her body through the small window. She knew it would land her on the staircase that led down to their dressing area. She slipped to the ground effortlessly.

Once inside, and now able to add breaking and entering and trespass to her résumé, she felt her way down the stairs in the dark. A small amount of light came in from the window, and she knew the way well enough. She reached for the light switch, hoping the electricity was still on. Jackpot. The bulbs above the mirrors fizzed to life, and she thought of Connie's electric eels. Her breath caught in her throat as she traced her fingers along her place at the bench. No one had been here in weeks, and a fine dust had settled over everything already. At Edie's place, there was a shriveled white rose, the one she had received the day before the theater had closed. Grace reached out toward it but was too scared to touch it in case the petals disintegrated. She needed it to stay exactly as it was.

She circled the room and let it fill with her memories of being here when the place bustled with life and rustled with the satin of costumes. She imagined the girls all squealing with delight and tittering like birds when there was a change in the routine and a new outfit to try on. Gossiping in groups when one of them went on a date with a new man.

"He's here tonight, in the brown. He has a yellow feather in his hat-band."

"A what now?" Betty roared. "Are you dating a canary, Mae Fowler?"

Everyone had laughed, Edie giggling until she got the hiccups.

Grace stopped at a wooden bench and reached below it. Yes, still here. She pulled out a half-empty bottle of whiskey and pulled the stopper, drinking as she toured her own memories. Edie was in front of her, twirling in a much-loved full-length white silk dress trimmed with feathers.

"You look like a swan," Grace mumbled in unison with the Betty of her imagination.

"I feel like I'm inside a pillow," she said in time with her memory of Edie, as she wrapped her arms around herself, a satisfied smile on her face. She tipped the bottle back again and wished Betty was here with her. She was the only other person who knew what the world had really lost.

Her exhausting day had left her tired, and the whiskey was working quickly. She stumbled as she lurched toward the stage outfits, abandoned on their racks, never to be seen or worn again. She ran her hands along the rail, sneezing as the disturbed dust plumed, throwing dresses to the floor as she tried desperately to find what she was looking for. There. The swan dress. She held it to her and hugged it as if Edie were still inside it.

Taking another swig of whiskey, she curled up in the pile of dresses on the floor, like a rainbow nest of silk and satin. She placed the bottle on the ground and draped the white swan dress over her body like a blanket, holding it tightly in her arms. There, as close to Edie as she could get, she wept until she finally fell asleep.

35

THURSDAY, JULY 24, 1930

Grace crept into the apartment. After looking in on Connie, who was asleep, she crawled into bed. It was the early hours of the morning, and still the Donohues made noise overhead. She found it comforting. At any time around the clock, there was always at least one of them awake and moving around.

An hour earlier, she had awoken in the abandoned dressing area of Dominic's with a banging headache and a desperate need for water. For a moment she had jolted upright, worried that she was late for work, until she realized where she was. Catching sight of Edie's dress, the flood of sadness came rushing back, a yawning chasm opening in her chest. There was no work, no dance career, and no Edie. Exhausted and depleted, she'd climbed back out the window and gone home.

When Grace was a child, the O'Connells' neighbors had kept a dog, and one day he'd lain down and stopped moving. He'd stayed there for two days, wouldn't eat and wouldn't drink. He didn't want to move, didn't want to play; he just watched the world from sad, heavy-lidded eyes until he slipped away and peacefully died. Grace was now that dog. She had no energy to move, no desire to carry on. She had endured too much. She would just stay in her bed, watching the world from her own sad, heavy-lidded eyes, her brain nothing but fuzzy static, protecting her from the truth.

When the door cracked open, she found her head too heavy to even move to see who it was. A glass of water and a plate of food was placed on her bedside cabinet. She pushed her slug of a tongue to the roof of her mouth and tried, but no words would come. She wanted to ask how Connie was, in bed just the other side of the wall, but her mouth wouldn't cooperate, so she went back to sleep.

Hours later, Mary knocked and opened the door.

"Grace, your young Italian friend is here to see you."

Grace slowly moved her head from side to side. Mary nodded once and disappeared out of the room. She returned a moment later. "He said he'll be back tomorrow."

Grace closed her eyes.

36

FRIDAY, JULY 25, 1930

All Grace could manage to do was sleep. Her body was a lead weight sinking into the bed; she couldn't have moved even if she'd wanted to, and she didn't. When she guessed it was probably afternoon, her stomach cramped with the thought that everyone on the construction site would be getting their pay packets but she wasn't. And neither was Seamus, or the Gagliardis. She closed her eyes, waiting for oblivion to take her.

A while later, she opened her eyes to see a small pale face framed in blond curls a few inches from hers. She looked at her sister but didn't move, unsure whether she was dreaming or if Connie really was well enough to get out of bed. She saw that tears clung to the girl's long eyelashes and felt a flutter of panic. How could there be more bad news? She tried to reach for her, but her body didn't respond.

"Ma told me what happened. I'm so sorry. And sad. I liked Edie a lot." Two fat tears fell from Connie's eyes. "I feel better, Grace, do you? Are you getting up today?"

Grace managed to shake her head.

"Too sad?"

She nodded once.

Connie nodded too, as if she understood. She threw her arms around her sister and kissed her on the cheek, the way Grace had done to her many times before. "I love you, Grace," she whispered, her breath warm on Grace's face, and then she left.

Later, her mother opened the door. "Joe?" she asked, and Grace shook her head.

Mary closed the door.

37

SATURDAY, JULY 26, 1930

"Grace?" Connie crept into the room. "Ma said not to bother you, but I just wanted to tell you that I love you." She replaced the food on the bedside table with something fresh, kissed her sister on the forehead, and crept out. Grace hated that she was wasting food she knew they couldn't afford, but she couldn't make herself eat.

She spent hours lying on her back staring at the ceiling, her body pinned down beneath her sadness. She had no concept of how much time had passed, when there was another knock on the door and Patrick cracked it open. "Grace," he said softly. "It's seven o'clock. Joe is here to see you."

"No," Grace said. Her voice was rough. It was the first word she had spoken in days.

Patrick nodded and left, returning with the message, "He said he'll be back tomorrow."

Grace started to notice that the world was creeping back in when she heard her mother and brother talking about her through the wall.

"I'm worried, Patrick."

"I'm sorry, Ma. This is all my fault."

"Ach no, don't blame yourself, no one could have known. It's grief, son, and shock. We've all experienced enough of it to know it can give you a rough ride. She's been through so much. I just don't know how long to let this go on."

"Edie's funeral is on Monday. She won't miss it, I know she won't. She'll be up by then."

Grace realized three things. One was that she desperately needed water. The second was that she was starting to smell in the hot, stuffy room; and the third was that perhaps her brother knew her better than she thought he did.

38

SUNDAY, JULY 27, 1930

On Sunday, Grace got up. She wasn't sure what time it was as she pushed herself upright and lowered her feet to the floor. They tingled to feel a solid surface, and she wiggled her toes to assist her circulation. Slowly standing, she made her way to the door and opened it. Patrick and Mary were sitting at the table, both startled to see her.

"I need to get clean," she said. They watched her carefully with concerned faces. "I'm done," she added as she headed to the bathroom.

Mary nodded; she understood. "Sometimes you have to rest," she said, reaching for a skillet, knowing that this time Grace would eat the food she was about to make.

"Until your arms get stronger," Grace said, and recognition flickered on her mother's face.

"It's good to have you back," Patrick said, standing to help his mother set the table. "Connie is doing really well."

Grace washed and soaped her entire body, including her hair. She scrubbed her face clean and let the water run as hot as she could get it until her skin was left pink and soft. Afterward, she sat at the table to eat eggs and bacon.

"Your arm," she said, noticing that her brother's cast was gone.

"Good as new," Patrick told her, and Grace closed her eyes, reminded of her failure and how, because of her actions, he didn't have a job to get back to.

"Another hospital bill."

"Don't you worry about that," he said.

"So what do we do now?"

Patrick and Mary looked at each other and back to Grace.

"Let's not think about that today," Mary said, patting her arm.

Grace stared at the water jug where Betty's letter had been the day before. But no, not the day before. It had been several days. She had been in bed for days.

"I have to do something." She tried to stand up, but Patrick pushed her gently back into her seat.

"Grace. Tomorrow you have a funeral to go to, and I'll go down to the site and get your pay for last Monday. Let's just get through all that, and then we'll sit down and come up with a plan. Because of you, we are in a better position than we might have been."

"I've been saving as much as I can from what you give me," Mary said.

"And Connie is getting stronger. Also thanks to you. We'll be okay." Patrick patted his twin's hand.

Grace couldn't believe that. She might be out of bed, but she still found it hard to imagine that anything would ever be right and good again.

At seven that evening, Grace was sitting on the stoop of her building when she saw Joe Gagliardi walking down the road toward her, the low sun trailing behind him. Her body tingled with anticipation. She didn't know what he was going to say and worried that he was angry with her. She dreaded his sharp tongue telling her how she had let both their families down, how stupid and reckless she had been, and how much trouble they were in already, having missed their first pay packets.

He picked up his pace when he saw she was there waiting for him, and Grace came down the steps to meet him on the sidewalk.

Without saying a word, he stepped forward and wrapped her up in a hug. She let her body sag against his, the tension released. He wasn't angry with her. At least, not much. It had been almost a week since they had seen each other, and it wasn't until this moment that she realized how much she had missed him.

"Grace, I don't think I have ever been so scared in all my life as when you fell and I thought that I . . . we had lost you."

Grace loved the way her name sounded on his lips, so smooth and effortless.

"And then when you ran off and I had no idea where you were, and then for you to not want to see me . . ." He shook his head. "This has been the worst week of my life."

"I'm sorry. For all of it." She stepped back out of his embrace. It was important that he could see her face; she wanted him to look in her eyes and know that she meant it.

Joe's own eyes were soft. "Will you walk with me?"

Grace took his arm and felt a fizz of excitement. It was a strange feeling after days of feeling nothing at all, like her body was switching itself back on. She had stood next to him all day, every day for five weeks, but this was different. His hair was slicked and shiny, his olive skin clean, and he smelled of cologne and Italian cooking rather than smoke and sweat. Her sensory deprivation of seeing nothing but the same four walls for days had heightened her senses and made her notice everything. He looked smart in his street clothes. The sleeves of his freshly laundered shirt were rolled up to the elbows, and the white undershirt he was wearing, visible beneath three open buttons, sat tight against his skin. There was a sharp crease up the center of his crisply pressed slacks.

"Patrick is worried. He said you are too sad."

"I am, but it's not just the job," Grace admitted. "Oh, believe me, that would be enough, but then there was Connie, and I found out that my friend has . . ." She paused, forcing herself to say the word. ". . . died."

"Yes, Patrick told us this, too. I'm sorry. It's terribly sad."

Grace didn't have anything to add. The emotions were still too thick and sticky in her head and throat and mouth for her to be able to form them into words.

"This city is tough, and I can't imagine how it would be to face it alone, with no family." They walked along the sidewalk. The streets were still busy with cars, streetcars, and the elevated trains that rumbled above them. People hurried past with their heads down or strolled arm in arm, all with their own problems, all with somewhere to be.

"*I* should have been her family," Grace said quietly.

Joe stopped walking mid-step. "That's what you think? You were risking your own life for your family and mine. You worry for everyone all the time and you still think you should have done more? You can't be in so many places, Grace. You can't save everybody. What about you? What about what you want and need? Who is saving you?"

Grace carried on walking, forcing him to keep up. "I don't need saving."

Joe snorted a laugh. "I thought the same. I thought I should always be alone."

"Why?"

"The job I chose. We know when we go to work every day that there is a chance we won't come home. It is a difficult thing to ask of someone, to understand and to accept."

Grace nodded. It made sense, but it didn't seem to stop Frank from having love in his life.

"But I was never truly alone. Everybody needs someone to carry on for. For me it is my family: my brother Bruno, Mamma, my nephews and nieces. Your friend, she didn't have the reason to stay and fight, and so she went. It's hard, but now she has no more loneliness and no more pain."

Grace partly agreed with what he was saying, and she knew he was trying to comfort her, but the thought of Edie having no reason to live was too upsetting. She had fought so hard to make it to a better life; she'd just had no one there to stop her from giving up. Grace had to push the thought away.

"And now?" she asked. "Do you still want to be alone?"

The low light of a lazily setting sun caught the line of his jaw and lit his profile as he turned to face her. They had walked to nowhere in particular, and something tightened in Grace's stomach as she stood gazing up at him on this unfamiliar street.

"No," he said with the tiniest shake of his head. "I think coming to see you every day even when you wouldn't let me in should tell you that."

Grace looked into his brown eyes and felt them unstitch her and sew her back together. Everything that had been before spooled away and dropped to the floor like a shed skin. Left behind, raw but fresh and clean, was the truth of everything that was yet to come. She had known in some unspoken place that he felt this way, and she did too, but to hear him say it was still so unexpected. She had thought he would be angry with her. Not telling her this.

Joe tilted his head toward her, and Grace felt warmth rush through her whole body as he leaned in to kiss her, their soft lips touching in the golden light.

It wasn't her first kiss, but there hadn't been many, and none of them compared to this. It felt so natural to be here with him like this, as if there was never any possibility of it being any other way. His chest was wide and his shoulders broad, muscles honed from endless hours of bucking rivets. His body was the only solid thing in her whole world.

"Joe." The word was small, but it contained everything she had to give, and when he held her tight in his arms, Grace felt as if he was melding all her broken pieces back together. Her heart tripped over itself as she stroked her fingers along his jaw.

The feeling only lasted a second before a wave of guilt crashed through her. It seemed unthinkable that she could even contemplate being happy with Edie gone. The thought of her friend's dreamy eyes and excited clapping when she would have told her about this moment sent a fresh stab of pain through Grace's heart. She hugged Joe close to her. He pulled back to look at her and quirked a questioning eyebrow, but didn't let her go.

"I'm just thinking of when we first met. You hated me."

He shook his head. "I never hated you. From the moment I saw you, I wanted to keep you safe." He squeezed her tighter. "I was angry at Patrick, and all of us, for making you do it. I didn't want you to have to go on the steel, but I could see no other way."

"There was no other way."

"When you walked across that washing line, I thought you were insane. And when you saved me, I knew you were the most incredible woman I would ever meet. I have thought of nothing else since that day."

A grin broke across Grace's face, then. She couldn't help it, and she knew that wherever she was, Edie would understand. Her stomach squirmed and sparked with delight at his words. She reached up around his neck and boldly pulled him to her for another kiss, longer than the first.

"I have to say goodbye to her tomorrow," she whispered when they broke apart.

"She will always be here." Joe placed his hand over her heart. "Do you want me to come with you?"

That he would do that for her brought fresh tears to Grace's eyes, but she shook her head. "Thank you, but I have to do it on my own." She thought of what her mother had said. This was her grief to carry, but it felt a little lighter with her hand in Joe's.

39

MONDAY, JULY 28, 1930

A hammering on the front door made Grace jump as she pulled on her black dress and hat, the feelings of the night before with Joe temporarily squashed by heavier ones. The last time she had worn these clothes had been for her father's funeral, and the memory of that day caught the grief she felt for Edie and wrapped around it like an anchor, threatening to pull her under. It was too hot for the thick material, and the dress no longer fit her properly, pulling tight across the shoulders, but she didn't own any alternatives and hadn't had time to dye any of her more appropriate summer dresses.

She poked her head around her bedroom door and gasped when she saw the huge man standing face-to-face with Patrick. For a second, she thought it was Bergmann, but when she heard the familiar voice, she realized it was the rent collector. Of course. It was Monday morning.

Patrick closed the front door so as not to reveal where they kept their money tin and took out the bills, returning to hand them over. With the rent increase, they were now paying thirty dollars a week.

The big man shook his head as he took the money. "Sorry, there's been a change, we take a month now, not a week."

"You can't do that," Patrick said. "A week at a time, that's how it's always been."

"Not anymore." The man held out his hand.

Patrick turned to Grace, not wanting to disturb Mary and Connie. Grace collected her savings from their hiding place, carefully counting out the extra ninety dollars and passing them to Patrick. Then she went back inside her room and closed the door, feeling sick to her stomach and fighting tears, unable to watch Patrick hand the money over. In just a few days she had lost more than half her entire life savings, and there wasn't enough left for another month. After everything she had done, it still wasn't enough. She hadn't managed to save anyone. There couldn't have been a worse start to the day, and it wasn't going to get any better. She had a funeral to get to.

It seemed wrong that the sun was shining on a day of such sadness, when Grace was so heavy with grief and worry. She was grateful for the first time that she didn't have to go to work. She couldn't have missed this. She hadn't expected many people to be able to make it, but as she arrived at the funeral home, she immediately spotted faces she recognized and her hand went self-consciously to her bare neck. She pulled her hat down a little farther. If anyone mentioned her short hair, she would have to pretend it was a daring statement rather than the result of duplicity and deception. She was pleased that so many people were here, but also reluctant to share her grief with them.

"Oh, Grace, hi," said Mae from Dominic's, her Southern drawl making each of the words longer than they had any right to be. "How are you?" she asked, stepping closer. "Ain't it just so sad?" She dabbed at her dry eyes with a white kerchief, her hands clad in black lace gloves, her mouth pulled into an exaggerated pout.

"Very," said Grace, wanting to get away as quickly as possible from this performance. Mae had barely known Edie, had rarely spoken to her. She bowed her head in the hope she could avoid further conversation and headed for the building. She had her hand on the big brass door handle when another, far more welcome voice called her name.

"Miss Grace." Andre bowed his head and reached out to hold the door open for her.

"Oh, Andre." Grace was tearful just seeing him. Andre fully belonged to her old life, and she had feared she would never see him again.

"It's nice to see you." He grimaced, hearing the words as he spoke them and realizing they weren't quite right. "I just wish it were in better circumstances."

"Me too." Grace squeezed his arm and together they headed inside the building to the chapel of rest, where wooden chairs were set up on either side of a central walkway. It reminded Grace of a wedding, except instead of a happy couple at the front there was a casket. A shiver raced down her back. The whole building reeked of death. It had seeped into the furniture, the floors, and the walls, and the stink of it hooked its talons into her. The coffin was mahogany with brass handles, draped with white roses. The thought that Edie was inside it was unbearable.

"Shall we sit?" Andre asked, offering her his arm. She was grateful for it and nodded, following him.

She heard a rustling of fabric and turned to see Betty striding down the carpet toward them, draped in a black coat, despite it being midsummer and pushing one hundred degrees. She slipped into the row next to them and took off the coat, revealing a black dress underneath and black satin gloves. She wore a black cloche hat with black satin roses sewn on, the only color being the sweep of her signature red lipstick across her mouth and her blond hair slicked close to her head.

"Gracie," she whispered. Grace turned and hugged her friend for a long time. Betty whispered in her ear, "Our poor little bird."

"Just awful." Grace felt tears forming at the corner of her eyes and sat back to compose herself as Betty and Andre greeted each other.

Betty fanned herself with her glove. "It's too damn hot for a funeral. It's too hot, period. I didn't spend time putting all this makeup on for it to just slide down my face without even telling me." Had there ever been a more Betty thing to say? Grace had missed her terribly.

They sat together in companionable silence, lost in their own thoughts and memories as they waited for the other mourners to join them. Out of nowhere, Betty spoke. "I made sure she was buried in that damn fur coat of hers."

Grace couldn't help it, she laughed. So did Betty, and they sat there laughing until they realized that their laughter had become tears, and then they sat and held each other as they cried.

"My makeup is definitely ruined now."

The service was short. Edie had no family, and few people had known her well. Betty stood to thank everyone for coming. She spoke about what a sweet girl Edith Jane McCall had been, and what a travesty it was for the world to lose her at just twenty-three. Grace let her tears fall silently, and in her head she told Edie she was sorry and that she loved her.

As they headed out, she saw a tall Black man slip from the back of the room and was sure it was Vernon. Howard had decided not to come.

Outside, the sun was getting stronger and the heat was seeping into their black clothes. Betty had provided a car for them to travel to the cemetery, and they invited Andre to join them on the solemn journey. As they sat in silence in the back of the car, Andre reached into his pocket.

"I know this is perhaps not the best time, and I mean no disrespect," he said, "but I heard in the club of an audition coming up in a few days for one of the big Broadway shows. I knew I would be seeing you today, so I got the details for you." He handed Grace a napkin with a name, the address of a theater, a date, time, and telephone number scrawled in blurry ink. "You should be on that stage, Miss Grace."

"Thank you," said Grace with a small smile, slipping the napkin into her pocketbook. She didn't think she would ever be auditioning again, but she still put it away safely to make sure she didn't use it by accident and blur the information any further with her tears. Betty watched with interest.

"If something good could come out of us all being here together like this," Andre said, "I think Miss McCall would have liked that." He smiled quietly to himself.

"I agree," said Betty, sitting back and looking out of the window.

Standing at the graveside, Grace's grief for both Edie and her father threatened to overwhelm her. She imagined Edie in a giant dance hall in heaven, with healthy, glowing skin and a smile to light up the world, dancing with a handsome man. Maybe Da would be there too and they would share a dance. A small smile crossed her face, and she stood there lost in her own thoughts, not realizing at first that the service was over and people were leaving.

"I must go," said Andre. "I'm sorry." He gave both Grace and Betty a hug and then disappeared. Grace couldn't help but wonder if she would ever see him again. She hoped so. He had always been a good friend to her.

Back in the car, they traveled once more in silence, with Betty only speaking to give the driver instructions to drop them off at the corner of Central Park West. When they got out, a strange sense of finality settled over Grace as Betty led her into the park. The dappled sunlight through the trees was a comfort as they found a bench.

"It was a lovely service," she said, squeezing Betty's hand. "Thank you. You did her proud."

"I'm just glad her roommate found me," Betty said, her face a grim line as they sat arm in arm, looking out across the grass at all the people playing and strolling with no idea that their friend wasn't alive anymore. "She had nothing and no one. I let her down; I should have done more. I didn't realize things were so bad. Or did I?" She turned her desperately seeking eyes to Grace. "We knew she wasn't doing well, we both did. I can't let myself off the hook and pretend I didn't. And I'm the one who could have helped her more." A single tear fell from her eye and disappeared as if it had never been there at all.

"You did more than anyone," Grace said, her voice thick. "If you let her down, we both did. But she had a lot of pride and she wouldn't let us help. She could have come to us, but she didn't. She kept telling us she was fine, and we were dealing with our own problems, so we decided to believe her." She sighed. "When I went to see her at that damn dance marathon, I tried to get her out of there, I swear to God I did."

"Me too," said Betty sadly. "More than once." This last detail was news to Grace, and it eased her conscience a little. If even Betty couldn't get her out of that place after multiple attempts, then no one could have. Poor Edie. All she had ever wanted was to solve her problems for herself by working hard.

"It's heartbreaking," Grace said. "But you, Betty, you've given her dignity in death. At least she had a proper burial, and she'll have a headstone. She would have really loved that. Just think of how her face would have lit up to know." She took a breath, exhausted by the emotion of it all. "She's not an unclaimed body sent out to Hart Island with all the rest. She knew we loved her." She shuddered at the thought of her dear, sweet friend dumped in a mass grave in a plain pine box. Betty had made sure she had the very best, and would rest in peace in the luxury she'd never had in life.

"Believe me, it took some convincing to get Howard to pay for it, but it's the least I could do. I could have saved her," Betty said, blunt as ever. "But I was too busy, caught up in my own dramas."

"We all were." Grace nodded, feeling the same. She had been risking her life for her family every day, but Edie was like family, too, and all the signs had been there. "You've just got married, Betty—"

"It was a mistake, Gracie," Betty cut in, twisting her body to gaze straight at her friend, gauging her reaction.

Grace swallowed hard, not sure what to say.

"Regretted it the moment it was done," Betty went on with a wry smile. "So my mind was a little distracted by other things, not that it's an excuse. Howard, he's a good man." She twitched her shoulders in a shrug. "Mostly. But the truth is, he deserves a wife who loves him, and I can't do that. Not when I'm in love with someone else." She sucked on a cigarette she had just placed between her perfectly red lips and blew out a cloud of smoke.

"Oh, Betty," said Grace, because what else was there to say.

"It's my own fault, I know that. I'm not looking for anyone's sympathy."

Grace nodded, but rubbed her friend's back anyway. "What are you going to do?"

Betty's bottom lip trembled for just a second before she painted a smile back on. Lily Lawrence was always performing. "Well, to be honest, I was going to put up with it. I'd made my bed, even if the wrong man was in it, but all this, Grace, losing Edie, it's really put things in perspective. I always thought money was the thing that was going to make me happy, the security of it." She shook her head. "But damn Edie was right all along."

"Vernon adores you. There are far worse things than a life of love," Grace said quietly.

"Now *you* sound like Edie."

They both smiled, full of sadness.

"Who's to say he'll even take me back? I married another man, for Christ's sake." Betty sighed heavily. "I guess I have a trip to Harlem to make."

Grace grinned at her.

"Okay, calm down. Anyway—" Betty changed the subject. "It's you we need to worry about right now. I won't make the same mistake with you I did with Edie. Don't think I didn't notice when you took off your hat. There is a story behind that awful hair, and I wanna damn well hear it."

Grace sighed. "I'm not sure you'd believe me even if I told you."

Betty raised an eyebrow and blew cigarette smoke out into the air. "Not much would shock me, kid."

Grace took a deep breath and told her everything. She told her about Connie's sickness, and Patrick's broken arm, and how she had spent five weeks working on the steel impersonating her brother. She explained how she had tightroped across a crane arm hundreds of feet in the air and saved a man's life, even though it had nearly cost her her own, and how it had gotten her thrown off the steel anyway, along with three other men whose families were now going to go hungry. Lastly, she recounted her subsequent frenzied dance audition failure at Mulroney's. She left out the part where she had been unable to get out of bed, too sad to even move.

"Holy smokes, Irish, and I thought I was going through the wringer."

"It's been a rough few weeks," Grace said quietly, taking the cigarette Betty held out to her.

"You really learned how to rivet steel?" Betty shook her head, clearly impressed.

"I did. Edie knew about it. I saw her dancing at one of the bars all the men go to. I took her home with me for dinner and she told me she was fine."

Betty took in the information about Edie but didn't react to it; in fact, she ignored it completely. "You are one tough dame. And the circus hooey too, that high up? You coulda been killed, and they fire you for it? Jeez. These guys make Texas look like boss of the century. Assholes!"

"I lied, Betty." Grace shrugged her shoulders. "We all did. We made them look stupid with me going up in my brother's place and them not even noticing. They were embarrassed, I guess. Besides, it broke every rule and protocol there is."

"They didn't notice because you were good. You did the job, and when it came to it, you were braver than anyone else up there, even though you knew what it would cost you." Betty puckered her lips angrily and shook her head. "It ain't right. You remember on our last day at Dom's, what I said about you sticking up for everyone else but yourself?" She raised a perfect eyebrow so high, Grace thought there was a danger it would disappear off the back of her head. "If it had been me, I woulda left that guy. *Fuck* that guy, Gracie, your family is your family. But you, you can't help yourself, you're just a good person. Not that I'm sure you know it. But Edie did, and it ain't anyone's fault she was too proud to ask for the help she needed, it's just a sad fact. And as for that audition, I have a mind to go and pay them a visit."

Grace smiled, grateful. Betty was nothing if not loyal. "There's no need. And anyway, they were right. How can I argue with what they said?" She pulled up her sleeve, revealing the scars and burns up her arms. "I'm damaged goods."

Betty gasped, cradling Grace's arm in her hands to take a better look. She looked as upset as she had at the funeral home, to see Grace's once beautiful smooth skin ruined and charred.

"Come with me," she said, already up off the bench and heading out of the park gates. "It took months for you to finally go to an audition, and that took guts. I knew you had it in you, Gracie. And now you've found your moxie, there ain't no way in hell I'm going to let you give up. We're going to fix this right up and get you back on that stage. Lord knows you deserve it, kid."

"What do you mean?" Grace asked, having to skip a little to keep up with Betty's purposeful stride.

"Trust me," Betty called over her shoulder. "You ain't done. Not if I have anything to say about it."

Fifteen minutes later, Grace found herself in Saks Fifth Avenue, with a clear view of the Empire State Building. Betty glanced up at the towering structure on their way in and paused, shaking her head in disbelief, before looking back to Grace with a whole new respect. Grabbing her by the arm, she steered her directly to the cosmetics counter.

"Afternoon," she said to the clerk, a young woman of around nineteen with a tiny waist and a flawlessly made-up face. She looked so perfect she could have been a store mannequin.

"Hello, welcome to Saks Fifth Avenue, how may I help you?"

"I have a challenge for you," Betty said, her eyes flashing with mischief. "One for which you will be handsomely rewarded in sales."

"Why of course, ma'am." The girl smiled. "Sounds fun."

"Is there somewhere private we can go?" Betty asked. "And bring these." She gestured to the powder compacts and makeup arranged in pretty formation on the counter.

The girl considered for a second, Betty's obvious moneyed appearance quickly making her decision for her.

"Sure," she said, scooping up armfuls of cosmetics. "Marjorie, cover the counter!" she cried over her shoulder as she led Betty and Grace to a store closet packed with boxes a few feet away.

Grace stood in the tiny room, looking awkwardly at her feet. Betty swept in like she owned the place and sat on a pile of boxes. She reached for Grace's sleeve and pulled it back, revealing her forearm. To her credit, the shop girl didn't even flinch.

"Can you cover these marks?" Betty asked.

"Of course," said the girl. "These aren't even that bad. I once had a lady who had been in a house fire, terrible mess her face was. When I'd finished, you would hardly even have known." She started setting up a makeshift workspace on the cardboard boxes.

Betty beamed and caught Grace's eye. "I like this girl."

Grace watched in mute amazement as the shop girl mixed creams and powders, smoothing them onto her arm, her bottom lip trapped between her teeth in concentration. Betty paid close attention, picking up each product as it was used and examining it. Within ten minutes, Grace's arm looked as smooth and unblemished as it had six weeks ago. A lump settled itself in the back of her throat as she twisted it this way and that, her trauma erased by a powder puff. She'd never thought she would see her arms look good again.

"This is excellent work," Betty said, examining the arm.

"Thank you."

Grace caught the girl's eye. She didn't have the composure to say anything.

"It's nothing," the girl said with a shrug.

"We'll take everything you used. In fact, two of everything." Betty stood decisively.

"Why of course," said the shop girl, stacking the products into neat piles to take back to the counter.

"Betty, no," Grace said as they stood at the cash register. "It's too much." A stack of pots and compacts were being rung up, with each one costing at least a dollar fifty.

"I'll decide that, thank you, Gracie." Betty paid with a handful of folded notes, and in return was handed a pretty paper bag, each product wrapped in dainty tissue paper sprayed with lavender. She handed the bag to Grace and thanked the assistant, telling her that she would be back to buy from her again soon.

"Betty," Grace hissed. "You can't afford this."

Betty stopped and spun on her heel, dipping her head close to Grace's, her eyes sparkling. "I may not be a rich man's wife for much longer," she whispered, "but I am right now, and how I spend my allowance is up to me, so let's make the most of it. What else?" she asked out loud, but it was clear she was talking only to herself. She ran her eyes over Grace.

"Hand it over."

"What?"

"The audition details Andre gave you."

"Oh, but—"

"But nothing, Grace, give me the napkin. I need to know what I'm working with. Opportunities like this can't be wasted."

Reluctantly Grace found the napkin and handed it over. She hadn't even read the details properly herself. Betty stood in the middle of the shop floor and studied the slightly smudged writing.

"Excuse me," said a nasal voice, clearly annoyed.

"There's room to go around," Betty replied without even taking her eyes off the napkin. The voice tutted and was roundly ignored.

"This is soon," Betty said. "On Thursday, in fact. And it looks like it'll be a hell of a show."

"Is it?" Grace craned her neck to look. Betty folded the napkin and handed it back to her.

"Your hair."

Grace's hand went self-consciously to the back of her neck again, but a devilish smile was working its way across Betty's face.

"What is that look for?"

"We can't do anything with your hair, but I still have my wig from Dominic's. It's yours. Who the hell would ever have thought that Texas and his stupid rules would actually come in useful?"

Grace turned the idea over in her head. Wearing a wig to hide her short cut and with makeup covering her arms, she just might look almost like herself again. The thought brought a sheen of moisture to her eyes.

"Really?" she whispered.

"A'course! Now let's get you a new audition outfit and you'll be ready to take on the goddam world, Grace O'Connell."

"I really will."

"That's my girl." Betty dragged Grace to the fashion department. "Now, which one of these is the most Broadway? We need to find something with plenty of razzle-dazzle that Edie would have approved of."

Smiling, Grace let her hand trail through all the satin and silk, so far away from paint cans, tongs, and the clang of hot metal.

That night, Grace could not find sleep no matter how hard she tried to tempt it to her. She tossed and turned in fresh sheets, her mind whirling with too many thoughts and worries. She thought about how soon the money would run out, of rivets flying through the air toward her, of how it had felt in that moment she was falling and was sure she would die, and how similar it felt to the moment Joe had kissed her. She thought about whether she should have saved Mick or left him, and of all the people now affected by the choice she'd made. She thought of Frank holding baby Mateo as his other children laughed and chattered, climbing over him like monkeys. She thought of Mamma Gagliardi and of sweet Bruno with his huge brown eyes and kind heart. His big eyes made her think of Edie and her father and Lukasz Kowalski, and her cheeks became wet with tears.

She thought of her own mother and of Connie, of Betty, and of how hard she had tried to make things right for everyone, but had managed to fail them all. She rolled over once more in her tangled sheet and froze. There was a body on the floor. She shouldn't have been able to make out anything in the darkness, but there was a faint glow coming through the window and she knew without question who it was. Lying there in the white nightshirt she had worn the only time she had ever been in this room was Edie.

Grace didn't know if she was dreaming, hallucinating, or had truly been visited by a ghost; the only thing she knew was that she wasn't afraid. How could she be scared? She was getting to see Edie again, and her beloved friend was smiling. Grace didn't dare move or even blink in case she went away. And then, from the floor, Edie reached up. With a sense of calm, Grace held out her own hand, and a peace washed over her as she felt Edie's cool fingers touch her own.

They held hands in silence for a few seconds before the version of Edie lying there in the dark opened her mouth and whispered, "It's all going to be okay now."

Grace remembered nothing else; she was already sound asleep.

40

TUESDAY, JULY 29, 1930

The next morning, Grace woke feeling calmer than she had in weeks. There was no reason for it; all her problems were still exactly where she had left them the night before, but she remembered vividly her visit from Edie and felt comforted by it in a way she could not explain.

She dressed and wrapped her hair in a headscarf before stepping out to use the telephone in the hallway, the scrap of napkin in her hand as she called and booked herself in for the audition. It was two days away, and she could do nothing now except wait. As she finished her call, she looked out of the grimy window and saw a suited man with a hat in his hand and an unmistakable mustache approaching their stoop. She was sprinting back to their apartment before she even realized what she was doing.

As she burst in, Patrick was sitting with the newspaper open in front of him and a faraway look in his eyes that suggested he wasn't really reading it. Having two working arms again was a definite bonus, but he still had to try and find a job, and they were as rare as hen's teeth. The situations vacant section of the newspaper was empty. Mary was at the table, counting out small piles of bills with her crooked fingers, allocating the money to their various expenses.

"Mr. Gilligan is here!"

"What?" Patrick folded the newspaper and stood, brushing his hand through his hair to neaten himself up. "Are you sure?"

Mary swept the money back into the metal tin she kept it in and put it back on the shelf.

Grace was sure, and she could see no other reason for him to be in this neighborhood or just walking by. She looked at the clock. It was still early, but he should definitely be at work. Her earlier calm disappeared as her insides coiled tightly with the thought that she was in trouble. Perhaps he was here to fine her for lying, or to have her arrested.

There was a knock at the door and her knees went weak. She could see that Patrick felt the same way, but he was hiding it better as he stepped forward and opened the door.

"Mr. Gilligan." The shock in his voice was only slightly less than it would have been if Grace hadn't warned him of their visitor. "What can I do for you?"

"May I come in?"

Mary's eyes darted desperately around the room, taking in everything the foreman would see in the small space. There was the sagging armchair, the chipped crockery, the tiny table, the crack in the wall, and the tap that bounced unsteadily against its fixings.

"Of course," Patrick said, stepping aside. Joseph Gilligan's eyes made a fleeting tour of the room, his face expressionless. "This is my mother, Mary, and my sister, Grace."

"Yes, I believe we've met," Gilligan said to Grace before turning to Mary. He shook her hand, wrapping it in both of his own. "Hello, Mrs. O'Connell, sorry for barging in like this, particularly so early, but I'm due on-site as it is."

"Not at all," Mary said. "You're very welcome. Take a seat—can I get you a drink?"

"Very kind of you, but I can't stay long." He turned his attention back to Patrick. "How is your arm?"

"Cast came off last Friday, sir, good as new." Patrick held out his arm and flexed his fingers.

Mr. Gilligan nodded, his eyes trailing along the floor before they came back up to meet Patrick's again. "In that case, I want to see you back at work tomorrow. You can tell your boys, all of you, back on the steel at eight sharp."

Mary couldn't hold in her gasp of relief as she slumped back down into her chair.

"Thank you, sir," said Patrick, not sure of what else to say.

"Turns out good ironworkers are hard to find. And my daughter can be very persuasive," Gilligan added, with a twitch of his mustache. "Told me all about your . . ." He paused. "Family situation. I didn't realize the two of you had been spending so much time together. Or any, in fact. Are there any other secrets? Anything else you ought to be telling me?"

"No, sir, I swear to God. I'm very sorry for what we did, but I just couldn't afford to lose my job." Patrick swallowed, not sure if he should go on. "If Grace hadn't saved that man, I would have been back on the steel and no one would ever have known."

"Hmm." Gilligan made a noise in the back of his throat. "You nearly got away with it. But I'm not sure that is something to be proud of."

"No, sir, that's not what I meant. I just mean that Grace . . . she put that man's life before her own, even knowing what it would do to her own family. And others."

"You don't need to convince me, O'Connell, I'm here, aren't I? I've heard nothing else from Florence for days."

Patrick bit his lip, still unused to the fact that it was the women in his life who seemed to be in control of events these days.

"And you," Gilligan turned his attention to Grace, studying her as if seeing her for the first time. "You might be the bravest, most stupid person I have ever come across."

Grace said nothing as he looked from her to Patrick and back again. "You are mighty alike. But it takes a lot more than that to do what you did. Your work was as good as any man's, and your bravery even greater. You saved a life and that can't be ignored. *That* is why I'm giving your brother his job back."

She nodded her thanks. She didn't have any words in her throat to offer him.

"I know a thing or two about strong-willed women. I married one and I'm raising two others." Grace thought she could see the traces of a small smile under his mustache. "So thank you. And know from me that you catch rivets as well as anyone."

A small laugh escaped from her. "Thank you, sir. I sure do."

"And as for my strong-willed daughter—" His attention was back with Patrick. "She tells me she intends to marry you, O'Connell."

Grace and Mary shot each other a look to confirm that this was news to both of them.

"Yes, but not yet, sir. I was going to speak to you about that and ask your permission, of course, but I thought I had lost my job and was waiting for better days, when I had my prospects in order. I wasn't hiding anything from you, I swear."

Joseph Gilligan chuckled a little. "I think we both know the only permission that matters is Florence's. I could no more stop her doing what she wanted than I could stop the Sixth Avenue El." He paused. "I think she could do far worse than marry into a good, strong Irish family. I have seen enough to know you are fine people."

Everyone in the room could sense the "but" coming.

"But I can't give you my blessing."

Patrick's head dropped.

"I have seen what this life has done to my wife, and I have visited too many desperate widows with children to look after. I don't want her to marry a man who works the steel. It's honest and honorable work, but I don't want that life of constant fear, danger, and worry for my daughter."

"Neither do I, sir." Grace had never heard Patrick so sincere. "I feel the same way. Breaking my arm was a wake-up call, and I've been studying hard every day. I'm going to be an accountant. I will keep working construction until I've qualified and can find a position, and that might take some time, but I have a plan, sir, to get myself off the steel. I will have a job in an office where there is no danger except a paper cut from time to time and I know I will come home every day. I want Florence to marry a man who has all his fingers and his hearing."

Grace shot her mother another look to confirm that once again she hadn't known any of this. So that was where Patrick went every day. It seemed her brother's life was a mystery to her. Instead of lamenting his broken arm or going off womanizing, he had been busy making plans for the future.

Gilligan gazed intently at Patrick before giving a curt nod and placing his hat back on his head. "In that case, come and see me one lunchtime and we will see what we can do about those studies. You're a sensible man." With that, he was done and making to leave. "I must go. Mrs. O'Connell, a pleasure to meet you. You must be very proud of your children."

"Yes, sir," Mary said quietly.

"Grace." Gilligan tipped his hat to her as he left.

Patrick closed the door behind him and rested his forehead on it, all the breath in his lungs racing out in relief. "I got my job back," he said in disbelief, as if they hadn't all been in the room. Mary gave him a hug, her eyes watery, before she released him and started to get ready to go out.

"Where are you going?" Patrick asked.

"Shopping," Mary said, reaching for the metal tin and removing a few dollar bills. "If you're going to be marrying her, you need to invite that girl of yours around for dinner. First she helps with Connie, and then she gets you your job back. She's an angel, and tonight she will sit at my table and let me feed her. It's the very least I can do." She had her shoes on, her shopping bag on her arm, and was at the door before there was even a chance for any protest. "I'll let you tell Connie the good news when she wakes up."

"So, Ma's happy," Grace said with a lilting smile once Mary had left.

"It was you as much as Florence that got us here."

"I guess we did it," Grace conceded. "One way or another, we did what we set out to do. Your arm is healed, and you go back to work tomorrow."

Patrick looked like he was struggling for words, so Grace didn't give him the chance to say any. "And you're in love," she added, her eyebrows shooting up her forehead.

"I am." His response was solemn, yet Grace could see that his love for Florence was fierce as flames. She recognized the look.

"I know the feeling."

"You do?" Patrick's own eyebrows shot up to match hers, and Grace smiled. They really did have the same face.

"I've met someone, yes," she said, suddenly coy. "You know him."

"I do?" His face creased in concentration, and then smoothed as he seemed to reach a conclusion. "No, wait, it can't be. It is, isn't it?"

"Joe," Grace said simply, the word like honey on her tongue.

Patrick barked out a laugh and put his hand over his mouth, eyes sparkling. "Of course. Well, he's a good man." He pulled his sister into a rare hug. "I'm happy for you." He started to laugh, and Grace pushed him away.

"What's funny?"

"You better start learning how to make pasta, Grace O'Connell. You're going to be an Italian!"

Grace smiled to herself, content enough with the person she was becoming. Dancer, daughter, sister, riveter. "I think I'll just be Grace, thanks."

41

WEDNESDAY, JULY 30, 1930

Patrick was nervous as he approached the elevator to head up onto the Empire State Building for the first time in more than six weeks. The heat of the day was already oppressive, and his newly healed arm ached. He had spent a lot of time over the last twenty-four hours putting his forearms side by side to compare them; one pale and one tanned, one looking decidedly thinner and weaker than its mate. He gazed up into the cloudless blue sky and swallowed hard. The building had doubled in size since he had last been on it; they would be working on the fiftieth floor, five hundred feet in the air.

"Patrick!" The Gagliardis were coming out of the office, holding their ID discs. "Never thought I would see this again!" Frank joked, holding up his disc like a shiny new dollar before kissing it and dropping it into a pocket.

"And you shouldn't have," said a man waiting for the elevator, shooting all of them a dirty look. Another man grunted in agreement.

"You should never set foot on steel again after what you did," a third said, spitting on the dirt in front of him.

Patrick said nothing. There was nothing he could say. The men were going to have an opinion on what had happened, and many of them would feel this way. He and his friends would have to watch their backs for a while until things settled down and another scandal or drama took people's attention.

The elevator cage arrived and the door screeched open. "It's not right," a man mumbled as they all got in. Patrick and the Italians stood in uneasy silence.

When they reached the fiftieth floor, Patrick felt dizzy, but he couldn't afford to show it. He was getting the smallest taste of what his twin sister's life had been like for the last few weeks, and he was just out of practice, not a total novice.

"O'Connell!" a voice yelled. "Is that you? Or have you sent a woman in your place?"

"It's me all right," Patrick said, his face burning with shame and embarrassment.

"Well, that's what *she* said, so how can we know? I think you oughta prove it." The men all laughed and jeered.

"Back off!" Frank shouted. "Just worry about your own jobs and get to work."

"Excuse me if we don't listen to *you*, Gagliardi. You're a liar."

Frank balled his hands into fists and clenched his jaw.

"Francesco, come," said Joe, pulling on his brother's arm. "We have work to do."

Frank turned away and they headed to the gang box. Patrick reached in and pulled out the black catching cone. He looked at it, confusion on his face.

"Grace used it," Frank said in a low voice. "But your can is still here." He rummaged through their tools and pulled out the battered paint can. Patrick felt out of his depth as he realized these men had become used to working with someone else. He was a cuckoo in the nest; he no longer fitted smoothly into his own life.

As he stepped off a headache ball and onto the beam, he felt his knees go weak. He had never been so high, and the paint can felt alien and awkward in his hand. He flexed his fingers, which hadn't gripped anything for a while, and tapped the tongs in his other hand nervously against the beam.

"It's good to have you back, Patrick," Frank said with a grin before starting up the riveting gun. Patrick touched his cap with the tongs and set his body. There seemed so much less room on the beam next to Joe than he remembered. He pulled his elbows into his sides and turned to signal Seamus, who sent the first rivet of the day up toward him in a looping arc. Patrick's nerves got the better of him, his hand shook, and he missed the rivet entirely. Joe had to duck out of its way.

"It's okay," yelled Frank. "Just a little out of practice." He signaled a thumbs-up to Patrick to tell him it was nothing to worry about. Patrick turned his head to see a group of men laughing at him.

"We can tell which O'Connell has the skill!"

The words barely made it to Patrick over the noise on the site, but he heard, and his arm ached. He took a deep breath, ready to try again.

"You aren't as good as your sister!" Bergmann's huge voice boomed, everyone hearing this time. Patrick gritted his teeth.

"Don't worry, Patrick," said Joe with an easy smile and a shrug. "Not many are."

His comment broke the tension, and the three of them laughed up on their tiny corner of the metal frame. Patrick nodded and gestured to his cousin for the next rivet. Seamus sent up a perfect delivery, and the rivet made a clean ping as it settled into the bottom of Patrick's can. *Off we go.* Relieved that he could still do the job, he felt his shoulders relax. He took the next two cleanly, too, and when he glanced across the beams, he saw Joseph Gilligan leaning against a column, watching him. They gave each other a nod.

42

"Betty's here," Grace said in response to an insistent knocking at the door. She jumped up and answered, her friend sweeping into the room with an armful of bags. Connie gasped at the sight of her, and Mary self-consciously raised her hand to her hair.

"Hello, O'Connells," Betty said, hugging them all and offering kisses. There was a particularly loud bang from above, and she looked up from under her long eyelashes at the ceiling. "And hello to you up there, too!" she called, making Connie laugh. "It's lovely to be here. Thank you for inviting me to your home, Mrs. O'Connell."

"Well, it's not much," Mary said, eyeing Betty's expensive clothes and her white shoes full of intricate cutouts that made them look like they were made of lace. They must have cost a fortune. "But you're very welcome."

"Nonsense." Betty waved her hand. "This place is great. It's a real home."

"Can I get you something?"

"We'll take two root beers," Grace answered for her friend. "And I'll get them, Ma, don't worry." She moved to the cupboard and removed the bottles, unashamed of how little else was in there. She had bought the drinks especially for the occasion on her way home the day before. "Does anyone else want one?"

Mary shook her head.

"Yes please!" said Connie, as Grace had known she would, and she reached for a third.

"Drink it slowly, please," she said, handing it to her sister. "You're still recovering. We're just going to head to my room. We're doing a practice run for tomorrow. Con, we'll need your help later, if that's okay? We want to get everything done before Patrick gets home from work."

"Fine." Connie tried and failed to hide her disappointment that she wasn't invited to the first part of the transformation.

"You can be in charge of lipstick and jewels, Miss Connie," Betty said with a wink. "The most important part."

Connie grinned back and nodded, nursing her root beer bottle to her chest.

In the bedroom, Betty dropped her bags onto the narrow bed.

"Sorry, it's not very big," Grace said as she tucked herself into the corner of the room to make space for her friend.

"It's fine. The light isn't great, but that's okay for now." Betty rustled in her bags, pulling out her wig from Dominic's and a beautiful emerald-green leotard with elbow-length sleeves and matching skirt. Grace had never seen it before, never seen anything like it for that matter, unless it was on a ballerina. It definitely wasn't what they had bought at the store.

"I was thinking, if they want you to dance, you have to look like a dancer. This getup will make you look like you were born in ballet slippers. The sleeves will help with the shoulder issue. Plus, green is your color. Luck of the Irish, Irish."

Grace was speechless as she took the silky material from Betty's hands.

"Can I really wear this?" she asked in a hushed voice.

"Well, sure," Betty answered. "You'd better. It cost me half a week's allowance. I asked around. This is just like what they audition for the big shows in, but they normally wear black, maybe pink. I betcha no one else will be wearing green. You'll stand out." She shot Grace a look. "In a good way."

Grace nodded slowly, then raised her face to her friend to give her a huge smile. "I love it."

"Of course you do. Now hurry up and try it on, I really want to use these products on those arms of yours."

When Grace left her room thirty minutes later, she was in her new audition outfit. The parts of her arms not covered by sleeves were smooth and blemish-free, and Betty's wig gave her untold confidence. It was a thrill to have hair again, even if it wasn't as shiny or lustrous as her own. Her makeup was applied perfectly. The only thing left undressed was her lips. She held out a lipstick to Connie, then knelt on the floor in front of her, face upturned.

"Gracie," said Connie excitedly, "you look like you again." Grace smiled and then pouted her lips for her sister to apply the color with studied concentration.

When Connie had finished, Grace stood in the center of the room, looking round at the three most important women in her life.

"Will I do? How do I look, Ma?"

"Beautiful," Mary said simply.

"Right, well, my work here is done," Betty said. "I need to run some errands."

"You're leaving already?" Connie asked. "You won't stay for tea?"

"Another time, sweetheart." Betty collected her belongings together. "Oh, one last thing. I have something for you."

"Me?" Connie asked, shocked.

"Yes, you. I heard I just missed your birthday. I hope it fits." Betty reached into one of her bags and pulled out a rectangle wrapped in tissue paper.

Connie took the parcel and laid it on the table to unwrap it. Inside, she found a black beret and a beautiful purple silk dress. It was knee-length with long sleeves, trimmed with a black collar, cuffs, and buttons.

"Is this really for me?"

"Well, it won't fit me, doll."

Connie jumped up and lunged at Betty, grabbing her in a hug.

"Be careful!" Mary warned. "You'll knock her down!"

"It's fine, Mrs. O'C." Betty smiled. "Takes more than a ten-year-old to knock me over."

"Eleven," whispered Connie.

"Them too."

"Betty, thank you so much," Grace said, still in her green splendor, her eyes sparkling. "You really are the best."

"Sometimes I am," Betty agreed. "And now I must go. If this practice run is anything to go by, you're going to knock them dead tomorrow. Call me straight after, although I already know you're going to do great." She hugged her friend and reached for the door.

"Oh my, there are children everywhere," she said, looking out onto a landing crawling with Donohues. "What a hoot! Goodbye, Connie, Mrs. O'Connell," and with that, she was out the door, and Grace heard her say, "Who wants to earn a nickel and carry my bags?"

"Well, she really is something," said Mary, leaning back in her chair, exhausted by the encounter. A slow smile was spreading across her face. "Good for her."

43

THURSDAY, JULY 31, 1930

As it turned out, the theater for the audition was only ten blocks from where Grace lived. If she managed to get a part in this show, she would save money on travel. She could walk there and back most days. These were the thoughts filling her mind and keeping her occupied as she waited for her turn backstage. The area was filled with girls, a few looking nervous, but most with levels of confidence Grace could only aspire to, despite all the things she had been through and achieved over the last few weeks. She had expected to be auditioned in a group, as she had been for Dominic's and at Mulroney's, with everyone dancing together and the best dancers being picked to stay, but it seemed here the auditions were individual only.

Girls in woolen tights and leotards were called by name, one by one, to go out onto the stage. Everyone left via the other side so no one waiting was given any clue what to expect. The nerves were rising in Grace as she sat in a corner keeping her breathing calm and trying to channel Betty's attitude. She had worked out that they were auditioning alphabetically, so she had a while to wait.

"Grace O'Connell?" called a small, sparrowlike woman in a brown dress.

"Yes?" Grace replied in surprise. Half the heads in the room turned to look at her, taking in her face and her outfit. Thank goodness Betty had gotten her the green outfit. Anything else and she would have looked out of place.

"You're next," said the woman. "Get ready, please."

Grace stood and started to warm up. She had no idea why she was being called now; she'd thought she would be waiting for hours. She tried to remember the name of the last girl as she focused on the whitewashed wall in front of her, stretching her leg against it, keeping her breaths long and slow. Beulah Collins. That had been the name. They must have put Grace under *C* rather than *O*. That was why she was being called so early. Still, she didn't mind.

"Action is the enemy of fear, eh, Da?" she mumbled under her breath. She would rather be moving than sitting, waiting, and thinking.

"Miss O'Connell, they will see you now."

Grace nodded her thanks and glanced down at her arms to check that the makeup she had applied was still there. Then she headed up the steps to the stage, where the lights were blinding.

"Grace O'Connell?" a male voice was asking, brisk and all business, before Grace had even reached the center of the stage.

"Yes."

"Age?"

"Twenty-one."

"Previous dance experience?"

"I danced at Dominic's on Forty-Second Street before it closed." Realizing that didn't sound particularly impressive, she added, "And I trained with Russian ballerina Irina Ivanova." She didn't think her circus skills or the fact that she could catch hot rivets from a distance of seventy-five feet was going to help her with this particular audition, so she decided to leave those out.

"You're a ballerina?"

"I'm a dancer," Grace answered. "If you can dance it, I can do it."

It wasn't until this point that she was in a position to see who she was talking to. In the second row, she could just make out two men. One was large, tall and broad, wearing a white shirt and light-colored trousers held up with brown suspenders. He had a cigarette in his hand and the smoke curled up into the air. His nose was wide and his white hair swept across his head. The other man was birdlike and thin. Grace absently wondered if the sparrow woman was his wife, or maybe his sister. He was wearing a dark suit and a bow tie. His black hair was slicked down across his head, and he held round spectacles in his hand but didn't put them on.

"Speak these lines, please." The bird man came forward and handed Grace a sheet of thin paper with some typewritten words on it. She felt panic surge in her throat. She was a dancer; she had come here to dance, not speak.

"Whenever you're ready," the large man said, putting his cigarette between his lips and leaning back, one leg across the other, balancing a clipboard on his knee.

Grace worried whether all the time she had spent imitating Patrick and smoking cigarettes had damaged her voice, but it was too late now. She took a deep breath, wiped all the Irish from her accent, and started speaking.

"Great." The bow-tie man stopped her after a few sentences. "Clear as a bell. Now sing it."

Grace was no singer, not really. Not like Betty, who loved to sing. The paper started to shake in her clammy hands. There was no musical accompaniment, no instruction about how to sing, or in what key, nothing. She looked down at the two men and then around the stage, checking she hadn't missed a piano or something obvious.

"Just sing it, however you want," cigarette man told her, waving a hand at her to tell her to start.

Grace thought of how scared she had been the first time she'd stood on the steel beams, all that way above the ground, and how she'd felt when Joe had nearly disappeared over the side of the building. She thought of how terrifying it had been when Connie was lying in bed slick with fever, and of those free-falling seconds when she had slipped from the loop and been surer than sure that she was about to die. Singing was nothing to be scared of, and she was in no doubt that the two men in the seats in front of her had never been through half the things she had. She started to sing.

"Yep, enough, okay." Bow Tie held up a hand to stop her. "Thank you." The two men looked at each other.

"And lastly, the dance." The one with the clipboard scribbled something, not even looking up. "You have prepared something to show us, I assume? Where is your music?"

"Oh, I, uh, thought you would ask me to do something." Grace squinted against the lights, feeling the most stupid she had ever felt in her life. When she had telephoned to book her audition, no one had told her to bring her own music.

"You don't have a routine? No music?" The bow-tie man was staring at her, an incredulous look on his face.

"I'm sorry." She felt her voice croak and break. "I didn't know. I've never been to an audition like this before. Normally they teach us a routine and then watch us perform it. I thought I would—"

"Miss—"

"I can do anything," Grace cut in, confidence rising in her chest. "You pick the music, I can dance to it. You pick the dance you want to see, I can do it."

"This is most unusual," Bow Tie said. "But I'm intrigued." He got up and headed to the phonograph. Some music Grace had never heard before started up, and he nodded at her to begin.

She cleared her mind and heard nothing but the music. She picked up the beat and started to move to it in a way that felt effortless and natural, using different steps and skills to show how well she could dance. She felt the meaning of the lyric deep inside and told the story of it with her body. One of the men called for her to stop, but she didn't hear, so much was she loving just dancing again on a stage. The music cut out and she stuttered to a stop.

"Okay, thank you," the large man said, raising his voice a little. He looked down and wrote something in his notes. Grace knew he was dismissing her; she was done. Except she wasn't done. The music had inspired her and she knew instinctively how the piece was going to end, so she started to dance again in the silence, her body moving only to the beat in her head. She suddenly felt sure that this was music from the show, and she just had to be the one to dance to it every night. The two men watched, at first puzzled and then with interest, before becoming annoyed.

"Enough, Miss O'Connell!" the man in the suit called out, but Grace was nearly finished, so she completed her last few steps before stopping in the center of the stage and looking straight at him, defiantly. *Now* it was enough.

"You can go now." The man with the clipboard finished his cigarette, dropped the butt on the floor and stomped it, offering nothing else.

"Wait." A female voice spoke from farther back in the theater. Grace couldn't see against the lights until a woman who had obviously been sitting back there walked down the aisle to the front of the stage. She had dark hair piled up on top of her head and looked no older than Grace, but she was clearly important, and the two men waited for her to speak.

"I like her," the woman said, hands on her hips, looking up at the stage. "She's got something."

"Miss Merman," one of the men started, but she wasn't listening. Grace had heard that name before. Ethel Merman. This woman had been singing in Brooklyn, and there was a big buzz about her and her voice. If Grace hadn't been busy being Patrick for the last few weeks, she would have gone to see her.

"What's your name?"

"Grace. Grace O'Connell."

The woman nodded to herself. "Do you want to be in this show with me, Grace O'Connell?"

"Yes, ma'am, I sure do." Grace looked at her, and something passed between them.

"Well, okay then," Miss Merman said, and without even a glance at the men, she walked back up the aisle to take her seat in the dark again.

Both men looked angry; the one with the clipboard was lighting another cigarette, his face red. The other put a swift end to the audition.

"You may go now. We'll be in touch shortly with our decision."

"Thank you," Grace managed to squeeze out through a throat that felt like it was swelling shut, choking her of all air.

She left the stage on the opposite side to the waiting girls. As if by magic, her belongings were there. She grabbed them, pulling a sweater and a skirt on over her leotard, before bursting out into the sunshine of the street. She started to run, and nearly got run over by a man on a bicycle. She gasped and ducked out of the way, calling an apology after him. She had to be careful. What a dreadful shame it would be if she was hurt or killed when everything was so close to finally working out. She shouldn't get carried away; they hadn't said anything yet, no decision had been made. Except it had, she knew it had. Despite the fact that there would be better auditions that day, prettier and better-prepared girls the two men preferred, it didn't matter. This time it was her the light was shining on. She had been seen and understood. Ethel Merman had told her with one look, woman to woman. She was going to be in that show.

44

FRIDAY, SEPTEMBER 19, 1930

"Come on," Joe hissed, waving Grace toward him. She made one final check that her hair was tucked up inside her cap and hurried across to him, shoving her hands deep into the pockets of the overalls she'd never thought she would wear again.

"Are you sure this is—" she whispered, but Joe put his hand over her mouth and pulled her into the empty elevator. Everyone else was already up top. He removed his hand and darted his head forward to kiss her quickly on the lips.

"Joe!"

"What are they gonna do? Fire me? The job's already done."

They stood in silence as they went up through the finished floors. Getting out, Grace felt a small pinch on her arm, and Joe tilted his head to tell her to follow him. They were getting into another elevator. This one was far smaller and more rickety than the first, which had been taken straight from the old Waldorf Astoria hotel that had been on the site previously. Grace had no idea where this one came from, but it made her palms sweat as they went up, ever higher. She watched the ground get farther and farther away, her insides wriggling with a mixture of nerves and excitement. Even after this one, there was still a way to go. She and Joe stepped onto a crane jib to be lifted yet higher.

When they finally arrived, Grace joined the back of a large group of men, instantly blending in. She caught the eye of her twin, who grinned back at her and reached for her hand, giving it a quick squeeze. Seeing each other up on the steel was strange for both of them. Grace had never been even half as high. She wouldn't have been able to work at this height. The wind whipped around them like they were eggs in a bowl.

At the front of the crowd, a guy in grubby white shirtsleeves rolled up to his biceps was leaning his full weight on a cable, inching out and up. Another, in dark coveralls, sat a few feet above him. After a few words and a lot more jeers, they unfurled the flag and tethered it. A huge cheer went up as the Stars and Stripes snapped and rippled in the wind. The steel was complete. The other teams would continue to work for months yet, completing the rest of the building, but the skeleton was there. The only thing left to add was the mast, where dirigibles would dock. Grace looked up and imagined fancy people like Howard arriving by airship. Men in their banker-gray suits and fedoras helping their rich wives with headbands trimmed with feathers and jewels onto staircases one thousand feet in the air.

"Photograph!" The word made its way through the crowd in mumbles. Grace started to move back, but Joe and Patrick pulled her forward into the group, where she stood smiling with all the others who had helped to complete this miraculous building. After the photograph, a couple of people did a double take as they realized there were two Patrick O'Connells.

"Time to go," Grace murmured, joining the crowd waiting to get down off the steel, as Joe was swept up into a bigger group of Italians and Mohawks, who were congratulating each other on their achievements.

"Excuse me!" Grace could sense the call was for her, but she tried to ignore it and wriggled deeper into the crowd. "Excuse me!" The caller was insistent, and she felt a hand grab her arm and spin her around. She found herself looking at a man she didn't recognize. She knew this had been a terrible idea. Joe had convinced her she had every right to be at the topping-out ceremony, and that there would be so many people there, no one would even notice. It had been foolish of her to believe they could get away with it, madness for her to have ever come back up here.

She looked at the man. "I'm sorry, I'm going now, I swear."

The man looked confused. "No, miss, I'm glad you're here."

"Oh?" Grace was shocked.

"The man you saved? Mick?"

"Yes." Grace took a step closer. "You know him? How is he? Is he okay? Is he here?" She started to look around for him.

"No, he's not here." The man pressed his lips together in a sad grimace. "He's my brother, miss. And I just wanted to thank you for what you did. I never got a chance before. He's not been on the steel since, and I dare say he never will, but he's alive and his kids still have a father, and that's down to you."

Grace swallowed hard. "Well, thank you. I'm just glad he's okay."

The man took her by the hand and pulled her out of the crowd. "There's no need to rush away. You deserve to take a look around. No one will bother you, I'll make sure of it."

Grace smiled her thanks and squeezed his hand, stepping around him and looking for Joe. He was sitting on the edge of a beam with Frank, looking out across the city with their arms around each other. They had managed to find work on a construction project in Brooklyn. It was only a ten-story building, nothing like this one, but she was secretly glad about that. She had taken to heart the conversation she'd heard between her brother and Mr. Gilligan about how hard it was to have loved ones up here, and she hoped that one day Joe would find his way down off the steel. It didn't look to be happening soon, though. The Gagliardis were already trying to get jobs on the clearance of the Rockefeller site, and that project was slated to last four years. Patrick was still planning to stick with them for now, but he was working hard on his plans to be an accountant someday.

"Not a bad view." Her twin was suddenly at her shoulder. This side of the building gave them a perfect view of Central Park, an impossibly large rectangle of green in the middle of the city. From here you could see it was so much bigger than most people imagined when walking around inside it. The grass and trees seemed to stretch for endless miles, the sunlight catching on the lake. The nearest buildings, in their brick and limestone, were tiny in comparison to where the two of them stood, not even half as tall.

They moved away from the crowd to a corner of the building that was still nothing but bare beams. The horizon was endless before them; Grace was certain they could near enough see the whole world.

"Can hardly believe we're here," Patrick said. "After everything it took."

Grace knew he was talking about the building, but she was thinking about the bigger picture. She looked out across the city and leaned her head against a steel column.

"Da would be proud," Patrick said, and she turned toward him.

"How did you know that's who I was thinking about?"

"I didn't. But I was thinking about him too."

"He'd be proud of both of us." She nodded. She knew it was true. "All that time when I was at Dominic's," she went on, "do you know the reason I always held back from auditioning for the big shows?"

Patrick shook his head, the wind ruffling his collar.

Grace swallowed hard. She had never told anyone this. "I couldn't bear the thought of getting a part, reaching that dream, and having to step out onstage without Da there to see it."

"I understand that." He paused for a second. "But when your big opening night comes in three weeks, do you think he would really miss it? I like to think he's everywhere, and at the very least he's in each of us. Always will be. Besides, if there really is a heaven up in the sky like Ma believes, then right now we're about as close to it as we'll ever be."

Grace reached for her brother's hand, and they both gazed up into the sky.

"What are we looking at?" Seamus and the Gagliardis came up behind them and stepped across onto the same beam. All five of them stood looking up into the sky. Grace turned her head to look at Joe.

"The future," she said, holding Patrick's hand on one side and Joe's on the other.

"Hello, Miss O'Connell," said the dark-haired boy who opened the door for her.

"Hello, Ciaran. How many times, please call me Grace!"

Ciaran Donohue grinned back. "Sorry, Miss O'Connell."

Grace growled in her throat and mussed his hair as she glided by. She had managed to get Ciaran a job in the theater, paying two dollars a week, and his older brother Connor worked upstairs selling refreshments in the interval and eating his weight in popcorn, no doubt. It helped keep the noisy Donohues living above them, and Grace was happy about that. It would be too quiet if they were to go. She hurried from the stage door to the dressing rooms, a little late and a lot out of breath.

"Gracie!" Her castmates greeted her, handing her water and taking her by the arm.

"You look like you've had quite a day," said Prudence, who changed next to her. Every time Grace was here, she felt a pang for Edie and Betty, but these girls were lovely too.

"I've been up the Empire State Building," she said, her breathing returning to normal.

"Oh, how lovely!"

"I can't wait to go up there!"

"Was it magical?"

Grace looked around at all the smiling faces and couldn't keep the beaming grin from her own. "Oh, it was certainly magical." The faces waited expectantly, knowing instinctively there was more to come. "Joe proposed up there! I'm getting married!"

The girls gasped, whooped, and cheered as they all piled forward to shower Grace in hugs and kisses.

"You're so lucky," sighed Prudence, and Grace nodded.

"I feel it."

An hour and a half later, Grace's friends and family poured into the theater, taking up a whole row.

Mary held Connie's hand as the girl bounced excitedly in her seat, rattling the box of Milk Duds on her lap. She was wearing her beloved black beret and her special purple silk dress. It wouldn't fit her for much longer. Florence and Patrick sat on her other side, then came Frank and Maria with their two oldest children, and a very proud and newly engaged Joe, holding the hand of Bruno at his very first show. Next there were two empty seats, left on purpose, for Edie, and Grace's father. Adjacent were Andre and his girlfriend, who was looking the height of fashion in a sparkling blue number. The last two seats were for Betty and her husband, enjoying a rare outing together.

"Isn't this just wonderful?" Betty asked as she settled herself, a look of glee and fierce pride on her face.

"It sure is," said Vernon, taking her hand and leaning over to kiss her. She tilted her cheek toward him to accept his kiss with a look of pure contentment.

Howard had wanted a quick divorce. The truth was, he really had loved Betty and he didn't want to see her destitute, but he also wanted to protect his reputation as far as possible. Betty had cried genuine tears as she told him how sorry she was, and how she had never wanted to hurt him. Howard's nod had been curt and his instructions simple. She could keep all her things, as much as she could take with her, and he would also give her one thousand dollars to leave quickly and quietly. Betty was grateful and moved into rooms with Vernon in Harlem.

Vernon was over the moon to have her back, and in true Betty style, she walked straight into a new job, becoming the first female emcee of the Hallelujah Club in Harlem. It suited her down to the ground. She and Vernon had married as soon as they were able, and Betty had never felt happier as she sat waiting for her best friend to fulfil her dreams on the Broadway stage. As she looked down the row of seats, her breath caught in her throat at the symbolically empty ones. Edie had been right all along, about both of them. Grace had made it in the big time, and Betty had married for love. It was just a crying shame that she wasn't there to see it.

Grace stood backstage and stretched her arms above her head and from side to side before she shuffled quietly with the other performers into the wings. She took a deep breath. She was filled with nervous excitement, as she still was every time she stepped onstage. It had already been quite the day, but to have everyone she cared about sitting in the audience filled her heart to bursting. It had been emotional to see the Empire State Building open, knowing she had played a small part in its construction as the only woman to have caught rivets on the most famous building in the world. And now it was cemented forever in her history as the place Giuseppe Gagliardi had asked her to marry him. She smiled at the thought that one day they would take their Irish-Italian American children there to enjoy the view.

"Two minutes!" The hushed whisper spread through the crowd of performers, and they all nodded to show they understood.

Grace smiled. No one might ever find out she had worked on the Empire State Building and danced on air, but everyone would know she had danced on Broadway. She pulled back her shoulders and looked up toward the ceiling, hoping her da was watching, wherever he was now. The curtain drew back, to rapturous applause, and Grace stepped out into the spotlight.

AUTHOR'S NOTE

I first had the idea for this novel more than ten years ago. I have an American Studies degree, and throughout, we touched on the defining moments in the history of America. More often than not, it was the exploits of men we learned about, and I often found myself wondering, "Where were the women?" The construction of the Empire State Building did not, as far as I am aware, involve any women, but I couldn't help thinking—what if it did?

Once I realized the way to get a woman up on the steel was to make her a twin pretending to be a man, the story started to come together in my mind. I still knew very little about how to build a skyscraper, and I used many, many resources to learn all I could about the process. If you are interested in learning more about the iconic building, in far more detail than I could ever include in the book, I would recommend *The Empire State Building: The Making of a Landmark* by John Tauranac; *Building the Empire State*, edited by Carol Willis; and *Thirteen Months to Go* by Geraldine B. Wagner. *Gotham Rising* by Jules Stewart also provided a lot of great information. The incredible photographs of Lewis Hine, documenting the construction, gave me a real sense of the height and danger, and I urge you to take a look.

I have tried to keep the details as accurate as possible, but I have made some minor changes. For example, the crane that Grace walks along in the rescue scene is not the type of crane used on the site, but I hope you will forgive this and a handful of other tweaks I have made to the facts in service of the story. Any accidental inaccuracies or mistakes are all mine.

Lukasz Kowalski is a completely fictional character, but there were men who died in the construction of the building. The official records state that five men died, but six names came up several times in my research—Luis DeDominichi, Giuseppe Tedeschi, Frank Sullivan, A. Carlson, Sigus Andreason, and Reuben Brown. Their sacrifice should not be forgotten, and you will notice that two of my characters were named to honor these men.

A lot of the detail of 1930s New York became clear in my mind after reading the *WPA Guide to New York City*. As a Federal Writers' Project, it was commissioned to create paying jobs for writers during the Great Depression. The whole book is fascinating and packed with so many brilliant details. It is responsible for a number of scenes making their way into the book, including Connie's birthday trip to the aquarium.

At the time of its construction, the Empire State Building was seen as a beacon of hope for the struggling city. People believed that if a project so ambitious was still continuing, the tough economic and financial situation was surely only temporary. No one would construct a building so large without businesses to fill it, would they? As it turned out, the building's beginning was pretty rough, resulting in the nickname "The Empty State Building," on account of its lack of tenants. However, it was built to last, and we can safely say it has stood the test of time. It is now one of the most recognizable structures on Earth, and the most photographed building in the world. Although the O'Connells and the Gagliardis never existed, thousands of people did who climbed those steel beams, risking their lives every day to, as Frank says, "gift this view to the world." I'm grateful they did, and I will certainly be thinking of them the next time I visit.

ACKNOWLEDGMENTS

F irstly, thank you to you, the reader. With so many brilliant books in the world, thank you for choosing mine. I hope you enjoyed it, and please know that by reading it you are making my dreams come true. So many people are involved in getting a book into your hands, and I'm grateful to all of them.

Anita Frank, a huge and heartfelt thank you for all your help, advice, encouragement, and support. Sending you my manuscript changed everything. To my wonderful agent, Julia Silk, thank you for making any of this possible, and for your wise advice. Thank you also to Sam Edenborough and the rest of the team at Greyhound. Huge thanks to an excellent international editorial squad—Sherise Hobbs and Priyal Agrawal in the UK, Lexa Rost in Germany, and Abby Zidle in the US. Thank you for your enthusiasm for the book, and for loving Grace right from the start. Working with you and having the benefit of your combined expertise was a dream.

Thank you to all the writers who have cheered me on, with a special mention to Book Campers Cesca Major, Isabelle Broom, and Kirsty Greenwood. Helen Lederer, thank you for creating Comedy Women in Print, a marvelous competition that has put so many wonderful witty women my way. To all the CWIPsters, you make me laugh, and that's the greatest compliment I can give.

Thank you to my Hammerson and JLL colleagues past and present for your support—Kiran and Gina, thank you for lending me your jobs! Phil Drinkwater, thank you for being a friend, down the road and back again, and for being a cool boss. Aaron Sanchious (aka Defcon Lawless, check him out on Spotify) thanks for being the most fun person to share an office with.

Chloe Smith, I will be the first in line to buy your book one day. Most times you can't believe a word she says, most times, but this time it was true.

Oscar Wilde said a sign of true friendship is that you can grow separately without growing apart, and with that in mind, a huge thank you to my parallel lines: Alexa Barlow, thank you for being on this writing journey with me for twenty years. Fancy twenty more? I love you more than Claudia Winkleman loves a great fringe. Stephanie Lazarczuk, you are the mojito to my pizza. Traveling the world with you will always be one of my favorite things. Leoni Munslow, you inspire me endlessly. Thank you for caring as much as I do, and never letting go. Felicity Brodrick, you are the kindest, wisest, most gentle soul, and I am forever grateful to have you in my corner. Kate Ridout, I'm so glad the universe put you in my life.

Jane McDougall and Claire Sharp, thank you for teaching younger me so much about the sort of person I wanted to be. Jane, I will never forget that you were my first publisher!

And lastly, thank you to my parents, Peter and Jackie, to whom this book is dedicated. Thank you for everything, and then everything else. Mum, thank you for the endless childhood trips to the library and giving me your love of reading. Dad, thank you for always encouraging creativity and teaching me the importance of hope. And thank you both, for always believing in me and my dreams, and knowing this would happen one day, even when I didn't. You were right. I love you.